Mark Watson, who I taught at Bedwas School; a Falklands War veteran who gave me an insight into the horrors of that conflict. He suffers to this day from his experiences as an 18-year-old. One day a schoolboy and the next a combat soldier.

Gemma Lewis, who I taught at Rhymney School. It was an honour to help a pupil from a former Welsh mining village to achieve her dream to study medicine at St John's College Oxford. The empathy in her poem informed me that here was a truly outstanding student.

Mr Goff Davies, headteacher of Hartridge High School, Newport. He was the inspiration for Foggy Head of Galaxy High. Goff was a truly inspirational character for staff and pupils. I owe him so much.

My long-suffering wife Val who has been my rock and the love of my life. Matthew and Hannah, my exemplary children who I love so much. Lucie, Matthew's lovely wife, who joined the tolerant female members of the family. My grandson Alex, a little ray of sunshine and a real gift to us all.

John Orchard was much more than a teaching colleague. He was a true friend and mentor who once told me a school was a gold mine.

Jimmy Stokes has spent his working life teaching and dealing with young people's problems. Having worked with secondary school pupils in areas of social deprivation, Jimmy strived to ensure that each one aspired to fulfil their potential. Recently, he has been involved with homeless people where he became aware that this situation was responsible for a loss of human capability.

Jimmy enjoys spending time with his family and travelling.

Jimmy Stokes

DIGGING FOR GOLD

AUSTIN MACAULEY PUBLISHERS™
LONDON • CAMBRIDGE • NEW YORK • SHARJAH

A CIP catalogue record for this title is available from the British Library.

ISBN 9781398451124 (Paperback)
ISBN 9781398451131 (ePub e-book)

www.austinmacauley.com

First Published 2022
Austin Macauley Publishers Ltd®
1 Canada Square
Canary Wharf
London
E14 5AA

Thanks to Austin Macauley for bringing *Digging for Gold* to publication.

And to Canon John Kelly and Cliff from St Helen's Church who help organise the night shelter.

Introduction

Billy Davies was lying in bed at Tooting Evangelical Church, knowing his death was imminent. With the end approaching, he began to think about his life and how this place of worship had been his home since 2012. At the time, two sixth form students, both church members named Antoinette and Simeon, rescued him from the dire poverty of homelessness. He reflected that he was one of 320,000 marginalised individuals in British society and if it had not been for their intervention, he would have been dead years ago.

It was now 2040 and his life was nearly over. Being 76 years of age, he contemplated the good fortune he'd enjoyed following some harrowing early life experiences. During the intervening years, he had worked for the church and although his achievements were legendary, he had not set out to achieve status. He just wanted to help marginalised people. He realised he'd been blessed, owing his survival to the unstinting generosity of this community who'd provided him with a home. He was so pleased he had been endowed with a sense of loyalty having repaid the chivalrous gesture of this religious institution.

Billy had worked tirelessly to enhance the church's status in the community and the wider world. He appreciated that without their intervention 28 years ago he would have entered the records as another deceased homeless person. At the time he was given shelter, Billy was 47 years of age which was the average life expectancy for a homeless person in the United Kingdom.

When he was growing up in Wales, he'd been suspicious of religious people, referring to them as Bible bashers. This lack of understanding disappointed him making him appreciate how misguided he had been. He owed his very existence to the love and care the church had shown him. Billy was delighted Simeon and Antoinette married despite their different backgrounds, knowing their concern for social justice had brought them together. As a homeless man alienated by society, he was thankful to be the beneficiary of their compassion.

Thinking about the chronic illness, causing his chest to rattle and wheeze incessantly, he was glad he adamantly refused to go to hospital, determined instead to die in the church. In his opinion, there was no better place to end his days than Tooting Evangelical Church, having found sanctuary there 28 years ago. Although desperately ill, he was stressed not by the thought of his inevitable passing but by the longing for the arrival of his two best friends, Simeon and Antoinette. Simeon was jetting in from the United Nations in Geneva and Antoinette was rushing from Parliament.

Chapter 1

It was one of those cloudless days in Clapham with an azure winter sky. Throughout the day the temperature remained below zero, the continuous sunshine taking the biting edge off the bitterly cold wind. Wrapping up against the elements ensured that one could be pleasantly warm. It was the type of winter day where the public had a spring in their step, thanks to the invigorating effect of the elements.

It was an emancipation from those days where the damp and drizzle made one's bones ache. Some people depressed by the continuous lack of sunlight, alleviated this problem by looking into a light box producing the necessary endorphins to make them feel human. They were released from this Purgatory as natural light struck their bodies. This day, nature's rejuvenating effect appeared to give everyone a desire to work.

Billy Davies sat outside Clapham tube station, observing the hustle and bustle of the London suburb. Constantly flowing traffic produced a din making it difficult for Billy to pick up people's conversation. Flash cars produced an ear-splitting sound as they accelerated away from traffic lights. Drivers of these vehicles had little concern for the noise or atmosphere pollution they induced. They appeared totally oblivious to the potential danger they could cause to pedestrians and as for the 30 mile per hour speed limit, it may as well have been non-existent.

Compounding the noise and pollution problems were the buses, lorries, taxis and motorbikes, all vying for a place on the limited tarmac of a London street. Most people went about their business oblivious to the plight of this homeless man, suffering profound psychological issues. Nevertheless, Christian churches had provided him with a thick winter overcoat and a good pair of trousers. Badly matching clothes were unimportant, the priority was warmth. For somebody who was homeless, Billy was not particularly scruffy, his glad rags provided by the generosity of local places of worship who also supplied food and shelter at the coldest time of the year.

Many homeless would sit barefoot in the hope people would notice their plight and contribute some cash. Billy knew this was a risky strategy, possibly causing frostbite to the feet, turning them black, sometimes resulting in amputation. An intelligent, widely read man, Billy unfortunately needed charity to survive. Severe mental health issues and alienation from his family prevented him holding down a job, leading to this dire situation. Depression and intermittent panic attacks were a constant problem for Billy, blighting his life.

He sat on a sleeping bag with three layers of cardboard underneath, donated by a kind supermarket manager as insurance against the damp and cold. Most days this store manager would buy Billy something warm to eat.

Being London, Billy showed gratification in the usual way, 'Thanks, Guv.'

Pleased Billy had acknowledged his benevolence the manager spoke up, 'I can't see you go hungry,' as he retreated to the store.

Obsessive about avoiding frostbite, Billy always wore two pairs of socks in the winter. He realised how important this was from his time in the army. Empty sandwich packets encircled Billy, marking out his patch of pavement. Although many people were totally detached from Billy's plight they would mutter, 'Lazy, druggy, bastard.'

Some of the more enlightened members of the public would enquire after his health, 'Are you OK or would you like a cup of soup or a sandwich?'

Realising no one in their right mind would aspire to homelessness, these people appreciated a myriad of reasons could cause the problem. Losing a job, relationship breakdown or as in Billy's case the trauma of war could just be some of the reasons why a person had fallen on hard times. The faces of these people exuded kindness as they empathised with the plight of the homeless person. In their mind, they were giving thanks for their own good fortune, while filled with sympathy for the poor person on the floor. These good individuals refused to take their advantage in life for granted, realising one missed mortgage repayment could mean they were in the same boat.

Receiving a gift from someone filled Billy with gratification. Realising some people empathised with his dire situation, filled him with hope. Equally perturbed by the large numbers of people believing all homeless people to be drug addicts or alcoholics, he was disappointed by their uncaring attitude saying to himself, 'Do these morons really believe anyone would choose to live like this?'

Regarding these ignoramuses as selfish, uncaring human beings, Billy gave them short shrift and would have an angry look on his face.

As the afternoon sun slid behind the buildings, Billy shivered. Absence of sunlight caused a significant temperature drop, dusk producing a grey, silvery and murky light. People were either rushing home to get into the warmth or heading to the pub to enjoy an after-work drink. Billy longed for a time when he could join them. Exhaling air, water vapour in his breath condensed, turning into a cloud surrounding Billy's head like a fog. Boredom resulted in Billy blowing rings with his breath then watching them drift above his head and dissipate. Just as the last ring of condensed vapour disappeared, a car screeched to a halt directly opposite Billy.

A white youth with a hoodie covering his head and a scarf around his face jumped from the vehicle plunging a stiletto into the chest of a black boy strolling along the pavement. As the weapon pierced the boy's chest, he let out a blood curdling high pitched scream, finally collapsing into a crumpled heap on the pavement. There was no need to withdraw the weapon because the knife withdrew automatically as the victim fell. Billy was able to see, this was a horrific knife, no more than a centimetre in diameter. Bearing closer resemblance to a needle than a knife, the weapon obviously punctured the boy's heart and a trickle of bright red-blood oozed from the perforation in his chest, quickly gathering pace, leaving a crimson pool on the pavement. Swiftly the once fresh, scarlet liquid darkened in colour as it dried.

Billy shuddered at this horrific assault occurring in such close proximity to him. Shocked by the assailant's lack of remorse and his haste at getting into the car which sped off, Billy was stunned at what he had just witnessed. Recording the number plate was impossible because it was broken. Witnesses were limited to saying that it was a red Renault Clio. Billy clung to the hope that CCTV would enable the police to identify the culprit. People screamed and a melee gathered around the corpse and people nervously prattled on, moving around almost like headless chickens uncertain as to what they should do. Billy put this down to the shock of what they'd just witnessed.

On hand to assist the victim was a nurse returning from a shift at St George's hospital. Any assistance was to no avail because the victim was pallid, all life drained from his face. Passers-by could see the casualty's eyes were back in his head, the perpetrator's knife had inflicted such a wound that death was instantaneous. Blood flowed across the pavement from the incision, forming a pool in the gutter. Billy thought what a sickening sight, a tragic waste of life. Taking out a mobile phone a young girl shook uncontrollably as she tried to phone the emergency services. She eventually succeeded in contacting the operator but being completely perplexed by what she had witnessed she had to be prompted to give the exact location and type of incident.

Time stood still because it seemed an age before the police arrived on the scene. Billy could hear the encroaching high-pitched siren and as it arrived at the scene, the whine made his ears scream with pain. High-pitched noises from emergency vehicles are a nonstop occurrence on London's streets. Each time Billy heard one, it had a profound effect on his hearing. Army experience led Billy to believe, there was no chance the boy could have survived such a brutal attack and the police would be dealing with a murder scene.

Chapter 2

Bystanders were shrieking because of the horrific sight on the pavement. Many were ashen faced at what they'd just witnessed because this was such a brazen attack in broad daylight, happening so quickly, leaving people transfixed and having no time to react.

'What sort of person could do that,' said one onlooker.

Another in a state of shock replied, 'Some people have no respect for anyone.'

Another interjected, 'Gang and drug culture cause this.'

Taking control of the situation the police supported passers-by who were in shock. It seemed to take an age for the ambulance to arrive. Large vehicles such as ambulances have difficulty in London negotiating the incessant traffic plaguing the streets. Deep in thought Billy wondered, how many people lose their lives when ambulances cannot negotiate the traffic.

Driving in the capital resembles being in a fairground on a dodgem circuit. Eventually arriving at the scene, a female paramedic jumped out and placed her fingers on the victim's throat. Absence of any pulse confirmed the boy's demise. The paramedic spoke confidentially to the police but as far as people were concerned, Billy may as well be the Invisible Man. His position on the pavement enabled him to hear many different types of conversation.

'Death was instantaneous caused by the weapon puncturing the boy's heart,' the paramedic explained to the police.

Her accomplice commented, 'The body will have to go to the hospital to confirm he's dead. Get a blanket to cover the body then bring the stretcher and strap the victim on.'

Removing the corpse from public gaze was done quickly, the crew being careful to treat the victim with dignity. Billy knew paramedics dealt with the aftermath of many violent incidents but he felt sorry for them because they were always affected by it. The female paramedic remarked to her accomplice, 'We will have to take the body to the hospital for a doctor to confirm death.'

Billy was rooted to the spot as the intense cold penetrated his bones, causing stiffness, slowing his movements. Freezing conditions reduced Billy's motion to that of an old man. Winter conditions eroded Billy's strength, significantly weakening him. A ghostly faced girl who had done her best to contact the emergency services was rigid with fear at what she had witnessed. Stuttering she made every effort to respond accurately to the police officer's questioning.

'Did you recognise the attacker?'

'It happened so quickly. It's just a haze, I didn't get a good look at him.'

Playing the instant over in his mind Billy asked himself, 'Why would a young person want to kill someone? They've got their life in front of them and what a waste of human potential.'

Thinking about what he'd seen Billy struggled to understand, why human beings are prepared to treat each other in such an appalling way. Witnessing horrific human behaviour through war convinced Billy that people could use their intelligence to resolve problems in a more civilised manner.

Hours sat outside Clapham tube station enabled Billy to read newspapers. He called them 'the freebies'. The Evening Standard and the Metro were always available allowing Billy to keep up with national and world events. Regular stabbings in London were reported by the press. There had already been 100 such crimes in the capital this year.

Perturbed by this fact Billy realised many of the victims were children. No amount of rhetoric from politicians had resolved this problem resulting in MPs debating the topic many times but it appeared they were only paying lip service to an incredibly serious issue. In Billy's thinking, the hot air they spouted was done to ensure they secured votes at a General Election, keeping them in power. He thought to himself, 'Many different groups needed to get together if this harrowing problem is ever to be resolved.'

Billy thought, schools could be a key player in helping rectify this problem and he started to think about his own time in school. Having so much time on his hands gave Billy lots of opportunity to ponder the past. Sometimes his thought processes produced positive vibes, equally negative thinking would blacken his mood. Teachers thought of him as bright enough, cooperative, however lacking motivation, preventing him fulfilling his true potential. Frustrated by his lack of effort they'd comment, 'Billy Davies, if only you spent time concentrating in class, you could do well.'

Billy's reply was always the same, 'I'll do my best.'

'Now how many times have we heard that Billy.'

Unfulfilled because of his apathy and with worsening mental health issues Billy thought to himself, 'It's too late now to improve my prospects.'

When Billy left school, jobs were two a penny. A career in the military seemed to fit his strengths, resulting in Billy joining the army. Realising society had moved on, meant achieving academic qualifications was now essential for youngsters in modern Britain. Failure today potentially means young people are in danger of being left behind. Billy resented his apathetic attitude to education; this indifference was partly responsible for his PTSD (Post Traumatic Stress Disorder) caused by war.

Newspaper reports highlighted the problem of youth crime and Billy agreed with their assessment of this dire situation. Realising that young, underprivileged children were being used to courier drugs, created a significant problem in the capital. Gangs formed, rivalries developed leading to armed attacks and the use of knives. Middle class recreational cocaine users were the beneficiaries from youngsters being used as mules to satisfy their habit. Billy found this disturbing because many of these users would pass him by making derogatory comments about his lifestyle but in fact, their behaviour was helping destroy young lives.

'How dare they,' Billy thought,

'I've never done that.'

He thought of these people as hypocritical scum of the earth, selfish and blinkered. Many had well paid jobs and their money provided them with pleasure, bringing misery to others. It was their crass hypocrisy which really got to Billy, his grandmother used to call this type of person a swanker because they put on a show but in fact, they were just hiding their wrongdoing. Billy thought to himself, 'Swankers be damned, I'd call them something else.'

Cutting youth facilities in London was another factor causing violent crime to escalate. Government austerity programmes had exacerbated the problem. New sports clubs, youth clubs and community centres might provide part of the answer to the problem but money was limited.

More police on the streets engaging with the youngsters would help reduce youth crime but police numbers had drastically been cut. It seemed to Billy that the solution to this knife crime problem could be straight forward if those in power decided it needed to change. Unfortunately, failure to commit money to the problem was preventing a solution. It irked Billy that politicians would talk about it but not actually do anything constructive to put it right. Cynically, he thought to himself they might do something if it was one of their own kids who had been knifed.

Stigmatising young people was a terrible mistake in Billy's mind. He wanted youngsters listened to because given the right facilities, most young people have the potential to do well.

Billy thought to himself, 'This problem relates to the social class into which they are born. It's totally unfair.'

In Billy's mind it was incumbent on the authorities to rectify it. Just as Billy finished thinking about this problem a policeman spoke gruffly to him, 'Move on and find a more appropriate place to doss down.'

Not wanting any trouble Billy replied, 'Yes officer. I'm on my way.'

Life was difficult enough for Billy but some people were just intent on multiplying his hardships.

'Yes,' he thought, 'I am a soft target, easy to get at but are the authorities prepared to tackle the real problems in society? I've never been in any trouble in my life.'

Rather than risk arrest, Billy went to the church night shelter for a hot meal. A very disturbing day all round.

Chapter 3

Next morning Billy returned to his own patch of pavement. London's hustle and bustle was at its most frenetic as crowds arrived and departed from the tube station. People busily went about their daily routine allowing Billy to pass his time watching people from all walks of life. Most were so busy and eager to get to the office, they failed to see a fellow human being living on the pavement. Whether they were a City high-flyer or a construction worker rushing to their site, they all exhibited London's manic lifestyle.

Time on the streets taught Billy passers-by fell into one of four categories. Vast numbers of people totally ignored the homeless, passing without having any time for the unfortunate individuals on the pavement. These self-centred narcissists only cared about their own problems and formed the largest group. Then there would be a small minority of people making disparaging comments. Pronouncements such as druggie, alky or idle bastard were commonplace for this group. One individual left Billy seething when he told his friend, 'uh look at him he's as rough as a robber's dog.' Lacking any empathy with their fellow human beings, they were totally clueless. It was more common for individuals to utter statements such as, 'How can he be homeless when he's got a dog or why is he smoking when he's got no money?'

Totally exasperated they would say, 'They're having nothing from me.'

Billy thought to himself, 'Ignoramuses, if they think the homeless are walking into kennels buying dogs. How misguided. They're too selfish to realise stray dogs are often adopted by homeless people and are a mutual source of comfort.'

Contemplating further Billy thought, 'Inconsiderate people think a homeless person smoking is unjustified and they should be spending their money on food. These individuals lack any sort of understanding of the problems confronting those living on the streets and the enormous pressures they face. Smoking is a coping mechanism and people do not understand, that having nothing to live for means it's futile for them to stop. Generally, those who think this way are middle class individuals with nice homes, flash cars and enjoying expensive holidays. Release from work pressures lead some of these to have a cocaine habit. Who are they to criticise! Bloody hypocrites thought Billy.

Billy appreciated the other two groups; these were compassionate people. One group go to the supermarket to buy food or a hot drink to give to the homeless. Worrying that the homeless might spend donated money on drugs or alcohol, these kind people hedge their bets. These are the steady eddies in society, never taking a risk with money, probably civil servants. There is no way they could be a business tycoon where calculated risk was a regular occurrence in their everyday life. Nevertheless, these were generous people.

Billy then thought about the final group. These people gave the homeless money, thinking even those on the streets have choices to make in life. How someone without a home spends money is at their discretion and donating money could stop these people stealing to survive.

A gentleman in a three-piece pinstriped suit handed Billy a sandwich, confirming his assessment of the groups who passed by each day. Suddenly a van appeared and a man hastily jumped out, flinging open the door. Taking out a bundle of newspapers he carelessly flung them, landing about a foot from Billy. Swiftly getting back into the van.

Billy shouted, 'Twat' they could have hit me. He must be on a bonus.'

If the bundle of newspapers had hit Billy, they would have caused considerable damage to a man whose resistance was seriously weakened by the situation he found himself in. The courier didn't care because Billy was just a vagrant who, in his opinion, shouldn't have been there. If it had been any other member of the public, he would have apologised but a homeless man was totally insignificant, just a blight on society. Certainly not worth worrying about, apparently less than human.

Inwardly, Billy was hurt by this behaviour but constant inconsideration had hardened him to these people's appalling actions. Taking a copy from the pile allowed Billy to retain contact with the outside world. On closer examination, he could see the headline referred to yesterday's murder. The police had detained a suspect and a local youth would be charged and named. Billy felt satisfied that there had been an arrest because justice had been done.

Being 18 the assailant could be named and press speculation was rife that the victim was a gang member who'd strayed from his area, infringing a rival's territory. Gangland culture ensured retribution had to be taken with the stiletto being the weapon of choice. Inevitably, gang violence evolved into a brutal business and consequently their behaviour became increasingly more callous. Brutality was the order of the day so survival of the fittest was the first rule of the streets. Using a stiletto ensured the weapon would pass between the ribs puncturing the heart, leading to instantaneous death. These young assassins were highly trained in this technique. Government rhetoric concerning deploying more police on the streets failed to halt London's knife problem.

Billy muttered, 'They make me move on but they don't deal with the real problems.'

Life on the streets had turned Billy increasingly more sceptical.

Saddened at the thought of young people dying needlessly, war had taught Billy about the futility of violence. To Billy, brutality demeans human beings resulting in society being the loser. Broken hearted families were forced to cope with the tragic, pointless loss of a loved one. Education could provide the answer, but Tony Blair's clarion call, 'Education, education, education,' seemed a distant memory and the system failed elements of society.

Billy mumbled to himself, 'These words just paid lip service to the public but nothing had changed. Surely, investment in Britain's children would benefit society.'

Billy's mood was darkening.

Chapter 4

London's rush hour intensified and groups of people came to the spot where the youngster was murdered. Adjacent to the murder scene was a lamp post where people attached flowers as a mark of respect. Public memorials of this type had become more common and Billy thought, it was a nice touch. Marking the passing of a life helped loved ones to grieve.

People in Clapham were shocked that this knife problem had come to their community; making Billy think, given the opportunity this youngster possibly had the potential to achieve great things. Fate dealt this boy a bad hand and his life had ended, making him another London stabbing statistic. Billy's thoughts on this matter were hypothetical because all that remained of the young man was a corpse in a morgue and dried blood stains on the pavement. Nevertheless, Billy was upset by the incident, despite having never seen the victim before.

As an adult Billy had developed into a sensitive man but as a teenager, he'd joined the army, which at the time seemed the macho thing to do but witnessing slaughter on the battlefield changed his perception of war. When he was young, he'd watched films glamorising combat but this was so far from the actual reality. When he signed on, he never visualised that he would have to fight in a battle as an adolescent and encountering death as a young soldier altered his psyche, making him see violence as degrading to our humanity.

Gathering his thoughts, Billy spotted a black schoolboy who he thought was about 17 or 18 come out of the tube station. Buying a single red rose from a nearby florist he walked to the memorial, reverently placing the flower on the pavement. People started fixing flowers to the lamp post. The community was adversely affected by the crime leading to large numbers of people arriving at the spot, forcing them to leave their mementos on the pavement. Immediately Billy could see symbolism in the boy's gesture, where he was paying his respects for a life curtailed by a stiletto and the red flower represented the boy's blood. He respectfully stood for a few minutes of quiet reflection with his head bowed.

Youngsters are often maligned for their behaviour but here was a young man, who was a credit to his generation. Surely, this boy was destined to make a great success of his life and his deferential behaviour at the hastily arranged memorial displayed a maturity belying his years. Billy thought to himself, what an impressive young man, really smartly dressed in school uniform, behaving in a dignified manner. Billy's innate compassion led to him being deeply affected by the boy's reverential act. This young man was obviously endowed with a lofty intellect and would surely never stoop to participate in London's gang culture.

Turning from the memorial the boy walked towards Billy, opened his bag and handed him a sandwich. Billy was touched by the generosity of somebody so young who could empathise with his dire situation. Obviously, part of the boy's lunch, his gesture brought a tear to Billy's eye.

'What's your name young man?'

'I'm Simeon Williams.'

'Which school do you go to?'

'I go to Oak Grove Academy in Balham.'

'You're immaculately dressed, you must be a high-flyer in school.'

'Sir, I'm proud of my blazer and I try to keep the creases straight in my grey flannel trousers.'

'Simeon, you must be over 6 feet tall and I bet you've broken a few girls' hearts.'

This was a tongue in cheek comment, Billy wondering if he should have said it. Such a statement although impulsive sounded a bit cheeky. He'd only just met the boy. Then on the other hand, Billy could be over-sensitive and Simeon didn't seem overly concerned.

Coyly Simeon replied, 'Why's that?'

Billy thought to himself I'd better give an answer now, I've started this conversation, 'Well, you're so smart and those shoulder length dreadlocks make you a sure-fire winner.'

'My parents have always insisted that I'm smart when I go to school.'

'I know the motto on your badge is Latin but when I was in school, we didn't study Classics.'

'Yes Sir, it says Bonna Tenete.'

'What does that mean, Simeon?'

'Hold fast to that which is good.'

'What a lovely school motto, you're a real credit to your parents.'

Simeon exuded humility and obviously had exemplary behaviour. Being a model pupil Billy wondered if he had to cope with bullying lower down the school.

'Did you have any problems with bullying in school when you were young?'

'Oak Grove is a comprehensive school where there could be considerable disruption in some classes. Not all pupils are motivated but their behaviour depended on who was taking the class. I always kept my head down and worked diligently. For me, it was important that I respected the teachers. They were the ones who were going to help me get to university. I was careful to avoid being judgmental and must say my classmates always respected me. Some kids would ask me for help with their work and although others were gang members, I would always encourage them, knowing some were facing awful problems at home.

Marcus Atwood, the murdered boy was in my class and in some lessons, I sat next to him. Yes, he was a gang member but he came from a poor family and was enticed into the gang culture by older, hardened criminals who used him as a drug mule. Being poor, he accepted payment for carrying drugs to users, seeing the money as justifying his actions. His parents had little spare cash to give to their children. This drug money gave Marcus the independence he craved. Many will think Marcus was a bad boy but while I couldn't agree with the direction his life was taking. I knew he was OK, just another victim of a burgeoning knife problem in London.'

Billy was impressed and astounded with what Simeon had just told him and responded, 'Young people are the victims of unscrupulous drug dealers snaring them into couriering this poison. Carrying a knife becomes a rite of passage for youngsters in gangs, making them feel big and invulnerable. It is a miscalculation of youth, failing to realise that their lifestyle could end in death.'

Simeon animatedly pointed out, 'Marcus was poor and his mother was a lone parent bringing up five children in a small flat. Trying to make ends meet is difficult, resulting in Marcus joining London's gang culture to get some cash. Although school provides great opportunities, some kids face terrible problems in their life. Through life's pressure, some parents are world weary but I'm fortunate. 'There but for the grace of God, it could be me.' After University, I want to help people suffering through poverty.'

Having underachieved in school Billy was pleased that Simeon was ambitious and he declared, 'It's really good you want to go to University.'

'Yes, I'll be the first from my family, which will make my parents immensely proud.'

'Getting a degree will give you a great start in life.'

'I've really enjoyed the chat but I need to run. There's no way I want to be late.'

Billy thought to himself, what an impressive young man but it was a terrible mistake for some adults to stereotype young people. This youngster had shown him respect, whereas many adults lived in their own little bubble failing to recognise the difficulties faced by some people. Contentedly Billy settled down, hoping they could chat again.

Chapter 5

Putting an empty shoe box in front of him, Billy hoped people would take pity on him by dropping in some spare cash. Local churches relieved any worry about clothing, having an endless supply of good clobber donated by generous individuals. People willingly discarded unwanted clothing, much of it designer gear jettisoned way before it should have been. Today, many people are committed to keeping up with the latest fashion and although, these clothes are thrown away before they're worn out, the homeless were grateful for any discards. Billy was disappointed for pessimistically thinking they wanted to clear their wardrobes. Unfortunately, the truth is we live in a throwaway world. Cynicism was a by-product of the situation in which he found himself.

Having plenty of time to think Billy visualised himself as well-heeled but he couldn't come to terms with why these people buy so many clothes. Waste like this jeopardised the world's resources with the fashion industry being responsible for 10% of all global carbon emissions. An article in the Metro highlighted the problem and Billy agreed. People thought the homeless were dirty but cleanliness was not a problem for Billy. He could frequently use the showers at a local sports centre. This was a Godsend, helping him retain his dignity.

Homelessness meant Billy owned few possessions but he did have one prized belonging. Billy treasured a silver mouth organ, given to him during military service. Taking every opportunity he could to shine this instrument, it gleamed so that he could see his reflection in it. Self-taught, this musical instrument was Billy's pride and joy and he could play a mean tune both sucking and blowing air into it. Being homeless nobody ever praised him for anything, so thinking he could play well lifted his self-confidence. In any case, some people respected his ability by dropping money in the box, for which Billy was grateful. Such acts of generosity helped make Billy's life a little more bearable.

Clapham's traffic intensified as rush hour drew near, pollution levels rising with it. At this time-of-day Billy's throat burned, resulting in his chest tightening. When he was young Billy suffered with chest infections, so on occasions London's pollution affected him. Today, his attention was drawn to a young adolescent white girl in a royal blue blazer with yellow braiding. Billy thought, she must be a sixth former even though some girls looked older than their chronological age, making it difficult to accurately tell how old they are. She was 5 foot 6 inches tall, attractive and exuding class.

Most of the other kids who passed by were in green blazers like Simeon but surely this young lady was in a private school. Billy thought there was an aura about her indicating an education at a fee-paying school. Approaching the nearby florist shop, she picked up a posy of flowers. Billy recognised these as Lily of the Valley. His grandmother used to grow them and they gave off an unforgettable aroma.

Sorely affected by the young boy's death, many people placed flowers at Marcus's memorial causing the grotto to extend across the pavement. This show of affection by members of the public caused people to side-step, to avoid trampling the flowers. Placing the bunch on the pavement the girl stood in a regal manner bowing her head. The girl's solemnity impressed Billy and it crossed his mind that surely this young lady could not know a gang member. Upbringing and privileged education would have cossetted her from this element in society. There could be no way the victim would have been in her friendship group.

Turning around the girl caught sight of Billy and walked towards him, took out her purse and dropped cash into Billy's shoe box. Billy was energised by her two acts of kindness.

'That was a lovely tune you were playing. Where did you learn to play a mouth organ?' she asked.

Billy was elated. This was the second time today a young person had spoken respectfully to him. Displaying compassion for one of society's down and outs lifted Billy's spirit. What was unimportant to other members of the public meant the world to Billy. Usually, he was sneered at with vile words being aimed at him and members of the public treating him as less than human. Mistreatment like this had a profound effect on his mental health, consequently blackening his mood. This darkness festered inside him making him very judgmental of those who passed by. Many people already looked at him as a vagrant and by giving vent to his inner fury would have exacerbated the ill feeling many members of the public felt towards the homeless.

'You're so kind miss,' Billy commented.

'I think it's important that people take time to speak to the homeless.'

'Very few people ever talk to me. I'm just thought of as a down and out.'

'Well, I realise someone could just be one missed mortgage repayment away from homelessness.'

Such sensitivity by a privileged schoolgirl produced a lump in Billy's throat, causing him to swallow hard preventing him from crying. Regaining his composure, he pointed out, 'I feel quite emotional. You're a great example to the majority of people who marginalise us.'

'Take it from me, I feel very strongly that greater support should be given to the homeless. In 21st century Britain, it's unacceptable that so many people are living on the streets.'

'What's your name and where do you go to school?'

'My name is Antoinette Spencer and I attend Hill House College, a private school in Balham.'

'Your attitude to the poor belies, your age showing a maturity beyond your years.'

'I hate the thought of someone who's fallen on hard times being rejected and discriminated against by elements in society. All forms of prejudice are wrong and my ambition when I'm older is to change society.'

'That'll be a big job and how do you want to do it?'

'Please don't think this is arrogant but I want to go into politics. However, I'm not sure if I've got the ability.'

'You've certainly got the compassion to make a difference.'

Antoinette was assertive and uncompromising in her thinking about those who were less fortunate and said, 'Poverty is a stain on society and I don't know why you're on the streets but no doubt there'll be a good reason. The murdered young boy is also a victim of poverty. There are still too many have nots in society. Numerous children grow up in crowded homes, lacking access to technology which is the norm in more affluent families.

Quite often poor facilities restrict the progress of children from poor homes. How can a first world country refer to itself as civilised if it has such a serious problem? Poverty is the root cause of homelessness and gangland murders. I have had the opportunity to have an excellent education but deprivation has meant, the murder victim didn't have a chance.

Ideally, people like him should have the same chance as me. We are all human beings and the first article of the United Nations Declaration of Human Rights, states **All Human Beings are Born Free and Equal.** Politicians sound off claiming they are going to rectify these problems but nothing changes. Austerity programmes have inflamed the problem and I'm desperate to change it. No doubt I will remain exasperated because unfortunately, I'm not doing that well in school which will prevent me fulfilling my aspirations.'

Billy was absolutely astounded by what he'd just heard. How could someone so young have such an old head on their shoulders? He declared, 'Antoinette, I've never met anyone so young who's as perceptive as you are for your age because you are able to discern between what's fair and unfair. You're 24-carat gold. We'll have to speak again.'

'I've got to rush or I'll miss my music lesson.'

Speaking to Antoinette produced a lump in Billy's throat and tears welled up in his eyes. Hearing these words Billy thought, he must be dreaming. Euphoria was not a sensation the homeless experienced but today Billy felt a million dollars. Intuition was telling Billy that these liaisons might produce a turning point in his life. Often wondering if there was a God, Billy felt it was best to hedge his bets and didn't totally rule out the possibility of a superior being controlling world affairs.

He wondered were these two young people God sent! Street life induced a feeling of hopelessness, producing negative attitudes; however these conversations helped Billy understand we are all united by a common humanity. Antoinette spoke eloquently, she just lacked a certain confidence. How could someone who had such insight lack confidence! It was hard for Billy to equate this lack of self-esteem with someone who was so astute. What this young lady said about poverty, placed her in a league of her own and her words were inspirational coming from someone so young and privileged. Would these two young people play a part in Billy's life, hopefully he would find out. Billy contentedly dozed off.

Chapter 6

Billy's meeting with Antoinette and Simeon the previous day was a temporary shot in the arm for a homeless man. A rumbling stomach convinced Billy to leave his spot outside the tube station. He travelled to Tooting Pentecostal Church where the homeless night shelter was located that evening. Billy was looking forward to staying here because the church was a vibrant faith community with fantastic facilities, a real five-star place where church members did all they could to give the homeless a pleasurable experience.

The church was one of a group of multi faith communities providing hot food and a bed for the homeless. Without this benevolence, homeless people would be desperate. Living on the streets in the winter was a harrowing experience, jeopardising lives. Providing a two-course meal and bed at the coldest time of the year, protected the homeless from the elements. Without this facility there would be a significantly higher mortality rate among these destitute people.

Entering the church hall, Billy's attention was drawn to a group of volunteers. Lo and behold Billy could see two of the volunteers were Simeon and Antoinette, the two sixth formers who had spoken to him 24 hours earlier. Bringing his thought processes to the fore, it crossed Billy's mind this was one in the eye for people stereotyping all youngsters as being disruptive. Simeon and Antoinette were a credit to their generation.

Billy ecstatically greeted them, 'How are you? It's great to see you again.'

Antoinette smiled and replied, 'It's great to see you here, it's freezing tonight.'

Simeon added, 'It would be dangerous if you were outside.'

'How long have you two known each other?'

'We met recently working in the night shelter,' said Simeon

Antoinette proudly pronounced, 'We're now dating.'

'I'm really pleased for the two of you. You're both lovely people.'

Antoinette chivvied Billy along, knowing the evening meal was ready, 'It's time to eat or the food will be cold and we can have a chat later.'

Sitting at the table was a luxury for Billy as his usual perspective on the world was a pavement view. From the footpath Billy experienced constant traffic and inhaling polluted air throughout the day was the norm. It used to cross Billy's mind, his lungs must have been clogged with microscopic pieces of carbon. Unfortunately, he amplified this problem when he smoked an occasional cigarette relieving the tension created by his lifestyle.

Nearby street food stalls produced delightful odours giving Billy a change from vehicles emitting poisonous odours. Inhaling these marvellous fragrances caused Billy's stomach to rumble. Tolerating hunger pangs was a real challenge for Billy making him irritable, however, stall holders were for the most part very generous donating leftovers as a freebie to the homeless. These small acts of generosity brought comfort, making a big difference to people living on the streets.

As well as food offerings Billy would get relief from the cold with wafts of warm air coming from the tube station. This warmth was produced by the braking tube trains. Although the tube walls were designed to absorb the warmth, age reduced their effectiveness and heat coming from the tube caused Billy to let out an appreciative shiver. Small acts of philanthropy and the emission of this warmth helped make Billy's life more palatable.

A pavement view allowed Billy to watch and work out which people had kind faces, in the expectation they would donate to him. Often disappointed by the public's attitude, he retained the same expressionless look on his face to prevent antagonising anyone.

Twice daily, London life became more frenetic when the morning and evening rush hour became the equivalent of the Serengeti migration of the wildebeest. During this time Billy's view was restricted to seeing thousands of pairs of legs whizzing past him. As rush hour escalated Billy's vision became blurred by this human stampede, everyone moving speedily, making it difficult for him to distinguish male or female legs. Moving away from the wall would result in Billy being trampled, so he sat rigidly upright against it. Looking at faces would have given Billy a cricked neck so there was only one thing to do, sit back and wait for the crowds to diminish.

Billy was grateful to be in the night shelter, hunger causing him to scoff the scrumptious food that he thought was fit for a king. Generosity from the volunteers filled Billy with gratitude that these kindly people felt called to give their time. Billy was really grateful that the homeless were referred to as guests. The churches insisted on this, giving the homeless dignity, something all humans deserve.

Volunteers went out of their way to treat the homeless with respect, contrasting with the attitude of some other people. Billy thought using the title guest implied people were expected to behave in a certain way and rules followed as they are in a hotel. No drugs, no verbal abuse, alcohol or violence. Smoking was permitted outside but guests did not generally flout the rules because they respected the generosity of the churches.

Tooting Evangelical church was a vibrant place of worship having a diverse congregation, with church buildings and extensive grounds marking this place out as exceptional. People from all social classes held the church close to their hearts, some donating large sums of money for its upkeep. Facilities were second to none with a roomy area for worship, a church hall and other rooms for activities. Billy was thrilled to use these facilities.

After cleaning up, washing plates and cutlery Simeon and Antoinette moved their chairs close to Billy. He was intrigued by this young couple who were poles apart in terms of upbringing and social class. Realising they were both compassionate people, they were obviously drawn together by a common cause, fighting the injustice of homelessness.

Billy was anxious to talk to both of them and asked Simeon, 'Were you born in Britain?'

'I was but my grandfather came from Jamaica to Britain in 1971. He was the last of the Windrush generation, who came here between 1948 and 1971. Being only five when he arrived in England, my dad remembers little about Jamaica but we still have family there. My aim is to have a good job and visit them.'

Antoinette knew nothing about the Windrush Generation and her inquiring mind led to her wanting to find out who they were. She said, 'Why were the Jamaican immigrants called the Windrush Generation?'

Considering, Billy lived on the streets his general knowledge was fantastic. He answered, 'They were given the title after the first Caribbean peoples in 1948 came on the MV Empire Windrush.'

Simeon wanted to know more, 'What does MV stand for Billy?'

'MV stands for merchant vessel as shipping falls into two categories. There are ships belonging to the Royal Navy, which are the warships. Then merchant vessels carry goods and people.'

Antoinette added, 'I'm really glad Simeon's father came here as it meant I was able to meet Simeon. The nice thing about Jamaica is that the sun shines all the time and it makes me wonder why people left.'

'I'm sure Simeon can answer that, Antoinette.'

'My Grandfather came here for work and a higher standard of living. Yes, the weather is lovely in Jamaica, unfortunately, it doesn't put food on the table.'

Billy wanted to elaborate further so he explained, 'In 1945 after the war, people came from the Caribbean to solve the shortage of workers in the country. Immigrants came from islands which were British colonies during the days of the Empire. We no longer have an Empire because the word points to people being subservient and countries which were part of the Empire are now called the British Commonwealth of Nations. Now independent, the Queen is their monarch and they're treated as equals, creating a mutual friendship where all people benefit.'

Antoinette remarked, 'Caribbean peoples have brought a rich heritage, benefiting us all. Unfortunately, some small-minded people discriminate against black people.'

'A total injustice. All men are created equal. For religious people there's equality in creation,' ranted Billy.

He continued to enlighten Simeon and Antoinette, 'Many Caribbean peoples have served our country with distinction in all walks of life and as such their contribution needs to be valued. A rich heritage was transferred from the Caribbean to Britain, so people with negative views need to think carefully about the ways in which our lives have been enhanced by the presence of these people. Jamaica and the other British colonies fought for the allies during World War Two with soldiers from these colonies giving their lives for freedom. It is unfortunate that people forget these things.'

Billy was really fired up because he understood injustice, having been forced to beg on the streets.

Antoinette was enamoured with Billy's general knowledge.

'It's really interesting talking to you. I find you an inspiration.'

Billy was really pleased. It was some years since he had been valued. These two young people were really lifting his spirits.

Chapter 7

Billy, Antoinette and Simeon moved to where they would be unobtrusive, allowing them to speak freely without disturbing other volunteers and guests.

Simeon continued speaking about the Windrush Generation, 'My parents and grandparents told me they experienced extreme prejudice when they first arrived here.'

Quickly making her point of view known, Antoinette spoke, 'Black people had been badly treated in the past and things are not as good as they should be today. Racism still exists in Britain within all generations but in particular some older people use racist language without thinking about the implications of what's been said. Although a minority of younger people can be racist, a lot of my generation do tend to accept people for who they are and don't judge them by the colour of their skin.'

Simeon had been told by his parents about the difficulties black people had encountered in the past and he remarked, 'Appalling names were applied to black people after they'd arrived in Britain. Today, the use of the word coloured is unacceptable even though, it was not thought of as disrespectful back in the day. Mind you my grandad told me discriminatory signs were put up in boarding houses when he arrived in the country, such as **Vacancies here but no Coloureds**. Discrimination was rife at the time but thankfully, today laws have been passed to protect ethnic minorities.

Antoinette asked, 'Why did the word coloured become a mark of disrespect?'

Billy answered, 'It is seen as discourteous today due to the segregation in the Southern United States during the 20th century. There was discrimination on the buses, in cinemas, schools, toilets and even drinking fountains were marked whites only or coloureds only. Simeon will be able to tell you the correct way to address a person of colour today.'

Simeon responded to Billy's remarks, 'It has to be black, mixed race or Asian. Today political correctness is important, particularly when one thinks about what happened when my family first came to Britain.'

Antoinette agreed with Simeon, 'Quite right too. The Bible speaks of us being created in God's image, teaching that there's equality in creation. Non-religious people should also be able to appreciate this.'

Having experienced life in the 1970s Billy was able to throw more light on the problem of racism. The three of them became engrossed in the conversation and Billy thought his experience could help elaborate some of the problems encountered by people of colour in the past.

'Television programmes in the 1960s and 70s used discriminatory language which would never be allowed today. Discrimination against black people was rife in the media. People of colour were distressed by the way they were insulted in both television programmes and stage entertainment. A popular stage and TV show the Black and White Minstrels fell into this category. From 1958 this show appeared on TV but during the 1960s a minority of white people started to see this show as racist.

Characters were blacked up, portraying them in a stereotypical manner. Accusations levelled at the show were that it trivialised racism in the Southern United States, where white supremacist organisations like the Ku Klux Klan victimised black people. Actors blacking up was seen as compromising the efforts of the Civil Rights Movement in the States, who were fighting for equality.

In Britain, the pressure group **Campaign against Racism** wanted the show ended. Such entertainment discredited the BBC and a campaign succeeded in bringing the show to an end in 1978. That was 20 years of hurt for people of colour in this country with white people failing to empathise with their black neighbours. They were not on the receiving end of the abuse and failed to understand the hurt caused by it. Consequently, this type of show helped racism to fester like a sore in British society.'

'So, during this time racism must have been rife in Britain,' exclaimed Antoinette.

Billy continued, 'Every facet of British life was affected by racism; British society was institutionally racist. Black sportsmen and women found difficulty representing sports teams as selection discriminated against them. Outstandingly talented sports people were denied the opportunity of representing their country because they were black.

Today, laws protect ethnic groups against this type of bigotry but even this does not mean the problem has been fully resolved. In most people's eyes, the first black person to represent England at football was Laurie Cunningham in 1977 when he played for the Under-21's. Six years earlier a black schoolboy called Benjamin Odeje represented England in 1971 at schoolboy level, when he played against Northern Ireland schools. History books seemed to have forgotten this but nevertheless well done to the school selectors for picking Benjamin. At the time this was a ground-breaking selection.'

Simeon interjected, 'Did Laurie Cunningham go on to win a full cap?'

'Yes, he did Simeon. Cunningham was an excellent West Bromwich Albion player winning six full caps during season 1979-1980. Nevertheless, the first black player to win a full cap was Viv Anderson in 1978 who went on to play 30 times for England. What a player! At the time he was playing for Nottingham Forest and even won the European Cup, the equivalent today of the Champions League.'

Antoinette had listened intently to what had been said and spoke up, 'Although I am not a big football fan, today there are numerous black players in the Premier League. Discrimination against black players has improved but is still far from perfect.'

Although brought up in a privileged home Antoinette's compassionate nature and inquiring mind hadn't distanced her from recent racist issues in Britain. Social justice was close to Antoinette's heart, nothing illustrating this better than her willingness to work with the homeless. Antoinette aimed to enter politics when she was older. However, she suffered from a lack of confidence in her own ability. This would have to be rectified, otherwise it would present an obvious barrier to her progressing in the political field. In the informal situation of the night shelter, she displayed an understanding of issues making her potentially a first-class conviction politician.

Billy picked up on the points made by Antoinette and he spoke up, 'Antoinette, you're quite right, saying there is less racism today in football but unfortunately, race issues still persist in the sport. Many black players represent England but statistically their chances of managing a Football League team when they retire are limited. Many see taking the FA coaching badges as futile. It is doubtful clubs would employ them, despite them having the potential to be outstanding managers.'

Simeon added, 'Football supporters are tribal, causing a small-minded minority to racially abuse black players and passing laws has still not fully resolved this problem.'

Billy's misfortune in life enabled him to empathise with these racial problems and he explained, 'Their ideas belong to the past and individuals purporting to be football fans are a disgrace. Football is doing its best to eradicate the problem, but these small-minded people need to remember black players are human beings with feelings. Football must work to put its house in order.'

Antoinette and Simeon could see Billy was emotional and well placed to express an opinion, having faced discrimination on the streets. Understanding the hurt caused by this type of behaviour he let out a tut.

Simeon became irate, 'Deluded fans deserve what they get. It needs to be a life ban from watching matches and anyone who thinks the punishment lacks proportionality are way off the mark. They just lack understanding of a hideous situation.'

Chapter 8

Antoinette remarked, 'Billy in no way do I mean to be condescending. You're such an enlightened man, when the general perception of homeless people is, they are vagrant scroungers. You obviously grew up in Wales as it's easy to recognise your accent.'

'You're quite right Antoinette. I was born in Wales and grew up in a mining village.'

'Which village Billy?'

Finding it difficult to understand why an intelligent man like Billy found himself in such a dire situation, Antoinette was determined to explore Billy's background and find out what led to his homelessness.

'I grew up in Llanen in a mining family. Mining was well paid at the time but dangerous work. Nevertheless, most men in the village worked in the pit. Mining was ingrained in the community and there was a wonderful camaraderie between the people. During the 20th century some horrific disasters in the mines led to many deaths. The worst of these tragedies occurred at Senghenydd in 1913, when an underground explosion at Universal Colliery caused by firedamp resulted in the deaths of 439 men and boys.'

Simeon was astounded to hear the figures quoted by Billy and joined the conversation.

'Billy that's a terrible loss of life.'

'Quite right Simeon and compensation for each man amounted to the equivalent today of just over 5 pence. Working class lives were cheap at that time. Today, the National Mining Memorial is located at Senghenydd, where visitors can see the names of the men and boys who died on October 14th, 1913, engraved along a wall.'

Astounded at the numbers that had died Simeon spoke up, 'Billy that's a paltry sum, probably symptomatic of the time when little value was attached to a working man's life. It was an absolute disgrace!'

Having been born in a village on the Welsh coalfield, mining history was ingrained in Billy and he continued, 'Then in 1966 a colliery spoil tip slipped down the mountainside in Aberfan, engulfing the local school. It was the last day before the half term holiday and there'd been a period of heavy rain causing the tip to move. Submerged by slurry, 116 schoolchildren and 28 adults were killed on October 21st. Despite numerous warnings by experts, nobody really took this information seriously. Although mine safety had improved by 1966, no one ever thought that a mountain would move.

Today, memories of these incidents are deeply entrenched in the minds of those living in former mining communities. These were two major disasters but there were plenty of other incidents that the public are not as familiar with. Disasters in the mining areas caused emotions to run high in Wales. People began to realise mining coal came at a great human cost when so many lives were being lost.

Today the pits in Wales are closed. Nevertheless, the history of coal is an integral part of Welsh culture, making our principality world famous. My father was a hardworking miner who married a girl from Llanen, my mother. She did some part time cleaning to supplement dad's wages. As children we were always well looked after. Saturday night at the Miner's Social Club was mam and dad's night out, giving them a chance to unwind following a hard week's work. Here mam had the opportunity to forget about the dangers in the pit but throughout the week her mind was tormented with the constant worry about dad.'

Antoinette was enthralled by Billy's childhood and what a complete contrast with her own middle-class upbringing in London. Intrigued by what she'd heard Antoinette wanted to glean more information.

'Billy where did you go to school?'

'I went to Ysgol Gyfun, Llanen.'

Antoinette's knowledge of the Welsh language was non-existent.

'What does that mean?'

'Ysgol Gyfun is Welsh for comprehensive school Antoinette.'

'Did you enjoy school?' Antoinette asked.

Billy did not really have to think hard about his reply.

'I did and there were some great teachers but, in many ways, school was different during my childhood. There was not the emphasis on exam results that exists today. During my school days pupils could leave school and go into well paid jobs or apprenticeships. Today, good exam results are essential for young people. One exceptional teacher used an analogy in assembly that a **school is like a goldmine**. He saw himself as a miner **digging for gold.** At the time I didn't get it but after leaving I realised, he was talking about the great potential existing in every child. Teachers must work hard getting the dormant, inherent ability out of pupils which can be as difficult as goldmining. In the end, good teachers succeed.'

Antoinette and Simeon were amazed at Billy's passion for Wales, realising here was a gifted individual with life experience they could learn from. Billy might not have gone to university, nevertheless he was well schooled in the University of Life. His intellect and common sense were coming to the fore, making it glaringly obvious Billy could hold his own in most situations. Antoinette's and Simeon's thoughts aligned, both wondering how unfortunate Billy had been and what contribution could he make to society if given the opportunity.

Billy was stimulated and bewitched by these two youngsters. He was in his element and spoke fondly about his school days.

'School was one of the most satisfying times of my life because I had no worries. There were always great friends and plenty of rugby. Some teachers would take us on rugby tours. Such occasions were absolutely fantastic, definitely one of the highlights of my school days. We used to go on tour to Cornwall, staying in a Falmouth hotel. What a fabulous place, right on the beach, a real playground for teenagers. Next to my room on the balcony the owners had a delightful looking parrot on a stand who persistently called out 'pretty Polly' and 'who's a pretty boy then.'

We spent hours retraining this alluring bird. He loved peanuts so much that eventually this fowl's narcissistic chatter transformed into foul language. Persistent tittle tattle was replaced with a tirade of four-letter words leaving the owners tamping mad. An investigation led to a tongue in cheek denial on our part. Well, it was only a prank wasn't it!'

Antoinette and Simeon were tickled pink and roared with laughter. However, Billy's joviality became more sombre, making it easy to see that his past experiences had seriously affected him. Both could see Billy's past had left an indelible mark on his life. They were thinking and hoping he would elaborate further.

Thinking about life after school Billy became melancholic and he spoke again.

'Life changed when I left school in 1980. Diminishing coal reserves meant I didn't want to follow my father into the pit as in time mining was destined to become uneconomic with the industry falling into decline. Deciding on an army career I enlisted in the Welsh Guards. For me this was an obvious choice, having enjoyed the affinity, fellowship and physical challenge of playing rugby. Little did I realise that two years after school I would be swapping rugby field battles for real combat in the Falkland Islands. Today, I realise that no 18-year-old should ever have to endure such a prospect.

Chapter 9

Antoinette and Simeon beguiled by what Billy had told them were now anxious to learn more about his past. Both were aware of the Gulf wars and Britain's commitment to fighting in Afghanistan but they were oblivious to the 1982 Falklands conflict. Many veterans who had fought in the Falklands felt it had become a forgotten war. Yet for those young soldiers who fought in it lifelong scars were inflicted on them, making life difficult.

Emotionally charged Billy began to speak about his experiences, 'When I finished school at 16, I signed forms to join the British army. I was fully aware that committing to military service might lead to a tour of duty in Northern Ireland and I was fully prepared for it. Never once did it cross my mind that I would have to serve my country in the hostile environment of the South Atlantic. Signing for the Welsh guards in 1980 I was filled with pride in the regimental badge. It meant having a leek and the motto Cymru am Byth attached to my beret.'

Antoinette was puzzled at the thought that a leek was part of a regimental badge and commented, 'It seems strange for fighting men to use a vegetable as a symbol.'

Billy was quick to enlighten Simeon and Antoinette.

'Leeks were used as a symbol in Wales. Legend stated it originated from a great battle against the Saxons. During the 7th century, St David advised the Welsh to wear leeks to show which side they were on. A myth has it that the Welsh won a great battle. New squaddies were regaled with tales of regimental heroism during past conflicts, all part of instilling new recruits with pride. Basic training went well but a conflict 8,000 miles from home was about to change my life forever. In 1981, a military junta came to power in Argentina.'

Antoinette had never heard the term military junta and was determined to explore further, 'What's a military junta Billy?'

Billy began to speak about his war experiences.

'Snatching power from the people turned Argentina into a military dictatorship, meaning the armed services controlled the country. Nobody in Britain envisaged our country involved in a war so far away. Throughout the centuries France, Spain, Britain and Argentina had all fought over the Falklands but from 1833 they had become a British colony. Argentina seized power in the Falklands to reclaim them from Britain. In the capital Port Stanley, the Union Jack was replaced with the Argentinian flag.

General Galtieri, the leader of the military junta thought, the British would never respond to this act of aggression as the islands were too far away. Invading the Falklands and South Georgia was a real 'faux pas' on the part of the Argentinian military. Margaret Thatcher or the Iron Lady as she was known wouldn't give up these distant lands without a fight. Naval commanders informed her that a task force could be assembled in days to sail to the South Atlantic. 5 April 1982 saw a British force comprising over 100 ships leave to engage the Argentinian invaders, a gamble which would either endorse Margaret Thatcher as one of the great Prime Ministers or bring her Premiership to an ignominious end.

Guarding Britain's Royal Family is one of the duties assigned to the army. I had been at Buckingham Palace two hours looking forward to a stress-free tour when our Sergeant instructed us, we were moving out. We'd been summoned to the Falklands. Prior to departure we were sent to Brecon for training. Brecon in May is nothing like the winter climate in the Falklands, sub-zero temperatures, four hours of daylight, constant sleet and snow and an unbelievably difficult terrain awaited us in these distant islands none of us 18-year-olds had ever heard of.

One could not imagine a harsher environment in which to fight a war. Government propaganda and intensive media coverage ensured the country was right behind the British task force. Conscientious objectors castigated the authorities for their action and in retrospect following the violence I experienced, I had some sympathy with their point of view. '**The first casualty of war is the truth'** and this old saying was well founded. Our government was economical with it.

One area where the British public were misled was the standard of equipment we were given. Some kit and equipment were substandard and harsh conditions ensured inferior footwear caused men to suffer trench foot and frostbite. Difficulties like this were preventable and were similar to problems encountered in the trenches during the First World War. Single shot weapons were another difficulty, whereas Argentinian soldiers carried automatic versions of the same rifle. Fortunately, advantage was gained over the Argentinians by them being young conscripts while we were professional soldiers.

Five Brigade left Britain on 12 May 1982 aboard the QE2. Belonging to the Cunard line this luxury cruise liner was requisitioned as a troop carrier and without this iconic vessel it would have been impossible to transport 3,000 soldiers preventing Britain defeating Argentina. Among those transported were Welsh Guards, Scots Guards and Ghurkhas. We arrived ten days later in South Georgia where Argentinian troops had also invaded and captured this island.

Fortunately, the Royal Marines and Paras had recaptured it before we arrived in this freezing, hostile region of the world. We transferred to another commandeered cruise ship the Canberra and sailed 965 miles to the Falklands. Amphibious landing craft took 120 of us to Fitzroy on East Falkland. Weather conditions were atrocious forcing us to wait 25 minutes in the landing craft before disembarking. Landing craft are open to the elements, creating an uncomfortable environment. Exposed to the South Atlantic winter climate was a circumstance nobody would relish; conditions were so cramped that your joints hurt through having to maintain one position for a long time.

Anxiety levels raised among the squaddies through the likelihood we would be facing enemy fire for the first time in our lives, compounding an appalling situation. Choppy seas doused us with sea water, icy cold on exposed flesh which chilled us to the bone. Ferocious waves hitting the craft washed vital equipment into the sea. Conditions were grim with a howling wind, continually whipping freezing sea water into the landing craft. It appeared as if the sea was saying, 'Welcome to the Falklands this won't be easy.' These weather conditions made me think that General Galtieri might not have to work too hard to defeat us. The elements could finish us off.

Eventually disembarking, our destination was San Carlos Bay, an 18-mile march where we'd meet up with the remainder of the Welsh guards who'd been transferred from the Canberra to the Sir Galahad. I was a machine gunner and with my teammate Russell Fouweather had to carry 150 pounds of kit across some of the worst terrain imaginable. Pragmatically, Senior Command decided a long march with kit was impossible and aborted the mission.

We were ordered to dig trenches, which was a futile exercise as the ground was sodden. Removing a spade full of earth, the hole immediately filled with water. Countering this problem, involved building sangars from stone for protection from enemy fire. What a waste of effort because 24 hours later we were ordered to board a landing craft for transfer to HMS Fearless. This took us to San Carlos Water where we were ordered to climb into a landing craft once more.

Unfortunately, we were forced to wait in the craft for eight hours prior to going ashore. Young soldiers were under terrible pressure causing tempers to fray. Even though we were going into battle, we were desperate to get off. Such confinement was physical torture. Once ashore, we built a second group of sangars while the remainder of the brigade were waiting to disembark the Sir Galahad. On board were 430 Welsh Guards, large quantities of ammunition, mortar rounds, anti-tank missiles and small scimitar tanks.

The rest of the brigade should have been quickly disembarked from the Sir Galahad, but the delay meant they were sitting ducks for the Argentinian Air Force. Four Argentinian Mirage jets appeared from nowhere at 2:00 p.m., flying low over our heads. Such a deafening, piercing sound forced us to cover our ears. Even then the noise was ear splitting. A strike was inevitable as they released their missiles at the Sir Galahad. Flying low they couldn't miss.

Devastation was inevitable as the explosion produced noise like an overhead thunderclap closely followed by an almighty inferno. Men trapped inside screamed as their skin began blistering, peeling off with the intense heat. Primal screams could be heard as men writhed in agony leading to survivors saying charred flesh smells like nothing on earth. It was nauseating, survivors said they could taste this holocaust. My mate who survived said the ghastly stench of human beings burning would haunt him for life.

Argentinian aircraft seemed to be moving at the speed of a meteor and to the naked eye they looked like shooting stars. Seeing flashes of flame hit the Galahad, I knew they'd used Exocet missiles. Rooted to the spot with fear we were like statues. Then quickly regaining our composure, we began firing at the aircraft. Uncertain if we'd hit anything, the sudden rush of adrenalin we experienced, prompted us to act in this way but was replaced by concern for our mates on board.

Inter regimental rivalry in the army is intense but that day any competitiveness was put aside in an effort to get the injured ashore. Marines, Paras, medics already at Bluff Cove rushed to help the injured. I know their speed of thought that day saved many lives. 8 June 1982 is etched in my memory as 48 of my mates were killed in one of the darkest days in British military history. Watching the dead being removed from the Sir Galahad, it never crossed my mind when I joined up that I'd ever witness carnage on this scale.

Army slogans stated, 'We will make a man of you,' never mentioning it could destroy you both physically and psychologically. Tears welled up in my eyes. Tough boys sobbed. None of us said a word. All were shocked at what we'd just seen. Welcome to the reality of war Billy but it was not over yet. I would witness more shocking scenes before the conflict ended.

Men with charred flesh were brought ashore. Such terrible injuries, produced by horrific weapons caused brave men to groan in agony. Intolerable pain disappeared as morphine was administered, many wishing their torment would end with death. Medication swiftly took effect causing pain to subside but unfortunately, we all knew our mates faced years of reconstructive surgery to lead anything like a normal life.

Hopefully, the public would not see these heroes as freaks but understand war lay behind these disfiguring burns. So many bizarre thoughts went through my mind. I could not help wishing I was back in Llanen. Etched into my psyche was the horror of what I'd witnessed. Although I'd no physical scars, my wounds were all psychological, triggering a chain of events lacerating my mind to the present day. Injured soldiers were transported to the hospital ship. Their war was over, mine was about to begin.

You would think that I'd have been exhilarated at not being on the Galahad. If I had been it might have resulted in me burning to death or being horrifically scarred. In fact, quite the opposite happened. I became overwhelmed with guilt having witnessed so many men being killed or maimed. Why did they die or get burnt? Why was I allowed to survive? It was fate being chosen to get in that landing craft. This good fortune was the starting point for my psychological scarring.'

Billy let out a huge sigh.

Chapter 10

Speaking with Antoinette and Simeon helped ease the grotesque demons tormenting Billy for years. Although not on the Sir Galahad, the thought that so many of his mates were killed, horrifically burned or injured produced feelings of guilt that he'd survived. Feeling culpable having survived Billy began to speak about his feelings.

'I should've been with them on the Galahad. After witnessing missiles hitting the ship, I had a heavy pounding feeling in my chest. All I could think about was I should've been on that ship. Not being with them made me feel remorseful. Over and over, I asked why was I one of the 120 chosen as an advance party. To me it wasn't fair that the other 430 were on that vessel, yet I had the good fortune to survive such a devastating event.'

Antoinette was moved by what she was hearing and her overwhelming sympathy for Billy consumed her.

'Look Billy, you're doing the best thing talking about your feelings.'

Although Antoinette offered kind words in an effort to comfort Billy, the Galahad bombing had left such a mark on him it would be nigh on impossible to change his perception of the incident. Billy was overwhelmed by guilt.

'I know it was a piece of luck, but I still felt guilty at not being on that ship.'

Simeon tried to placate Billy adding, 'These are normal feelings for anyone surviving a war. You have to realise you were not the one who killed your mates.'

Whatever Antoinette and Simeon told him, Billy still seemed to carry his escape as though he was carrying a millstone, slowly weighing him down. If he was not careful, he would eventually collapse under its enormous weight. Billy elaborated further about his war experience.

'This initial guilt was replaced by the need to avenge the dead and injured. They were our mates; we were going to pay the Argies back. At the time, I struggled to think of the Argentinians as fellow human beings. They were now the anathema of evil to be defeated. War definitely succeeds in changing people, bringing out basic animal instincts, belying our ability to reason.'

Simeon's inquisitive mind wanted to find out if there were further incidents playing on Billy's mind.

'What happened Billy after the incident on the Sir Galahad?'

Sapper Hill, 4 June 1982

'I was a machine gunner working with my mate, Russell Fouweather. We were part of an assault force made up of Two Company Welsh Guards and Forty Commando Royal Marines. Command ordered us to attack Sapper Hill where Argentinian forces were dug in. Fortunately, we were well supported by a naval bombardment and Harrier jets. Navy and air support were significant factors in the battle but it would be 'boots on the ground' that would eventually win the day.

We were a professional army with good fitness levels. Army command made sure we retained our fitness on the journey to the Falklands. Huge deck space on the QE2 provided us with a training area. We needed to be fit to counter the challenging Falklands terrain. The ground was reminiscent of the Scottish islands, boggy under foot making our boots sink into the ground with a gurgling, squelching sound. Carrying 150 pounds of equipment was a further handicap, making our progress painfully slow.

A hilly landscape allowed the Argentinians to set up vantage points, making it difficult to flush them out. Another problem was the Falkland's winter with only four hours of daylight. Consequently, most combat took place in poor light, creating a significant problem for machine gunners. Tracer from the guns is red, making it easy to pick out those firing it. Countering this problem meant continually moving position to avoid being hit.

Continual movement was exhausting, causing every muscle in our bodies to ache. Pushing pain to the back of our minds, survival was the priority. I worked well with my mate, Russell Fouweather, ensuring we covered each other's backs. Teamwork was essential if we were to stay alive. Any lapse in concentration was quickly remedied by your mate reminding you it could cost you your life, making mutual trust the main ingredient if we were to stay alive.

Training exercises always involved using blanks. Sapper Hill was real conflict, something you prepare for but hope you will never participate in. Adrenaline courses through your veins, nerves jangle but you forget the

Argentinians are trying to end your life. Drinking inadequately purified water, particularly using it in dried food produced diarrhoea making an added complication for us all. Staying alive was our focus. We could not allow any one problem to become a distraction because death was one lapse of concentration away.

Battlefield smells linger in my memory with cordite pervading the atmosphere reminding me of bonfire night, as a kid at home in Wales. Your chest tightens, smoke causing you to gasp for breath. Uniforms become impregnated with battlefield chemicals, producing nausea. Losing concentration could have put me in the sights of an Argentinian sniper. You're in danger of your mind wavering making you think whether military service was an appropriate career choice. It was disconcerting thinking that Army life meant others were controlling my destiny.

Decisions about our future were being made by politicians from the safety of their Westminster offices. I wondered whether they'd find it as easy to make life and death decisions, by sending us to war if they were the ones being shot at. Intense noise, created by aircraft, exploding shells, mortar and gunfire was deafening and stomach churningly frightening. I allowed my mind to wander for a split second to the tranquillity of a Welsh Valleys Sunday afternoon. Very quickly I was brought back to the present when an Argentinian shell exploded close to our position.

Russell screamed, 'Billy keep your focus. We need to move because the Argies have picked our position.'

Picking up our weapons, we moved slowly through the grass and gorse. Such long vegetation meant we couldn't avoid catching it around our boots. The thought crossed my mind that even the terrain was trying to trip us up. Peat bogs are difficult to move around in normally but under the pressure of gunfire and the weight of our equipment, it was a real handicap.

Assembling the equipment at another sangar we fired again on the Argentinian positions. Naval and air support began to turn the tide in the battle giving us the advantage. This superior firepower meant we were able to overcome the Argentinian defenders.

Death is a smell pervading any battlefield, mingling with the odours produced by the explosive material. Beginning to retch through the stench, we move up the hill, passing dead Argentinean bodies mutilated by the horrific violence created by modern warfare. Limbs blown off, some of the enemy missing parts of their skulls, others with huge holes blown in their torso made me want to throw up. Initial feelings of revenge for the sinking of the Galahad subsided and were replaced by sadness at the carnage inflicted on our fellow human beings. Dumbfounded, I couldn't believe that I'd participated in this horror.

A final mortifying act followed when the dead had to be cleared from the battlefield. Corpses were searched in an attempt to identify individual Argentinians. We came across photos of wives, children and other family members. Each of us had families and when you do a job like this there is a realisation that these bereavements will bring heartache to many families. The magnitude of what had taken place hit home as if I'd been battered with a sledgehammer.

Following their surrender prisoners of war were taken and I was struck at how young the Argentinian soldiers were. They were obviously conscripts, not professionals. Many looked as though they should be in school, not on a battlefield. Although I was only 18, they looked younger than me.

Fear was etched on immature faces, many were crying. Any feelings of reprisal were replaced by thoughts that these youngsters needed to be treated with compassion. Anything less would have demeaned us as human beings, contravening the Geneva Convention. My whole thought process had been transformed by what I'd witnessed. Gone was the urge to take revenge, replaced by feelings of sympathy and tolerance for the enemy.

Working alongside prisoners we had to dig a mass grave to bury the Argentinean dead. Thankfully, the Argentinian soldier's bodies were exhumed at a later date and given a dignified burial in their own military cemetery on the Falklands. Our inhuman sentiments after Bluff Cove were replaced by sympathy for the enemy and empathy for men whose service was mandatory. It dawned on us these victims were pawns forced to fight promoting a dictator's ambitions. They'd been given no choice, thanks to a fanatic coercing them into war.

Filled with sadness at young lives cut short, my heart went out to them. I came to appreciate the futility of war and the fact that former enemies now contact each other through Facebook exemplifies this. During the 1980s we were sworn enemies fighting a senseless conflict. Without a doubt we temporarily lost our humanity. It took the horrible consequences of the conflict at Sapper Hill to bring me to my senses, making me appreciate we all belong to one human race.

I have paid a terribly high price for what happened on that day, but I'm not alone. There are many others who have agonised over what happened in that battle. British and Argentinian soldiers now united as friends regularly contact each other. Thank God common sense prevailed in the end.

Sapper Hill was a British victory. Luckily, I survived as did Russell Fouweather. Port Stanley, the capital, was recaptured with the Argentinian flag being taken down from outside the Governor's house to be replaced by the Union Jack. Falkland Islanders celebrated their liberation welcoming the British troops as heroes having just restored their freedom.

Quite rightly the Paras and Marines triumphantly walked into Stanley first to liberate British citizens 8,000 miles away from home. This group of soldiers had been fighting in the Falklands, the longest period of time and, were fully deserving of the plaudits. Port Stanley had to be secured, a job which fell to the Welsh Guards, Scots Guards and Gurkhas. General Galtieri wasted no time signing a peace treaty but would he still have felt his actions were vindicated or would he have felt great shame at his miscalculation. The Argentinian people would be judge and jury.

Today, Argentina is a great South American country. Issues remain over the sovereignty of the Falkland Islands but hopefully politicians have learned from past mistakes avoiding a repetition of 1982. Any dispute needs to be settled in an amicable way respecting the sanctity of human life. My witness at Sapper Hill convinced me war can never be the answer.

Our final duty in the South Atlantic was the repatriation of prisoners of war to their homeland. A shock awaited us in Argentina when nobody turned up to meet these defeated brave youngsters. Having survived, these were the lucky ones but it was so sad to think of their compatriots who would have had ambitions for the future destroyed on the battlefield. I was terribly saddened that these survivors had to cope with the humiliation of their own people rejecting them.

Today I hope they've recovered from their experience and are leading meaningful lives. Contrast their homecoming with ours in Portsmouth. In a show of nationalism, we returned to thousands of people waving Union Jacks, treating us like returning heroes. Bands played; soldiers waved from the decks of ships to the people standing on the quayside. Locating wives, girlfriends, mothers and fathers was virtually impossible, there were so many people in the crowd.

Margaret Thatcher was feted as an inspirational leader. She was lucky. The task force she ordered to the South Atlantic could so easily have been routed owing to the distance it had to travel. Victory resulted in a Conservative government being re-elected with an enhanced majority. A Welsh miner's son had helped the Prime Minister who would, in a short period of time, become a figure of hate in the valleys through her attitude to the coal industry.

Returning in such a way seemed OK at the time but the scars of war were deeply rooted in my persona. My mental health would deteriorate as the years passed with depression setting in. There were many restless nights festering on what happened and I could see no way out of this despair. Desperation drove me to go to the garage one afternoon to end it all. Throwing a rope over the rafters I climbed onto a chair. Having created a noose, I put the rope around my neck. Stepping from the chair my wife and two sons came in to get their bikes. She let out a scream as the rope tightened.

Immediately my eyes started to bulge and my neck veins protruded as the strangulation process had begun. Survival depended on the swift actions of my family. My wife rapidly pulled herself together telling my young sons to hold my legs, relieving the tension on the rope. Sprinting into the kitchen she returned with a knife, climbed onto the chair severing the rope. Collapsing on the floor into a crumpled heap I was gasping for air on top of my two sons. This was a terrible thing to put my family through. I just could not cope. It was the last straw for them. Unable to take anymore I left home going into a bedsit in Cardiff. Having no money to pay the rent forced me onto the streets, eventually ending in London.

Although the Falklands War ended more than 30 years ago, the psychological trauma affecting me is ongoing. I am better away from my family, sad as it was to break from people I genuinely loved. Post-traumatic stress takes years to establish itself but overtime, it slowly demolished me. Living with my family became impossible because of the stress I'd put on them. Post-traumatic stress disorder was triggered by the terrifying events of Bluff Cove and Sapper Hill, creating anxiety more debilitating than any physical illness.

On my return to Britain, I was delighted to have survived. Given six weeks wages I just pissed it up for two weeks until this windfall had gone. Thirteen years after the cessation of hostilities intrusive thoughts began. Negative thinking resulted in emotional outbursts where I would harbour violent thoughts. Family members failed to understand these psychological changes and I was back at

Sapper Hill reliving the carnage. Unable to speak about my experiences, memories were bottled up inside me. I was slowly imploding.

Family abandonment was inevitable in these circumstances. There was no way they would be able to appreciate the guilt I was feeling at surviving the conflagration in the Falklands. Numerous times I have asked, could I have done anything about my feelings. There was no support for soldiers suffering post-traumatic stress disorder. Although some progress has been made today for soldiers returning from war, many still suffer. Thirty years on I know war is the result of human selfishness, to be avoided at all costs.'

Antoinette profoundly affected by Billy's recollections remarked, 'Psychological scars are worse than physical injuries. The suffering is ongoing. You are a man with amazing life experience, which could benefit society. Anyone who'd witnessed war at 18 years of age would be traumatised.'

Simeon added, 'Billy, I wonder if the church could help you. Pastor Robbins is the one to talk to and I'll speak to him. It might just be the therapy you need.'

Chapter 11

Pastor John Robbins was devoted to the life of Tooting Evangelical Church. It was important to him that he lived life in accordance with biblical teaching, consequently fighting for social justice. He was never judgemental but would express a point of view if he needed to. The Pastor's mantra involved continually fighting for the less fortunate.

Consequently, people from all strata of society respected him for his commitment to people's welfare. Devotion, to his work led to many flocking to his church for worship, creating a vibrant community supported by people of all races and colours. Sunday services generated a unique atmosphere with people glorifying and venerating God at this unique place of worship.

Antoinette and Simeon viewed the diversity at the church as a model for wider society to replicate. People who'd never been churchgoers were captivated by Pastor Robbins's commitment. Those who'd previously avoided church found themselves drawn to this captivating Christian sanctuary.

Simeon's parents had worshipped at the church for many years whereas Antoinette's induction followed after meeting Pastor Robbins at a fundraising event for world poverty. His sincerity made an immediate impact on her and she became a church member. She met Simeon at the church, both enjoying the lively worship where modern music was central to the glorification of God. No fuddy-duddy old fashioned music at Tooting, rather electric guitars and drums producing a melody catching the attention of all ages, particularly the young.

Many outsiders referred to the worshippers in Tooting as happy-clappy Christians through the inspirational way in which they praised God. Large numbers of the congregation were endowed with Gifts of the Spirit, giving them the ability to speak in tongues. Sceptics questioned the legitimacy of this act, wondering if it was a case of mass hysteria whereas participants viewed this as a gift of the Holy Spirit, a language that God alone understands.

Tooting Evangelical Church bucked the national trend with the size of its congregation. Hundreds of members flocking there on a Sunday for worship whereas growing secularism in society meant conservative churches struggled to attract decent numbers for worship.

Simeon went over to see Pastor Robbins who was speaking to some of the homeless guests. He was so completely devoted to his work that he would always speak to anybody needing his counsel.

Simeon approached him to promote Billy's cause.

'One of the guests, Billy Davies has suffered with PTSD for nearly 30 years after fighting in the Falklands War as an 18-year-old. What he witnessed there was horrific and he's been psychologically traumatised ever since.'

'Is he a Londoner Simeon?'

'No, he's Welsh but Billy was depressed as a result of what he saw as a young man during the Falklands War. He separated from his family after trying to take his own life. He only failed through his wife's intervention.'

'That's incredibly sad Simeon.'

'I wondered if there's some way the church could help him. He's intelligent and has extensive life experience. What he needs is a leg up in life. I'm sure if he had one, he could make a good contribution to society.'

'It's really kind of you Simeon to think about Billy and I'm sure we could help by employing him as a church caretaker. You know how many activities we have going on here. His help could be invaluable. As well as being a caretaker he could help me. I'd be prepared to pay him a small wage to go along with his own room at the church.'

'Oh, that would be fantastic, Pastor, you've come up trumps again. He would really appreciate it. Thanks, Pastor.'

Simeon could not wait to tell Billy that he was going to have the opportunity of a fresh start in life. It was time his luck changed.

Billy ecstatically said, 'I never thought I'd meet people who are as kind as you. Working hard in the past has never been a problem. I'm going to make every effort to get my life back on track.'

For the second time in his life Billy was about to experience the generosity of a religious fraternity. During his school days Billy had experienced the magnanimity of a religious community. The Pastor's generosity excited Billy.

'I was not a real troublemaker in school but I was rough and ready. However, I'd readily admit I could have worked harder.'

Antoinette was puzzled as Billy had spoken so eloquently about the issues in his life, making it difficult for her to understand how he'd under achieved in school.

'Billy, you don't seem to be the trouble making type.'

This was the cue for Billy to speak about an experience he had in school. Animatedly he said, 'During form four, the Head teacher came to my class to ask if he could have a word in the corridor. He told me I was one of 15 pupils selected by the school to go to the Hebridean island of Iona, located off the Scottish West Coast.

Iona is a stunning, crime free place, where no citizen ever locks their doors. Here was an example of a harmonious society where everyone could be trusted. There are only a few vehicles on the island needed to transport provisions. Staggering scenery with white sandy beaches reminiscent of the Caribbean greets visitors and if you didn't know better, you'd think you were in Barbados.'

'Have you ever been to Barbados Billy?' asked Simeon.

'No, don't be daft, the only place I've been beginning with B is Barry Island but I've seen pictures of Barbados.'

They all laughed. Billy continued.

'Some years previously, a religious community had been established on Iona. At the beginning of July 1979, there was a youth week on the island. The Head told us there was no charge for us to go. Money had come from the local council as part of a crime reduction grant, to pay for the travel and accommodation. Two teachers would accompany the group from Llanen to Iona.'

'That was a long way, Billy. I bet you were ecstatic,' said Antoinette.

'Hearing this invitation from the Head my face beamed with joy. I had difficulty sleeping and couldn't wait. I had barely been 5 miles from Llanen, let alone 500 miles to Scotland. This was one of the highlights of my school life.'

'You seemed to like your trips, Billy. When you went to Cornwall you taught a parrot to swear. Did they call you tripper Davies?' Simeon asked.

'No, I was only on there because I was one of the naughty boys and girls.'

The three of them laughed again. Being goody goodies in school Antoinette and Simeon were tickled pink with Billy's school days tales.

'I'd willingly admit to being a bit naughty in school though never a criminal. In fact, the teacher who accompanied us said, we were the best-behaved criminals he'd ever met.'

'And he was right,' said Antoinette.

'You didn't know me when I was in school, Antoinette.'

Antoinette kindly exclaimed, 'I wish I did. You would have been a bit mischievous but no doubt the life and soul of the class.'

Billy was in his element as he began to tell Antoinette and Simeon about the trip.

'We set off from Llanen station on 14 July 1979, catching the Valley's train to Cardiff. The adventure of a lifetime had begun. Arriving in Cardiff one of the boys asked, 'Where do we catch the next train?' Leaving the valleys train at platform 7, we were told to go to platform 3 but, quick as a flash, one of the boys, Jason, jumped from the platform and ran across the tracks. No words could describe the look on the faces of teaching staff.

Dumbfounded, stunned, emotionally drained, petrified, terrified, the staff stood rooted to the spot. Quickly coming to his senses, the teacher, we called Doc sprinted to platform 3 bellowing, 'What are you playing at?' Doc was as white as a corpse. Jason retorted, 'See in Llanen we always go across the line.'

Realising that Jason had never been outside Llanen in his life a smile drifted across the Doc's face. Jason's only experience of a railway station was a single-track railway in the valleys. All of us came from working class homes which were not affluent. We also had limited experience of the wider world. Here was a genuine case of a child lacking any insight into the world outside his little enclave in the valley.

Following the near-death experience in Cardiff we boarded the train to Manchester. We had to leave the train at Crewe to board the Glasgow Express. Arriving at Glasgow Central we walked across the city to Glasgow Queen Street to catch the train to Oban. Our teacher stressed the importance of our party getting on the back two carriages of the train. At Crianlarich, the train would split with the front two carriages going to Fort William in the Highlands, while our two carriages would go to Oban.

Miraculously considering our naivety, we all managed to get in the right carriages. The whole party arrived in Oban to spend the night in a youth hostel. Next morning after a Scottish breakfast, we embarked the Charles MacBrayne ferry to Craignure on Mull. Following a 50-minute crossing we boarded a service bus for the one-hour journey to Fionnphort. Mull's scenery was stunning, rugged ridges, black basalt crags, blinding white sands on the beaches and emerald sea water left us mesmerised.

We had never left the Welsh valleys; such amazing scenery was awe inspiring. Mull is a wildly beautiful island leaving us wonderstruck by its splendour. Departing the bus at Ffionphort our party walked down the slipway to board the ferry to Iona. Hanging over the rail we could see the holy isle from the boat. All that remained of our journey was a crossing of less than a mile. Our 500-mile journey was about to come to an end but our adventures on the island were about to begin.

At the quayside, we were met by one of the Iona Community who escorted us to the McCleod Centre where we would be billeted for the week, with many other young people from different countries. All this was mind blowing for a boy from Llanen who'd never been anywhere.

Unfortunately, the visit could have been a disaster without the Doc's quick thinking. Three of us were put in a room with a Canadian boy who left his money on the bed. One of the boys in our room decided to pocket the cash. Unfortunately, he was a youngster from an extremely poor family who'd little in the way of material possessions. Seeing the wallet on the bed tempted him to nick the cash. It was a bad thing to do but his poor background was a mitigating factor. How dull was that? There were only three others in the room, so he was certain to get caught except that we didn't actually see him do it.

Nevertheless, we knew it was him. Obviously, the Canadian boy was well off but he was visibly upset. Our irate roommate complained to the Doc that his money had been stolen. Quick thinking by Doc saved the day. He didn't threaten us but told us the future of our trip was now in our hands. Putting us in the bedroom we were told we had a choice. It was up to us we could stay in the room two minutes, two hours, two days or the rest of the week if we didn't bring the money out. As long as the money was put in the Doc's hand the matter would end.

Giving us this amnesty was the lever needed to encourage the culprit to give me the money. Having recovered it, I took it out and delivered it. We never said anything. He only handed it over when we threatened to beat hell into him. The last thing we wanted was a good trip ruined by an act of pilfering, so grabbing him by the throat we could hear his knees knocking. As quickly as he nicked it, he handed it to me. To the Doc's credit, he kept his word. Handing the money over to a delighted Canadian youngster, the matter was closed resulting in us having an amazing week.

Our Canadian roommate had a Scottish father who had taught him to play the bagpipes. When we left, the Canadian boy piped us off the island. This proved to be a highly, emotionally charged occasion.

Our time at the McLeod centre was amazing. We were treated like royalty by the Iona Community. Charles McLeod had set up the centre for impoverished Glaswegian children giving them a holiday away from the poor surroundings of their everyday life. Meals at the centre were mostly vegetarian, except for fish on Friday and meat on Sunday.

Movements like the Iona Community protecting Earth's resources have gathered momentum and in this respect the Community was ahead of its time. There is an Abbey on Iona standing on the site of a monastery founded by Saint Columba and is one of the oldest religious buildings in Europe. Quickly it dawned on us that most of the other young people with us were religious as they attended the service in the abbey every evening. It was not compulsory for us to attend church, nevertheless by the end of the week we were participating in services.

Among our group were some good singers, who were brave enough to perform a solo while others read aloud to the congregation. Many of our group pinned prayers to a cross in the abbey, something which our teachers found emotional. These prayers asked for help with family problems highlighting the difficulties some youngsters have in their everyday lives. I am sure the trip helped change the teacher's perspective on life as much as ours.

Glorious weather and pristine safe water allowed us to swim in the harbour. One afternoon following an hour swimming, the teachers asked us to go back to the centre while they had a cuppa. Allowing time for the teachers to disappear out of sight, some of the boys sneaked back thinking they would have an extra dive into the harbour. In the case of a Welsh valleys boy, the old adage 'boys will be boys' rings true.

Jason dived first, failing to consider the tide had started to go out. Emerging from the shallow water he had a gash on his forehead which was bleeding profusely. Having just finished their tea, the teacher we called Doc calmly said, 'What have you done?' Thankfully, he was a tolerant guy. He certainly needed to be. Jason answered in his valleys accent. 'Dur Sir. See when we was diving earlier on, I was just going into the water then I came back to have another go and hit something rock hard.' Doc roared with laughter saying, 'You bloody buffoon, the tide went out. You hit something rock hard alright. It was a rock you nutter.' Docs response was brilliant.

All the ferries had stopped for the night. To get Jason medical help on Mull, Doc smooth talked one of the locals into taking him over in a small motorboat. When Jason came back, we all called him Frankie. Those stitches in the middle of his forehead made him look like Frankenstein.'

Antoinette and Simeon howled with laughter, 'Why haven't we had school trips like that?'

'I felt really valued by the Iona community. It was terribly upsetting to leave. Being piped off the island by the Canadian boy whose father was Scottish, the same one who had money stolen, made us feel like superstars. Today another religious community has treated me in a compassionate way rescuing me from the streets. I have had so many low moments in my life but I am happy, this opportunity will hopefully change things for me.'

Chapter 12

Climbing into bed Billy was more relaxed than he had been for years. He now had two new friends and the thought of working for Pastor Robbins sent him into a deep, restful slumber. Lethargically pulling the blankets back in the morning, the delightful aroma and hissing of cooked breakfast greeted him. Volunteers were buzzing around preparing to serve breakfast for the homeless guests.

Filled with fresh vitality Billy was hoping his desperate situation on the streets had finally concluded. He always had an apathetic attitude towards prayer. Such were his expectations he decided to invoke the Almighty in the hope God would change his desperate situation to a positive one. The prospect of a hearty breakfast put a spring in Billy's step. Revitalised Billy thought to himself, what more could anyone want? Optimistically, he would now have a real purpose in life, not just exist.

Simeon and Antoinette were helping prepare breakfast for the guests. Linda, who was in charge was a jovial lady always offering words of encouragement. When breakfast was ready, she mutated from a convivial human being to a doughty lady where all were expected to run to the tables. Prior to the morning fayre being served, one could hear pans clinking as Linda prepared the food then there was the occasional damn and blast as droplets of fat leapt out of the pan, landing on her arm. She would scream, 'Cor, that's heavy.'

When she was ready Linda would blurt out at the top of her voice, 'Grub's up.'

Rolling and storing mattresses was the first task of the day for the homeless but on Linda's command everything had to be dropped. All were expected to sprint to the tables to avoid upsetting Linda. Orange juice, cereal and hot cooked breakfast were enthusiastically devoured. Outstanding hospitality was a life saver for people living on the streets. Gratitude was obvious by the way guests repeatedly thanked volunteers.

Following breakfast, a meeting had been arranged with Pastor Robbins to discuss the work he wanted Billy to do. Although he would receive remuneration for his efforts, the most appealing part of the arrangement would be his own room giving Billy a base for the first time in years. Prior to the meeting there were 30 minutes for the group to watch breakfast television to catch up with the news.

To Billy's astonishment, the first news item was the stabbing at Clapham South tube station. Gang culture where knives were used had become a major issue in London developing into a significant problem. It was no wonder it was a lead news item. An 18-year-old man had been arrested and was in police custody. Interviewed by the news correspondent the police spokesman read a short statement.

'The man who's been charged is named as Dennis Fouweather. Being 18 years of age, we can name him and he'll appear in court today.'

As the police spokesman finished, the camera switched to the boy's grandfather who wanted to make a statement. Billy was nonplussed at what he was seeing on the screen. It was Russell Fouweather, the squaddie who'd been his machine gunner mate during the battle for Sapper Hill. Billy could see his former mate looked emotionally drained as he spoke to the BBC correspondent.

Shaking and stuttering he made a statement, 'The family is appalled by the actions of my grandson and the hearts of our family go out to the victim's parents, relations and friends.'

The BBC correspondent asked Russell, 'Have you got a message for London's youth?'

Russell with tears in his eyes made a heartfelt appeal to the capital's youngsters, 'My grandson's in pieces following his monstrous action but it's too late to bring the victim back. Using a knife is a tragedy, costing many lives in London, couriering drugs and the endemic gang culture has to stop.'

Billy had always known Russell to be honest. This incident involving a family member would have devastated him.

'My grandson will be pleading guilty in court. He's genuinely filled with remorse and again, I can't emphasise the folly of young people carrying a knife.'

Russell emotional and looking completely demoralised by what had happened spoke out, 'My grandson's actions are those of an impulsive, hot headed, disturbed individual for which the only appropriate punishment is a long custodial sentence. Such an abhorrent crime, inflicted through a spur of the moment decision has taken an innocent young life, brought heartache to two families and ruined my grandson's life. Justice must be seen to be done and although a long prison sentence would take away some of the best years of my grandson's life, the most devastating punishment will occur as he gets older. This action will continue to play on his mind. In some ways he will be a prisoner forever, always carrying the mark of Cain.'

The BBC correspondent asked Russell, 'What do you think should be done about the knife problem in London?'

Obviously, this was difficult to answer because his grandson had just committed a heinous crime. Russell's intrinsic honesty came to the fore in his answer.

'Money needs to be invested to counter this problem. I am reluctant to offer an excuse for Dennis's crime but my son, the boy's father has suffered from PTSD after fighting in Afghanistan. During his childhood, Dennis found his father's mood swings overwhelming. Mixed up, he sought security in the gang culture. Social services need to be on the ball offering help where children are struggling. It has taken this monstrous action for Dennis to realise that his miscalculation will cause grief for himself and a large number of other people.'

Billy knew many viewers would have little sympathy for Dennis Fouweather. Significant numbers would advocate the death penalty for his sickening, detestable action. Personal experience of PTSD from the Falklands War, particularly the way this psychological trauma impacted on his own family, enabled Billy to empathise to a point with Dennis Fouweather's tragic life. Lacking love in his home life led to him compensating by becoming a gang member. Billy's experience gave him the vision to appreciate here was another human tragedy where war was at the root of the problem.

Hoping Tooting Evangelical Church would give his life direction, there was every possibility he was now in a position to contribute to improving society where all people are valued.

Chapter 13

Billy's life had just received a fresh impetus creating a newfound determination in this homeless man. He was set on utilising his inventive mind to benefit others. There was a problem with this as he was the only one who knew he possessed such novel thought processes. Billy had become aware of this talent he had during his time on the streets where he would dream up strategies solving fictitious problems. God willing, his new role at the church would give him the opportunity to use this latent gift. Buoyed by this new opportunity produced a dynamism in him which had been missing since he was a child. Having new status Billy's confidence grew, giving him the fortitude to discuss problems with Pastor Robbins.

Living in the church created a desire in him to participate in many aspects of church life. One of his favourite involvements was playing the mouth organ in the church band. All this allowed Billy to become a popular member of the church community. Many church members with a fundamental approach to Christianity asked Billy to consider Believer's Baptism. Although Billy could take or leave organised religion, he'd been baptised as a baby. He certainly appreciated the significance of this rite of passage, pointing out to church members the importance of the sacrament he'd taken as a child.

'I was christened as a baby. Christianity teaches baptism is a once in a lifetime event. Even though you people have made your own vows as an adult in the baptismal pool, my vows were taken on my behalf by Godparents. I might have been a baby but I retook the vows for myself when I was 13. In my thinking it means I don't need to be re-baptised.'

Pastor Robbin was really delighted Billy had such a good understanding of Christian initiation ceremonies. He agreed with Billy.

'It's immaterial whether you're christened as a baby or baptised as an adult. The most important thing is a person leads a life where they help their fellow man.'

Simeon and Antoinette's relationship continued to develop. Billy could see the couple were gradually falling in love and wondered what they were going to do after school. One evening after band practice, he popped the question about their academic futures.

Knowing both these young people were academically gifted, he asked, 'Antoinette and Simeon, you're both in your last year in school. Do you know what you'll be doing next year?'

Simeon was the first to embrace Billy's question.

'I've done well at GCSE but I'd like to go to Oxford to study Philosophy, Politics and Economics. However, there's one problem. Nobody from my school has ever studied at Oxford. What's more, I don't know whether there's a member of staff who will be able to help me get in. Oxford is different to other universities because it functions through a tutorial structure.'

Simeon was reticent about his chances having been brought up in a Balham council flat with his four siblings. Although not from an affluent family, Simeon's mum and dad worked incredibly hard giving their children the best educational opportunities they could. Growing up the family didn't have the luxury of being able to afford lots of books or have their own computer.

Technological poverty was no barrier to this family. Simeon's mum made sure they were well catered for by taking them to the local library. Here they had access to books and the free use of computers. Simeon's attitude to work together with his exemplary manners guaranteed he was popular with library staff. Unbridled enthusiasm for learning meant they were always willing to help him. Simeon's mum constantly instilled into him that the family's small income should never be used as a barrier to educational progress. Sometimes she irritated Simeon by quoting her favourite proverb at him, 'Where there's a will there's a way.'

Exasperated on occasions with his mum's determination to see her family succeed, Simeon realised her drive was pushing him on. Her fervour and Simeon's determination saw him make excellent progress at Oak Grove Academy. During secondary school, Simeon reinforced his learning by spending countless hours in the library which paid dividends at exam time.

Having reached an age where a decision about his future needed to be made, Simeon had to consider higher education options. Simeon was academically way ahead of anyone else in his year. Billy recognised the difficulty Simeon faced, making an Oxford application from a state school in a socially deprived area.

Oak Grove was no Eton but Simeon's natural academic ability gave him the tools to compete on a level playing field with anyone irrespective of their school. Values ingrained by loving, religious parents benefited Simeon, marking him out as an exceptional human being.

At Oxford, there would be no Bullingdon Club for Simeon. This covert, all male club, responsible for gratuitous damage was populated by very affluent ex public school elite, some progressing to high political office. Simeon would judge their behaviour as causing wilful damage, committed by a bunch of narcissistic individuals using wealth as a cover for hooliganism. Viewing this behaviour as vandalism, Simeon would think they needed to be prosecuted. Their behaviour was criminal. Having oodles of cash by birth right should not exempt these individuals from justice.

Billy could see Simeon needed a push to make an application to Oxford. Here was an opportunity to give him some advice.

'You must apply Simeon because I remember a girl in my class in Llanen, who was the first person from our school to go to Oxford. Her achievement was the talk of the village. Gemma was encouraged by the Head of sixth form after he heard a poem she'd written. This piece of literature had been read out at the school Eisteddfod.'

Simeon had never heard the term Eisteddfod before, so he enquired, 'What is an Eisteddfod?'

Realising that a London schoolboy would never have had access to this aspect of Welsh culture Billy threw some light on the subject.

'In Welsh tradition, an Eisteddfod is a festival of Welsh literature, music and performance. On 1 March, St David's Day, each school in Wales has their own version of this cultural event.'

Simeon's desire to continually get the best out of himself and his inquisitive mind meant that he would have loved to see the poem.

'I wouldn't have minded seeing a copy of that poem.'

'Neither would I,' added Antoinette.

Billy was pleased that these youngsters were so interested in what he'd just told them.

'When Gemma was 15, she gave me a copy which I've kept safe. I'll get it and read it to you.'

Billy went to his bedroom, fetching it from his treasured possessions. Antoinette and Simeon listened attentively as Billy read it to them.

Monster

To the reader. I am aware that this poem may evoke some strong and indeed upsetting emotions, but I believe there was no other way of expressing the fear and terror the girl was feeling and monsters really do exist and are not just a figment of our imagination.

Each time I go to bed at night,
I grasp my blanket very tight,
Pretending to fall into a warm, deep, sleep,
Begging God that safely I'll keep.
But I don't.
I hear the slamming of the door,
And the hard noise that is made when he stumbles,
Then falls to the floor,
He breathes heavily as he walks up the stairs,
I tremble nervously, yearning for a daddy who really cares.
My bedroom door slowly opens and the light floods in,
Daddy's fun is about to begin.
I feel a hand on my body that is not my own,
And I wish that mummy hadn't left me all alone.
The tears of anger and frustration run down my face.
Fearing the act which is about to take place.

Gemma Lewis

Antoinette's face was a conglomeration of emotions at what she'd just heard causing her to blurt out, 'I can't believe what I've just heard. I don't know whether to be amazed, shocked, flabbergasted or disturbed. How can a 15-year-old girl write about child abuse with such clarity?'

Billy was anxious to answer Antoinette's concerns about what she'd just heard.

'Gemma's work certainly triggered emotions in people. Obviously, some staff wondered if she'd personally suffered abuse. The issue was raised at the time but she was not a victim at all. Gemma was a student with unprecedented insight, giving her the ability to empathise with victims of this type of horrific mistreatment.'

Simeon was also astounded by what he'd just listened to. After thinking he was compelled to pass an opinion on the poem.

'She must have been an amazing student. Simple language but a stunning message, as she says evoking strong emotions. I am absolutely blown away by it.'

Billy continued, 'The new Head of sixth form shared your amazement at what he'd heard. He told her a hard-hitting message had been conveyed through using simple language everyone could understand. The simplicity of the written word marked it out as an iconic piece of work. Gemma was only 15.

'What happened to Gemma?' asked Simeon.

'Well, the Head of Sixth Form suggested that Gemma applied to Oxford.'

'Oxford is a collegiate system so which college did she apply to?' asked Simeon.

'Gemma applied to do medicine at St John's College Oxford.'

'I heard that is one of the most difficult colleges to get into.'

'You are quite right, Simeon; you really have done your research.'

'I was thinking of applying there but I don't know whether I'm that good.'

Antoinette was quick to support Simeon.

'Simeon, you'll never know unless you do.'

Billy elaborated further.

'Gemma had the same reservations as you, Simeon. The Head of Sixth Form encouraged her. Although I had left school, Llanen is such a close-knit community I remember her going to the open day worried about the public-school kids who were there. When she started talking to them, she realised her GCSE results were better than any of the students she'd spoken to.'

Antoinette quickly offered encouragement.

'Simeon, you've got 10 A*, you must apply. There's going to be a member of staff who can help you, just like there was for Gemma.'

Billy had further morale boosting words for Simeon.

'When Gemma went for the interview, she had to do an aptitude test based on the Stephen Lawrence case. After she had started at St John's, the Head of Sixth Form told her he had a letter informing him that the aptitude test she'd done was the best they'd ever read, fitting in with Gemma's ability to empathise with a victim. This innate gift had been obvious when she'd written the poem, again coming to the fore in the test.'

Billy had lit a fire in Simeon making him anxious to know more. Probing further Simeon asked, 'What's Gemma doing today?'

'She did her three-year pre-clinicals at Oxford, followed by medical training at the John Radcliffe hospital in the city. She is now working as a palliative care consultant. Unfortunately I've lost touch with her since I left Llanen.'

Billy's words resonated with Simeon, inspiring him. The idea that a working-class girl from Llanen went to Oxford convinced Simeon to apply.

'I'm going to apply, if you don't try, you'd never know if you were good enough or not. There's no reason why a Sixth Former from an apartment block in London, a descendant of the Windrush Generation cannot be the first from his family to study at university or the first from his school to study at Oxford.'

Billy now wanted to know about Antoinette's plans for the future.

'What about you, Antoinette. Would you like to go to Oxford?'

Antoinette managed a wry smile then proclaimed, 'I've no chance of studying at Oxford. It would be no more than a pipe dream for me to study at the city of Dreaming Spires.'

Many girls at Antoinette's school applied to Oxford each year while about 10 would be offered places. Such a prestigious school counted many well-known figures among its alumni. Unfortunately, Antoinette's lack of confidence led to academic under achievement, all down to a lack of stability at home. Her upbringing was quite the opposite of Simeon's. Having grown up in a broken home had a tremendous effect on Antoinette.

Reared in a large six bedroomed property worth millions, adjacent to Clapham Common, Antoinette wanted for nothing when it came to material possessions. Privately educated Antoinette surprisingly struggled with her confidence. This lack of self-assurance stemmed directly from her home life. Antoinette's mother was a high-flying barrister who put her career and personal life before Antoinette's need for a happy family life. A live-in childminder when Antoinette was young, was no substitute for a mother's love. Antoinette's mother thought deep pockets could compensate for a mother's obsession with climbing the career ladder at the expense of her family life. This led to Antoinette's dad divorcing her mother.

Although Antoinette would see her dad, who she related well to, it was no counterbalance to a stable home life. Such instability at home severely affected Antoinette, compromising her progress at school. Her mother's complicated love life created a web of problems and a succession of male partners brazenly flaunted in front of Antoinette was not something she could ever approve of. Antoinette always felt relegated in the pecking order behind these lovers. Her mum's vanity was another issue she had to cope with. Personal trainers, cosmetic procedures, beauty treatments all costing thousands of pounds were part of a regime, impacting on Antoinette's well-being.

Fortunately, meeting Pastor Robbins at a world poverty conference opened the door for Antoinette to attend church in Tooting where she met Simeon. Immediately struck by the contrast between her family life and his, Antoinette could see the benefit of having a loving family. It certainly relegated the financial advantage she had as a child into second place. Quickly appreciating bundles of cash could not compensate for genuine love, Antoinette related well to Simeon's parents. A short time ago she made up her mind, there was no value in constantly bickering with her mother. Endeavouring to keep the peace was far better, while totally disagreeing with her lifestyle.

'Antoinette, you're obviously very able so why shouldn't you study there,' exclaimed Billy.

'I haven't worked diligently in school. I should really be called the dreaming prospective politician.'

Billy had seen the perceptive side of Antoinette, which she'd failed to recognise in herself. Difficult circumstances at home continually eroded her self-belief creating a crisis of confidence for her. This needs rectifying, thought Billy. In a calculated way Billy began to address the problem.

'I am astounded at your assessment of yourself. All this is in your hands. You've definitely got the innate qualities to achieve in the political world. Look, I know you're making an honest assessment of yourself as you see it. That's not how I see it and your problems can definitely be rectified.'

Billy identified Antoinette had a confidence problem. Although speaking very directly, he aimed to illicit a response from Antoinette where she'd show the determination to fulfil her potential. She now began to talk about her problems.

'Concentrating in lessons is difficult. Although I do homework, I feel like I've a 'box full of frogs in my head.' I am all over the place leading to my once high standards slipping. Unlimited material possessions just can't compensate for this problem.'

Billy was determined to start instilling confidence in Antoinette. After considering what she'd just told him, he began to offer a measured assessment of the situation.

'Antoinette, your self-esteem is low. Potentially the world's your oyster. It's imperative you start to believe in yourself. Take it from me you've tremendous potential. Look Antoinette, I can tell you until I'm blue in the face. You must come to terms with it. Then change it.'

Antoinette's intellect spotted that this 'kick in the pants' was just what she needed. Despite Billy speaking in a very direct way, his words expressed a real concern for Antoinette's future prospects. She responded positively,

'Billy, you're so kind-hearted but unfortunately, I've allowed my dysfunctional family life to affect me. During Year 7, I was achieving well but my father and mother split up then divorced. Obviously, I live with my mother but there have never been any difficulties with my father having access to me. Since the split nearly five years ago my mother's seen numerous men, creating instability at home. Discussing this problem with her would be futile. She is self-obsessed with her own lifestyle. I've had to fend for myself, leading to this problem impacting on my schoolwork.'

Billy thought back to his schooldays remembering some of the dedicated teachers he'd come into contact with.

'Have you spoken to a member of staff about these things, Antoinette?

'It's really difficult speaking to a member of staff about this problem. Their focus revolves around getting exam results. Many of the girls do exceptionally well academically, making it easy for one person with a family problem to slip through the net. I'm definitely that one person. It's made me withdrawn, refusing to speak about it until now.'

Billy was thrilled that his willingness to speak about his own problems prompted Antoinette to discuss her difficulties.

'Divorce creates enough problems for youngsters but the way you describe your mother's behaviour is just exacerbating the problem. You're sensitive, leading to a preoccupation with your mother's actions seriously affecting your academic performance.'

'I agree with what Billy's saying,' exclaimed Simeon.

This discussion had created a spark in Antoinette and for the first time in ages someone had shown an interest in her problems. For years, these had remained bottled up inside her. Billy's concern had forced Antoinette to open up about her troubles.

'What do I do about it before it's too late?'

Billy was swiftly on the case.

'Right Antoinette, there are definitely extenuating circumstances. I'm certain a real effort to work now will enable you to go to University.'

'There's no way I could apply to Oxford.'

'Yes, I can see that Antoinette.'

Billy's voice became assertive again.

'You must apply now to university. You will still be able to get in to study Politics. Don't let your mother's behaviour stop you achieving.'

Billy's encouragement was the trigger Antoinette needed.

'My minds made up. I will.'

Billy was euphoric at Antoinette's response realising this was a new friendship, mutually beneficial to the three of them.

Chapter 14

At the end of September, Antoinette went to Cardiff University to study Politics. Frantic last-minute revision attributed to Billy's pep talk paid dividends and she was accepted onto a politics course. Simeon excelled in his A-levels enabling him to take his place on the Philosophy, Politics and Economics course at St John's College, Oxford.

Billy was ecstatic, having instilled both with the confidence to achieve well. He might not have helped them academically but he'd given them the encouragement needed to do well. Self-esteem had been a problem for both, but in completely different ways. Simeon might have missed the 'Oxford boat' and Antoinette might never have gone to University without Billy's intervention.

Continually focusing on family issues was preventing Antoinette achieving at school. Although she'd gone to Cardiff University there was still so much more to come from her. Billy was convinced, in time she'd fulfil her considerable potential. Distressing times seemed to be behind Billy and he became absorbed by his work at the church. Having been raised to a new life by Simeon, Antoinette and Pastor Robbins, he'd started to repay them for the faith they'd shown in him. New friends had mutually benefited each other, leading to an improvement in all their fortunes.

Billy's innovative thinking started to come to the fore in his new role at the church. He spoke to pastor Robbins about his desire to bring the wider community together, irrespective of whether they had a religious commitment or not. Having witnessed the incident at Clapham station, Billy was perturbed by the level of knife crime in London and wanted to do something to improve this problem. Government oratory was all well and good, but Billy thought it was time to do something about this proliferating issue.

Youngsters of secondary school age would be Billy's target group; they were the people he would have to influence if this problem was going to be resolved.

For any initiative to be successful Billy needed the support of the authorities. He decided to speak to the Chief Superintendent at Tooting police station.

Knife amnesties had been tried before with limited success. People who owned and carried a knife were reticent about handing them in at the police station. Lack of trust between the two parties was a huge obstacle needing to be overcome. Billy wanted to use an alternative strategy, encouraging youngsters to hand in their weapons at Tooting Church. Handing knives in at the church would be less threatening, encouraging youngsters to submit their weapons making the streets safer.

Billy contacted the head teacher at Simeon's old school, Oak Grove Academy to explain what he intended to do. A perceptive man, the Head, realised this was a necessary initiative needing his support. At the Head's invitation, Billy was invited to the school for a preliminary chat. Captivated by the reception he received, Billy was fortunate the Head already knew about Billy's role in encouraging Simeon to apply to Oxford. This notable success was responsible for the school gaining positive press coverage.

Simeon's achievement thrilled the Head, who was particularly impressed that a former homeless man was the catalyst for this accomplishment. Billy asked if he could speak to the youngsters about his military service, with the purpose of pointing out that violence discredits human beings. Young people carrying knives for protection was certain to result in unnecessary deaths, devastating families and ultimately the perpetrator's life as they'd be forced to live with the consequences of their crime for the remainder of their life.

Speaking openly to them about his war experiences and the destruction of his family life caused by post-traumatic stress, Billy pointed out if they murdered someone, they might well serve a prison sentence. Unfortunately they'd also be facing a life sentence as their actions returned to haunt them. Experiences during the Falklands War had left a mark on him, rearing its ugly head when he was older. Combat deaths on both sides were harrowing, tormenting him to the point where his family could no longer cope with his disturbed psychological state.

Billy implored the students to give up any weapons by surrendering them at Tooting Evangelical Church. He was at pains to point out that they'd be giving a knife to him and no police would be present. Later the knives would be deposited at the police station where an amnesty would give those who submitted their weapons anonymity. Billy stressed the difficulties he'd encountered in his own life explaining how Simeon a former pupil had played a part helping him overcome these.

Giving them the same opportunity was important, one they shouldn't spurn. Using a knife might seem the big thing to do but there would come a time when this impetuosity would create a void in their lives. Forcefully stressing, people change as they grow older and today's actions would come back to bite them. Billy thanked the pupils for listening, accentuating there were no religious motives behind his visit. The only rationale was removing weapons from the street, saving young lives.

Leaving the school Billy felt a sense of achievement at what he had done, wondering if his talk would have any impact at all. Cooking his evening meal, he heard footsteps coming down the stairs. An adolescent black boy appeared at the door. Removing a machete from his sports bag he told Billy his weapon was always stashed outside the house because he was desperately concerned, he didn't want his mother to know about it. Having been given the chance of an amnesty he wanted to hand it in.

Shuddering as he took the fearsome weapon from the boy, the thoughts crossed his mind that one thrust with this machete would mean certain death. Such a huge razor-sharp blade would easily decapitate someone. The surrender of this armament brought a sense of joy to Billy. He was at pains to reassure the youngster when it was handed to the police there'd be no repercussions. Billy commended the boy for making a wise choice and saying goodbye, he wondered if there would be others. Possibly thought Billy, the boy is bound to have friends who are armed.

Hoping a drop would become a trickle and eventually a torrent, Billy went to bed. He would soon have his answer when the following evening three other boys brought their weapons. Drums had obviously been beaten and news gone out that the bloke from the church was sound. Billy was overjoyed at this turn of events.

Over the next few nights what happened filled Billy with unbridled joy. He now had 20 knives in his possession. Protecting the young people's identity Billy handed the knives to the police, who were staggered at this initial success. In the following days, more young people handed in their knives and the local press began to take notice of Billy's achievement.

Tooting's Superintendent contacted London's Mayor at City Hall. Rhetoric had achieved little. However, the efforts of a former homeless man produced results. There was a realisation by the authorities that churches could play a substantial role in reducing the capital's knife crime. Youngsters willingly cooperated knowing churches posed no legal threat to those carrying weapons.

Billy set about contacting vicars, priests and ministers in order that the amnesty could be extended. An amazing response led to countless weapons being removed from London's streets. Every church and parish had someone with the skills needed to help halt the knife epidemic. The initiative brought forward people with real charisma who could relate to youngsters.

Billy thought, the best people to deal with this issue were those who'd encountered problems when they were younger and had managed to overcome their difficulties. The kids had no problem identifying with these people and the fact they had changed their own lives around prompted youngsters into relinquishing their weapons.

Billy went into other local schools, receiving a warm welcome from pupils who eagerly listened to his story. An ever-growing number of youngsters came forward with weapons. This was not a government official but a former homeless man who had enormous personal problems to overcome. Billy's story created an impression with the youngsters helping them realise that all people have problems which can be beaten with encouragement.

Billy's star was certainly rising and London's Mayor invited him to City Hall for afternoon tea. Having no need to ever wear a suit, a church member loaned Billy a pin striped one for the occasion. This former homeless man was revelling in his newfound status, even putting him on first name terms with the Mayor. It made Billy think that people in Llanen would never believe this.

Tooting was now Billy's new home and he could not have felt better if he had won the lottery. Billy had just dug a few nuggets out of the gold mine, making his teacher from all those years ago right about what can be achieved with hard work. The knife amnesty certainly convinced Billy that changing lives fills someone with a great sense of achievement.

Chapter 15

Traditionalists referred to Billy's efforts as unorthodox but effective. Although pleased, Billy knew the job was incomplete. Better facilities were required for young people if a long-term solution to the problem was to be found. Ingenuity was needed if the majority of young people in London were going to fulfil their capability.

Billy again spoke to Pastor Robbins explaining his vision for counteracting boredom among young people in London. Facilitating his vision called for a meeting of the London Council of Churches to present a plan managing the issue. Worshipper's skills could be utilised by providing expertise on a voluntary basis. Church facilities could be used to set up homework clubs allowing youngsters from deprived backgrounds to get help after school. As he did when he was sitting on the streets Billy had thought fully about the problem and a possible solution to how it might work. He spoke to Pastor Robbins.

'How many retired teachers are there worshipping in churches? Surely, they would want to give their time as part of their Christian calling. How many other worshippers would be capable of taking a sports team or setting up a boxing club?'

Pastor Robbins was always impressed by Billy's innovative thinking.

'Carry on, Billy, I like what you're saying.'

Giving Billy the green light led to him elaborating further.

'Pastor, the potential opportunities are limitless giving Christian churches an opportunity to reinvent themselves in the 21st century.'

'Yes, Billy I agree with what you're telling me. Many churches have large unused spaces needing to be utilised. Without doubt this would benefit individual youngsters and wider British society.'

'I also think businesspeople might want to get involved, Pastor, particularly if they attend church. Surely these people would want to invest in helping youngsters, suitably equipping tomorrow's workforce. What about local entrepreneurs who might never have been near a church, they would see this as a golden opportunity to promote their companies, as institutions which care about today's youth, seeing them as worth investing in.'

Pastor Robbins was always looking for ways to promote the Christian message and Billy's initiative would give churches a chance to refresh themselves in the 21st century.

He said to Billy, 'I'm really taken with what you're saying Billy. It's a great idea. Although it's very much in its embryonic stage it has serious potential and could well bring youngsters into the different churches. It will give places of worship an opportunity to make a provision that is appropriate to the 21st century. Churches should not just be available for Sunday worship. It is our duty to ensure a wide range of activities are provided.

Children might be reticent about attending church for worship, making it imperative that we provide opportunities, drawing youngsters in. Historically places of worship have been venues where people were educated. Christianity has evolved during the last 2,000 years, so it is important that our provision adapts to the needs of our time. If we don't do that we'll just stagnate, subsequently only appealing to a small minority.'

The Pastor's willingness to initiate change further enthused Billy.

'Yes, it could well do that, Pastor. If this is to pay dividends the emphasis has to come away from worship. Young people will not buy into it. Caring and setting an example will provide the church with a totally new focus where young people learn skills benefitting both the individual and wider society. Underprivileged youngsters would have a place to do homework. Young people will be in contact with adults capable of instilling good standards of behaviour and caring about them.'

'Billy, if youngsters like what they're doing it could lead to them coming to church.'

'Yes Pastor, that is how I see it, but in the first instance put Sunday worship to the back of your mind. Helping youngsters in this way will be more important to them. Giving youngsters the help they need means many will go on to achieve their potential. Suddenly, churches will be contributing to social order. Whereas churches have been side-lined by the secularism dominating modern life, they will be given a new impetus and quite rightly held in high esteem by the general public having been prepared to adapt and change.'

Just as all clergy agonise over how to make churches more appealing to 21st century society, Pastor Robbins saw this as a wonderful opportunity for places of worship to promote themselves.

'Billy, there's a lot of talk about how churches can be made more attractive for youngsters. People now need to pull together. This would certainly give the churches an opportunity to do that.'

Billy felt encouraged by the Pastor's response.

'I'm really pleased you're thinking this way, Pastor. Churches must learn to work with schools, police, local councils and government. It is important because the greatest asset we have is our children.'

'There could be a lot of people who will give their time Billy as long as we are organised.'

'Society will definitely be the winner, Pastor.'

Billy's ideas invigorated Pastor Robbins.

'I will contact the Roman Catholic Archbishop, the Church of England Bishops, the Presbyterian and Methodist synods. The Evangelical churches meet regularly and I know all these church leaders.'

'Excellent, Pastor. If we harness the respective strengths of these individuals, there could be a 21st century Reformation.'

Laughing loudly, Pastor Robbins exclaimed, 'You're really getting carried away now, Billy.'

Pastor Robins used his extensive connections to call a meeting of the London Council of Churches at Tooting Evangelical Church. Tooting was one of a small number of churches where attendance was booming whereas many of the traditional churches had dwindling congregations. Religious leaders were continually looking for answers to the diminishing attendance problem causing large numbers of clerics to attend the meeting including the Archbishop of Canterbury and the Catholic Cardinal for England and Wales.

Many of these learned men and women had countless academic qualifications with many letters after their names. Despite their formidable intellects they couldn't find an answer to contracting church numbers. Billy thought about the many doctrinal arguments throughout the centuries causing Christianity to fragment. It is absolutely ludicrous he thought to himself.

'Why should it matter if a cleric is a man or woman? A person providing inspiration for the public should be the primary focus, not their gender. Surely, God intended there to be equality in creation. No wonder there's a problem with numbers attending church. If a female is considered unfit to lead worship, churches are bound to stagnate. Many modern-day women are feminists. They will not buy the line Jesus did not appoint any woman disciples. During the 1st century women had no status and if women had been appointed as disciples, then Christianity wouldn't have spread. These sexist attitudes today are totally unacceptable. Convictions like these are firmly entrenched in some churches, causing institutions to falter rather than moving with the times.'

Billy was really pleased, Tooting Evangelical Church was a forward thinking, thriving Christian community where men and women could be leaders.

Billy began to think deeply to himself about why church unity was impossible to achieve. It began to dominate his thought processes as he pondered on the following.

'A divisive issue is the Catholic belief in transubstantiation when the bread and wine at the point of consecration becomes the actual body and blood of Christ, whereas other churches treat Communion as a memorial of Jesus's sacrifice on the cross. Billy had been brought up in a Chapel background in the Welsh valleys, so the thought of the bread and wine becoming Jesus's body and blood was risible to the people who worshipped in this way. He thought none of this should matter, they are all insignificant arguments. What counts is what Christians hold in common, that Jesus became incarnate, died for man's sin and rose from the dead.'

Billy let out a huge sigh as he concluded, it's ironic if these religious leaders had nothing to argue about, they'd look in the mirror in the morning and argue with themselves. Such a thought lit up Billy's face with a wry smile.

Mentioning any of these religious differences during a London Council of Churches meeting would lead to outright rejection of his ideas. He might think it but was not stupid enough to voice these opinions at one of the meetings. If Billy learned anything in the army, it was that unity is strength.

Billy and his pal Russell Fouweather formed a great team in the Falklands, their togetherness keeping them alive. Sometimes in life you need to be canny and this was one of those occasions if Billy was to win the Council's support. Success would depend on him performing well in front of these church leaders. One advantage was they knew about his triumph in initiating the knife amnesty. The result was a substantial reduction in young people carrying knives in London, leading to less children being killed. How would these religious leaders receive the latest line of thinking by Billy? He was about to find out.

Meeting of the London Council of Churches

Pastor Robbins introduced Billy to the Council.

'This is Billy Davies, a former homeless man who has been adopted by the church in Tooting. Billy fell on hard times following war service in the Falkland Islands. He struggled with PTSD to the point where he tried to take his own life. Quick thinking by his wife saved him but the stress he was living under, sadly ended the relationship. He was part of the homeless night shelter in Tooting leading to us adopting him. You will know he's taken a lead in addressing the knife crime problem in London. The knife amnesty he set up has produced amazing results. I don't want to waste any more time on introductions so over to Billy.'

The religious leaders showed their approval by either muttering or nodding in unison.

One of the senior clerics spoke out, 'It is really important that churches adopt a positive attitude to the homeless. How easy is it to underestimate a person looking bedraggled, in second-hand clothes sat on a sleeping bag in the street? Obviously, Billy is a man with a rare talent, he's knowledgeable, more importantly his work reducing knife crime portrays a creative mind. Pastor Robbins has told me that Billy's plan is to take churches forward in the 21st century.'

This scholarly audience applauded loudly.

Continuing he said, 'None of us lack compassion yet sometimes we become concerned with unimportant aspects of organised religion such as ways in which individual churches worship and miss opportunities to help the underdog. Billy's ideas could be the epitome of Jesus's work and we need to listen carefully then consider its merits.'

Billy came forward to the lectern to speak. The last time he'd experienced nerves on this scale was at Sapper Hill. At least this lot were not firing bullets at me, he thought to himself.

He began, 'Attitudes to religion have changed but it doesn't mean there's no room for faith communities in Britain. If traditional churches continue as they are, all the rhetoric in the world will not prevent church attendance diminishing further. We have to accept we're living in a secular age. What I'm proposing is that greater emphasis needs to be put on encouraging youngsters. Many centuries ago, the church gave the poor a vision of heaven with elaborate buildings, music, incense, beautiful artwork and prayers. This was OK during the Middle Ages.

Life for the poor was hard. Reformation in Europe brought change, through division, creating Catholics and Protestants.

In England, the Church became an integral part of the establishment. Church and monarchy became closely tied together. Later came John Calvin's influence, leading to the development of Presbyterianism and Methodism. During the 20th century, Pentecostalism began in the United States, eventually spreading to Europe, promoting gifts of the spirit as a core belief, particularly speaking in tongues. Differences of opinion have always been present in the church but core beliefs are the same for all Christians. Certainly there is more that unites churches than divides them because all worship the same God. Despite not being a good Sunday Christian, I realise churches can add real value to society. You surely must ask the question,

Is the church maximising this value?

Unity can change this. I am proposing a 21st century Reformation digging for spiritual gold. You all recognise that the church is moved by the Holy Spirit but it's time to open the cage and let it out!

Young people are society's future and all youngsters want to achieve but many lack the correct guidance to do well. London's churches need to utilise their space as often as they can. People who attend for worship on Sunday should be encouraged to volunteer to help youngsters. Many would be willing, but it needs organisation and what could be better than staffing homework clubs. It is important children from underprivileged homes have the opportunity to attend so they can access good facilities, maximising their academic progress. Correct me if you don't think Jesus would approve.

Many churches have retired teachers who would willingly give their time in a church environment, seeing it as an opportunity to live out their faith. Churches should refrain from thinking that worship and studying the Bible is their only responsibility. Broadening horizons is essential because society demands youngsters need to be competent at English, maths and science. I can hear you thinking but we are religious institutions! Quite right, you are but when I was in school, I was one of a group chosen to go to the Macleod centre on the Scottish island of Iona.

A crime reduction grant paid for the visit, so we were not exactly the 'crème de la crème.' A criterion for being at the centre was to attend the evening service in the Abbey but because none of us went to church, the leader waived this condition. However, the community and environment infused us with a desire to find out what happened in the Abbey. By the end of the week all of us were going to church. Some of the group even read or sang in the Abbey, all a by-product of not being forced to worship.

Churches in London should open to kids from all backgrounds. Surely you are able to see disadvantaged kids would be the greatest beneficiaries but so would your places of worship. A secular society would hold your churches and chapels in high esteem through Christian places of worship making a significant contribution to youngster's lives. Continuing as you are will only further erode church attendance. Some church worshippers have excelled in sport. Their expertise could be used to set up sports teams.

A league system could be set up encouraging competition and fair play. I am not naive enough to realise, a project like this would need oodles of finance and management creating an effective organisation. Professionals must be employed centrally orchestrating everything. Then there needs to be advertising and money made available to buy equipment. All these ventures would be run by volunteers freely giving their time to enhance children's lives.'

The Archbishop of Canterbury thanked Billy but he now wanted further discussion.

'Can we divide into smaller groups to discuss Billy's proposal.'

Dividing into small groups, these esteemed ministers of religion went into side rooms to scrutinise Billy's proposal.

Chapter 16

Returning from the meeting rooms a profound, ominous silence descended on the hall, as delegates waited for one of the senior clerics to take a lead. Acting as spokesperson the Archbishop of Canterbury acknowledged churches were always looking for ways to attract new worshippers and as institutions needed to broaden their appeal to the wider public. The Archbishop was at pains to stress that churches needed to continually evolve but many had stagnated and were now in need of re-energising to fulfil their vocation. Raising his voice, he exclaimed, 'Carpe diem [seize the day], Quo Vadis [where are you going].'

Billy had a limited understanding of Latin. The learned church leaders had no problem grasping the point being made. It was obvious from these pronouncements, the Archbishop had taken a positive view of Billy's proposal. His glasses rested on the end of his nose. Peering over his specs with a glowering look of determination, he wanted to leave those delegates with conservative leanings that this moment needed to be grasped. Although prepared to innovate to make Christianity more attractive, he wondered about some of the other clerics who were more set in their ways, holding fundamental beliefs.

'I would like to say that Christianity is at a crossroads in this country. One Anglican Bishop resorted to setting up a golf course in a cathedral in the hope of enticing people inside. Unorthodox it might be, but at least the Bishop is thinking about how the church could appeal to the wider public.'

A few of the more fundamental leaders tutted at this innovative thinking failing to see any value in it.

Britain's foremost cleric then proclaimed, 'Billy has stepped forward to show us the way giving us a proposal and we now need to grasp the mettle.'

The Catholic Cardinal was quick to support the Archbishop. Although Catholicism had the greatest numbers of worshippers throughout the world, Western Europe had seen a considerable decline in attendance at Masses. He realised Billy's initiative offered hope at a time of encroaching secularism. The Cardinal would not want to be left behind.

'Billy's suggestion could breathe new life into the church in London. Where London goes the provinces follow, possibly revitalising churches throughout the land. Homework clubs are a really good idea. At the time of Jesus synagogues were places of learning. We need to look back 2,000 years by trying to emulate these ancient Jewish places of learning. Supporting this initiative transcends our doctrinal differences and is an outstanding example of the unity we should all be aspiring to. Apathy is not something we should tolerate and like the Archbishop of Canterbury the proposal has my full support.'

Again, the Archbishop of Canterbury spoke, 'In my previous employment, I was a business executive before I took holy orders. I have retained enough contacts for one of my former associates to draw up a business plan promoting Billy's ideas.'

The Catholic Cardinal wanted to ensure the Church of Rome participated fully in the initiative.

'There are many wealthy Catholics attending churches who could act as benefactors for a worthy cause. Great kudos would be attached to supporting this type of effort, presenting any of their businesses in a favourable light.'

Pastor Robbin's face was a picture, knowing Billy had won over a discerning audience. He told the gathering, 'This initiative would support schools by giving less privileged children the opportunity to achieve through accessing after school facilities. Unfavourable home conditions are an impediment to their progress. Surely the New Testament teaches Jesus supported the disadvantaged. This is what we should be using as our yardstick! The police would also be ecstatic to think youngsters were being presented with opportunities to enhance their development, hopefully keeping them from trouble.'

A minority of leaders raised the point that some older members might see the church as selling its soul in return for populism. The Archbishop of Canterbury quickly jumped on this objection.

'The church is not just for middle aged and older worshippers to promote their own agendas. It's important we encompass and nurture all ages in particular children. Remember Jesus said, 'Suffer the little children to come to me, for the Kingdom of Heaven belongs to such as these.'

The Archbishop was at pains to express his gratitude to Billy, 'I'd like to thank Billy for his contribution.'

Billy responded, 'Your Grace I'd just like to raise one other point. We need to consider Muslim, Jewish, Hindu, Buddhist and other faiths, incorporating them in this initiative. I know we wouldn't exclude these children but their leaders need to be part of this programme. To this end I'd like to propose that we change the name of this body from the London Council of Churches to the London Council of Unity when we discuss this issue.'

Leaders acclaimed this idea and began to cheer. The Archbishop of Canterbury concluded the meeting saying, 'This is a potentially unifying idea, helping heal divisions within different faith communities. We could encounter bigotry in the future. It is a bridge to be crossed at the time. We need to revel in the potential this idea offers. It means different institutions uniting to work together setting a good example to the rest of society.

It is important we contact leaders of other faiths; ever mindful they need inclusion in this project. Senior church leaders will contact potential benefactors. A press conference needs to be organised to launch the initiative. I would just like to thank Billy, while he might not be a Sunday Christian, he certainly is a God sent man, whose ideas are providing a guiding light.'

Billy left the meeting invigorated ready to meet more fresh challenges.

Chapter 17

Billy's ideas for uniting different communities had been so successful that he featured in the press, made television appearances and was invited to prestigious functions. Life was the best it had ever been. Billy became a well-known face in London. This level of acclaim could easily go to someone's head but Billy retained his dignity, acting with modesty at all times. Many people wanted to know why Billy didn't move into his own home. He just told them the only place he wanted to live was Tooting Evangelical Church.

Children from disadvantaged backgrounds attended places of worship to be helped with their homework. The prelates of the two main churches kept to their word, using their influence, getting businesspeople to provide large sums of money to purchase equipment for use with the children. Boredom was not an issue for Billy as many people made great demands on his time. However, he did take pleasure in his newfound status having left his troubled past behind.

2015 was a special year for Billy because the young couple Simeon and Antoinette were graduating. Simeon achieved a first-class honours degree from Oxford in Philosophy, Politics and Economics, while Antoinette fulfilled her potential achieving the same degree classification in Politics.

Early self-doubts about her ability disappeared as she was awarded a politics prize for the best student in her year. She also excelled in political debate prompting many to earmark her as a future politician. Academic success ensured Antoinette would be an outstanding recruit for any organisation. Having been interviewed at the Home Office, she gained a post as a researcher for the Home Secretary. Simeon's call did not lie in the world of politics, rather his compassionate nature guided him into a post with Save the Children.

Following their educational success there was a small matter of their graduations. Each was allowed to take three people to their respective ceremonies. Billy went with Simeon's mum and dad to Oxford in June. He was awestruck by buildings dating back to Tudor times. What an institution he thought! Simeon had been rubbing shoulders with academic high-flyers for three years.

Simeon's dad had a tear in his eye while Billy had a lump in his throat when Simeon's name was called out. He proudly stepped forward to receive his scroll from the Vice Chancellor. Previously Billy had borrowed a suit, but this occasion warranted him splashing out on a new one. Never one to overindulge Billy bought a £79 pound suit from Marks and Spencer and a shirt online for £6. Billy could never understand why people spent hundreds of pounds on a suit as he looked a class act, or so he thought!

Following the degree ceremony at Oxford, Billy attended a banquet. As he looked around him, he kept thinking back to those dark days as a homeless person living on the streets. Academics recognised Billy from media photos, quickly praising his work. One even suggested, his efforts were worthy of an honorary degree. Such acclaim filled Billy with satisfaction at his achievements.

July 2015 was another great day for Billy. Antoinette was going to be awarded her Politics degree at St David's Hall, Cardiff. She managed to put aside any difficulties with her mum, realising a difference of opinion, leading to a war of words about her multiple relationships would not change anything. Maturity convinced Antoinette that insecurity was at the root of her mum's problem, appreciating even someone who is a high-flying professional could have mental health issues. Seemingly her mum needed a partner to give her confidence.

In the past, this had affected Antoinette, but at university she'd come to accept her mother's lifestyle. Time in Cardiff gave her the space she needed away from her mother's situation, where she came to realise all human beings have demons, even those with a privileged existence. Wealth and status did not exempt her mother from this aspect of life.

Billy attended the ceremony with Antoinette's mum who was there with her umpteenth partner. Antoinette commented to Billy with tongue in cheek, 'My mum has had so many partners she couldn't remember their names.'

Billy thought to himself, 'That's my girl, she's beginning to see some humour in what was a really difficult personal situation.'

Taking their seats in the auditorium with large numbers of Welsh people caused Billy to think about his childhood in Wales, reflecting on how happy it had been. Suddenly Billy refocused on the ceremony when the orchestra began playing a classical tune. As their names were called out students filed across the stage to receive their award. St David's was a huge venue, so Billy used an old pair of opera glasses to improve his view. Antoinette's name was announced and she walked elegantly, at an appropriate pace across the stage. What a wondrous moment. A few years previously, Antoinette would have thought this impossible. Her satisfaction in what she'd achieved was apparent in her deportment, Billy thought, 'Here's a young woman who's going places.'

Next to be called was a graduate named Steven Davies. Keeping his theatre glasses focused on this individual, Billy initially thought this was just another graduate. Taking a prolonged look, Billy was astounded as this degree holder was the elder of the two sons from his marriage. Here he was gaining his degree from the same class as Antoinette.

Wonderstruck Billy felt butterflies in his stomach. He began thinking about how his son would respond towards him if he saw him. Surely this was fate. Would he also bump into his ex-wife? How would she react towards him after these years? Countless emotions agitated Billy, causing anxiety to wash over him.

In trepidation, Billy left his seat knowing he would have to go to the foyer. Moving down the steps Billy was in a trance at the thought of meeting his family. Graduates stood around talking in small groups. When Antoinette spotted Billy, she ran towards him giving him a hug. Billy focused on another group including Steven Davies who stared back at him. This was Billy's equivalent of the OK Corral. The two men were like western gunslingers facing each other, wondering who was going to draw their gun first. Steven looked bewildered; Billy was equally nonplussed. It was Steven who budged first.

He blurted out, 'Dad, what are you doing here after all these years?'

Uncertain what Steven would think of him Billy played a straight bat.

'Well, I came with Antoinette but this is an added bonus.'

Steven hurried towards Billy. In the intervening seconds Billy wondered if he would be decked thinking his son hated him for the way he'd behaved. Any thoughts of Steven being angry were allayed when he stuck out his hand to shake Billy's. Handshakes quickly turned to hugs.

Steven exclaimed, 'Now I'm older, I know exactly what you went through when you were young. Any anger at you leaving home has been replaced by an understanding of the torment you must have endured from your experiences. Many times, I've asked myself, 'would I have been able to cope with experiencing battlefield horrors at such a young age?' It has caused me to shudder at such a prospect, I also know what you've done in London making me extremely proud of you.'

Immediately Billy's spirits were lifted. Here was a reconciliation he never expected. At that moment Billy's ex-wife Linda with her youngest son came into view. Their expressions said it all. Here was the man she could no longer remain with because of his depression. Difficult to understand at the time, Linda now realised that a serious mental health issue instigated by war had led to the break-up of their marriage. Initiating the first move, Linda hugged Billy and he reciprocated. As Linda removed her arms from Billy, his youngest son Wayne embraced him. Billy overflowed with emotion following such a positive response from his family.

He'd been wrong, all along thinking they would reject a man who had run away. Fortunately, his family understood the psychological damage inflicted by war. Antoinette found it difficult to grasp that a student in her classes was Billy's son. All were emotionally drained at this reconciliation; Billy was dumbfounded by it all. Nevertheless, he was thrilled Antoinette had done so well at university. What a bonus that his eldest son had also achieved a top degree. What a tremendous double, Billy thought, but more importantly the reunion helped in a small way to alleviate any guilt for his leaving home.

Immediately Linda was able to see the change in Billy, expressing her pleasure at his transformation. She had seen his achievements in London on the television but was afraid to contact him, worried he would see her as intolerant towards the mental health issues he'd suffered. Billy pointed out nobody was to blame. Difficulty coping with his PTSD would have been a problem for anyone at the time. It was understandable that Linda couldn't cope.

'The way you've put yourself on the road to recovery is a testimony to your determination,' said Linda.

'I can assure you I was lucky to meet Antoinette. She is one of the people who helped straighten my life out. Without help from Antoinette and her boyfriend Simeon I could still be on the streets.'

'A lot of people obviously think highly of you. It's really important that you continue the work you've been doing. Remember you're always welcome in Llanen. By the way, the boys will want to see more of you. You didn't realise it but you've made them really proud.'

This was a remarkable day in Billy's life. Billy, Antoinette, Antoinette's mother, her partner and the Davies family all went for a meal.

Antoinette suggested, 'We usually go to Cardiff's famous Chippy Lane, but we'll have to splash out today. Won't we mum?'

Billy nodded in agreement.

Chapter 18

The commitment made by the Anglican and Catholic prelates delighted Billy. Having been impressed with Billy's ideas for engaging London's youngsters in the churches, they were determined to bring it to fruition. A business plan was drawn up, wealthy businesspeople contacted to finance the projects with other people and churchgoers donating to the cause. Billy was bowled over with the generosity of the financiers, enabling appropriate professionals to organise the different projects.

Academic standards among underprivileged children rose as a result of the support available in the different places of worship. Schools were delighted churches were giving their work added value, helping create a more level playing field for pupils from disadvantaged backgrounds. Favourable conditions were something those from privileged backgrounds took for granted. This project gave underprivileged youngsters the opportunity to 'join the party.' Ever improving pupil attitudes excited London's teachers with schools eagerly awaiting exam results day, hopefully confirming the success of Billy's innovative programmes.

Sports teams were also uncovering some very skilful players. Many Asian cricketers were bewilderingly accomplished, thanks to their unbridled passion for the game. Youngsters whose descendants came from India and Pakistan were so smitten with cricket, being not only a national sport in these countries but also a national obsession. Some Imams in the London mosques helped coach sports teams and the Islamic spiritual leader in Tooting was particularly active in this area. Muhammad al Mahidi was a Sunni Muslim who had struck up an excellent relationship with Billy and Pastor Robbins. This was a friendship based on a mutual respect for each other.

Large numbers of Muslims in Britain are Sunnis' while a smaller number belong to the Shia branch of the religion. In many ways, there are parallels with Catholic and Protestant Christians who separated during the Reformation, when Henry VIII was King. In Islam division occurred after the Prophet Muhammad's death. United until the seventh century, one group believed Muhammad had no rightful heir and this needed to be resolved through electing a religious leader by a vote among the Islamic people. Consequently, Muhammad's friend Abu Bakr was appointed as successor. Followers of Abu Bakr formed the Sunni group. In contrast, the Shiites believe only Allah can select religious leaders leaving Muhammad's descendants as the only successors. Ali, Muhammad's son in law and cousin was appointed as successor causing the religion to develop two distinct branches.

Billy and Pastor Robbins would regularly visit Tooting Mosque where Muslim children would go after school to learn the Quran. Children could also get help from Muslim worshippers to do their homework. Some non-Muslim children opted to go to the mosque with their Muslim mates, creating an inclusive group. Billy was particularly pleased with this cordiality. Here was a model for how people of different faiths can live together in harmony. A classic case of interfaith cooperation.

Youngsters would naturally come to appreciate differences between religions, helping create a more tolerant society. Imam Muhammad al Mahidi was liberal thinking, possessing a generous spirit, qualities appealing to any fair-minded person, irrespective of their faith. One of his greatest strengths was his openness about the way hate preachers were undermining Islamic ideals of peace and obedience. Some British youngsters had been radicalised online and joined ISIS. What might have seemed a good idea to them at the time, eventually began to unravel. Some were killed in targeted drone attacks. Others wanting to return to Britain were prevented from doing so, leading to their detainment in refugee camps.

Britain's security services uncovered plots in the United Kingdom leading to long prison sentences for misguided youngsters intent on bringing terrorism to Britain's streets. Imam Muhammad al Mahidi was saddened by these events as impressionable young minds were infiltrated by these purveyors of terror, leaving lives in tatters. This magnanimous spiritual leader was determined to do all he could to prevent this problem by encouraging youngsters of different faiths to participate in Billy's scheme. Muslim youngsters were offered advice by the Imam, keeping them from being influenced by evil pronouncements from ISIS.

The Imam spoke openly with Billy about this problem, 'Refugees coming to this country from war zones, need to be given a leg up into British society.

Learning to adapt to the British way of life is difficult if you cannot speak the language.'

Billy was upset to think of people being excluded because there was nothing in place to help refugees and he replied, 'Yes, I can see how much of a problem that is, Imam. Refugees who come to the country as a result of war, famine, religious persecution or criticising an authoritarian Islamic regime could potentially be radicalised. They are at a disadvantage in a foreign country, being easy prey for unscrupulous hate preachers.'

'Yes Billy, language is an obvious problem for refugees. Without it they cannot access the British way of life or for children, the education system.'

'Imam, last week a boatload of refugees landed at Saint Margaret's Bay in Kent looking for safety and security in Britain. Many were Afghan and Syrian refugees including children who surely deserve the chance to live in peace.'

'Billy, this situation is desperate if they're prepared to cross the busiest shipping lane in the world aboard the flimsiest of vessels. Desperation leads them to believe it's a risk worth taking.'

Billy deep in thought exclaimed, 'I have an idea. We need to extend the work we are already doing to include refugees. There's no doubt many of the people are bright with skills to benefit British society. Imam, we need to dig for more gold.'

'That's an unusual turn of phrase, Billy.'

'Yes, it's something I picked up in school. I'm going to speak to the London Council of Unity about the contribution we could potentially make to migrants if we have the will to do so.'

'That'll be fantastic, Billy, because many caring people would be only too willing to give these migrants a leg up.'

'In Wales, we call our mate 'butty'. I'm going to suggest every migrant coming into London has a butty who will help them with language, education and employment.'

'You're right, Billy, refugees can only benefit from spending time with someone who can help them adapt to British society.'

'If the professionals organising homework and sports clubs in the different places of worship are able to sort out the logistics, we need to formalise it, Imam. Finance shouldn't be a problem because there are billionaires donating to these programmes.'

'It would be nice to call it the 'Butty System' in recognition of your idea, Billy. This will thrill the Muslim community if it happens, helping further cement the good interfaith relationships we're trying to promote.'

'It will happen, Imam. I'll raise it at the next meeting.'

To Billy's delight the London Council of Unity was thrilled by this suggestion. It was just the type of work they were looking to do. The Archbishop of Canterbury and the Head of the Catholic Church were ecstatic, seeing it as a perfect way to deliver their religious ideals. Providing this type of support would substantially reduce the risk of undervalued and abandoned migrants being radicalised by terrorists. The prelates thought the government would be interested in such an initiative ensuring Parliamentary support. It would certainly help endorse Britain as a welcoming, caring society.

Billy's star continued to rise. Importantly, he kept his feet firmly on the ground. There would be more problems to resolve but the support he was getting, gave him the incentive to continue improving conditions for the needy.

Chapter 19

London's disadvantaged children excelled in their GCSE exams through the churches adopting Billy's initiative. Success on this level created a favourable impression with the Prime Minister and Government. Billy's work persuaded the Prime Minister to invite him to Downing Street for tea. Places of worship succeeded in attracting children to their homework clubs.

His proposition for resolving London's knife crime issue had also borne fruit, initiating a dramatic decrease in violent incidents. Using the places of worship as venues, where youngsters could get help with schoolwork was the icing on the cake, without any strain being placed on the public purse. Business leaders were falling over themselves to participate in these ventures, guaranteeing prestige for their companies.

Dignitaries including government members, religious leaders and benevolent businesspeople attended the Downing Street tea. All were anxious to speak with Billy. Many MPs were effusive in their praise for his innovative thinking. Although delighted with his achievements, Billy knew there was no time to sit on his laurels. There were more battles to be fought. Achieving social justice for marginalised members of society allowed people with low self-esteem to feel valued. Having lived on the streets, constantly reminded Billy how many different groups of disadvantaged people needed help.

Billy was mesmerised as he looked around 10 Downing Street. He was amazed at the black and white checkerboard floor, resembling a giant chess board. It reminded Billy that political shenanigans involved engaging with opposition politicians trying to force a checkmate. Glancing towards the main staircase he noticed the walls were lined with the photographs of former Prime Ministers.

Billy knew the Cabinet Room was upstairs. He was not taken there, denying him the opportunity to look closely at the photographs of former Prime Ministers adorning the staircase. Maybe he'd have the opportunity sometime in the future.

The reception in his honour was held in the Pillard Room, where the portrait of Queen Elizabeth I hangs over the fireplace. Billy's mind wandered making him think about the dignitaries from Britain and foreign countries who had stood here. Gazing at the portrait of Queen Elizabeth I, Billy felt a tap on his shoulder. Turning Billy was greeted by the Prime Minister.

'We can't thank you enough for the exceptional work you've been doing. Religious leaders from the churches and the Islamic Ambassador for Intercultural Dialogue are unrestrained in their praise for your work.'

'I've been fortunate to have their support, Sir.'

'Having been through dark periods in your life, I'd like to offer my personal gratitude for your bewildering work. Long may it continue. Your initiatives have enhanced the lives of young people in London.'

'Thank you, Prime Minister, for your invitation.'

The Prime Minister moved to speak to other guests as Billy sipped his tea. This was a momentous occasion for the former homeless man who a short time ago appeared to have little hope of ever achieving anything.

At the conclusion of tea, Billy left number 10. Turning left he walked to the gates protecting Downing Street, where a cab waited to take him back to Tooting. Reflecting on his afternoon, Billy suddenly remembered the Imam had asked him to go to the mosque.

'Could you please take me to Tooting Mosque.'

'No problem, Gov.'

Imam Mohammed al Mahidi had asked Billy to call around after his appointment in Downing Street. As the cab drew closer to the mosque, the dome and minaret came into view. Such prominent features made it easy to identify the mosque. Billy commented, 'Architecturally it's so different to the other buildings, it stands out like the iconic building it is.'

'How much do I owe you, Guv?' Billy asked as he left the taxi.

'Nothing, this one's on the house. You have done so much good work; a free ride is the least I could do for you. My son did his GCSE exams this year, exceeding our expectations by passing them all. What you put in place was the icing on the cake.'

Billy was really grateful. He felt a sense of great pride at what he'd achieved.

Billy walked through the main entrance into the ablutions area being careful to remove his shoes in accordance with Islamic law. Making his way into the hall where Muslims worship, Billy could see there was a significant difference with Christian churches. Muslims prostrate themselves in prayer on the floor so there are no need for seats. There were no paintings of people or statues. Walls are bedecked with amazing patterns. Attached to the walls were highly decorated lamps. Islamic law states that no image of men or animals can go on the walls. Their creation is the preserve of God alone who is a higher authority than a man. Standing beneath one of these aesthetically pleasing lamps was the Imam accompanied by a youngster. The young boy had a swarthy Middle Eastern appearance, possessing luminous, extremely world weary, sunken eyes. He looked forlorn.

Approaching Billy, the Imam spoke, 'Meet Payam, he's an Iranian refugee whose mother has been given asylum in Britain. Her estranged husband has been imprisoned in Tehran. He's considered a political dissident.'

'Where did he come from before he came to London, Imam?'

'From Newport in Wales.'

'Does he speak English, Imam?'

'His spoken English is excellent. His mother's grasp of the language is limited.'

'What about his written English, Imam?'

'Well Billy, he's had problems with his written English. He doesn't expect to pass GCSE in the subject.'

'What about his other subjects, Imam?'

'He tells me his maths and science are excellent. It's a bit of a dilemma for him. His ambition is to be a doctor but he's in a predicament about where he wants to study in the sixth form.'

Billy shook Payam's hand and said, 'You've just finished your GCSE exams and it's really important that we do all we can for you to fulfil your ambition. Tomorrow, I am speaking to the Oxford University Union about homelessness, my rescue from vagrancy and the projects I've set up to unite London's people.'

'Billy, will you be able to speak to anyone about the way forward for Payam?'

'It's almost certain that I'll be able to talk to someone about him.'

'That's good, Billy.'

'Just leave it to me. I'll come back to the mosque on Friday after worship to see you both. Hopefully, we'll get Payam sorted. He definitely deserves a hand to fulfil his ambition to be a doctor.'

Gratefully the Imam said, 'Thank you, Billy.'

Payam followed suit, 'Thank you, Sir.'

As he left Billy said, 'See you both on Friday. '

Chapter 20

Billy left London Paddington on the 2:30 p.m. Great Western train to Oxford. He was on his way to address the Oxford Union regarding the work he'd done, particularly its impact on London society. Many politicians, stars from the world of the arts and sport had addressed this distinguished group. Billy's achievements had earned him the right to speak to this prestigious gathering.

Here was a man from humble beginnings in the Welsh valleys about to engage with these young scholars. He had made his mind up to speak about his war service, the subsequent mental health issues, homelessness and his ideas for social justice. Billy was in no doubt, this academically gifted young audience would ask searching questions about his life. Such an intellectually demanding convention meant he would really have to be on his mettle. However, they were young, lacking the type of life experiences Billy had. Although he had little in the way of formal academic qualifications, when it came to speaking about war and life on the streets, Billy's first-hand experience guaranteed he could enthral his audience.

Leaving the train at Oxford station Billy hailed a taxi.

'Where are you going, sir?' asked the driver.

'Can you drop me at the Oxford Union, please.'

'Why are you going there?'

'I'm speaking to the students this evening.'

'Blow me down, the people I normally take there are real toffs. I don't want to be rude you don't look smartly dressed enough. They always wear dinner suits. The last one I took there was that dickhead politician who looked like he'd stepped straight out of Victorian England.'

Billy laughed loudly, then proclaimed, 'It's a debating society, not a fashion parade. Besides, I haven't got a dinner suit.'

At that moment, the penny dropped with the taxi driver.

'I've seen you on the telly. Let me tell you, there's no one gone there who's done as much good as you.'

'It's good of you to say that.'

'Most of the politicians who go there are bloody liars. They're only interested in power, meaning they'll say anything to get it.'

'I take it you don't think much of politicians.'

'You've got it. Oh and the football players who have been there have got more bloody money than sense. Their way of life just don't belong in this world. They don't understand what ordinary folks have to go through. Sock it to 'em mate.'

The car pulled up at Frewin Court.

'How much do I owe you,' said Billy.

'Give me six pounds, mate.'

'Here's eight pounds. Keep the change.'

'Thanks and good luck.'

The Oxford Union had been founded in 1823 providing a platform for debate. Participating students were given the opportunity to broaden their horizons receiving instruction from people who'd made a considerable mark in life. Billy had to pinch himself. It was difficult for him to comprehend how his life had changed. On entering the building, he was struck by how ornate the decor was. Many of the rooms were named after figures from the Union's past. From an office an older male appeared, introducing himself to Billy as the President of the Union. He was accompanied by a few students who were all a couple of years younger.

'Welcome to the Oxford Union, Mr Davies. It's a pleasure to have you here.'

'The pleasure is all mine.'

'If you follow us to the debating chamber, we will show you where you will be speaking tonight.'

Billy walked into the chamber and was overwhelmed by the number of busts of distinguished people interspersed around the room. Glancing left and right Billy was able to pick out Roy Jenkins, Edward Heath and Michael Heseltine. He fixed his gaze on an old grand piano which had pride of place.

As he looked at it the president spoke, 'We found this wonderful musical instrument dusty, just forgotten in the music room. Determined to restore this to its original grandeur, the Union took great pride in the project.'

'It's a wonderful piano which wouldn't look out of place in the social club at Llanen,' Billy said jokingly.

Normally used to invited guests 'playing a straight bat', Billy's comment made the group giggle. Billy thought to himself, what a grand place for a miner's son with limited education, speaking to some of the finest academic minds in Britain. Initially alarmed at the thought, he was comforted by the fact his experiences were alien to all those who were going to listen to him. Inquisitive minds guaranteed their total attention. Surely, these circumstances would inspire him in the face of such an esteemed audience.

Initially looking at the room gave Billy an understanding of the layout and ambience of the place. He started to appreciate the daunting task faced by any individual speaking here. Any trepidation was replaced by pride at the honour of being asked to address such an acclaimed audience.

Following a satisfying meal Billy made his way to the debating chamber to address these erudite individuals whose academic prowess would take them to the very pinnacle of British society. His introduction by the President made him appreciate his significant achievements, impressed even the most learned members of this fellowship.

Billy opened his speech, 'Thank you very much for your kind remarks. It's a great honour to address this chamber, having originated from such a humble background in the Welsh valleys. My father was a miner and I left school with some CSEs (Certificate of Secondary Education) to join the Army. My academic qualifications wouldn't be good enough to get me into Oxford Technical College today. However, my harrowing personal experiences have taught me the importance of human beings learning to get on together and seeing each other as members of one human race.'

Many in the audience smiled when Billy mentioned his academic qualifications. Nevertheless, they applauded his opening remarks. Billy continued talking about his experiences during the Falkland's war and his descent into darkness as a result of his experience from the conflict. This was followed by homelessness and his subsequent rescue by two young members of Tooting Evangelical Church.

Having time to reflect on this experience during those murky years made Billy realise, he had qualities to draw people together. He referred to it as an innate gift locked away for years. The ideas he was now bringing to the fore were rooted in his life in Wales as a youngster. Billy reserved special praise for

Simeon, Antoinette and Pastor Robbins who'd released this gift, providing him with the launch pad to carry out his work. He was anxious to impress upon his audience, we are all interdependent on each other. Rapturous applause followed from this intellectual gathering. The Union President then asked if there were any questions.

A young student in a three-piece pin striped suit questioned Billy, 'Do you think it was appropriate for Britain to go 8,000 miles to fight a war in the Falklands, particularly after your experiences since?'

Billy had spent long periods of time thinking about this over the years and he replied, 'Throughout the years many countries have fought over the Falkland Islands. Even though the islands were in close proximity to Argentina, they were ruled by Britain when they were invaded. Our government in 1982 had a moral duty to defend its citizens against Argentinean aggression. One needs to remember that Argentina was ruled by a military dictatorship, making it impossible to know how the islanders would have been treated under Argentinean rule.

An important factor is the desire for the population wanting to remain under British rule. Following the war, democracy quickly returned to Argentina when the military junta was discredited. In that respect, British intervention helped the Argentinean people as well as the Falkland islanders.'

A significant proportion of the Union's audience would enter politics when they completed their studies. Billy's answer delighted this judicious gathering, prompting a rapturous applause.

A young lady with an awareness of feminist issues asked, 'When I observe homeless people on the streets there appear to be an increasing number of females living as down and outs. As a former homeless man, I wonder if you could throw some light on the reasons for this increase.'

'Your observations are spot on. There are definitely more homeless women on the streets for a variety of reasons. One of the most disturbing factors is the number of women who are victims of coercive husbands. Threats of physical violence by these men result in some women having no choice other than to leave their homes. Many fear for their lives and the streets are a last resort. In 2015 this type of bullying behaviour became a serious criminal offence. A minority of men resort to humiliating or intimidating their partner, making women subordinate and dependent on them. Threats of violence drive women onto the streets rather than seeking police help. Today police authorities handle these issues with greater sensitivity leading to men who use strong arm tactics against women being imprisoned.

One case involved a woman being forced to sell her wedding and engagement rings in a pawn shop so her husband could use the money for gambling. She knew this wasn't love and there'd been red flags from the beginning of their relationship. For years she felt trapped but eventually, plucking up courage to go to the authorities, he is now serving a two-year jail sentence.

Equality in a relationship is essential and the assumption by any man that his wife is her husband's property is now redundant. During church wedding services, the word obey in the vows is virtually obsolete. Couples now repeat the words love, honour and cherish. Browbeaten by self-obsessed men, placing them under duress pushes some women into homelessness. Street life is menacing for all homeless people. Unfortunately, women on the streets can find themselves in grave danger.'

Delighted with Billy's reply the young lady said, 'This country needs to help all homeless people. However, women in such, a perilous situation need to be a priority.'

The President addressed the audience once again, 'One more question please.'

A number of hands were raised but the President asked a female student in the front row to ask a question.

'Your idea to set up a London Council of Unity is ground-breaking, particularly working with refugees where your Butty System is a great idea. How is this progressing?'

'This has been a great success because young refugees arrive in a foreign country disorientated, most with little or no English. Initiating the Butty System gives refugees access to a committed individual, helping them adjust to British life. Buying into the British education system is demanding enough. Without support it would be a harrowing experience. Schools do a terrific job, but the Butty System gets the youngsters up to speed by helping break down language barriers. Looking after them reduces the risk of radicalisation. Hopefully, they will go on to fulfil their potential, contributing positively to British society.

Most pleasing of all is that Muslim men and women are involved with this initiative. Quite rightly, all religions have the opportunity to belong to the London Council of Unity. Inclusivity was achieved by separating it from the

London Council of Churches, making all members equal partners, helping create social cohesion, where all are valued.'

Billy's response brought this group of intellectuals to their feet. A two-minute standing ovation left him feeling on 'cloud nine'. A final act by the Union President involved him thanking Billy for his enlightening lecture. Taking plaudits for his contribution to London society made Billy realise that informed members of the public held his work in high esteem. Leaving the debating chamber, Billy returned to the bar for a well-earned drink.

Chapter 21

Whilst he relaxed in the bar, a member of Oxford's academic staff introduced herself to Billy. Dressed in a smart blue suit, she informed him she was admissions tutor at Oriel College. Here was the opportunity Billy had been waiting for. He now had the opportunity to ask about schools for Payam, the Iranian refugee he'd met at the Mosque.

'If you knew a very able refugee who'd come to Tooting hoping to study A Levels. Where would you suggest he went to school?' asked Billy.

'If you've the opportunity there's one school I would choose above any others.'

'Which one is that?'

'It has to be Galaxy Boys High School. Their motto is 'Aspire to Reach for the Stars' tallying with the school, setting the highest academic standards in London. It is a requirement that a proportion of their intake are children from underprivileged backgrounds. Originally set up as a charitable foundation, this is one of the conditions. You really need to contact the Head.

'I'm really grateful for the advice, I'll look into it.'

Returning to Tooting Billy decided he would see Imam al Mahidi and Payam tomorrow afternoon. Following a comfortable night's sleep Billy ate a late breakfast, then set off for the mosque. Passing a newspaper stand, Billy could see his Oxford talk had made the newspapers. One billboard read, 'Former homeless man beguiles the Oxford Union.'

Being Friday, this was the Muslim holy day and worshippers were streaming from the mosque following the conclusion of prayers. Because of his friendship with the Imam, Billy had taken a real interest in Islamic worship. These special prayers were called Salat al Jumu'ah. He knew they were held just after noon. Jumu'ah means Friday taking the place of the daily Zuhr prayer. This is a special act of worship obligatory for Muslims. Billy could see the Imam speaking to Payam and he approached them.

'Payam there's a chance I've found an excellent school for you to study for your A-Levels,' proclaimed Billy.

'Where's that?' asked Payam excitedly.

'Galaxy Boys High School. It's one of the best schools in Britain. If you want to give it a go, I'll phone the school to make an appointment with the Head.'

Payam's luminous, brown eyes exuded determination. Here was the opportunity he had been waiting for. Billy sensed this young man would grasp every academic opportunity allowing him to fulfil his ambition to study for medicine.

Billy explained to Payam, 'Only the highest academic standards are acceptable at Galaxy High. A place there virtually guarantees educational excellence.'

'Suits me fine. I will love it. Studying hard is no problem for me.'

Anticipating Payam's determination to succeed academically Billy had already phoned the school to make an appointment with Mr Davies, the Head. Billy and Payam caught a bus and tube for an appointment at Galaxy High with Mr Davies the Headteacher.

'He's a lucky man having the same surname as me. He must be Welsh. With you having gone to school in Newport, this really will be a Celtic meeting,' Billy said jokingly.

Payam delved a little deeper, 'What are the Celtics, Billy?'

'It's like this Payam. The people in England are descended from tribes called the Angles and Saxons while the people in Wales, Scotland, Ireland and Cornwall are descended from a tribe known as the Celts. This is why there is so much rivalry when Wales play England at football or rugby. It's competitive because both sides want the bragging rights.'

'I understand, Billy. It's like the rivalry between Liverpool and Manchester United.'

'Yes Payam, you've got it. Bragging rights are really important to the fans.'

As they approached the school Billy thought, the building had an aura about it, strikingly similar to Oxford University. In contrast to a London state school, it stood in its own grounds with extensive playing fields, enclosed by metal railings with an arched shaped wrought iron gate. Galaxy High in large letters went from one side of the arch to the other.

Passing through this arch-shaped entrance, Billy and Payam walked along the path to the front door. Approaching the school door Billy noticed a sign pointing left, indicating where the Headteacher's office was. Once in the corridor Billy and Payam could see the Head's office. On the opposite wall were last year's GCSE and A-Level results, showing exceptional academic standards to be the norm at this establishment. A sixth former met Billy and Payam to accompany them to the Head.

Addressing them in a confident manner, 'You've come to see Mr Goff Davies.'

'Yes, we've got an appointment with him,' said Billy.

Suddenly the boy changed tack from formality to what many older people might consider familiarity towards a man in such an important position.

'Ffogy's really great. All the boys and Parents love him.'

Billy thought what a peculiar name. It brought a smile to Billy's face.

'Why do you call him Ffogy?'

Laughing the sixth former enlightened Billy and Payam, 'The old Head was dour and puritanical lacking any sense of humour. Ffogy as we call him has a really easy manner and is so supportive. When we need help, he always comes up trumps. He's Welsh and two of the boys found out online that in Wales ff in a word is pronounced in the same way as an f in English, whereas a single f is pronounced as an English v. These two boys are very bright and they reverse everyone's name. I am Nigel but here everyone calls me Legin. Consequently, Mr Davies's name is Goff, so the boys refer to him as Ffogy. It's a really appropriate name for him.

When any of the boys go to him with a problem he always says, 'When you come into my study, you're in a fog, not having a clue where you're going. It's my job to lift the fog, helping you see clearly.'

Going to see him with a problem is an amazing experience as Ffogy straight away makes you feel comfortable. He removes any jitters you might have, unlike the previous head who'd intimidate us. You'd prefer to see the Grim Reaper than see him. Everyone is comfortable in Ffogy's presence and the boy's love him. Mind you, we wouldn't call him Ffogy to his face. We're not daft. He's always Mr Davies.'

Reversing names in this way convinced Billy these boys at Galaxy High were bright pupils. When he was in school if you liked the teacher, you called them Mr or Miss and then the surname. If you didn't like them, you would just use their surname but not to their face. Billy thought what the Galaxy boys were doing was clever. It was impressive the way the boys had connected the ff to the

Welsh language. Correlating these letters was a masterly act, making Billy think Payam would fit in well here with these academically gifted boys.

Further along the corridor Billy could see the school's prestigious academic record on display. Names displayed on the wall showed that many former pupils had been awarded places at Oxford and Cambridge. In addition, an array of individuals had represented England at rugby and cricket. Galaxy High created such a positive feeling in Billy. He was praying Payam would get a place at this elite school. Surely a place here would guarantee him fulfilling his ambition to be a doctor.

Approaching the Head's study, the door opened, revealing this tall figure with thinning hair. What an impressive individual, Billy thought to himself. Wearing an academic gown, allied to the speed of his exit from the room made Billy think Batman had arrived on the scene. After what the sixth former said, Billy's assessment was valid.

Taking on the demons in the boy's heads was Mr Davies's forte. The Joker or the Riddler aside, nothing was too hot for this caped crusader. Mr Davies thrust out his hand for Billy's. Such a firm handshake indicated a meeting of minds caring passionately about other people. Before Billy had a chance to introduce Payam, Mr Davies spoke.

'I'm Mr Davies, Head of Galaxy Boys High. Billy you've really made a name for yourself. Your work has been phenomenal, fully deserving the plaudits you've had. The boys here seem to think I'm good at clearing up problems for them and I know they call me Ffogy. Mind you they're always totally respectful when they come to see me. It surprises many people that such able boys from time to time have problems. Most of their issues are academic ones but I'm really delighted that they're not afraid to call in and see me. It thrills me these young men are not only keen to listen but also willing to act on the advice I give, making this the best teaching job I've had. What can I do for you?'

'Mr Davies, Payam is an Iranian refugee who is hoping to study medicine. Having just finished his GCSEs in Newport, his mother has moved to London. Payam is now looking for a place to study A-Level.'

'Payam what grades are you expected to get in your GCSEs?'

'I should pass maths, physics, chemistry, biology and computer studies. With a bit of luck, I might pass religious studies.'

'When you say you'll pass what grades are you likely to get?'

'Well Mr Davies I should get A* in maths, chemistry, physics and computer studies. There's a lot of writing in biology making it more difficult for me but I hope to get an A.'

'Payam, what about religious studies, you said that you hoped to pass?'

'Well, 'I'm hoping to get a C. Although there's a lot of written work, my knowledge of Islam is good. I've been brought up in the faith giving me an advantage.'

'Payam, excellent, but the 64,000-dollar question is what about English Language?'

'Mr Davies, my spoken English is good. However, I do struggle with the written element of the exam, so I probably won't get a C grade.'

Mr Davies's question perturbed Payam. His large brown eyes filling up thinking his English Language would prevent him from getting a place at Galaxy High.

Mr Davies allayed any fears Payam had. 'I can see you're in a fog, Payam. You needn't worry, your previous school has written an amazing reference. The English Language problem can be addressed by you entering the 'Test of English as a Foreign Language.' That exam will guarantee you entry into university if you pass your A-levels.'

Any fog that descended when Payam was asked the question about English Language lifted. Payam could see why the boys called him Ffogy. A light had been shone in the murk by this Headteacher who was totally devoted to his work. Mr Davies proclaimed, 'Payam, you pass six GCSEs and you're in. Oh, by the way, did you play rugby in Iran?'

Payam laughed. Here was a Headteacher with a great sense of humour who had just given him the chance to be a doctor.

Chapter 22

During their time at university Simeon and Antoinette's relationship continued to develop. Constrained by the demands of their academic work, they took every opportunity possible to visit each other. University vacations gave them extended periods of time together to enjoy each other's company. Following graduation both worked in London. Being employed in the capital provided the opportunity for them to get engaged.

August 2017 would be a momentous year in their lives, having decided to marry at Tooting Evangelical Church. It was a day the whole church community looked forward to, even though most worshipers at the church couldn't go to the reception. Their popularity meant they'd have needed City Hall to accommodate such numbers. As totally committed church members, it guaranteed the place would be packed to the rafters.

Pastor Robbins officiated. Keeping with tradition he waited at the church door for Antoinette to arrive. Never one to be late for anything, she decided to observe the matrimonial convention that a bride arrives a few minutes late. This ancient heritage derived from the idea the groom is made to sweat, not taking the brides attendance as mandatory. Simeon needn't have worried. Antoinette couldn't wait to arrive at the church but she was anxious not to incur any bad luck by breaking with this custom.

Antoinette stepped out of an open topped vintage sports car belonging to a church member. Although divorced, her parents retained an amicable relationship. A few years ago, Antoinette made her mind up to sit on the fence regarding their matrimonial problems, leaving her parents to resolve their own differences. Even though she couldn't agree with her mother's behaviour, taking sides would have been counterproductive. She chose instead to hold her counsel on the matter.

On this special day in her life, Antoinette would be given away by her father. Behind the sports car a white Bentley pulled up, the doors opened and three bridesmaids and a page boy stepped out. Pastor Robbins welcomed Antoinette with a hug, then he turned to enter the church. Sticking with convention, Pastor Robbins led the procession, followed by Antoinette arm in arm with her father. The remainder of the entourage behind them. Diana Ross and Lionel Ritchie singing 'Endless Love' played as the procession made its way to the front of the church.

Walking serenely, Antoinette wore a traditional white wedding dress and veil. Tiny flower posies were attached to the end of each row of seats, enhancing the church's appearance. When she arrived at the front of the church one of the bridesmaids removed the veil covering, revealing Antoinette's face. Simeon and his best man stepped into the aisle to stand alongside Antoinette. Pastor Robbins said the marriage vows and as is tradition they were repeated by the couple. Nervously reciting their vows, the couple drew strength from the loving gazes they gave each other.

Words of encouragement from Pastor Robbins followed the taking of these important oaths. He was at pains to stress the importance that those attending the service supported the couple throughout their lives. The service culminated in the exchange of wedding rings and the best man fumbling in his pocket trying to find them. Audible gasps were heard from some members of the congregation thinking he'd forgotten where he'd put them. Turning around, giving a wry smile the best man mischievously pulled them from his top pocket. Following the exchange of these significant, symbolic, important pieces of jewellery the Pastor proclaimed, 'Those whom God has joined together let no man put asunder.'

Antoinette and Simeon smiled at each other as the Pastor explained the symbolism of the rings where only the death of one partner should end a marriage. Simeon was asked to kiss the bride, drawing a rapturous round of applause from the congregation. Pastor Robbins led the couple and witnesses to a table to sign legal documents, required by British law. At the conclusion of these legitimate formalities the couple walked towards the door to the sound of 'Can't help falling in love' by Elvis Presley. Billy waited outside with a box of confetti, taking an opportune moment to empty it over the newly-weds.

Despite Antoinette's past differences with her mother, she looked as pleased as punch that her daughter had married Simeon. Although many people spoke of Antoinette's mum as 'posh totty', she'd always loved and admired Simeon. Originating from backgrounds which were poles apart, Simeon's academic achievements were a source of great pride for Antoinette's mum. Sycophantic at times, she was extremely perceptive, appreciating how difficult it was for someone from a background like Simeon's to win a place at Oxford. Always very hospitable to Simeon's family, Antoinette's mum made a point of stressing how compatible the young couple were.

Leaving the church, Simeon and Antoinette climbed into a sports car to go to the reception at the Feathers Hotel in Wimbledon. Money being no object for Antoinette's estranged parents meant one hundred and fifty guests didn't have to put their hands in their pockets. Champagne flowed but Billy drank in moderation following Antoinette's request that he say a few words. Speaking to the Oxford Union had been straightforward enough, in comparison with enunciating the high esteem in which he held this young couple. Billy quickly acknowledged the part they'd played in his redemption from homelessness.

During the speech Billy was so overcome with emotion it tongue tied him, preventing him getting his words out. Guests were sympathetic, recognising the difficulties he'd encountered during his life and his gratitude for the people who'd helped him. Such an emotional occasion had overwhelmed him when he needed to speak. Dwelling on Simeon and Antoinette's role in saving him from the streets reduced Billy, who previously had eloquently addressed the Oxford Union to a stuttering wreck. Numerous media outlets had focused on Billy's innovative approach to solving problems, ensuring the public had regular exposure to his story. He was held in high esteem by people in Tooting who were au fait with Billy's initiatives improving life chances for the less fortunate.

Once he'd stumbled his way through the speech, Billy was ready to participate in the celebrations by drinking a few glasses of beer in the couples' honour. A superb evening was enjoyed by every guest but there'd definitely be a few sore heads in the morning. Before the reception concluded, Antoinette and Simeon left for Heathrow catching the flight to Jamaica. Simeon was returning to the land of his ancestors fulfilling a long-held ambition. A well-earned break awaited the couple, where Simeon's Jamaican relatives would treat them like royalty. Billy was left to reflect on what the future might hold for an aspiring politician and a charity worker with a heart of gold. Billy knew, their prospects were bright.

Chapter 23

Returning from Jamaica at the beginning of September, Antoinette and Simeon set up home in a rented two bedroomed flat in Colliers Wood. Determined to stand on their own feet, they refused the offer of a deposit from Antoinette's mother to buy their own place. Their plan involved saving enough money for a deposit to buy a property when they were ready.

Antoinette had changed jobs and was now employed as a political assistant to the Liberal Leader. Hopefully, this opportune move would put her on the first rung of the political ladder, helping Antoinette fulfil her ambition to enter politics. Such a role involved providing secretarial research and publicity support, giving her an insight into and familiarising herself with the intricate workings of a political party. Working in this environment gave her an understanding of the considerable demands made upon a Member of Parliament.

Meanwhile, Simeon's role with Save the Children saw him assigned to northern Syria. This responsibility coincided with politicians debating endlessly about what should be done with children born to British mothers who'd been killed after leaving Britain with the promise of a wonderful life in the ISIS Caliphate. These children were fathered by ISIS fighters and were now orphaned.

Politicians viewed this as a contentious issue, consistently pushing it to one side in an effort to avoid confronting the matter. Naturally, public opinion was divided through their being a potential threat to security in the United Kingdom. A protracted bitter dispute took place where some people thought the country was in danger of spawning the next generation of terrorists. Others with a liberal outlook took a more compassionate standpoint, promoting the idea these were children who should be brought home. They viewed these children as the innocent victims of a tragic situation, making them Britain's responsibility.

Visiting these Syrian camps gave Simeon a greater insight into the problem. He viewed the children as innocents caught up in an appalling situation for which they did not deserve to be held responsible. Prior to their liberation, these camps had been indoctrinating children in an academy for the next generation of terrorists. Although their British mothers had died in bombing raids, the children were exposed to IS evil at an impressionable age. Infiltrating these young minds in preparation to use them as the next generation of terrorists was the wicked ambition of the ISIS Caliphate.

Frightened children were brainwashed by extreme factions among these ISIS women who'd survived the raids but supported the barbarism of this terrorist group. Such grisly women had set up their own courts, religious police and punishments. It was impossible to police this extreme behaviour in the camps. In these places there could be 70,000 inhabitants enabling monstrous women to freely commit horrific crimes.

European governments maintained many young impressionable women had joined the Islamic State, posing a significant threat to national security in their mother countries. Countries refused to repatriate them. Britain's government had stopped dragging their heels with regard to the children born to British mothers who'd been killed. A groundswell of opinion thought the children should be brought home. Although Simeon was charged with accompanying these young victims back to Britain, he was not naïve, realising the children could pose a threat to national security and would need careful monitoring. Immediately thinking of Billy, Simeon contacted him in the hope he would have some ideas about how the children's needs could be catered for.

Billy listened sympathetically to Simeon and said, 'It's important these youngsters are helped now before ISIS propaganda takes a hold of them, making it too late to successfully repatriate them.'

'Thanks Billy, I knew you could be relied upon to help.'

'I'll raise the issue with the London Council of Unity to see if an appropriate provision can be made for them. Failing to create the right conditions could create significant problems.

'Do you think the council will be willing to help, Billy.'

'I would bet my bottom dollar the different faith leaders will want to support the children. They won't want the 'sins of the fathers and mothers heaped upon the sons and daughters.'

Billy hastily convened a meeting of the London Council of Unity to discuss the issue of the children. Knowing he'd be speaking to a receptive audience Billy spoke, 'The only way these children can be saved is by providing them with loving homes, so they can forget the horrors they've witnessed in their time in the ISIS Caliphate. It's not good enough to just bring them back, we need to change their whole outlook on life.'

The Archbishop of Canterbury replied, 'We need swift action; these children have witnessed horrors on an unimaginable scale. I agree with Billy. We need to provide caring homes to integrate these youngsters.'

Billy spoke again, 'People volunteering to take on this role need patience and have to be totally committed if the children are to be saved from what they've witnessed in these ISIS camps.'

Billy's words struck a chord with the faith leaders who by virtue of their vocation were compassionate people. They willingly agreed to convey his idea to their worshippers.

Speaking for the group the Catholic Cardinal proclaimed, 'We have been called to act and cannot afford to fail. Love will conquer the horrors witnessed by the children. If we fail these children, we are falling short in our calling to serve God.'

Media opinion was divided on this issue. Some of the tabloid press were guilty of putting the boot into Billy's idea, singling him out for special attention from journalists who enjoyed playing devil's advocate. Headlines referred to him as the 'Tooting Taff with a Bleeding Heart.' Editorials stressed that by carrying on with his humanitarian work, he could introduce young terrorists into the country. Newsmen were stoking unnecessary fear by saying other people would shed their blood if the country continued along this path.

Always negative, these pathetic journals were gutter press, little better than comics, deliberately aggravating people's fears. Undaunted, Billy was encouraged by the faith leaders whose support and efforts would give the children a chance. Fully endorsing Billy's work, the faith leaders expressed the belief that in God's eyes children were a gift and a blessing. Putting criticisms by these trashy tabloids to one side, Billy was determined to find the right people to foster the children, proving to these sensationalist reporters, their attempt at a populist viewpoint was an appeal to a minority of hate filled right wing sympathisers.

An appeal by the faith leaders resulted in people coming forward ready to foster these displaced youngsters. Some worshippers at Tooting Evangelical Church embraced the project, filling Billy with the expectation that all these people would provide the necessary guidance and care needed for the youngsters to prosper. In total 60 children arrived from northern Syrian camps. Their world-weary faces bore testimony to the horrors they'd witnessed during their short lives.

Billy praised these committed members of the public for providing the gift of a home for the displaced children. He was at pains to stress these youngsters might encounter serious problems adjusting to British life. The Government were anxious for this rehabilitation to succeed and in recognition of their commitment to the project, they provided a team of psychologists to help with their introduction to a new way of life. Billy knew this was a gamble but when he was young, people in Llanen would compliment him, 'Billy Davies, you're a glass half full.'

He hoped they were right for the children's sake.

Chapter 24

London's Council of Unity had no difficulty finding sixty families ready to foster the orphans. Politicians debated vigorously whether these youngsters could be repatriated but fortunately, there were enough compassionate MPs to let Billy's plan proceed. For Billy, it was a no brainer. These children could never fend for themselves, so bringing them to Britain was the altruistic thing to do. Billy and Simeon were grateful that people with a kind disposition had volunteered to offer a home for these displaced youngsters. Hopefully, psychological support would counter the horrific experiences they'd encountered in the Middle East, smoothing the path for the project to succeed.

Members of Parliament commended Billy and Simeon in the House of Commons for their efforts. Unconcerned with the plaudits coming their way, their anxiety centred around the children's welfare since they were born to British mothers. Unfortunately, they were innocent victims having been born to deluded parents who'd populated a horrendous terrorist Caliphate. Both Billy and Simeon were committed to Britain, giving these refugees an opportunity. As they saw it, the country had a duty to children who in time would be young enough to hopefully forget what they'd witnessed.

At 3:00 p.m. on 7 May 2020, a British Airways jet landed at Heathrow airport. Billy accompanied by the Archbishop of Canterbury, the Roman Catholic Cardinal, the Tooting Imam and the Foreign Secretary went to meet the group. A lounge had been set aside for the children to meet the families who would foster them. Simeon and other charity workers accompanied the bewildered children from the plane.

Each child was shabbily dressed, most suffering malnutrition. Their emaciated bodies bore testimony to the fate confronting them, if Simeon and Billy had not intervened. Jaded, melancholy faces looked bemused by their new surroundings. Most were aged between 7 and 8 years of age. Many were crying but sympathetic charity workers offered comfort. It was imperative these young people received some stability in their lives if they were ever to adapt to British society and fulfil their potential. Billy clung to the hope that a loving home would provide the remedy needed. Here they would receive love, care and guidance to turn around the ghastly start they'd been given in life.

Religion would be a secondary issue for these youngsters but the prospective foster parents had been vetted for their suitability to provide the necessary buttress needed to underpin the lives of these disturbed young people. Immediate disorientation created by unfamiliar surroundings was alleviated when the children were given a choice of soft drinks, sandwiches, cakes and biscuits. A welcome on behalf of the government was delivered by the Foreign Secretary who acknowledged the vital part Billy and Simeon had played in this humanitarian venture.

In his speech, special mention was made of Billy's integrity, resourcefulness and ingenuity in setting up the London Council of Unity. Praising the mainstream churches and the Tooting Imam for their part in finding homes for the children, his words of gratitude indicated the government's delight at resolving an issue debated in Parliament on many occasions. London's Council of Unity had reconciled this issue, leading the Foreign Secretary and Government to think this venture could be successful.

Warm words delivered by the Government were reserved for families opening their homes to these youngsters, giving them a fighting chance in life. The Foreign Secretary alluded to this venture resembling the Kinder transport evacuation of Jewish children from countries overrun by the Nazis prior to World War II. Unfortunately, he stressed this group of young people had been born into families who advocated gratuitous violence in the name of religious extremism. Gratefully, the Foreign Secretary pointed out there were not enough adjectives to describe the benevolence of those giving the youngsters a fresh start in life. Finishing, the Foreign Secretary said the Government was indebted to these families and they would get all the support needed for this rehabilitation to succeed.

Billy had been informed that 60 children were being placed with families. Names were called and children introduced to new foster parents. Looking around, Billy could see one youngster remained. Sweating profusely, Billy had butterflies in his stomach. Had he not accounted for this youngster who looked older than the others. Billy had difficulty assigning an age to him because he was gaunt and needy. In the valleys they would refer to the child as having 'poor dab syndrome'.

Anxiously Billy approached Simeon but before he could speak Simeon proclaimed, 'Billy you've not made a mistake, this little boy is 12 years of age and a special case. The Foreign Secretary has been informed that I would be bringing this boy back from Syria with me. Understanding this is a special case, he has agreed that the country should take him in. He's a Yazidi boy and he's coming to live with Antoinette and me.'

'Lucky fella,' said Billy.

Chapter 25

Billy was staggered to hear that Simeon and Antoinette would be fostering a Middle Eastern refugee. Media outlets reported the plight of the Yazidi people in the Middle East. Billy knew they'd been brutalised by ISIS, as the terrorist organisation claimed Yazidi land while expanding their Caliphate. Although the Yazidi's had a unique set of unusual religious beliefs, ISIS referred to them as devil worshippers. Knowing this to be a distorted and warped point of view, Billy was aware that they were a tribe with ancient monotheistic beliefs, making ISIS discrimination against their belief system totally unjustified.

Life had always been difficult for the Yazidis, forcing them to live in small groups away from other religions. Yazidis simply means worshippers of God but ISIS persecuted them for their belief that Yazidis were descended from Yazid ibn Muawiya. The belief system of this ancient people had its root in Christianity. Consequently, Yazidis revere both the Bible and Quran, believing the creator God made the world, then ending His involvement with it. Yazidis believe it to be controlled by seven divine beings. Such beliefs conflicted with ISIS extreme interpretation of Islam.

Simeon anxiously wanted to enlighten Billy about why he'd decided to foster the Yazidi boy. His story was a real eye opener. Anyone with the remotest sense of compassion could not help being moved by the plight of the Yazidi people. Members of the British Government found the story heart breaking prompting an agreement to give the Yazidi boy refuge in Britain.

Simeon explained to Billy, 'The Yazidi boy is 12 years of age and is named Amir. His Story is nothing short of an absolute tragedy. If he's ever to find peace, he needs love, compassion and understanding. I realise this is a huge undertaking, but I think we can achieve something really rewarding if we can rebuild his shattered life.'

'Where did Amir live, Simeon?'

'He lived in the mountains near Mosul in Iraq. Unfortunately, his village was attacked by ISIS forces.'

'What happened to the village, Simeon?'

'ISIS showed the Yazidis no mercy. They thought of them as devil worshippers. Entering the village, they ruthlessly began slaughtering unarmed inhabitants.'

'Why was Amir not killed with the rest of the village?'

'Initially Amir's family escaped the village in a car but were pursued by ISIS who eventually caught them. Spotting the lead vehicle was flying the black ISIS battle flag, displaying the seal of Muhammed in a white circle, they knew mortal danger confronted them. Above it was a quote from the Quran stating, 'There is no God but Allah.'

'Were Amir's parents killed straight away, Simeon?'

'No Billy, they were taken to a house where his father was removed to a separate room with the other men. Amir and his mother were held in a different area.'

'I couldn't think of anything more frightening for a youngster, Simeon.'

'It didn't end there, Billy. Amir was roughly dragged from his room as his father was hauled from his gaol into the courtyard, where one of the ISIS monsters hit him with a club across his legs, forcing him to kneel. Another ISIS brute, face covered to protect his identity, drew a gun from its holster placing it against Amir's father's temple. Droplets of sweat fell from his brow leaving indentations in the sand. Shaking with fear but resigned to his imminent death Amir's father waited for the terrorist to discharge a bullet into his head.'

'Amir must have been petrified, Simeon. No youngster should have to witness the execution of an innocent parent whose only crime was to belong to an ancient tribe wanting to live their lives out in peace.'

'Amir was held by the arm as his father's life was about to be terminated. Another man grabbed him up by the hair forcing him to look at the execution.'

'Simeon, I just thought Amir would have closed his eyes.'

'Billy, the monster holding him told Amir he would be next if he looked away. Big Brown eyes swollen with tears; he was forced to witness a terrible crime. As the gun discharged its bullet, Amir let out a shriek leading to the brute holding him, twisting his hair.'

Billy was astounded at what he'd just heard and exclaimed, 'Simeon, that's monstrous. These terrorists deserve to face the harshest of punishments for their crimes. No words can describe how I feel at such a violation of human life.'

'This was the beginning of Amir's indoctrination Into Islamic state's perverted philosophy. He was seven years of age. Amir was able to tell me Islamic state burned 500 people alive in an appalling act of barbarism after invading one village.'

'Simeon, what about Amir's mother?'

'After he was removed from the room to witness his father's murder, he never saw his mother again. It seems any young women were taken to satisfy the ISIS terrorists' sexual needs, while the older women were killed. Amir doesn't know what happened to his mother. To be perfectly honest with you, it's probably better he doesn't.'

'What a traumatising situation for a youngster, Simeon.'

'Amir was then taken to an ISIS training camp with the other young boys.'

'What he's faced in his young life Simeon beggars belief.'

'His willingness to speak out about these horrors convinced me to support him in trying to rebuild his shattered life. During his time in the ISIS camp, he was forced to train as a young Jihadi. In an attempt to get him to forget his Yazidi upbringing, he was made to take the Islamic name Muhammed. ISIS only allowed him to speak Arabic.'

'What is his native language, Simeon?'

'Yazidis speak Kurmanji. They read the Bible and Quran, meaning they also speak Arabic. Amir was told the only language he was to use was Arabic. ISIS indoctrinated him with their ideology where killing westerners or infidels is an accepted part of their philosophy. Amir was instructed in the ways of the suicide belt and told his reward would be the promise of martyrdom with eternity in Paradise, guaranteed for those who detonate these weapons. Refusal to comply with ISIS commands would have resulted in Amir having his hand or foot cut off as punishment.'

'Simeon, these are depraved people whose actions are alien to any God I have ever been taught about. He obviously witnessed grisly behaviour on an unprecedented scale.'

'Yes, Amir witnessed brutality on an appalling scale by these monsters who incarcerated him. Along with other boy soldiers, they were forced to execute ISIS opponents as a measure of their loyalty to the movement.'

'I know you have brought Amir with the other 60 children, Simeon. His case is unique. I can see why you and Antoinette are his only chance and fully understand the government's sympathetic view of his case.'

'To let you know, Billy, Amir witnessed a Jordanian pilot captured by ISIS being burned alive in a cage. In addition, he witnessed convicted gay people being thrown from a building, followed by stoning to death. ISIS viewed homosexuality as an affront to Islam, justifying their actions.'

'Surely his worldview has been changed forever, having suffered so much psychological damage. Could he ever be rehabilitated into British society?'

'We've got a chance Billy. Fortunately, Amir remembers his time as a Yazidi boy with his family and village. Although suffering great psychological damage, he escaped from ISIS making his way to a Syrian refugee camp.'

'Is that where you met him, Simeon?'

'Yes, hopefully with the right support and love the psychological damage can be countered, giving Amir a chance of adapting to British life.'

'I'm right behind you with this, Simeon. I'll fight your corner to get Amir successfully integrated into British life.'

'It won't be easy. I just think between Antoinette and myself, we can resurrect Amir's life.'

'You're doing exactly the right thing, Simeon. Some people might say Amir committed murder but anyone in their right mind could see he was given no choice. What a horrendous, utterly confusing situation for someone so young. Amir has to be exonerated from any blame. He's too young and what could he do, he needed to survive. Amir had no choice and if he hadn't killed those people, somebody would have done it. I hope the British people will understand the horrendous situation he's come from and show him the compassion he deserves.'

Chapter 26

Amir was fostered by Antoinette and Simeon, who worked hard helping him adjust to life in Britain. Both plugged away, talking through the problems he'd encountered at the hands of ISIS. Having to convince him he'd done nothing wrong was difficult as Amir was riven with guilt at what he'd witnessed. Persistence eventually started to pay dividends. Slowly his outlook began to change but fully adjusting to British life would take years. No doubt there would be bumps in what would be a long and difficult road ahead.

Antoinette and Simeon's stable home life provided the foundation Amir needed to succeed. Both worked diligently with him at his spoken and written English, improving his language skills, making access to school lessons less demanding. Persistence brought gradual improvement in these skills, allowing Amir to thrive in the British education system. Amir briskly adapted to life in school, revealing his academic potential to all. However in spite of throwing himself into his schoolwork, it was difficult to fully eradicate Amir's harrowing early childhood traumas where he'd witnessed gruesome acts.

At home, Amir experienced the love he needed and deserved to cope with his transition to a civilised society. Both Simeon and Antoinette were indebted to the government who could have scuppered Amir's introduction to Britain. As a family they began to prosper and their dedication meant Amir's change to a new way of life was as smooth as it could be.

Billy's activities had not gone unnoticed, prompting high praise from elements of the media who were quick to acclaim his work. Television channels were always on the lookout for a humanitarian story and Billy's work fitted the bill, making him one of the most recognisable figures in London. His story was a personal triumph against adversity, providing a feel-good factor for the British public. For individuals concerned with social justice, Billy became an iconic figure.

Caring members of the public would invoke the ideal that 'there but for the grace of God goes your child or my child,' believing that anyone who suffered as a result of war would want to find sanctuary in a peaceful, civilised country giving them security, education and employment opportunities. Simply put, Billy's mantra was that we all belong to one human race so anyone suffering should be helped.

Many in British society supported Billy's work; however, a minority element resented the government's immigration policy viewing Billy as a do-gooder the country could do without. This right-wing faction accused Billy of watering down British culture. These individuals thought preserving white Britishness went right to the heart of their doctrine. Some areas of London were a hot bed for this type of ideology where certain individuals were at pains to present Billy as a hate figure, responsible for destroying white culture. Refugees became the scapegoats for these extreme elements blaming them for taking jobs and positions of authority which should in the extremists' opinion be the exclusive preserve of white British people.

The British Loyalists, a far-right neo-Nazi terrorist group appointed a new leader, Tooting resident Tommy Gunn. As in other European countries this group's numbers increased as a response to the number of refugees being admitted into the country. A hard-core of extremists played on fear created by new immigrants in the country. Racism was at the heart of this organisation and their behaviour emboldened through a proliferation in their numbers. Linked to this increase in membership was a belief that their activities should be legalised. Outlawing these organisations was seen by members as an affront to their freedom of speech as large numbers of people held far right views.

Sixty Syrian child refugees being brought to London led to the movement campaigning for the youngsters to be forcibly deported. Referring to these young refugees as 'junior terrorists', this hate filled doctrine was garnering large scale support. Tommy Gunn's supporters openly displayed Nazi symbols. Social justice advocates were perturbed by this burgeoning problem in British society. Billy animatedly pointed out that he thought this type of organisation had been confined to the bin when Oswald Mosley's fascists attempted to gain a foothold in British politics during the 1930s.

Tension increased when a newspaper told Amir's story. British Loyalists failed to appreciate the child had no choice but was pressurised to execute a condemned ISIS prisoner. If it wasn't Amir, who was young and had no choice in the matter, it would have been someone else carrying out the assassination. Their limited understanding of the situation Amir found himself in, combined with the loss of his parents showed this organisation to be hell bent on destroying the inclusive fabric of British society.

Tommy Gunn called a meeting of neo-Nazis at a Tooting theatre where his racist, Islamophobic pronouncements succeeded in indoctrinating the right-wing audience with hatred against children who'd suffered horribly at ISIS hands. Attendees at the meeting were ominously dressed in black paramilitary style uniforms. On view, hanging on the auditorium walls were posters showing Tommy Gunn making a Nazi-style salute. Each member of the British Loyalist organisation had a swastika attached to their black shirts. Gunn described Amir as an abomination of a human being belonging to a mediaeval religion engendering revulsion in people.

Utterances of this nature were so far from the truth when one thought about the kindness of Tooting's Iman, a really good Muslim spiritual leader and in any case, Amir was born a Yazidi. Tommy Gunn's statements were uttered with the intention of inciting maximum fear in his audience, coercing individuals ready to support fallacious statements from an abhorrent figurehead. Amir was a little boy being verbally abused through the herd instinct of a vile gathering. Witnessing this any fair minded, tolerant individual would be frightened by the intense hatred spouted against a minor.

Newspapers have a duty to report the truth but unfortunately space devoted to these articles was helping perpetuate this organisation by drawing it to the attention of small-minded individuals. Billy's view that the government should outlaw this movement made him a hate figure for the organisation. Having successfully integrated refugees into British society, Billy was an obscenity in their eyes, making him the primary target of this poisonous group.

Tommy Gunn's hate message was spreading, drawing discontented people to its ranks. Odious material readily available online, radicalised disgruntled individuals fulfilling Tommy Gunn's aim for the movement. Spreading further afield, the British Loyalist's message reached Llanen where Johnny Jones had lost his job when his factory ran into financial difficulty. Traditionally, Llanen had been a coal mining area but following pit closures in 1985 conventional industries had to be replaced. Failure to do this would have caused the area to decline. An industrial estate had been built in Llanen replacing the coal mine, allowing many of the villagers to work in the factories.

Johnny Jones was employed in a well-paid job making car parts. There was always plenty of overtime giving him excellent take home pay. Unfortunately, there were repugnant traits in Johnny's character. It was not unusual for him to make racist and Islamophobic comments. As time passed his thinking became ever more extreme. In private, he was looking at far right websites promoting hatred of immigrants. Johnny would spend time in chat rooms with likeminded individuals from London and the North of England. However, his behaviour was unusual for someone living in the Welsh valleys. The only people in the community from ethnic minorities were running the Chinese and Indian restaurants.

Highly regarded by valley folk because of their willingness to work hard, Johnny's thinking was bizarre as he was a regular customer at these eating places. Reserving his ire for Muslims, he developed an intense hatred of this religious group. Dramatic fiscal problems precipitated the closure of his factory with Johnny failing to recognise the reasons for his workplace closing. Determined to blame someone, he looked for a scapegoat. Unfortunately, he latched on to the appalling message of the British Loyalists as he looked to apportion blame for the termination of his employment.

Johnny blamed Billy Davies, a son of the village for bringing immigrants into the country. Determined that Billy was going to take the blame for his misfortune he set off from Llanen to London. Johnny's indoctrination occurred through continually watching and reading far right material, consequently impregnating his mind with the poison they were promoting. Contacting likeminded individuals online further proliferated his hatred. Johnny's perverted worldview was complete with immigrants becoming the focal point of his hatred. Billy's benevolence to refugees caused Johnny to become obsessed with ending his life. Johnny saw Billy's work as undermining British society.

Johnny pulled into Leigh Delamere services to buy a coffee. Lifting the drink to his lips his hand shook, agitated by the thought of the crime he was going to commit. Adrenaline coursing through his veins was motivating him to perpetrate this heinous act. Finishing his coffee Johnny went to the toilet, returned to his car then reached under the dashboard, taking out a vicious looking knife. A razor-sharp blade glinted in the sunlight. This hideous looking weapon was approximately 9 inches long culminating in a formidable point, capable of inflicting a fatal wound. Rubbing his index finger along the length of the blade brought a glimmer of a sinister smile to Johnny's face. Infiltrating his mind was the thought that he would end the life of this man who'd helped refugees, ultimately costing him his job. Giving little thought to his own future he started the car, heading for London, impatient to get the job done.

Johnny knew Billy's home was at Tooting Evangelical Church because the media were always reporting his work. Arriving in Tooting, Johnny drew his car up outside the church. Getting out he approached a woman and asked, 'Do you know where I can find Billy Davies?'

'It's Friday, Sir. Billy always visits Imam al Mahidi when Friday prayers are finished at Tooting Mosque. They are great friends and do a lot of work together.'

'How far is the mosque?'

'It's less than a mile down the road and you can't miss it. The dome and minaret are obvious landmarks in Tooting.'

Little did the lady know what the man who was speaking to her was planning. Johnny grunted, got back in the car and made his way towards the mosque. Typical, Johnny thought to himself, he is now mixing and worshipping with Muslim scum. As Johnny's thought processes went into overdrive, aggression welled up inside him as he drove the short journey to the mosque, giving little thought to the consequences of his impending action.

Driven on by revulsion at the thought that Billy Davies befriended Muslims, nothing was going to stop Johnny killing his fellow Welshman. He was overcome with the thought as to why Billy Davies was helping refugees when he'd lost his job. He was obsessed with the idea that in his opinion he'd lost his employment because the country was willing to open its doors to immigrants. Such notions had scrambled his thought processes. Far right literature Johnny read, lay the blame for his misfortune on immigrants infiltrating British society. Johnny's brain washing was complete, making him determined to succeed in his quest, irrespective of the ramifications of his crime.

Johnny's plan involved leaving his car around the corner from the mosque then travelling on foot to find Billy. Rounding the corner, he could see a group of six men standing by the mosque gate. Instantly recognising five of the group were Muslims, wearing white robes called kandura, loose fitting trousers and a traditional taqiyya headdress. Billy was easily identifiable in his western clothes. As this menacing figure slowly approached the group, Billy was unaware of what this skulking potential culprit was planning. Concealing the hideous blade under his jacket, Johnny's hand was shaking uncontrollably, impatient to finish Billy Davies off.

Reaching the group, he asked, 'Are you Billy Davies?'

Billy replied, 'Who am I talking to?'

Shouting at the top of his voice Johnny blurted out, 'You're the scum of the earth'

Reaching inside his coat he pulled out the weapon, raising his hand to inflict the fatal stroke. The Imam reacted quickly, pushing Billy just as the knife made its downward thrust. Without the Imam's swift action, the weapon would have contacted Billy's chest, killing him. Fortunately, the downward thrust missed Billy's torso, catching him on the arm, leaving only a superficial wound. Acting quickly, the other Muslim worshippers put the man on the ground, restraining him.

The Imam dementedly screamed, 'Set an example, hold him but don't hurt him. Keep him there until the police arrive.'

Maintaining composure, the Imam phoned the police giving the communications officer any details. Billy was bleeding but alive. He would need stitches but was comforted by the Imam until he could go to hospital. Swiftly the police were on the scene to arrest Johnny and the Imam was praised in the media for his swift reactions but more importantly for encouraging the Muslim men not to harm the assailant.

Chapter 27

Billy was taken to Saint George's hospital to stitch his wound and have his arm put in a sling. Following his discharge Billy went to thank the Imam and the men who had restrained the attacker. Well aware that his work antagonised people with far-right views, Billy was determined not to cower to these tyrants. Allowing these people, a substantial foothold in British society would fragment society and be detrimental to the wider British community.

When he first arrived in Britain, Amir made a positive start helped by Antoinette and Simeon working hard to introduce him to the British way of life. Having witnessed the death of his father and the abduction of his mother, no amount of love and compassion from Antoinette and Simeon could compensate for his great loss. Following the initial feel-good factor of being out of harm's way, 'the bump in the road' arrived as Amir's mind-set slowly began to change.

Past horrors returned to haunt him. Psychological damage suffered at the hands of ISIS produced nightmares causing melancholic distress. When Amir did manage to sleep, he was haunted by the thought his tormentors had forced him to execute an innocent man. During nightmarish spine-chilling visions, he would see the ghastly look on the man's face as he was about to administer the fatal bullet. Then waking screaming in a bath of sweat, Amir's body convulsed violently as his religious upbringing convinced him he would be going to hell for this mortal sin.

No matter how many times he was told he had no choice in the matter, his conscience and innate goodness slowly shredded his mind. Without drastic action Amir's mental state would disintegrate, slowly destroying him. Despite Antoinette and Simeon's best efforts, they went to Billy for advice.

'Amir is finding life difficult, Billy, after the success of his initial introduction to British society. He's now dwelling on his time in the Islamic state. Have you any ideas?'

'I know a man who would be only too willing to help, Simeon.'

'Who is that, Billy?'

'A first-class education with the right person in charge could help change his focus. We need to see Mr Goff Davies, Head of Galaxy High for Boys. He is such a compassionate man who'll want to help. I'm sure he would be spot on for Amir. The boys call him Ffogy with a double f.'

'That's odd, Billy, why a double F?'

'The school is full of very able boys who knew straight away Mr Goff Davies was Welsh. When one of them looked online he found out a single f in Welsh is pronounced v, but a double f is pronounced like a single English f.'

'So why did they call him Ffogy, Billy?'

'He's like chalk and cheese, with the previous head who did little to help the boys. By contrast Mr Davies can't do enough for the pupils. Many go to see him with problems, claiming their state of mind leaves them feeling as though they're in a fog. Numerous boys leave Mr Davies room saying everything is much clearer now.'

'Ah I see it now, Billy, Mr Davies solves the boys' problems making things much clearer for them. His Christian name spelt backwards is Fogg.'

'He knows they call him Ffogy, but they don't do it to his face. His nickname Ffogy is a mark of respect for the high esteem he's held in. The boys love him.'

Antoinette spoke up, 'Let's hope he can help Amir. Hopefully, it might make all the difference.'

Simeon made the appointment to go with Billy to see Mr Davies, who was delighted to see them both. Being such a compassionate man, he was thrilled to meet Billy for a second time. Sharing a common trait through their willingness to do the best for people, both men warmly shook hands. Simeon relayed Amir's story to Mr Davies who was visibly moved by the heart-rending narrative he'd heard.

When Simeon finished Mr Davies spoke movingly, 'Anyone who's suffered like Amir would have difficulties adjusting to a new life. What he witnessed happening to his father and mother and the subsequent traumas at ISIS hands, would play on the mind of any youngster.'

Silence descended on the room. Billy knew Ffogy would want to help. Having previously shown sensitivity towards Payam, the Iranian refugee; Ffogy was swiftly assessing Amir's situation. On the other hand, these were moments of trepidation for Simeon who had never met this Head with the gift of being able to empathise with someone who had suffered such mistreatment.

The hush was broken by Mr Davies proclaiming, 'Amir's in. We'll start him in Year 7. He'll have my best year tutor to look after him. Oh and of course, he can come to see me at any time if he's feeling low.'

A beaming smile came across Simeon's face removing the concerns he had gone into the room with.

'Thank you so much for your kindness, Mr Davies.'

'Simeon, we've got a duty to help youngsters who've suffered so badly. We'll see him on Monday.'

As they turned to leave, Billy smiled at Ffogy, who reciprocated with a wink. A problem distressing Antoinette and Simeon had been resolved. Walking to the tube station Simeon praised Billy for his intuition.

'That was a great idea to see Ffogy.'

'I told you he was a top bloke, Simeon. All Welshman are.'

'Oh, you're such a tease, Billy. On this one I agree with you. He's a man who puts the person first. He didn't even ask about Amir's academic ability.'

'At the moment, he'll just be concerned with integrating Amir into school life, providing him with challenges and care that will ease his torment. Ffogy is a special human being, Simeon. The academic matters will follow once he's settled.'

'Billy, Antoinette will be thrilled.'

Sixty-one youngsters had come from northern Syria's refugee camps and Amir was not the only one having difficulty putting the past behind them. All had adjustment issues. Depending on the problems they'd suffered in the Middle East, these youngsters would hopefully settle at different rates to life in Britain. Billy was determined to support these young people in any way he could.

Thinking back to his time in school it struck him these children could benefit from a trip to the McCleod centre on the Inner Hebridean island of Iona. Their experiences in the refugee camps would have traumatised any human being but the calm and solitude of the holy Isle could complement the work of their foster parents. Such a visit would be a complete contrast to their life in London. Here was an opportunity to change their focus, helping relieve the horror of their time in the ISIS Caliphate. Life in 21st century London was always frenetic. Time spent on this Hebridean island would revitalise the kids, helping them temporarily forget the nightmare they'd been forced to live through. 'What a tonic,' Billy thought to himself. 'I need to put this idea to the London Council of Unity.'

Billy couldn't wait for the April meeting of the council. He then put the proposition to those present.

'Wouldn't it be fantastic to give these children the experience of a trip to Iona?'

'That's an odd place to suggest,' remarked the Archbishop of Canterbury.

'When I was in school, a grant paid for a group of us to go there. It was one of my school highlights, an unbelievable week.'

'I must say. Although it's an odd place to choose for children it could be an inspired choice, Billy,' commented the Archbishop of Canterbury.

'However, there's one problem Billy. Iona is a Christian community and the vast majority of the children are Muslims.'

Immediately Imam Muhammad al Mahidi spoke up, 'That's not important at all. My understanding of the Iona community is that it's an ecumenical community. There are absolutely no reasons why Muslim children can't participate as we are all children of the one God.'

'I think, its important Imam you are one of the adults who accompanies the party,' added the Catholic Bishop.

'I'd be delighted to accompany the youngsters. It's a fantastic opportunity to promote interfaith relations. It'll be a great experience for the Muslim children to encounter the special way of life on Iona. Muslims don't need a mosque to worship Allah. It can be done anywhere.'

'I agree with the Imam,' proclaimed the Archbishop of Canterbury.

He continued, 'The early Christians didn't worship in churches, rather they met in each other's homes. Churches are the people, buildings came later. This is a wonderful opportunity, one we mustn't allow to pass us by.'

Billy was thrilled by the responses from the different faith leaders.

'Thanks to all concerned for your support. It's all systems go then for July, a great month in Scotland because of the long days. There's only one issue, the money to pay for the trip.'

'Money's no problem,' said the Archbishop of Canterbury.

He continued, 'Between us we've enough contacts to pay for this trip. Remember Billy, the Lord will provide. Helping these youngsters adjust psychologically to their new life is the most important aspect of the trip.'

Billy smiled, 'Oh, I do know that, Your Grace. God also works through men. I expect one of our benefactors to cough up.'

All at the meeting were amused by Billy's quick tongue, nodding in full agreement with him.

Billy enthusiastically moved ahead with booking the trip. Flights, coaches and ferries were chartered so the group could enjoy the designated youth week at the McCleod centre. Media interest in this venture was high. The majority of people having a positive outlook, believed it to be a wonderful opportunity to prove worshippers of different faiths could interact with each other. Understandably negative attitudes persisted among extreme elements in society who saw this as pandering to a group of youngsters who should be extradited from Britain. Tommy Gunn was particularly vociferous in his opposition to the venture.

He would openly say, 'The money should be spent on British children not the children of terrorists.'

Billy was adamant he would rather die than give in to such a foul individual. To Billy, such a divisive character had no place in British society. Inclusivity, so all are valued, was needed if there was to be harmony within communities. Hopefully, this trip would show people what could be achieved if people kept an open mind. For this reason, there was no way Billy Davies would draw back in fear at such a disparaging human being.

Sixty-one former refugees were picked up at Tooting Evangelical Church to be transported to Heathrow for a flight to Glasgow. Rescued from the insecurity and the hell of a refugee camp in Syria, the children had been lovingly fostered by London families. These children were embarking on an adventure, hopefully helping erase the scars of the brutal treatment inflicted on them by ISIS. Billy was not normally a man to pray. Even he was imploring the Almighty to allow this trip to succeed.

He kept saying to himself, 'Surely a beautiful Hebridean island would be certain to leave an indelible mark on these youngsters who had endured such trauma in their young lives.'

Boarding the flight, the group bubbled with excitement. Cabin crew greeted them, treating the party like royalty. Extensive media coverage ensured this party couldn't possibly travel incognito. BBC Breakfast Television thrived on heart-warming stories and a reporter was at the airport to interview Billy and the children. After fastening seat belts, the Captain welcomed the party aboard, extending his best wishes for their trip. Engines accelerating quickly, the chatter in the cabin increased in volume to counter the din of the engines. Excitement was tangible, but the youngsters settled when refreshments were served.

An hour later the jet landed at Glasgow Airport, where they were picked up by coach transferring them 93 miles to Oban. Leaving the bus at the quayside, the party boarded a ferry to Mull. Disembarking at Craignure the party got on a bus for the 35-mile journey to Fionnphort. Captivating scenery slowly reduced the children's noise level until there was a deathly hush in the bus.

To this point the children's life experience extended to desert refugee camps populated with unsavoury characters ready to exploit innocent youngsters. Following their rescue, London's hustle and bustle was the environment they were now adjusting to. Stunning Scottish vistas had transformational qualities, immediately helping improve the mental health of the children. Already they were beginning to appreciate the beauty of this wild, barren landscape. Billy was hoping their psychological state would start to be reshaped on this trip.

Exploring this beautiful island could possibly prompt a permanent change in their lives. As Fionphort came into sight, the children could see the slipway leading to the small ferry which would transport them to Iona. Aboard this boat, Billy appreciated the serenity of the surroundings as he was transported back to his school days. The importance of Billy's first visit to this holy Hebridean Island remained unchanged, having made a significant impact on his life. Would it do the same for these children? Billy thought there was a good chance.

Chapter 28

It was not much more than a quarter of a mile to the McCleod Centre from the quayside of this staggeringly beautiful island. The children would be billeted here. Belonging to the Iona Community, this building was a centre for the ecumenical Christian organisation founded in 1938 by George McCleod, a Church of Scotland minister. Most of the children from London were Muslims but this was unimportant as all faiths were welcomed by the community. The emphasis for the week would be arts, crafts, music and outdoor activities. Tooting's Imam accompanied Billy with other adults ensuring the children were well catered for.

Food at the centre was vegetarian for five days of the week. Fish and meat would be served on two days, as part of the community's concern for the planet's resources. Meat served to the Muslim children was Halal meaning lawful, complying with Islamic dietary laws. Meat is processed and prepared in accordance with accepted Islamic requirements. It has to come from a slaughterer using halal practices where animals have to be killed using a sharpened knife. Undertaking this means a quick, deep incision into the throat, resulting in an expeditious death. As the animal is killed an Islamic prayer called Bismillah is recited. Muslims regard this method of slaughter as the most humane.

Catering for the children's religious needs meant a room had to be provided as a place to pray five times a day in accordance with Islamic tradition. Daily prayers are called Salat, one of the five pillars of Islam, a compulsory religious rite for all Muslims. Ensuring these religious observances were met provided a welcoming environment for the children and Imam Muhammad al Mahidi. George McCleod founded the community in 1938 to provide for the most vulnerable in Glasgow society who spent their life in poverty. Such a visit by the children from London gave the community an opportunity to display its relevance to life in modern Britain. Such a provision made the Imam appreciate how much the children could benefit from being in such a tranquil, harmonious, crime free community.

An amazing aspect of life on Iona is the safety of the place. Being crime free gave the children an opportunity to roam outside at will. This made life on Iona the polar opposite to London where such a busy city had the potential to jeopardise any child's safety. Billy had to reassure the children there were no dangerous individuals living on Iona.

Reticence was to be expected having spent time in a refugee camp where danger lurked at every turn. Consequently, the children's confidence grew as they started to meet local people. Many made friends with children from Edinburgh and Glasgow, whose parents had holiday homes on the island. Friendships were forged, then developed giving rise to Syrian youngsters being invited into Scottish homes on the island, further developing their self-assurance.

Art sessions with the children were a revelation providing many of the youngsters with the opportunity to display remarkable artistic talent. Unbelievable representations were produced by extraordinarily talented children. Islam bans the depiction of animate beings, so the children could not draw animals or humans. Two reasons exist for Muslims refraining from drawing living beings. The first prohibition stems from the worship of idols, linking to the second, a belief that God alone creates life. Artwork of the highest standard, involving the use of geometric patterns was produced by the children. Such high-quality work drew praise from everyone at the centre.

Imam Muhammad al Mahidi was particularly thrilled with the work created by the youngsters. Producing work built on a combination of squares and circles meant the finished efforts were a real eye opener. Such unique work needed to be displayed, as they were a complete contrast from anything ever produced before at the Centre. Each piece received pride of place on the walls of the main hall. Children signed their design, further affirmation of the groups growing self-confidence. Another highlight of the art sessions involved the children designing a minaret, the slim tower attached to a mosque, used by the Muezzin for the call to prayer. Designing this tower was another first for the Iona Community, drawing great praise from those who saw it. Local people were invited to view this construction and were effusive in their praise.

Art sessions gave rise to Amir coming to terms with the ordeal he had been through at ISIS hands. Unlike Muslims, Yazidi's can draw animate objects, giving Amir the opportunity to release the pent-up emotion he felt as a result of

ISIS brutality. Art sessions acted as psychotherapy, healing his trauma. He was able to draw very moving paintings, highlighting the violence his people suffered at the hands of ISIS. Terror reflected in the facial expressions of the characters depicted in these art works gave those who looked at them an insight into the terror faced by the Yazidi people.

One of the prime aims of the Iona Community is the promotion of peace and Amir's paintings left an indelible mark on all who saw them. Such therapy seemed to give Amir the platform needed to come to terms with the horrors he'd witnessed. Portraits drawn by Amir were so detailed, displaying war weary images of people brutalised by a barbaric terrorist organisation. All viewing them could see they conveyed the misery of the Yazidi people's suffering.

Traditional music played a significant part in restoring the confidence of the young Syrian children. Music was generated by using a stringed instrument called the oud. Catering for this aspect of the work meant borrowing a number of these implements from Glasgow. Some of the youngsters were accomplished musicians who could play traditional instruments while the remainder formed a choir. A concert held in the Abbey presented the children with an opportunity to display their talents. So impressive was their performance they were given a rapturous applause by the audience.

Amir sang a solo leaving the audience transfixed by his rendition. Yazidi music is reputed to be between five and seven thousand years old, having never been formally written down or recorded. Tradition dictates that songs are handed down from one generation to the next with musicians memorising pieces. As a young boy Amir had been taught some folk songs by his parents. Thankfully, ISIS attempts at indoctrination failed to remove these from his memory so he could sing accompanied by a traditional Yazidi frame drum. Unusually the compere asked for a standing ovation, such was the impression left on the audience by his amazing recital.

Iona tradition dictates Tuesday is a pilgrimage walk around the island. Although a Christian place of pilgrimage, Billy asked the Imam if the children wanted to join in. He saw this as a sublime opportunity for the Muslim youngsters to experience such a religious undertaking. Islam demands Muslims make a pilgrimage to Mecca once in their lifetime. Being the holiest city in the world for Muslims, there's a pilgrimage tradition dating back to Muhammad, the founder of the religion. Muslims call this journey the Hajj and thousands of worshippers flock to this holy city annually.

Worshippers in different religions make religious journeys reminding them of their life's journey. Throughout life, humans experience a conglomeration of experiences. Any pilgrimage can have easy and difficult sections making it symbolic of our life's journey. Tooting's Imam thought this short pilgrimage would give the youngsters a chance to experience this aspect of worship. Importantly it would help explain the places of historical and religious significance on the island to the youngsters. Climbing over stiles, walking through boggy ground, balancing on stepping-stones was enormous fun enjoyed by all the children, a marked contrast with their experiences in Syria. Revelling in this freedom, Billy's idea to bring the youngsters to Iona was certainly bearing fruit.

Finishing the pilgrimage at the Abbey, Billy and Amir walked to the nearby graveyard named Reilig Odhrain or St Oran's Graveyard.

'This is a really peaceful place, Billy,' remarked Amir.

'Yes Amir, this is a significant burial place.'

'Who's buried here, Billy?'

'There are at least seven Scottish Kings buried here, Amir.'

'If there are kings buried here it must be important.'

'Quite right, Amir. If you come over here, there's a special grave.'

Amir followed Billy making every effort not to walk over graves as a mark of respect to the dead. Arriving at the grave Amir wanted to find out more, 'Billy it says, John Smith. Was he a King?'

'No Amir, he was an extremely popular Labour politician who became leader of the Labour Party.'

'I can see he died young, Billy. He was just 55.'

'Quite right, Amir, you worked that out quickly.'

'I've always been OK at maths.'

'I can see that, Amir.'

'Did he live on Iona.'

'No but he was Scottish. The locals kicked up a fuss about him being interred here. In the end, they agreed to his burial as he was such a popular politician.'

'It seems a bit mean not to allow him to be buried here, Billy.'

'Traditionally, only people with ties to the island were buried on this site. The Islanders were concerned that many people would visit the grave and tramp across other graves. In fact, so many visitors came to pay their respects, five graves collapsed.'

'I can see their point, Billy, but how did he die?'

'It was a massive heart attack. He was so popular that the BBC extended the news on the night he died.'

'Would he have been Prime Minister, Billy?'

'It's quite likely because of his popularity. It also begs the question would Tony Blair have become Prime Minister. He succeeded John Smith.'

'I like the words on the grave Billy, **An honest man, The noblest work of God.**'

'Yes, Amir this is a quote from an essay by a great poet called Alexander Pope.'

'He must have been a good man.'

'He was. Let's go back to the centre now, Amir.'

A sensational week was quickly passing but the day before returning to London would be one to remember for the children. This would be the climax to a fantastic trip. Boarding small boats at the quayside Amir and the Syrian children were going to make the seven-mile journey to the island of Staffa with the purpose of visiting Fingal's cave. Staffa was named Pillar Island by the Vikings after the basalt columns there.

Mendelssohn, the German composer visited Fingal's Cave, discovering it was an amazing natural theatre. Resounding acoustics in the cave inspired him to write his musical composition, named after this amazing cavern. Boat crew encouraged the children to sing in the cave giving them the feel for Mendelssohn's motivation to compose his formidable work.

Landing on the island, Billy and the adults took the children to the summit of this isolated piece of rock where puffins were nesting. Mesmerised by these beautiful birds with bright orange beaks, the children couldn't believe how tame they were. Some birds returned to their nests with small fish in their beaks. What a highlight for the children! Billy was filled with gratification that the week-long trip had surpassed his expectations.

Returning to Iona for a farewell dinner, Billy thanked everyone concerned for making the trip such a great success. Memories lasting a lifetime had been created. More importantly, the children were ready to take these experiences back to their life in London, ready to fully embrace the British way of life. It wouldn't be easy to forget the ingrained horrors they'd witnessed. However, Iona had a therapeutic ability, contributing to the healing process. Billy thought only time would tell if there were any lasting benefits.

Tooting's Imam praised the Iona community's willingness to bring different religions together in a spirit of friendship. Endorsing Billy's words, the Imam impressed upon the children the importance of them returning home where they could focus on the week's positive experiences. Such an irrefutable experience would play a part in easing past negativity. Hopefully, they'd return to London ready to prosper in a free society.

On Saturday morning a happy, contented group left the island enriched by their experience. For Billy, there was a sense of pride in a job well done. The cloud on the horizon was the growth of right-wing extremism who resented diversity in society. Billy put that to the back of his mind and pondered on the huge nugget of gold, he'd just dug from life's goldmine.

Chapter 29

Amir and the Syrian children profited from the trip to Iona. Miserable lives had been revitalised by a visit to this holy Scottish island. Such an odyssey surpassed all expectations, providing the youngsters with a fruitful experience. Iona's unique qualities had given the children freedom and positive experiences they could have only craved in the Syrian refugee camps. Mr Goff Davies (Foggy), Head of Galaxy High School for Boys reported that Amir's academic progress had accelerated since the trip. Considering the brutality he had witnessed Amir's development was remarkable, gladdening Antoinette and Simeon.

Settling down to his commitments at Tooting Evangelical Church, Billy would be trolled online by far-right supporters. Enunciating violent threats capable of frightening many people, Billy refused to be intimidated by these crass individuals. Fortunately, made of stern stuff, his resilience prevented him from being menaced by people with Fascist viewpoints. Although there'd been one attempt on Billy's life, he was unperturbed by these people's attitude, drawing strength from the countless numbers of people attaching great value to his work.

As Billy relaxed one evening, two women entered the church looking for him. Billy was watching television, unwinding with a cup of tea when there was a knock at the door.

'Hello, who's there?' shouted Billy.

The door opened and two women stood in the doorway.

One said, 'My name's Elzbieta and this is my partner, Anna.'

Looking at the two women Billy could see that Anna had a large red area extending from the right side of her forehead, disfiguring her eye socket and cheek. When Anna's hair moved, he could see some ear cartilage had been destroyed making him wonder whether this was caused by a burn or possibly something more sinister.

'How can I help you, ladies?'

Anna spoke nervously, 'We are both Polish and gay which would not be an issue in Britain. In Poland, many people are intolerant of same sex relationships. For Polish people gay culture is a bone of contention.'

'That's certainly different to Western Europe where diversity is important,' said Billy.

'Whenever there's a General Election in Poland gay culture is a significant issue. In fact, the leader of the ruling Law and Justice Party has openly declared, 'We consider one man, one woman and their children as the only correct family.' Now this party are in power, gay people have been further ostracised from Polish society,' Elzbieta added.

Billy was disturbed by what he'd been told and commented, 'But the Catholic Church is strong in Poland so when the Pope was asked to give his opinion of gay relationships, he replied by saying, 'Who am I to judge?' Surely the Catholic Church will fight discrimination against gay people.'

Anna was keen to enlighten Billy about how the Catholic Church had exacerbated the problem in Poland.

'Poland's Catholic Church has amplified the problem for gays through their support for the ruling party. LGBT issues are seen by the Polish Church leaders as an affront to family values. Catholics in Poland adhere rigidly to church teaching, stating having two mums or dads is an anathema, contrary to God's will. In the church's eyes, any gay person is expected to remain celibate and expressing love for a person of the same sex is forbidden. Unfortunately, church thinking in Poland is back in the dark ages.'

Billy was perturbed by these revelations when he considered how strong Catholicism is in Poland. In Billy's eyes, the church should have been taking their lead from the Pope.

'Anna, I'd have thought the church should support love between two people irrespective of their sexual orientation. Surely this is what the New Testament teaches through Jesus' life, where he stated, love one another as I have loved you.'

'Krakow's Archbishop has denounced gay relationships, identifying the LGBT lobby in the country as a new threat to Polish freedom,' said Anna.

Billy was able to empathise with Anna and Elzbieta's feelings, having been alienated and discriminated against as a homeless man.

'I've experienced discrimination at first hand as a homeless person. Any intolerance aimed at a particular group of people is an affront to their humanity.

Everyone has a right to lead a life without being threatened. You would find some people worshipping in this church literally interpreting the Bible, pointing to the book of Leviticus for guidance on gay issues.

This Old Testament teaching states, 'You should not lie with a man as with a woman. It is an abomination.'

However, that needs to be balanced with Jesus's teaching on love. Nowhere in the New Testament does it mention gay issues. While these people would be in the minority with their thinking on this matter, none of them would openly discriminate against a gay person.'

'That's not the case in Poland where equality marches have faced violence from right wing activists,' said Anna.

Billy enlightened the couple on the position in Britain.

'We have right wing organisations in London disagreeing with the Government holding out the hand of friendship to refugees and having discriminatory viewpoints about gay people.'

Elzbieta responded quickly pointing out, 'Unfortunately, organisations in Poland having links to fascists carry banners warning the public that members of the LGBT community are paedophiles.'

Anna re-joined the conversation saying, 'Catholic Bishops in Poland have taken their own stance on the issue and in direct contrast to the Pope's statements, they call gays sinners.'

Billy was adamant that a Catholic country should be taking its lead from the Pope.

'If the Pope is expressing a conciliatory tone, then the bishops should be following suit, Anna.'

'That's not what's happening in Poland where the most vociferous opponent is the Archbishop of Bialystok, who wrote a pastoral letter stating LGBT campaigners insulted Christian values and blasphemed against God.'

Elzbieta was upset by the situation in her homeland so she added, 'He further claimed the equality marches were an initiative alien to our land and society, dividing the church and depraving our youth. These inflammatory proclamations have led to people on the equality marches having bottles thrown at them. Some people even spit at them.'

'Crowds chant keep Bialystok free of perverts,' proclaimed Anna.

Having listened, Billy was thinking to himself there was no way the LGBT community would have just taken this lying down.

He asked, 'Well, how did the equality marchers respond to this?'

'We carried banners stating that the Holy Mother would protect people from the church and priests who think it's OK to condemn others. I carried a banner with an image of Mary on it wearing an LGBT halo. Police involvement led to my computer being confiscated and I was charged with offending religious feelings, a crime in Poland.'

Elzbieta continued where Anna left off, 'Others in the LGBT community stuck photos on rubbish bins of priests who'd abused children and the bishops who covered it up.'

'What a measured response. It's not easy to throw stones when you've been involved in sexual crimes against children,' said Billy.

Elzbieta began to speak about the retribution faced by the LBGT community, going into detail about what had happened as a result of this action. She declared, 'Unfortunately, the situation grew more volatile because pasting photos of paedophile priests to rubbish bins actually poured petrol on a fire, gradually getting out of control. One evening while watching television somebody knocked our door. Anna opened it to find a man stood outside, dressed in black with a balaclava covering his identity. Before I had time to ask who he was, he screamed, 'gay bitch'. Taking a bottle from his jacket he squirted acid into Anna's face.'

Billy was upset at what he'd just been told but not surprised that something as vicious as this had happened. When he saw Anna at the door, he could see she'd been burnt in some way.

'When I first saw you, I wondered what had happened to Anna's face.'

Anna spoke up, 'These attacks are common in countries like Bangladesh, particularly where girls look to escape forced marriage, but this sort of assault should not be happening in Europe. In Bangladesh, it's an expression of control over a woman's body and damaging the face is a means of limiting her marriage chances. Persecution of gay people in Poland has dramatically increased because the authorities turn a blind eye to the problem, making the whole situation toxic. Why jeopardise our lives in a country which is intolerant to people like us, so we came to England where there is a more tolerant attitude to the LGBT community.'

Billy could see these two women were distressed by the situation they'd found themselves in. He realised they needed help.

'How can I help you, ladies?'

'We've heard Tooting Evangelical Church and you in particular are at the forefront of the fight for social justice so we would like to join the church,' replied Anna.

'I'll speak to pastor Robbins but I'm sure everything will be fine.'

Pastor Robbins was delighted to count Anna and Elzbieta among his congregation. Theirs was a high-profile case in Poland and right-wing extremists in this Eastern European country were tracking the women's movements.

British media reported the women's story, paying particular attention to Billy's involvement with them. It resulted in Polish fascists liaising with their counterparts in London, who not only discriminated against refugees but were intensely homophobic. Billy was certain some significant problems might lie just around the corner.

Chapter 30

A considerable majority of openminded worshippers at Tooting Evangelical Church welcomed Anna and Elzbieta into the congregation. Disappointingly, a narrowminded minority clung tenaciously to Old Testament teaching, interpreted as apparently condemning gay people. Pastor Robbins pointed out that this tenuous evidence from the book of Leviticus was written down over 2,500 years ago, having been superseded by Jesus' teaching on love. Importantly the Pastor insisted these people should put aside their bigotry, recognising all people deserve to be treated with respect.

He was at pains to point out nobody could possibly be a complete human being without giving and receiving love. The Pastor was adamant that this love could come from a same sex relationship. Billy was thrilled with the Pastor's stance. Referring to their narrow mindedness, he succeeded in quelling this intolerant element within the church. Following the Pastor's words, Anna and Elzbieta were welcomed into this unique place of worship.

Repressing right-wing elements in British society was an altogether more complex issue. The venomous creatures populating these groups were determined to inflict their toxin on the British public. Scurrilous right-wing movements were gaining in popularity throughout Europe. Tommy Gunn leader of the British Loyalists viewed Billy as a pariah in British society, portraying him as a buttress for immigrants, who'd now resorted to supporting gay people from foreign countries. As Tommy Gunn watched breakfast television, Billy, Anna and Elzbieta were being interviewed about the forthcoming Gay Pride March in London.

Tommy Gunn's innate homophobia initiated an increased, pounding heart rate followed by shouting, screaming, ranting, swearing and finally animal like noises. Raging against British law failing to discourage people from expressing their sexuality in ways he found distasteful, brought on an apoplexy with the potential to kill him. Violently bringing his fists down on the arm of the chair, he vowed to take revenge on Billy for his liberal views. Tommy Gunn wouldn't be happy until Britain recognised the folly of allowing immigrants into the country and stopped tolerating gay people.

During the interview Anna explained that the London Pride march would promote the plight of Polish gays.

'Pride in London has asked Elzbieta and me to lead the March. They want Billy to march alongside us. He'll address the crowd in Trafalgar Square.'

Hearing these words Tommy Gunn was seething, causing his eyelids to raise, displaying enlarged eyeballs making the small arteries in his eyes protrusive. He emitted countless profanities with the potential to fill a swear box in record time. He swore Billy Davies would never make that speech. Contacts with likeminded fascists in other countries would help him achieve his objective. Using a foreign fascist to kill Billy would make it difficult for the authorities to trace the criminal, whereas using a British Loyalist member would give the police a good chance of catching the perpetrator. Using a foreigner with similar ideology to his own would guarantee success, preventing the act being detected.

Trawling through his associates on the continent, Tommy contacted Kurt, a neo-Nazi in Germany. Sharing Tommy's philosophy of white nationalism and an obsessive hatred of gays meant he was only too willing to assist in stamping out someone supporting obscene minority groups. He saw immigrants and gays as polluting pure white society and was delighted to be asked by Tommy to eliminate Billy. Discussing the crime on the phone Kurt showed no flicker of emotion as they spoke about ending Billy's life. Right-wing extremists were always careful to cover their tracks, using 'pay as you go' mobiles to avoid detection.

Tommy Gunn was well aware that Kurt was a highly intelligent scientific whizz, possessing a doctorate in chemistry from Bonn University, equipping him with the knowledge to assassinate Billy without having to leave Germany. Kurt decided to use a letter bomb to eradicate this British social justice campaigner, where he would be able to pack the necessary explosive chemicals into a restricted space allowing detonation to happen the second the envelope was opened. Trying to trace the culprit would be an almost impossible task for the authorities. Any evidence would be obliterated by the explosive force. Tommy Gunn was thrilled with Kurt's strategy.

Chomping at the bit at the thought of ending Billy's life Tommy grew more infuriated.

'We'll show that Muslim and gay loving bastard. It'll be the end of him, sending an important message to anyone else supporting immigrants and perverts that they don't mess with us.'

Tommy really had a way with words and his adrenaline levels started to swamp his brain at the thought of the impending assassination.

Kurt's intelligence was 'a given'. Unfortunately, any good he could do by creatively using his scientific knowledge was ruined through his right-wing sentiments. Innate hatred gave him an obsessive aversion to certain minority groups. With an evil glint in his eye he said, 'I can get working on it straight away, Tommy. The most complex bit of the work is getting the detonator into the envelope but I'll figure it out.'

Showing off to Kurt who spoke fluent English, Tommy's German extended to a few words. He said, 'Danke schoen, Kurt.'

Ending the phone call, the two men decided there would be no further discussion between them. Surreptitiously, Kurt enjoyed concocting the chemicals for the letter, hastily dispatching it as soon as he completed his incendiary cocktail. Sitting back, he eagerly awaited the news that another supporter of people blemishing white, heterosexual, European society was dead. Lacking any emotion Kurt thought, it would be two or three days then he and Tommy would lift a glass toasting Billy's death.

Billy received large quantities of mail from people who admired and supported his work. Correspondence arrived from many different countries, so a letter with a German postmark would not arouse any suspicion. Picking up the letter with a German stamp, it crossed Billy's mind that it was heavier than usual. He didn't really give it a second thought, Billy opened it. As he held the envelope the detonator ignited the explosive, producing a limited bang.

Kurt had created an inflammable device, cruelly burning Billy's hands, singeing his eyebrows and hair. Part of Billy's face was burnt and he was temporarily blinded by the intense white light from the explosion. At first it shocked Billy, producing a piercing scream, bringing Pastor Robbins running to the room. Fortunately for Billy, the device had produced more of a phut than a bang, reminiscent of Billy's efforts to set gunpowder alight from bangers on Bonfire Night.

Acting swiftly, Pastor Robbins put Billy's hands in cold water then putting a cloth in cold water, applied it to his face. Other people ran to help, one comforting Billy who was now displaying signs of shock, while another phoned an ambulance. Billy's mind was transported back to the Falklands War where he witnessed men horrifically burnt on the Sir Galahad. There'd already been one attempt on his life by someone with extreme views, now a more sophisticated attempt had been made. Billy came to his senses. Although burnt, he was not going to let these extremists win. He would not be deterred from fighting for social justice. An ambulance arrived and Billy's initial shock at the attempt on his life was replaced by a steely resolve.

Chapter 31

Fortunately most wounds were superficial. Given time they would repair without treatment. However, the medical staff thought his hands might need skin grafts. Despite this, burns specialists were hopeful Billy would make a good recovery. People were appalled that somebody was vindictive enough to commit such a cowardly, odious crime. Although shocked by the explosion, Billy made light of the situation.

He quipped, 'I've never been an oil painting or even a watercolour. You never know I might get a modelling contract now.'

As Billy's hands suffered the worst damage having taken the full force of the blast, medical staff decided to apply a petroleum-based ointment on the burns, covering them with sterile bandages. Treating Billy in this way, there was a good chance that restorative work could be avoided. Only time would tell if this would work. In the meantime, Billy had an appointment at London Pride. Determined not to miss this march gave him another chance to express the importance of diversity and inclusivity in British society.

7 July in London was a glorious day, absolutely perfect for the Pride March. Billy knew thousands of liberal minded, forward-thinking people would attend this annual event, expressing support for the LGBT community. Unfortunately, a minority of small-minded individuals failed to recognise the importance of an inclusive society and were intent on generating discord.

Billy, Anna and Elzbieta set off from Tooting Evangelical Church, making their way to the tube station. They headed for Portland Place, situated in Marylebone. The Pride route involved marching along Oxford Circus, Regent Street, Piccadilly Circus, Pall Mall, ending at Trafalgar Square. Here Billy would address the crowd. He began to feel unusually anxious, realising how important the Pride Rally and march were to the LGBT community. There would be countless thousands of people celebrating the importance of this event, all expecting to hear an inspirational message.

'This is our first march in London and we can only hope it's different from the Polish Pride marches where we're outnumbered by confrontational homophobes,' remarked Anna.

'You won't need to worry. So many people will support the LGBT community that far right organisations will stay away. Like all bullies they're only brave when they're in the majority,' said Billy wanting to ease Anna and Elzbieta's apprehension.

Arriving at Portland place, Billy, Anna and Elzbieta were greeted by a mindboggling throng of people. Rainbow banners were everywhere and clusters of coloured balloons were being held by vast numbers of participants.

Elzbieta was stunned by what she saw.

'I can't believe how many people are wearing quirky costumes. It's like we're attending the world's biggest fancy-dress party.'

Anna was absolutely astounded by what she was witnessing.

'Elzbieta, look how many people have dyed their hair different colours. It looks like a giant rainbow's dropped from the sky.'

Many women carried rainbow fans to cool themselves, while other gay people painted their faces different colours, entering into the spirit of the day.

'Look,' said Billy.

He continued, 'Some people have even decked their pets out in different colours. Obviously, these animals want to support their owners.'

Groups of people had coloured garlands draped around their necks, seemingly everyone had entered into the spirit of the occasion.

Elzbieta was amazed by what she saw.

'Look, same sex couples are kissing. Isn't it lovely that people are not afraid to express their love for each other in this country! How different is this to Poland! It's amazing how tolerant people are here.'

One bisexual woman carried a banner stating, 'God said Adam and Eve, so I did both.'

Snaking its way along London's streets this legion of marchers were a riot of colour, bellowing out songs. What a joyous occasion, liberal thinking people eagerly supporting the LGBT community. Anna and Elzbieta responded euphorically, inevitably contrasting the occasion in London with the marches in Poland where participants were treated with disdain. London's Pride organisers had been made aware that Anna and Elzbieta were participating. They were accommodated with a prime position at the front of the procession.

Arriving at Trafalgar Square, a stage had been erected for speakers to address the crowd. Billy's address to the crowd would be the highlight of the day, having become a popular British figure. Thousands of marchers claimed different vantage points to listen. A raucous crowd fell silent as Billy climbed onto the platform. Laughter, singing and chanting was replaced by a muted response. Such a deathly hush wouldn't have been out of place at a funeral.

Thousands of participants with painted faces some carrying rainbow-coloured posters waited in anticipation for Billy to begin. Such a huge audience with anticipation etched on their faces were looking forward to the address from this former homeless man, who through his humanitarian work had become such an iconic figure. Billy adjusted the microphone as he looked out at the crowd, flabbergasted by the size of his audience.

'Thank you for inviting me to this bewildering gathering. Your presence here is testimony to the fact people in this country can freely celebrate their distinct individuality. Respecting the unique and diverse nature of the human race ensures we treat each other with dignity and a spirit of toleration. The LGBT community needs to feel valued for their achievements.'

The crowd applauded, cheered, whistled and gradually fell silent again.

Billy continued, 'During the 1980s, London's LGBT community won the respect of the Welsh mining communities. Miners and their families in my own village were helped by them. The Miner's Strike lasted a year putting mining families under intense pressure. Margaret Thatcher wanted to close uneconomic pits but the Miner's Union led by Arthur Scargill went on strike in an attempt to prevent closures, believing the mining communities would be decimated by such action.

During a year-long strike, miners and their families had no income. Thankfully, communities rallied round providing mining families with the essentials to survive. What a harrowing episode in the history of coal mining in this country. During the summer of 1984, a group of lesbian and gay activists in London decided to raise money to support struggling mining families. Such an act of benevolence took place at a time when gay people were facing enormous prejudice through the AIDS issue. Gay activists saw the miners as another group being ostracised by the government, making it easy for them to identify with the miner's plight.

Eleven thousand pounds was raised by the London group and Welsh miners took this group to their hearts allowing both to draw strength from each other through their mutual support. Welsh miners fought the Thatcher government, while the LGBT community were facing raging homophobia. Miners renowned for their toughness and physical strength were moved by the commitment of the London LGBT community who collected money in pubs and held concerts. More importantly, they wore a badge 'Coal not Dole.' In recognition of the kindness shown, the miners from my village hired a bus to take part in the 1984 London Pride march. Mark Ashton who led the gay community died from AIDS in 1987 at 26 years of age. He and all other members need to be remembered for their kindness. What the LGBT community achieved during the strike touched the hearts of mining families.'

Grateful for Billy's address the crowd applauded rapturously. They eagerly wanted to hear more.

'I never worked in the mine but my father did and I know he would come back to haunt me if I hadn't mentioned the generosity of the LGBT community in my address. Today, the mines are closed but the scars of that year long strike still remain. Communities have tried to move on but they still fondly remember the LGBT community in London, remaining indebted to the work they did during a dreadful period in the history of mining. Today most people accept the LGBT community for who they are but unfortunately a minority of individuals with far-right views preach hate against those who they see as falling outside the mainstream. It is essential we stand united proving them wrong.'

The crowd cheered uncontrollably, waving their rainbow flags. Billy realised his words struck a chord with the marchers allowing the party to begin.

Fortunately, the burns on Billy's hands healed. Although left with some dark patches of skin there was no need for skin grafts. Two attempts on his life by far-right extremists convinced Billy, he needed to remain vigilant. Deluded individuals would be a constant threat to him and by supporting the LGBT community, the far right's hatred of him intensified, making him more determined to stay alert but not to be intimidated by them.

Chapter 32

Antoinette and Simeon were high-flyers forging successful careers for themselves. Simeon's humanitarian work had not gone unnoticed involving him in Third World crises. War's human cost was a constant reminder that man had a long way to go before they could truly regard themselves as civilised. Simeon was employed by Save the Children. His work involved feeding 11 million children on the Arabian Peninsula, the innocent victims of famine.

Amir excelled at Galaxy High School for Boys and was now in his second year at medical school in Cardiff. Mr Goff Ffogy Davies had promised Amir would get the support he needed to achieve. Such a caring individual as Ffogy stuck to his word and Amir overcame the difficulties he encountered at ISIS hands. Antoinette and Simeon were indebted to the staff at Galaxy High having displayed the care and concern that Amir's situation demanded.

Mr Davies had been an inspiration for Amir constantly taking an interest in his progress. Amir finished school, at the same time Mr Davies retired. Considering his commitment, he was understandably given an unforgettable send off by the school community. Boys still in school were upset, Ffogy had retired before they'd finished but he left an indelible mark on the place. Without a doubt his successor would have a difficult task measuring up to his achievements, in particular matching the personal attention he gave each pupil.

Antoinette's work as a researcher for the Liberal Party instilled her with the determination to become an MP. Single-mindedly, she diligently worked to achieve her ambition. Following the 2016 Brexit referendum Liberalism rejuvenated in the country and the party was looking to steadily garner more votes and parliamentary seats.

Chapter 33

An unprecedented calamity afflicted Yemen, a country on the Arabian Peninsula. Prolonged civil war displaced many people causing the country to be ravaged by famine. Yemen's problems began when the Arab Spring changed the political situation in the country. Beginning in 2011 as a series of uprisings it spread across the Arab world, causing chaos in some countries.

Initially aiming to bring stability to a politically hostile region, the purpose of the insurrection failed. Unfortunately, the Yemeni people encountered horrendous suffering caused by this insurgency. Instability caused by Jihadist attacks and a breakaway movement in the South of the country destabilised the nation. Troops continued supporting Mr Saleh, the President with government corruption leading to Yemenis losing their jobs, followed by a dreadful famine.

Internal weakness in the country opened the door for a breakaway Islamic movement known as the Houthis to emerge in opposition to President Saleh. Accusations of financial mismanagement created this toxic situation. To counter these fiscal problems the President sided with the United States and Saudi Arabia. This move caused hardship for the Yemeni people through civil war.

Initially revolutionaries belonged exclusively to the Shia Houthis, one of two main Islamic groups. Eventually disillusioned, Sunnis joined traditional adversaries against the Government. Poverty not religious belief was the common cause bringing these two Islamic groups together. This was an extraordinary alliance due to the discord between the two groups dating back to Muhammad's death in the 7th century AD. Thirteen centuries ago dispute occurred over who should be Muhammad's successor causing these two Islamic groups going their separate ways to the present day.

Having taken the lead in this civil war, Shia Houthis were joined by Sunnis perceiving intervention to be in the national interest. Long serving President, Ali Abdullah Saleh was forced to hand power to his deputy Abdullah Mansour Hadi. Faring no better, he proved himself another inept Yemeni leader. Failure to manage the country's problems showed Mr Hadi had serious shortcomings in his attempt to govern. Weak governmental structures opened the way for Houthi rebels to capture Sanaa, the capital. An action by the revolutionary group forced Mr Hadi the president to flee to Saudi Arabia for safety.

Alarmed at these developments, Saudi Arabia a largely Sunni country launched a campaign against the Houthis who were backed by Iran, a country with a Shia population. Logistical intelligence support was provided by the United Kingdom, United States and France helping the Saudis prop up the Yemeni government. Saudi expectations were that the conflict would last a few weeks but the Houthis proved a resilient enemy with the discord dragging on for years.

Hardship and misery for the Yemeni people were the result of this bad blood with Aden in the south of Yemen remaining under government control. The chaotic situation in the country had been exacerbated by rogue Islamic state groups taking advantage of the carnage caused by the insurrection. ISIS groups carried out deadly attacks in Aden showing little mercy to the local people.

Simeon's advisors at Save the Children informed him that a town to the North of Aden called Ad Dali had been attacked by an Islamic State group. For an Islamic town Ad Dali was relatively liberal by comparison with other towns in the region. Women were given the opportunity to express themselves in ways other towns did not permit. Tolerance in Ad Dali gave women the freedom to fulfil their potential.

They dressed respectively in line with Islamic teaching, rather than the extreme standards demanded by the Islamic State. Ad Dali women could work and drive cars, contravening Islamic State beliefs. As a result, Islamic State's imposition of their interpretation of the Quran forced women to comply with the extreme conditions of this demeaning code of conduct. Lacking any credibility if the religious principle of equality in creation was observed, Islamic State's demands were contrary to the will of God. Here was proof that their extreme religious philosophy was nothing short of a code of conduct belonging in medieval times.

Unwilling to give up their freedoms without a fight, a group of Ad Dali families failed to comply with medieval impositions laid down by the Islamic State group. Brave families were rounded up by these barbaric monsters who proceeded to sexually abuse the women. Such a hideous organisation prepared to commit gruesome crimes were led by an aggressive, cowardly bully dressed in black, with a hood covering his face, preventing him being identified. Such a spineless individual was prepared to impose his perverted thinking on defenceless people. He failed to appreciate these people had moral fibre, alien to such a lily-livered individual as himself.

Husbands were held back as they strained every sinew in an effort to save their wives from the violation of these behemoths. Devoid of compassion and a moral code, the black hooded one gave the order that following the sexual abuse of the women they should be taken and stoned to death. Husbands and children were forced to watch as this barbaric practice was carried out. Men and children screamed as women were dropped from the roof of a house. Breaking legs first was the Islamic State's way, preventing any woman from running away.

Islamic supporters were given licence to bombard the women with rocks, inflicting terrible injuries. As each woman was hit, they emitted bloodcurdling screams, noises diminishing to a whimper as lives slowly ebbed away. Children bellowed in desperation as punishment was inflicted on the mothers who'd given birth and reared them. Bowing their heads in desperation caused tears not to run down their face but hit the desert dust like rain droplets. Forcing families to endure such punishment demeaned any god these devils worshipped.

Traumatised, children with hands tied behind their backs were forced to stand upright by an ISIS tyrant who placed the barrel of their gun under each child's chin compelling them to watch as their fathers were beheaded. Venting their fury on the fathers was the ultimate ignominy. Children hunched shoulders, wide eyed and open-mouthed trembled as they were forced to watch such atrocities. Colour drained from children's faces leaving them deathly white like any corpse, anticipating it would be their turn next. ISIS tyrants held each father's severed head by the hair, claiming this would be the fate of any non-believer. Relenting at this point, the ten traumatised children were taken and locked up in a house on the outskirts of Ad Dali.

Although saved from immediate death, the children faced a horrendous and macabre fate. Fanaticism is at the heart of ISIS philosophy; the children were so young these monsters would infiltrate their minds with ideals alien to the vast majority of human beings. Brainwashing would include teaching that Jews, Christians, Muslims and anyone else not submitting to the ISIS creed were nonbelievers and should be killed. Justification for their actions came from a draconian interpretation of the Quran. Such an understanding of this holy text was outside the thinking of any mainstream Muslim. After all Islam teaches peace and obedience to Allah. Nowhere does it teach the right to kill another innocent person.

Invading these youngsters' minds would involve manipulating their thought processes as preparation for them becoming suicide bombers. Following indoctrination, these young people would willingly wear suicide vests to kill or maim, with the promise that their reward would be in paradise. Immediate action was needed to prevent such a horrific outcome.

Chapter 34

Sitting at his desk in Save the Children's headquarters, one Monday morning Simeon was about to make a coffee when the phone rang. Answering he expected it to be an everyday call but to his disbelief it was the Secretary General of the United Nations. Antonio was Brazilian and his dedication to strive for justice for all, led to him acquiring the top job in the organisation. His commitment to the first principle of the United Nations Declaration of Human Rights, 'All human beings are Born Free and Equal' guaranteed him being held in high regard by world leaders. His status gave Antonio access to global statesmen but, on this Monday, he'd picked up the phone to speak with Simeon. Simeon thought to himself surely this call must be one of paramount importance.

The Secretary General extended a greeting to Simeon, 'Good morning, Simeon. I need to speak with you regarding a salient matter. The lives of ten young children are threatened by ISIS. Unfortunately, they have witnessed heinous crimes committed against their parents. It's imperative we bring these children to Europe where they can find security. Resettling them here will give them an opportunity to rebuild their lives.'

At first Simeon couldn't quite believe why the Secretary General decided to phone him but the fact children were involved, helped explain Antonio's reasoning.

'What's happened to the children and where are they, Secretary General?' asked Simeon.

'I will email you a copy of what has happened to these kids, read it, then phone me back. I'll warn you, Simeon, it makes for mortifying reading.'

Reading the email caused Simeon to shudder at the horrific details it contained and was reminiscent of the suffering Amir endured at ISIS hands. Simeon found difficulty believing what he was reading, wondering how human beings could ever behave in such a cynical, contemptuous way. These religious extremists were alien to anything the world had encountered before, making a mockery of the 'sanctity of human life.' Although stunned Simeon thought it imperative something was done to rescue these youngsters. Picking up the phone, Simeon was agitated as he dialled the Secretary General. Palpitations were not something he had ever suffered but what he'd just read would cause a snowman to break into a sweat. Antonio answered the phone.

'What I've just read is unbelievable. I'm fully supportive of any rescue. Could you fill me in on any other details?'

Antonio threw further light on the whereabouts of these imprisoned youngsters, 'They are Yemeni children, imprisoned in a small town 100 miles north of Aden called Ad Dali. My contacts tell me they are in a house guarded by one ISIS fighter. ISIS know these children are young and frightened and there's not much chance they would try to escape.'

Simeon expressed his disgust at what he'd been told. He declared, 'I can't believe what's happened to their parents. It beggars belief the children were forced to witness it.'

Witnessing the brutal deaths of their parents at the hands of this grisly organisation has left them distraught, psychologically damaged and in need of rescue', replied the Secretary General

Simeon was moved by the Secretary General's concern.

'How can I help?'

'I wondered if you had any ideas about how we can get the children out of Yemen. Obviously, this has to be a covert operation. ISIS will show no mercy to anyone who's caught.'

At university Simeon had undertaken parachute training, jumping on a number of occasions and the thought of rescuing a group of orphans who were in danger, filled him with a desire to help. However, these thoughts were tempered by dread at trying to attempt such a daring, complex mission. Amir's experience at ISIS hands motivated Simeon making him determined to attempt a rescue. Failure would certainly cost him his life.

Moreover, Antoinette would be petrified at the prospect of him endeavouring to carry out such an audacious liberation. She would definitely want the children freed but the precarious nature of such a rescue would create reservations in Antoinette making her believe any mission was doomed to fail. Simeon thought of Billy who although in his mid-fifties had served in the British Army and was certainly no shrinking violet. Surely, he'd want to rescue the youngsters, in the hope of giving them a new life.

Simeon didn't have to give it too much thought. He blurted out, 'Secretary General, I know just the man to help.'

'Who is that Simeon?'

'A man called Billy Davies who lives at Tooting Evangelical Church. He's done so much humanitarian work.'

Antonio was stunned to hear that Simeon suggested this could be undertaken by someone living in a church.

'He needs to be a bit special to free these children.'

Simeon wanted to allay any initial fears Antonio might have.

'Billy is a bit special, Secretary General; he was a homeless man who suffered with PTSD from fighting in the Falklands War in 1982.'

Antonio was concerned that Simeon might be miscalculating the level of danger involved in such a rescue.

'Will he be up to such a daring raid?'

Simeon had no doubt that Billy would be up to the task.

'Oh, definitely he helped solve the knife crime problem in London, which was endemic within the city gang culture. He is really astute, courageous and one of the most altruistic people I know.'

'Now you mention him I have heard of Billy. Don't you think Billy is past his best? He might be a bit old for this type of work, Simeon?'

Holding Billy in such high esteem Simeon was anxious to substantiate why he thought Billy was up to the task.

'Billy's very fit for his age, having received extensive military training when he was young which has been firmly ingrained in him. I will speak to him later and I'm sure he'll want to participate. I'll ring your office tomorrow.'

'Thanks for your help, Simeon. I'll look forward to your call.'

Simeon left his office at St Vincent House, Orange Street, Leicester Square catching the tube to Tooting. His mind was overwhelmed with the thought of rescuing the children. It also crossed his mind something could go tragically wrong. How would Antoinette react? Would Billy be prepared to help? Knowing the answer to both questions it would be a mistake to harbour any self-doubt. Undertaking something as daring as this rescue needed a focus obliterating negative thoughts from the mind. It was also important to play down the danger as not to worry Antoinette.

Arriving at the church it was lunchtime. Simeon walked into the main hall to be greeted by the wonderful aroma of bacon cooking in the kitchen. It was no problem finding Billy, the delightful smells were a giveaway. Billy heard the footsteps then looked up to see Simeon in the doorway.

'Hi Billy, that smells great.'

'There's plenty here for two. I'll put another two eggs in the pan. By the way what brings you here at this time? Surely you should be working.'

'If you get the meal, we can have a chat about the phone call I've had this morning.'

Once the meal was cooked and served the two men sat down to eat. Eagerly tucking into the bacon and eggs Billy asked,

'Well Simeon, what have you come to see me about?'

'How much do you know about the political situation in Yemen, Billy?'

'I know there's a civil war, causing many people to die from famine.'

'It's a real tragedy because a splinter group called the Houthis control the north of the country and are based in the capital Sanaa. Iran is backing this group in their fight for control of the country, whereas Saudi Arabia are supporting the official government based in Aden. To further complicate matters a renegade ISIS group has taken control of the town of Ad Dali, establishing a base there, about 100 miles from Aden.'

'Simeon, there's not much we can do about a civil war.'

'But there's more, Billy. This detestable IS group have executed a group of parents in the most abhorrent way imaginable, imprisoning their children on the outskirts of the town.'

Having remembered what happened to Amir, Billy expected to be told something he didn't want to hear.

'Were the children made to witness these acts, Simeon?'

'Yes Billy, it's really important they are rescued so their shattered lives can be rebuilt. This morning I was phoned by the Secretary General of the United Nations.'

'What did he phone for, Simeon?'

'He wanted to know if I had any ideas about a rescue attempt. As I am working for 'Save the Children' I want to help but the political situation in Yemen is so complicated that if troops were sent in, IS would have no compunction about killing the kids. Promoting their own warped ideology is their only concern. Totally lacking any humanity means they would not think twice about murdering the kids. It would be amazing if we could get them out.'

Billy suddenly sharpened his focus and began thinking about his time in the army, particularly his experiences in the Falklands War. Frequently questioning the validity of that war, he did not need to give a second thought to rescuing ten children who might be put to death at any time.

He quickly assessed the issue.

'This is a cause where no effort should be spared to liberate the children.,'.

'Oh, I'm glad you feel that way, Billy. I knew you would.'

Eager to get on with the job Billy declared, 'Can you fix a call to the Secretary General? We need to discuss it.'

'Consider it done, Billy. We'll have a zoom meeting with him in my office tomorrow.'

'What time, Simeon?'

'Can you be there at 2 o'clock because Antonio is based in New York and it'll be 9:00 a.m. there.'

Chapter 35

Having eaten an early lunch, Billy set off to meet Simeon at his Leicester Square office. Previous military training ensured his mind was awash with strategies to free the ten Yemeni children. Success depended on a thoroughly planned covert operation. Too many people knowing about the mission would jeopardise the children's safety. Secrecy was vital because ISIS had cells of supporters throughout the world supplying information to these Ad Dali terrorists.

Billy hatched a plan involving Simeon and himself undertaking a mission to rescue the Yemeni children. He was aware that disclosing information to the wrong person could result in certain death by them being unwittingly lured into a trap with ISIS lying in wait. In Billy's mind, there was no room for error and the only people to know about this secretive operation should be Antonio, the Prime Minister and some Cabinet members. Billy did not give his advancing years a second thought, considering himself to be as fit as a fiddle. Repetitive weapons training in the Army ensured he would swiftly re-acquire the skills needed for such a mission. Any reservations about using a weapon again were superseded by the thought he'd be helping to rescue ten children.

Billy walked from Leicester Square tube station to Simeon's office. This area of London was busy during lunch hour. It was nearly two in the afternoon when workers were returning to their offices. Many would leave their reappearance in work to the last minute, soaking up every last ray of sunlight on a glorious June day. Strolling along Orange Street, Billy approached the Save the Children offices wondering whether his zoom meeting with such an important dignitary would bring a satisfactory conclusion for the ten imprisoned youngsters. Crossing Billy's mind was the thought this call might just be a talking shop where nothing would be achieved. Billy was an action man and would the Secretary General be willing to pull enough strings for a two-man rescue mission to be set up?

At 1:55 p.m. Billy walked into Simeon's office and there was a warm embrace between the two friends. On Simeon's desk a laptop was set up for a meeting, hopefully resulting in an attempt being made to rescue the children. At precisely 2:00 p.m., Antonio appeared on the screen, introducing himself to Billy by his first name. Mesmerised at the thought of conversing with such an esteemed world figure, Billy was pleased the meeting started on time.

He thought this was a good sign auguring well for a rescue attempt being given the green light. People back home would never believe that a valley boy could chat with the leader of a world-renowned intergovernmental organisation. Immediately, Antonio allayed any fears Billy might have about his total commitment to a covert mission. Simeon reiterated the point about Billy having military training and that he was both innovative and forward thinking.

'If we send the military into Ad Dali, ISIS will immediately kill the children. Cruelty is endemic in this organisation. Although the children are young it will not matter one jot to these barbarians who are psychopathic. Such monsters are devoid of conscience,' said Antonio.

Billy was convinced Antonio was committed to freeing the youngsters.

'A covert operation by two civilians would give us the element of surprise. From what I know of IS they have supporters with their ear to the ground who would tip them off about a military attack. Our greatest weapon is the element of surprise. A charity worker and a former homeless man undertaking a covert rescue attempt will mean ISIS won't suspect a thing.'

Antonio was in total agreement with Billy.

'I agree with what you've said, Billy. It is surprising how good ISIS intelligence is. They get to know about plots against them. ISIS spies manage to infiltrate countries' security structures, alerting their spies on the ground. Keeping details of this operation among a small group of people will give us the best chance of success. What do you think, Billy?'

'I've thought about the consequences of undertaking such an operation. It's worth the risk. Treating a child in this way is abhorrent. They are in the hands of monsters.'

Simeon joined the conversation, 'I'd like to participate in the mission. My feelings about the way the children have been treated are the same as Billy's. It's really important we're successful.'

Antonio appreciated how unwavering the two friends were towards the mission.

'Right, we've established that you're both anxious to participate in this mission. We now need to plan it.'

Billy had spent all his waking hours thinking about this rescue from the moment Simeon had mentioned it.

'After looking at the map last night, I have already thought about how we can do this. Everything hinges on the level of support we can get.'

Antonio had bought into Billy's determination to bring the children to Britain and asked, 'Billy, just tell me what you and Simeon need. My informants tell me the children are being held on the outskirts of the town. Being so young and frightened, they're not going to be that well-guarded. IS won't be expecting a rescue attempt.'

Delighted to hear this. Billy excitedly said, 'That's really good. I'm confident, we can break the kids out.'

Reality hit home to Simeon that he could easily lose his life in this type of operation. Suddenly his heart was in his mouth. He began sweating uncontrollably. Quickly snapping out of this negative mindset, Simeon had great faith in Billy who had the knack of turning everything to gold. Hopefully, this Midas touch would lead to the children being freed and both of them getting back home alive.

Antonio was determined to give Billy and Simeon the support needed. As a father and grandfather he was dumbfounded that such a villainous organisation could exploit young children in this way. Possessing such primitive values which they're prepared to inflict on young children appalled the Secretary General.

'What do you need for this assignment to be successful, Billy?'

'This has been on my mind all night. We need your Yemeni contacts to pinpoint the children's exact location. Once in Yemen we'll move in quickly, liberate them and transport them to the coast. Ad Dali is approximately 100 miles from Aden and a Royal Navy ship needs to be ready to pick up the kids taking them to safety.'

'Have the two of you thought about how you're going to get into the country undetected?' asked Antonio.

Billy's mind had worked overtime from the moment Simeon had mentioned this to him and he said, 'I've looked at the map of the Arabian Peninsula. If you could persuade the Saudi government to fly us from Riyadh to Najran, a town near the Yemeni border, we could pick up a small plane to fly us to Ad Dali at night, where we could parachute out.'

Being concerned for the men's safety Antonio was alarmed by Billy's bravado.

'That all sounds great but how much parachute training have you and Simeon done?'

Billy grew impatient at being asked such a question knowing there was no time to waste.

'Antonio, there's no time to flaff around about parachute refresher courses or health and safety. I did so many jumps in the Army it will come straight back to me. Our main priority are these Yemeni kids.'

Antonio seemed to get the message loud and clear. Billy could not be deterred in any way.

'Well, I can see you're ok with it, Billy, but what about Simeon?'

'He did parachute training when he was at university. I'm sure he's not going to give it a second thought.'

Astounded by Billy's determination to rescue the children Antonio still wanted to ensure Simeon was on the same page as his friend.

'Are you OK with it, Simeon?'

Simeon was literally quaking in his boots but there was no way he was not going to participate in the rescue. Billy was in his mid-fifties and was ready to parachute into Yemen. There was no way he was going to be found wanting.

'Yeah, I'm fine, I'll take my lead from Billy.'

Mulling over the conversation he had with the two men Antonio declared, 'Let's get on with it. I'll speak to the Saudi Government. There'll be no problem with Saudi Arabia as they detest IS. Contacting the British Prime Minister to enlist his help is essential to the success of this mission and we need a Royal Navy frigate patrolling in the Middle East anchored off Aden ready to pick the children up. Rescuing these children will be a feather in the cap of the British Government. Your Prime Minister is renowned as a bit of a maverick, so he'll definitely want to help. I am convinced their cooperation is guaranteed.'

Antonio's compassion came to the fore. It was certain he was not going to abandon the Yemeni children even if it meant taking a punt on an ex-serviceman and a charity worker.

Billy continuing to think about the mission spoke again, 'Once we have parachuted into Yemen, we'll make our way by foot to where the children are imprisoned. We both need a weapon and it's really encouraging to hear that only one person is guarding the children, so overpowering the guard should not present a problem.'

All of a sudden Simeon's nerves jangled, agitating him. He began wringing his hands and pacing up and down. At no time in his life had he been so highly strung as he felt at this moment. Billy sounded unbelievably confident and 'his speak' would make someone think this mission was going to be a walk in the park. Any calculation Billy made included a no failure option. Single-mindedly Billy had only one thought in his mind. They were going to free the children and that was the end of it.

Simeon was concerned and exclaimed, 'Billy, I've never used a gun.'

Gloom did not fit with Billy's agenda. He confidently said, 'No problem, Simeon. I'll have an automatic weapon and you'll have a pistol. Hopefully, we can overpower the guard without using our weapons. The last thing we want to do is alert IS to the breakout.'

Antonio was confused, not knowing whether to be exhilarated or alarmed at Billy's confidence. Was he reckless or could he really pull it off?

'Is there anything else you need, Billy?'

Billy's planning was at an advanced stage.

'Antonio, can you arrange for two jeeps to be brought from Al Hudaydah. Then leave them in the desert about a mile from where we're going to rescue the kids.'

Antonio was well connected in many different countries including Yemen so there were many people he could call on for help.

He informed Billy, 'There are some Yemeni tribesmen, we can enlist to help us as their hatred of ISIS is well known. Mind you we'll have to pay them but leave that with me.'

Billy's 'game face' really was on. If there was such a thing as an adrenalin rush, then Billy was cascading it. Pumping through his veins this hormone infusion caused him to stutter with excitement,

'We've no time to waste and need to be ready to go in three days.'

Absolutely convinced nothing would deter Billy. Antonio said, 'Good luck to both of you. I'll get going on the arrangements.'

Simeon was astounded at how clearly and precisely Billy thought things through. However, his confidence in his own ability to get things done flabbergasted him. It crossed his mind that Billy could be an adrenalin junkie switched on by the thrill of doing something really dangerous. No, the most likely scenario was he was so overwhelmed by the situation the children were in, he felt compelled to act. Nothing would dissuade him. He'd remembered Billy's comment about the importance of digging for gold and getting the best out of people but it crossed his mind that by going to Yemen they might be digging their own graves.

Chapter 36

Antonio's allegiance to the emancipation of the Yemeni youngsters was unstinting. Logistically, many aspects of the mission were in his hands. Billy and Simeon needn't worry as his ability to connect with different groups of people was exceptional. Antonio communicating with and enlisting the help of the British and Saudi Governments would give the two friends their best chance of succeeding. Both men would be flown from RAF Brize Norton to Riyadh then transfer to a Cessna 172 dropping them near Ad Dali. Both governments' actions demonstrated their determination to liberate the youngsters.

Antonio's willingness to engage the contacts at his disposal was further confirmation of his strength of feeling about the plight of the children and the desperate need to free them. Trusted Yemenis conveyed information about the children's whereabouts. Acting surreptitiously gave Yemenis the opportunity to display their hatred of the Islamic State who'd infiltrated their country. Passing on this information was a risk worth taking to exact a small measure of revenge on these terrorists who thought it their right to grab land in the name of an ill founded extreme religious creed.

Antonio's contacts enabled him to pinpoint the children's exact location. Conveying this information in the form of compass bearings supplied Billy with the details needed to study maps as a precursor to attempting the rescue. Antonio's attention to detail was a crucial factor if Billy and Simeon were to succeed. Two Land Rovers were ordered, each capable of carrying six people. These were shipped from Eritrea 200 miles east of Yemen to Port Hudaydah which despite the civil war was still under government control. Arrangements were made to leave the vehicles in the desert, one mile from the property where the youngsters were being held. Cover for the vehicles was provided by a large sand dune and having compass coordinates would help Billy locate the jeeps.

15 June 2022 would be a momentous day for Billy and Simeon. Antoinette knew Yemen was a country in turmoil, causing her to question Simeon about his

reasons for going there. She was well aware that travelling to a country ravaged by civil war carried a high degree of risk, making her suspicious about Simeon's motives for going there. Simeon was enveloped by guilt, spawned by him being economical with the truth. It left him agitated and ill at ease about what he was doing. Being openly frank and honest with each other was a central pillar of their relationship but his secrecy on this occasion induced a sense of guilt making him apprehensive about his dishonesty. Such a complex mission left Simeon psychologically torn but he thought it better not to worry Antoinette.

In Simeon's opinion, remaining tight lipped was in everyone's best interests. Occasionally, delusional thoughts convinced Simeon there was a good chance that the rescue would succeed. At other times doubts would surface making Simeon consider any positive vibes were just wishful thinking. Islamic State would never suspect two insignificant characters having the gall to attempt such a rescue.

In Islamic State's eyes any rescue attempt would be made by a group of professional soldiers. There'd be every chance that informants with IS sympathies would alert them, in which case it would be the end for the children. It was incredible to think how far the tentacles of this villainous organisation reached making two inconsequential characters such as Billy and Simeon insignificant. Calculating that IS would drop their guard, could open the way for the two friends to conduct a successful mission.

Antonio began to pull the logistics of the mission together. His first point of contact was Jonny Free-Spirit, the British Prime Minister. Renowned for being a bit of a maverick he was delighted that two British citizens were undertaking such a venture. Affectionately known as Bohemian Jonny he phoned Billy and Simeon to wish them luck, also informing them that a government chauffeur driven car would be provided for their transport to Brize Norton. From there they would be flown by an RAF plane to Riyadh in Saudi Arabia, made possible through the good relationship between Britain and Saudi Arabia.

The Saudi king insisted his private Cessna would be used for the flight to Yemen. Such was the chaotic nature of Yemen it would be relatively simple for a small plane to fly undetected into Yemeni airspace. Billy and Simeon would make their parachute jump a few miles from Ad Dali.

At 5:00 a.m. on 15 June, Simeon set out from his home to meet Billy in Tooting. Equipment for the mission would be issued at Brize Norton. Strolling towards Tooting Evangelical Church, Simeon wondered if he'd bitten off more than he could chew. A second thought crossed his mind creating significant angst. Would he ever see Antoinette again? Compounding Simeon's perception was his failure to be less than totally honest about why he was going to Yemen. Sometimes thinking about it overwhelmed him with guilt. Coming to his senses he knew dwelling on negative thoughts created trepidation, something to be avoided if the mission were to succeed.

It was a few hours before London's people would set off for work and the streets once again became manic. At this time, the streets were relatively quiet but it was a pleasantly warm morning. However, this pleasant warmth paled into insignificance by comparison with the daytime temperatures in the Yemeni desert. The rescue was scheduled to take place at night when temperatures would be approximately 18 degrees centigrade, creating an ideal environment for emancipating the children and moving around in the desert.

Meeting Billy lifted Simeon's spirit. His consternation was the polar opposite of Billy's ebullience. An exceptional man who had overcome so many personal difficulties in his life seemed to be taking all of it in his stride. Simeon thought, surely, he must be feeling the tension of the situation.

Billy proclaimed, 'Good morning, Simeon, our lift will be here in the minute. I understand how you're feeling but it's important you get your mind set right if we are to succeed. Feeling nervous is natural but once we get going, you'll be OK.'

At exactly 6:00 a.m. a grey Vauxhall Insignia drew up outside the church. The driver jumped out, opened the doors for the two men to get in. Sitting either side of the car both settled down for the 70-mile journey to Brize Norton in Oxfordshire. At such an unearthly hour in the morning both said little but the mellow lyrics of the Carpenters provided a soothing background. Billy continued to obsess about the logistical details of the mission, desperately wanting nothing to go wrong, whereas Simeon drifted off to sleep.

Ninety minutes later, the car stopped by a large sign reading Royal Air Force. Brize Norton was printed underneath. Recognising a Government car, security waved it straight through. In their eye line the friends could see numerous buildings and a runway appearing to go on for miles. Simeon was amazed at what appeared in his line of vision.

'The runway's over 3,000 metres long to accommodate gigantic Hercules aircraft. When fully loaded these monsters need a maximum runway length to get it into the air. If you look to the right, Simeon, there's an Airbus 330. No doubt that's what we'll be flying in,' said Billy.

Billy was spot on. The car pulled alongside the plane. Before Billy could open the door, the chauffeur jumped from his seat and opened it. Moving to the far side of the car he opened Simeon's door, shook hands with both men, returned to the car and sped off. Boarding the plane by the steps attached near the cockpit they entered the cabin to be greeted by a female RAF officer.

'Good morning, Billy and Simeon. I'll be flying the plane to Riyadh today.'

With impeccable manners both men said, 'Good day to you, Captain.'

'Make yourselves comfortable, gentlemen, the staff will look after you. Your flight time to Riyadh is 6 hours 50 minutes. We will be taking off at 8:00 a.m. and Saudi Arabia is two hours in front of the UK. Our estimated time of arrival is 4:50 p.m. local time.'

Billy already in mission mode piped up, 'Thanks very much, we were led to believe that our kit would be on the plane.'

Billy wanted to check that vital equipment had been put on-board. Quickly allaying Billy's fears, the Captain retorted, 'I've been told to tell you that the rucksacks with the kit you need are on the plane. You will be able to check everything when we're in the air. You haven't long, so fasten your seatbelts ready for take-off.'

Taking window seats on opposite sides of the aisle both settled down for the flight. Simeon gazed out of the window to see two hares sitting attentively looking at the plane. Focusing on them he thought these animals must be used to the roar of engines, they probably won't even move when the plane taxis to the runway. No time was wasted closing the doors, cabin staff strapping themselves in ready for take-off. Jet Engines roared into life, followed by a grinding, squeaking noise as wing flaps were tested.

Unperturbed by the noise the hares sat bolt upright, continuing to stare at the aircraft, confirming Simeon's initial thoughts. Such noise didn't even fluster these fascinating creatures. Here was an everyday occurrence in their lives. Finishing its taxi, the plane stopped, waiting for an instruction to take off. Realising there was no going back, Simeon became engulfed by anxiety. This was their D-Day. Even though he'd flown many times before, the serious implications for this trip made it different. Once in the air, Simeon would normally do a crossword or read but this was unlike any normal flight and his thoughts were fixed on the impending mission.

Glancing across to Billy, he could see this astonishing individual who'd endured so much hardship in his life appeared totally unfazed, taking it all in his stride. No doubt in his mind Billy was sifting through the whole mission, focusing on every minute detail. At first the plane trundled down the runway, accelerated, creating the necessary forces, taking it into the air. Ten minutes after take-off the seat belt sign went off and a steward asked if the two men wanted breakfast. Simeon's stomach was knotted.

Billy said, 'It's important to eat, Simeon. You'll need those calories when we're in Yemen.'

Putting aside his queasy stomach Simeon quickly realised Billy was right.

'Could I have the full works, please?'

Billy then added, 'I know our kit will be there. We just need to double check everything to make sure it all works.'

Botching this mission could mean Billy and Simeon were on their last ever flight. The important venture made it difficult to appreciate the luxury of travelling in a private jet. Agitation resulted from the thought they might fail to set the children free. However, tension was relieved when the Captain made an announcement outlining the flight path to Yemen. This RAF flight would cross France, Germany, Austria, Croatia, Serbia, Bulgaria, Turkey, Lebanon, Israel and Jordan before entering Saudi Arabian airspace, finally descending into Riyadh.

Following the information Billy said, 'We need to check our kit.'

Walking to the back of the plane Billy and Simeon found their equipment. Simeon could see the parachutes.

'I hope these open,' he said nervously.

'You worry about everything, Simeon. That'll be the least of our worries. Attention to detail is uppermost in the mind of the packers and you know as well as me there's a reserve chute. Let's look through the rest of the gear.'

Billy emptied the rucksacks and found the automatic weapon he'd requested. On inspection he could see it was different to the one he'd used during the Falklands War. Previous experience enabled him to assemble and dismantle it very quickly. Ecstatic at being given a high calibre firearm he was also pleased by the inclusion of numerous magazines. Examining Simeon's pistol Billy could see that despite him being a novice, he'd have little difficulty with this weapon.

'All you need to do, Simeon, is load the magazine, point it and fire, a piece of cake even for a beginner. It's just the same as the ones in the fairgrounds. Easy peasy.'

Billy was adept at instilling confidence. He was quietly praying that a successful mission might mean Simeon wouldn't have to use his weapon. Of great interest to Billy was the compass they'd been given, an absolutely essential piece of equipment if they were to make it to Aden with the children. Many years had passed since Billy had used a compass but the one he'd been given was magnetic.

Confidently Billy declared, 'No problem with this beauty.'

Simeon found it bewildering. Billy appeared to be revelling in these circumstances, obviously in his element. Totally lacking any fear, Billy's sense of duty burgeoned rather than diminished. Worryingly Simeon didn't know whether Billy's confidence should inspire or unsettle him. Lacking any consternation at what lay in front of them, Simeon could only assume any anxiety felt by Billy had been superseded by the thought of rescuing ten children from a hideous fate.

Billy's apparent lack of fear and determination impressed Simeon, who was hoping his resolution would rub off on him. He knew it was essential any trepidation he was feeling be put aside if they were to succeed. Billy found packets of glucose tablets included to provide sustenance for the two men. There'd be plenty left over to give the children if they needed them. Included in the rucksacks were lengths of rope which could be used in a variety of ways. Walkie-talkie radios had been added for the two men to communicate with each other as they drove the Land Rovers.

'We've got everything we need. All we need now is a bit of luck and the Land Rovers to be in the right place,' said Billy.

Confidently Simeon declared, 'I'm sure Antonio will have taken care of that.'

Simeon looked out of the window to see a barren landscape making him realise they were nearing Riyadh. Saudi Arabia's capital was situated on a 600-metre-high plateau, surrounded by desert. Having a population of 8 million people, Riyadh was a wealthy city built on Saudi's oil production. Billy and Simeon knew the temperature would be in excess of 40 degrees centigrade when they landed but operating at night would be more conducive to Europeans unused to the excessive heat of a desert climate. Quickly losing altitude Simeon became aware that the plane would soon be landing at King Khalid airport. Oil reserves dramatically increased during the reign of King Khalid between 1975 and 1982 led to the airport being named in his honour. Continuing to descend the city came into view.

Simeon spoke to Billy, 'There are countless mosques in the city, Billy. Look at the number of domes and minarets. What a noise there must be in the city when the various muezzins call the people to prayer. It must be enough to give anyone a headache.'

Completely unresponsive, Billy was concentrating on the mission, making Simeon wonder if he had even heard what he'd said. Dropping from the belly of the plane the landing gear produced a loud clunk. As the Airbus continued to lose altitude, landing was imminent, then came a bump as the wheels contacted the runway. Braking, the plane quickly decelerated, further slowing as the wing flaps lifted upwards. Eventually halting, Billy and Simeon could hear the moveable steps being brought to the door. Billy was suddenly in mission mode.

'Don't forget your parachute and rucksack.'

'How could I,' replied Simeon.

'Let's go, Simeon.'

'There's a car with a small flag on the front coming towards the plane, Billy.'

'That's the royal ensign. King Salman must be providing transport for us to the small plane. Sunset is approximately 7:30 p.m. in Saudi and it's essential we fly under cover of darkness because they'll not expect us.'

'How far is it to Ad Dali from Riyadh, Billy?'

'Just over 1,000 miles, Simeon.'

'Will a Cessna have enough fuel to fly that far?'

'No Simeon, its range is less than that, so we'll have to refuel near the Yemeni border. I am sure the Saudis will take care of everything. Hopefully, Antonio's had the Land Rovers transported from Eritrea.'

'No need to worry, Billy, he's a man of his word.'

Disembarking both men thanked the Captain, commending her for such a smooth flight and landing. As Billy put his foot onto Saudi soil the chauffeur greeted them in perfect English.

'Welcome to the Kingdom of Saudi Arabia. I have to take you to a private reception area for a meal. A member of the Saudi Government will brief you about your onward journey.'

Neither man had ever sat in such an opulent vehicle. Slumping back in leather seats embroidered with the insignia of the Saudi King Simeon was struck by the mildly earthy, sweet smell of the leather. By contrast Billy's state of mind meant he could've been sitting on a mound of manure and he'd have failed to notice. Even for Simeon the impending mission made it difficult for him to appreciate such grandeur. Arriving at the reception Billy and Simeon were met by two Saudi Government officials in full Arabic dress.

The taller of the two men spoke, 'It's time for you to eat before we brief you with essential information for your journey.'

Traditionally Arabic peoples would sit on the floor to eat but Billy and Simeon sat at a table where coffee was given to them as a sign of Saudi hospitality. Following the drink, a meal of lamb in a spicy sauce, rice and dates was provided with cardamom cookies following the main course. Observing Islamic dietary law is important for Muslims and the meal conformed with these statutes. At the conclusion of the meal, it was suggested both men rested before the onward journey.

Saudis intensely dislike IS and were desperate for this mission to succeed. Despite both men being given comfortable beds to rest, it was difficult to switch off through the adrenalin rush they both experienced. Any mistake would cost them their lives and dwelling on this could engender panic. Capture would certainly result in them being beheaded.

Following a rest Billy and Simeon were taken to a briefing room by the two Saudis. Taking their seats, a Saudi Army officer entered the room and spoke.

'Welcome to Saudi Arabia. I would like to wish you all the best for your mission. You will be leaving for Ad Dali at 8:00 p.m. local time on a flight taking approximately five and a half hours. A Cessna has a range of 800 miles and Ad Dali is 1,000 miles away, meaning you'll need a refuelling stop for the pilot to get back across the Saudi Yemeni border. Refuelling will take about 30 minutes at Harajah, a small desert town. We need to leave six and a half hours for the journey, you'll be jumping at 2:30 a.m.'

Handing Billy an envelope the Saudi officer conveyed instructions to Billy and Simeon,

'In here are the coordinates for the house where the children are imprisoned. It'll take about 40 minutes for you to walk to the building. My understanding is that you're competent with a magnetic compass. You'll need to be because the house is in an isolated spot on the outskirts of the town. Our contacts tell us the children are guarded by two IS members with limited military experience. Setting the children free will be a real coup for the British Government and your Prime Minister is fully supportive of this mission. Fortunately, he appreciates the dreadful future facing these youngsters if they're not rescued.

ISIS will not be expecting a raid, making the element of surprise your greatest weapon. Here's a second envelope with the coordinates for you to locate the Land Rovers shipped from Eritrea on the UN Secretary General's orders. I have been informed they'll be out of sight on the far side of a sand dune about one mile from where the children are being held. These coordinates will lead you to the vehicles. Make sure you do a good job on the two guards. You should be able to get to the Land Rovers with the children in about 30 minutes. Drive immediately south to Aden and safety. I think that's everything. Good luck, you're two very brave men. Is there anything you'd like to ask?'

Billy glanced towards Simeon to see if he had cottoned on to what the Saudi officer had said about the men guarding the children. Simeon didn't respond, leaving Billy to assume his concentration had wavered, something that couldn't happen in Ad Dali. He decided not to mention it until they were in Yemen.

Chapter 37

Boarding the Cessna, Billy and Simeon took their seats behind the pilot. He turned around gave them a beaming smile and introduced himself as Muhammad. All the kit including parachutes were stowed behind them. No chances had been taken as domed shaped parachutes with a huge canopy had been packed, ensuring the two men could land safely. During his military service Billy had made numerous jumps and was certain the intervening years would make little difference to his ability to safely use the equipment. It was not that Billy was over-confident, he was just so focused nothing would deflect him from rescuing the children.

In Billy's opinion self-doubt and anything less than 100% commitment to the mission would result in failure. There was no way that could happen. Simeon had undertaken a parachute course at university and was quick to admit that he was 'bricking it'. Reassuringly Billy pointed out the chutes they were using were as safe as houses. Simeon didn't say anything but he couldn't help thinking, with the frame of mind Billy was in he'd think houses in an earthquake were safe.

There was no way anything would deter him. Billy referred to them as jellyfish, their shape resembling one of these marine creatures. Less than convinced by Billy's attempt to instil confidence Simeon settled down in the craft for the six-hour journey. Restricted space in the Cessna contrasted with the spacious Airbus cabin in which they had travelled to Riyadh.

Muhammad turned the key. The engine spluttered then fired into life. At first the propeller laboured with a puff of smoke coming from the engine making it easy to see the individual rotors. Very quickly the blades gained such momentum the individual components blended into one finally becoming a blur. Racing down the short runway the plane lifted into the sky. Billy looked straight ahead, while Simeon heart in mouth stared anxiously out of the window.

A Cessna 172 was the ideal plane for this journey, flying at 13,000 feet but dropping to 3,000 feet for the men to make the jump. Unperturbed at the prospect of jumping, Billy actually seemed to be relishing it, whereas Simeon swallowed hard trying to push his fear to one side. Cruising at 190 MPH the journey would take six hours including refuelling on route.

Muhammad said, 'You need to strap the parachute and kit on 30 minutes before you jump. I'll aim to drop you within 2 miles of the house. It will be 2:00 a.m. allowing us to fly undetected into Yemeni airspace. Chaotic government in Yemen means flight monitoring in their airspace is inadequate. I've brought some sandwiches with me because you need to eat.'

In a coordinated response both men spoke, 'Thank you, Muhammad.'

A sustained period of silence followed as both men contemplated the events about to take place in a few hours' time.

Billy broke the silence, 'Simeon, it's important you jump first just in case you get the jitters. There's no need to worry if you do, I'll give you a shove. We're making a static line jump and our chutes will open automatically.'

Simeon looked petrified at the thought of jumping into the darkness. Any jump he made in university had been in daylight.

Billy added, 'You've done it before and in any case, you don't need to worry. There's a spare chute as insurance.'

This was a first for Simeon. Even though he was petrified, there was no way he was going to jib out. Having time to think about what they were going to do was the worst part of it. Simeon was convinced when the time came to jump, he had enough courage to exit the plane unaided. Nevertheless, he thought Billy's idea to give him a shove if he needed it was a good insurance policy.

'Thanks Billy, I think you're right about me exiting first.'

Billy's words brought a wry smile to Muhammad's face.

Billy added, 'When you're on the ground, Simeon, just unstrap the chute, gather it up and secure it by placing some rocks on it. There'll be no time to bury it.'

'What should I do then, Billy?'

'Don't start thinking you're Rambo just stay where you are. I'll find you. Desert skies are clear and there should be good light from the full moon. Don't forget we've also got lights on our helmets, so we'll be OK.'

Four hours into the flight the pilot received clearance to land in Harajah for a refuel.

He announced to Billy and Simeon, 'We should be able to refuel in 30 minutes, keeping us on schedule for a 2:30 a.m. jump.'

Descending, both men could see the lights on the ground illuminating the landing area. Skilfully Muhammad put the Cessna down with very few bumps. Landing on a hastily prepared runway in the desert was no problem for an accomplished operator like Muhammad. Swiftly a tender was brought to the Cessna for refuelling and the pumps started.

Muhammad leaned out of the window and shouted, 'Thanks, Abdul. Can you get a move on because these chaps are in a real hurry?'

Throughout the journey having experienced more mood swings than a swing boat in a fairground Simeon was suddenly engulfed with apprehension as he heard the pilot's words. One minute he was positive about the mission but at this moment his thoughts filled him with dread. Meanwhile, Billy was in the zone, seemingly unaffected by what lay in front of them. His amazing attitude usually rubbed off on Simeon. On numerous occasions he'd been able to draw strength from this inspirational character, seemingly blessed with the Midas touch.

Simeon thought surely, they'd succeed, even if they had to kill the guard. Freeing the young children would ensure justice was done. Putting everything into perspective helped Simeon relax, knowing it was time to summon up his reserves of courage and put on his 'game face'. Abdul quickly filled the Cessna.

Muhammad shouted, 'Thanks Abdul.'

Abdul knew Yemen was a country in turmoil so anyone going there must be on an important mission.

'Any Saudi taking a Cessna to Yemen means these men must have important business there. May Allah give them the fortitude to succeed. All is in the Almighty's hands. Good luck,' said Abdul.

Taking off from Harajah, Billy and Simeon knew their date with destiny was close. Simeon's reticence about the mission was now replaced by a newfound optimism.

Billy took the opportunity to reinforce this optimism, 'Anxiety is a natural emotion. It was written all over your face, but I can now see you're ready. Abdul was right. All is in God's hands. If he's right the importance of what we are about to attempt means the Lord will guide us to succeed.'

Reference to God controlling world events was something Simeon believed but he'd never heard Billy allude to it. Re-energised Simeon was ready to play a part in a mission of such paramount importance.

Adrenalin fuelled Simeon boldly stated, 'Let's go, Billy. I'm ready.'

Chapter 38

'Kit on fellas, we're nearly there,' barked Muhammad.

Such an aggressive command meant the gravity of the situation had even taken a toll on Muhammad who managed to lose himself in the moment. Gradually descending, Muhammad would eventually drop the Cessna to 3,000 feet for Billy and Simeon to make the jump. Strapping their parachutes on in limited space created difficulty for the men. Succeeding, following a struggle with straps and buckles the men attached them to their backs. This allowed Billy and Simeon to have their rucksack and weapon in front of them.

Billy quickly commented, 'Dur, we look like a pair of GI Joe's.'

Simeon was dumbfounded by Billy's ability to make a throwaway comment when he was absolutely petrified at the thought of what they were going to do.

'Who's GI Joe?' said Simeon.

'Cor Simeon, you haven't lived. It was a model of a soldier we had when I was young.'

The noise of the aircraft allowed Simeon to tut without Billy hearing it.

Descending slowly at first the plane began to lose altitude, suddenly dropping quickly, causing the men to think they were about to plummet to earth. Eventually arresting the descent Muhammad had the Cessna flying at 3,000 feet. The friends knew they would shortly be exiting the craft.

Muhammad barked another order, 'Both of you hook the static line to the aircraft. Simeon first, then you Billy. Make sure you exit straight after one another if you want to land close together.'

'Got it,' exclaimed Billy.

'Nearly time to go. Be ready in two minutes and don't jump until I tell you.'

Anticipating this moment created tension in Simeon. Now the time had arrived he felt a surge of confidence causing earlier anxiety to disappear. Simeon was very able in school, rarely ever getting questions wrong but on one occasion when he was playing rugby for the school the teacher had said to him, 'Simeon. What's the first thing you put in your kit bag?'

'My boots, Sir,' replied Simeon.

Gently chiding Simeon, the rugby teacher said, 'Wrong, Simeon. Your guts.'

His teacher had been right and now they were about to jump 'his guts' were definitely in the bag.

This was consistent with what he'd experienced at other key points in his life where initial nerves were replaced by a conviction that he could succeed on this mission. Having too much time thinking about what he and Billy were attempting was the factor he found unsettling. Just as he was about to leave the plane Simeon was hopeful, he could provide excellent backup for Billy. Operating below par meant he would not be an asset possibly making his contribution to such an important venture woeful. There was no way he could allow that to happen.

'Jump now, Simeon,' shouted Muhammad.

There was no need for Billy to give him a shove, Simeon reacted immediately.

'Billy your turn, go straight away.'

Static lines instantly opened the chutes, allowing both men to sedately descend towards the Yemeni desert. Fortunately, very gentle breezes prevented Billy and Simeon being buffeted by the wind and blown away from each other. Jellyfish shaped parachutes used by the two men created significant drag, maximising wind resistance making for a sedate descent. Silhouetted against the night sky by the glittering full moon allowed both men to see each other as they descended.

Having time to think during the descent Simeon wondered what a daytime drop would be like when they could view the desert in all its glory from such a vantage point. Each desert landmark would magnify in daylight as the ground drew closer. Such thoughts were hypothetical as an eerie, profound silence accompanied any night-time descent. Personal prayer in church enabled Simeon to experience solemn moments but these were always punctuated with somebody coughing or clearing their throat. A fidgeting worshipper might drop something or rustle their service sheet breaking the silence at this contemplative moment. However, experiencing the silence of this night-time drop to earth was unique with a beauty all of its own, guaranteeing he would never forget it if he survived the mission.

Thinking of his own mortality he questioned whether he should have downplayed his reasons for going to Yemen. Antoinette was fully aware of the problems faced by the Yemeni people, however his being economical with the truth meant she was unaware of the significant dangers faced by her husband. Quickly approaching 'terra firma' jolted Simeon into the present. Hitting the ground with a gentle thud, Simeon unbuckled his chute, gathered it in then secured it to the ground with heavy rocks. Billy had landed 200 yards away but was able to quickly find Simeon using his helmet light. Picking up his rucksack Billy made his way towards him.

Locating him he said, 'There you are, Sim. That was OK, wasn't it?'

'I quite enjoyed the jump Billy, let's hope the next bit is as easy. Somehow, I don't think it'll be problem free.'

'Keep your wits about you and we'll be OK. Once we have the children, we'll find the Land Rovers. There's just one thing, Simeon. I don't know whether you picked up what the Saudi official who briefed us said about who was guarding the children.'

'There's one guard, Billy? That's what we were told.'

'The Saudi official said there were two. I didn't want to mention it at the time. It was obvious how nervous you were and the last thing I'd want to do is make it worse. Bringing up about the second guard would have compounded your anxiety so we will deal with it, Simeon. Once we have the kids, we'll find the Land Rovers. Job done, Simeon.'

Simeon was pleased Billy had kept it to himself. Being on the ground and ready to go, he would be able to cope with it. Having known earlier about it would have created unnecessary unease, something he'd find unsettling.

'Dealing with something' was one of Billy's sayings which Simeon perceived had originated in the Welsh Valleys, always bringing a smile to his face. Billy had the rare gift of being able to energise people in really trying circumstances. If ever Simeon needed his spirit lifted this was that moment and Billy was his man.

A desert full moon is a spectacular sight, highlighting countless other celestial bodies, sparkling like jewels in the night sky. Neither man had ever seen stars as numerous or prominent as those in the Yemeni desert. London's light and air pollution prevented the city's inhabitants ever seeing a vista as beautiful as this. Pollution free, a desert night sky presented a wondrous spectacle. Billy demanded Simeon's attention.

Speaking with authority, 'Come on, Simeon, stop star gazing, we've work to do. From my calculations the house where the children are being held should be 2 miles from here, taking us no more than an hour.'

Having jumped at 2:30 a.m. Simeon said, 'Well Billy, we should get to the house where the children are being held captive by 3:30 a.m.'

Always ready to make a quip Billy had a way of keeping these academic types grounded.

He said, 'Lucky you're good at maths, Simeon, you're quite right.'

Simeon could never be offended by Billy's sardonic wit. He just took it on the chin.

'It doesn't matter how good I am at Maths you can still add up the dart and snooker scores much quicker than me.'

'In Wales, we'd say that pointed to a wasted youth.'

Having had a laugh at each other's expense Billy said, 'Enough of this banter. It'll give us time to find the Land Rovers, situated approximately 1 mile south of the house, allowing us to start the journey to Aden in the dark.'

Taking out the compass Billy said, 'This way and we should be able to manage with the light of the moon so switch off your helmet light.'

'How are you going to read the compass Billy without a light?'

'Look it illuminates, Sim. Let's go set these kids free.'

Chapter 39

Glancing at the compass coordinates Billy and Simeon headed southwest in the direction of the house where the children were imprisoned.

Billy declared, 'Simeon, these readings should take us to the house.'

'I'm really glad you're here, Billy. There's no way I'd have a clue where I was going.'

Continuing walking in the right direction their initial thoughts about the difficulty of travelling on foot in the desert did not materialise. Compacted sand made it easier than expected.

Billy commented, 'Near the town the sand is always tightly packed. During the day groups of people have been in the vicinity possibly buying and selling animals or selling items they've made.'

'It doesn't make it any easier. My legs are still exhausted, Billy.'

'That's because you're expending physical and nervous energy. Grit your teeth, Simeon, we need to get to the kids.'

'I'm really digging deep, Billy. You don't need to worry I know how important this rescue is.'

Gentle desert breezes caused scrub grasses to whistle. Croaking noises from nearby lizards broke the calm night-time silence. Lizards didn't worry Simeon but he was scared to death of snakes. Billy swiftly put his mind at rest. He didn't have a clue about snake behaviour but now Simeon had gained some confidence he wanted to reassure him. Worried any negativity might put Simeon on a downward spiral Billy was concerned to stay upbeat. Positivity was the order of the day if they were to succeed.

Sounding like David Attenborough Billy proclaimed, 'Night is too cold for snakes. They like basking in the sun.'

Billy had never been in a desert before, nevertheless his words raised Simeon's spirits. Simeon always hung on Billy's every word and this occasion was no different. Failing to realise Billy was more of a serpent novice than he was, Simeon would never have the gall to question anything he said. At least Simeon had been to London Zoo, whereas the only snakes encountered by Billy were the two-legged type.

After walking for 50 minutes the men gazed at the silhouette of a building illuminated by the full moon. This would be their moment of destiny, needing guile if their mission were to succeed. Original information that the children were guarded by one IS supporter had been replaced by fresh information from the Saudis that two men were restraining the children. Discovering this new information changed the mission's perspective, whereas Simeon was hoping Billy would take care of the sentry. He now knew he'd have to deal with the second one.

Billy offered words of wisdom, 'Simeon, using our guns must be a last resort. Gunshot will alert the people in the town, making it much more difficult for us to get the children to Aden.'

'Billy, we must succeed. The thought of children being indoctrinated and used as suicide bombers leaves me cold.'

Shuddering at the thought of such an appalling outcome Billy said, 'Simeon, I totally agree with you.'

Drawing closer to the building the men slowed, assessing the structure in front of them.

Billy whispered, 'Look Simeon, there are steps from the ground to the roof, typical of Middle Eastern buildings.'

'Yes, this is usual for a Yemeni house. It'll be built of stones and blocks, with two storeys and a flat roof. Outside steps lead to the roof area and animals are usually kept on the ground floor, whereas people live on the second storey and the roof. Sleeping on the roof is the pragmatic thing to do because Yemen is such a hot and arid country.'

Assessing the building layout Billy had a good idea where IS would be holding the children.

'IS have probably locked up the children on the ground floor, Simeon. Those two guards will be holed up on the second storey preventing the children from escaping. My guess is the two of them will be near the door. Our job is to case the joint and act quickly. Failure is not an option. The last thing we want is ten young deaths. Grand promises will be made to the children by their IS captors glamorising martyrdom. Indoctrination will follow, then their deaths, along with many other innocents as a result of enforced suicide. We can't afford to fall short on this one Simeon.'

Creeping closer to their objective they could see this was an elaborate structure for a Yemeni house. IS commandeered this home from someone who was quite wealthy by local standards.

Billy whispered, 'Using our guns must be a last resort. Killing the guards with our knives is vital so as not to alert other terrorists in the town.'

Determination was etched on Billy's face, giving Simeon a fervent desire to draw the same tenacity from his friend's resolve. During the Falklands War Billy had killed Argentineans, leaving Simeon contemplating whether he himself would have the necessary will power to end a life.

Despite IS members being human monsters, Simeon's religious commitment led him to believe human life is God's creation and should be specially respected. Such a utilitarian problem led him to conclude the obvious course of action would be to kill the guards saving the ten children. There would be two less brutes, lacking any moral compass about murdering numerous innocent people to fulfil the aims of this fiendish organisation. Concluding the children deserved the chance of a better life, Simeon knew any future they had lay in their hands.

Reaching the bottom step, the two men drew knives from their scabbards. Slowly, cautiously they crept up the stairs. Efficient stealth was essential, otherwise the mission would be jeopardised. Walls of Yemeni houses were not particularly sound proofed, so this furtive approach was necessary. Billy was right about the children being detained on the ground floor. Behind the uninsulated, porous walls, snoring sounds could be heard. Twelve steps led to the second storey door, causing Billy and Simeon to climb purposefully to where the IS guards were sleeping.

An open door confirmed Billy's assessment of where the children's jailers were holed up. Peering through the door they could see two men propped against a wall, fast asleep. Saudi information about the detention and guarding of the children proved correct. Entering the room Billy gestured to Simeon that he would eliminate the guard on the right. Firstly, stalking his quarry then cunningly pouncing like a wild cat with a move belying his years, Billy efficiently attacked the first guard. He restrained, then quickly rotated him slicing the guard's throat with a single thrust.

For such a caring man this was an aggressive, violent action warranted by virtue of the guard's willingness to participate in terrorism. Death was instantaneous, through the severing of the carotid artery causing a jet of blood to squirt from his neck creating a gruesome mess on the wall. Such a well-timed action proved military training decades earlier had been ingrained and not forgotten.

Reacting to Billy's action Simeon pounced on the second guard, easily overpowering him. He had youth and strength on his side but religious devotion caused Simeon to momentarily hesitate. Overcome with guilt he faltered, refusing to press home his advantage. Letting out an ear piercing scream the second guard escaped death. As he was about to inflict the fatal wound Simeon had a crisis of conscience. Into his mind came Biblical teaching from the book of Exodus, 'Thou shall not kill.' Simeon's adherence to God's Commandment suddenly superseded necessitating the death of the guard.

Billy screamed, 'Do it Simeon.'

Simeon threw down the knife then picked up a stone pot. Billy dementedly shouted, 'Hit him on the swede.'

This was another Billyism Simeon would have found funny if it had not been for the life-or-death situation, they found themselves in.

Reacting immediately to Billy's prompting, Simeon hit the guard on the head causing him to let out a grunt. Imparted with such vigour the blow left the second guard unconscious. Meanwhile the commotion stirred the children.

Billy urgently shouted, 'Come on, Simeon, he's sparko. Use the inside steps to get the children.'

Many of the youngsters awoke crying uncontrollably with large droplets of tears flowing freely. The friends gestured with fingers to their lips for the children to regain their composure and keep quiet. Quickly untying their hands, the friends could see the children were relieved to be unshackled. Unable to speak English the children realised Billy and Simeon were there to rescue them and were nothing to do with IS.

Some of the nervier children shook with fear as they were bundled through the door into the darkness. Billy indicated they must follow him, while bringing up the rear Simeon chivvied the slower kids along. Having seen the compass coordinates he'd been given Billy knew the Land Rovers were one-mile due south in the desert. Sand, slowing their walking and disorientated children meant the journey could take up to 45 minutes. Billy hoped the guard hit by Simeon was either dead or deeply unconscious.

Billy dementedly barked an order, 'Turn on your helmet light, Simeon, so the kids can see where they're going. It'll be much easier to keep them together.'

Simeon thought to himself, 'It might be forty years since Billy was in the army but the curt, precise instructions he gave were typical of someone who'd undergone military service.'

Simeon constantly encouraged the children as they started to tire by putting his arm around them in turn in an effort to move them along.

Back in the house the IS terrorist who'd been guarding the children was starting to come round. Slowly regaining consciousness, he realised the children had gone. Immediately raising the alarm, he alerted the terrorists in Ad Dali. Reacting to the call IS vehicles raced at breakneck speed to the house, to discover a covert operation had liberated the children. Dressed in black, the leader screamed obscenities at the guard for failing in his duty.

Such hideous human beings behaving in a grisly way in the name of religion were not going to just let the children escape. Once their radicalisation had been completed, the youngsters would be useful to their masters in an attempt to destroy the lives of people who didn't subscribe to their perverted version of Islam. What sort of people indoctrinate children into strapping suicide vests to themselves, telling them that martyrdom awaits those who are faithful to Allah? Quite simply people such as these with a perverted worldview and guilty of horrendous crimes. Liberating the children was the reason Billy and Simeon came to Yemen. They couldn't fail.

Having their noses put out of joint by this rescue, four vehicles set off in pursuit of the children and their liberators. Billy, Simeon and the children were only 200 metres from the Land Rovers when they heard pursuing jeeps closing in on their position. ISIS commanders easily located their position knowing any escape would be heading for Aden, a region of the country still in Yemeni Government hands. Breaking into a trot Billy hurried the children along hoping Antonio, United Nations Secretary General was true to his word.

To Billy's delight as they approached the sand dune in front of them, the moon created a vision of salvation. They could see the moonlit shadows cast by two Land Rovers. Distant engine noises indicated IS were closing in on their quarry.

Billy almost seemed unbalanced as he screamed, 'There they are, Simeon, get the kids in. The keys should be in the ignition. Let's go.'

Hastily pushing children into the vehicles Billy and Simeon took their seats, then started the engines. Aden was nearly 100 miles away. It would be touch and go.

Simeon could not allow himself to be overwhelmed with guilt but it crossed his mind if he'd killed the guard, they would have had a free run to Aden. Both men hurtled south along the desert tracks. Fortunately, these vehicles were perfectly adapted for desert terrain. In their wing mirrors they could see the lights of the IS jeeps manically pursuing their prey. Willing the vehicles to go faster was useless. They were already flat out.

Looking to the east the sun emerged over the horizon like a flame from a furnace, quickly illuminating the desert, filling the sky with shades of orange and pink. Hurtling through a landscape of wind worn rock formations, interspersed with desert tracks, the race to safety had begun. Either side of the vehicles were clumps of different desert grasses bleached yellow by the heat of the sun. Erect cacti reminded Billy of the rugby posts back home in Wales. Seemingly devoid of water he thought to himself, how could such a place ever support life? Nevertheless, this land of fissures, sand and crumbling rock had a unique beauty, supporting a largely invisible diverse ecology.

Realising there was no time to admire this barren environment both men could see IS vehicles closing in on them. Handicapping their escape was the additional weight of five children in each Land Rover, creating a reduction in speed. Billy began to perspire at the thought they might not make it. After all they'd been through the thought that it could all end in the Yemeni desert petrified Billy. God forbid they were taken alive by IS. These monsters would certainly take revenge by 'making sport of them'. Gunfire from the IS vehicles caused Billy and Simeon to concentrate on survival, rather than their fate if they were captured.

Mounted on each IS vehicle was a machine gun turret. Soon they'd be in range, ending both this escape attempt and their own lives. Constant gunfire profoundly affected the children causing them to scream. Disconcertingly, Billy could make out a vehicle on the horizon. Were they driving into an IS trap with terrorists in front and their pursuers behind? It was time for a calculated gamble. Stopping would be suicide. Such a dire situation would normally lead to Simeon praying but there was no time to seek divine intervention.

Pursuing vehicles were only 100 yards behind them. Both men were thinking, surely this is the end of the rescue bid and their lives. Then a sudden boom brought an end to the leading IS jeep, as it exploded, blasting it to smithereens. In an instant the other three pursuing vehicles stopped then turned, realising they were now the quarry. Billy and Simeon continued driving towards the vehicle in front of them and hallelujah the vehicle displayed a Saudi flag.

'Praise the Lord, salvation,' said Simeon.

'No,' said Billy, 'we have been saved by the Saudi Arabian Army and their accurate gunfire.'

Simeon desperate to have the last word on this one and with a look of delight on his face.

'God works in mysterious ways and through men.'

Billy submitted, 'Who am I to argue with that.'

A Saudi officer raised his hand halting the liberating Land Rovers. Desperate to get out, both men jumped from their vehicles ecstatic that Saudi Arabian vigilance had saved them.

In perfect English, the Saudi officer said, 'Greetings to you all. We have been sent by our government following instructions from the United Nations Secretary General. We will escort you to Aden.'

Billy exclaimed, 'You don't know how delighted we are to see you. I thought we were goners.'

Any anxiety Billy and Simeon felt eased following their good fortune. Deliverance occurred just as they were about to be caught. Simeon was delighted. He would see Antoinette again. Success left him feeling vindicated at having taken on such a difficult mission. Bewildered Billy had sworn that after the Falkland War he would never take another life. Ten young lives for a dead monster in his mind justified his actions.

For Billy this was a euphoric moment, whereas he had felt totally empty as he helped clear the battlefield of dead Argentinean bodies following the conflict at Sapper Hill. Such young enemy soldiers seemed a waste of life, whereas killing the IS guard who had probably raped, stoned and beheaded other human beings substantiated his actions. Such a sense of achievement led to Billy and Simeon embracing.

Chapter 40

The Saudi officer waited for the two men to recover their equanimity. Such a responsibility had left Billy and Simeon physically and mentally drained. Appreciating the children were safe both men breathed a sigh of relief.

The officer said, 'It's about 25 miles to Aden. We'll be leaving immediately. The British Government have informed us they want you to accompany the children to the United Kingdom. Your Prime Minister has made it known that British families will have the opportunity to foster the children. Our King and the British Prime Minister, Jonny Free-Spirit have asked me to convey their thanks for what you've achieved. Waiting for you in Aden is a Royal Navy frigate ready to transport you to Cyprus.'

Saudi soldiers followed their commanding officer's instructions to help the children into a military lorry. Relieved all the kids were safe Billy and Simeon joined them in the vehicle. Traumatised by their experience, the children looked emotionally drained with pasty faces reflecting the horror of their ordeal. What they had been forced to witness would have left them overwhelmed with grief. The brutality doled out to their parents in front of their very eyes was a heinous crime.

Such an important mission gave the two friends no time to think about their own safety. Uppermost in their minds was the children's welfare and how their futures would pan out following their hideous experience. Temporarily intoxicated with adrenalin, the lorry journey gave Billy and Simeon an opportunity for a moment of reflection. It suddenly dawned on them how fortunate they were to be alive.

Motoring through the desert it took an hour to reach Aden. Leaving the lorry Billy and Simeon stepped onto the quay to be greeted with words of encouragement spoken by the Saudi officer.

Praising both men he said, 'Well done, you're definitely going home to a hero's welcome.'

Simeon blushed at the plaudits coming their way. Modesty was something he had learned from young and in any case, he thought Billy was the one who deserved the praise.

In unison both men said, 'Thanks very much to you all.'

Billy added, 'Your intervention definitely saved our bacon.'

'Too true,' added Simeon.

Although the Saudi officer spoke fluent English possibly having spent time at Sandhurst Military Academy, they doubted many of the soldiers would have the same grasp of the language. Any Saudi officer would have benefited from a privileged education. Nevertheless, the friends showed their gratitude by gesturing thanks to the soldiers. Smiles on the soldiers' faces indicated their understanding of Billy and Simeon's acknowledgement of their life saving intervention.

Anchored offshore in deep water was a Royal Navy frigate preparing to launch a tender to pick up the group. In the meantime, Billy wandered away to sit on a capstan. Such a stressful 24 hours had taken its toll. A few moments of solitude were needed for Billy to gather his thoughts. Slowly bowing his head Billy was overwhelmed with emotion. Spiritually drained, tears fell from his eyes like raindrops leaving imprints in the quayside dust. He was physically and mentally tough, nevertheless his emotions caused him to respond in a way Simeon had never witnessed before. Feeling compelled to comfort his friend Simeon put his arm around Billy, having realised even the toughest of men are human.

In Simeon's eyes Billy was a stoical character, seemingly taking in his stride all life could throw at him. Here was a lesson for Simeon that even the most resilient of humans have a breaking point. It dawned on him for all his academic success he still had a lot to learn about human nature. In the past Billy had attempted suicide prior to becoming homeless and this had slipped his mind. At this moment he failed to appreciate the significance of that tragic incident.

No human was exempt from pressure but Simeon's willingness to support Billy would help him quickly recover his normal poise. His achievement in saving the children had taken its toll and Simeon wanted to support Billy through this emotional crisis. Academically gifted he was well versed in diverse religious teaching.

Momentarily Simeon drew inspiration from a teaching in the Jewish Talmud, 'Judaism teaches that the person who saves one life saves the world in time.'

Simeon was determined to convey this inspirational religious teaching to Billy.

'Nobody knows what these children are going to achieve in their life. You have given them the opportunity to fulfil their potential. It's certain they will always be grateful for your efforts. What an achievement, Billy! You can be proud of what you have carried off.'

Billy recovering his composure responded, 'I couldn't have done it without you.'

'I nearly messed up because I didn't kill the guard.'

'That's unimportant, Simeon. It all worked out well. I've spent enough time moping. It's now time to move on.'

Smiling children boarded the tender, enthusiastically greeted by two British sailors. Handing sweets to the children brought delirious whoops of joy. Such a kindly gesture was guaranteed to lift their mood. Billy and Simeon stepped aboard, to be greeted by a Petty Officer. Effusive in his praise he said, 'Well done, fellas. What an amazing job. There'll be a hot shower and food when we get to HMS Vanguard.'

The tender's engines roared into life; they were on their way to the frigate anchored about three quarters of a mile offshore. All were amazed at the speed of the tender. Excited children couldn't help gawking at the wake produced by the engines. Billy and Simeon could see the ship's crew on deck. Crew members lowered the gangplank for the group to enter the ship's hull. Climbing tentatively onto the walkway, the group hastily scrambled onto the ship, conscious of the Arabian Sea's significant swell.

Billy led the way, followed by Simeon and the children being helped by crew members. Climbing the steps to the deck, the ship's Captain waited to greet them. An important naval tradition was observed when the boatswain ceremonially welcomed the group with a number of two-tone blasts on the pipe. Usually reserved for senior officers this was recognition that Billy and Simeon had achieved something truly exceptional. Piping aboard dated back years to the time when commands were passed to the crew in this way. Men couldn't be heard above the sound of the sea, making pipes an obvious means of instructing the ship's company. Obviously, the children failed to understand this aspect of naval heritage, but its importance was not lost on Billy or Simeon.

Shaking hands, the Captain said to them, 'Your heroism has brought great credit on yourselves, your family and country. Such an achievement should be a source of great pride to you and we're truly honoured to have you on board.'

'We cannot thank you enough, Sir. We owe so much to many different people. Without their help we couldn't have accomplished this mission,' replied Billy.

Billy's words spoke volumes for his modesty, recognising the contribution made by so many different factions.

Simeon added, 'Captain, this man's common sense, commitment and bravery is legendary. It's the primary reason we succeeded. He might be playing down his part in the mission but there's no way it would have succeeded without him.'

Billy blushed at such lavish praise, while the Yemeni children looked on in amazement having never seen a warship. Undoubtedly, they were glad to be safe and their minds were probably looking back to the horrific punishment meted out to their parents. Future psychological assessment would be an essential factor as they were integrated into British society. At least they now had the opportunity to rebuild their lives, giving them the chance to prosper.

That evening the children were looked after by the crew, who served Arabic food prepared in the Islamic Halal tradition. This was a relatively simple task for the catering staff on HMS Vanguard who were well versed in the preparation of this food, as some crew were Muslims. Meanwhile Billy and Simeon dined in the wardroom as guests of honour of the Captain. Sumptuous cuisine served by the stewards led to both men tucking into roast beef and Yorkshire pudding. Concluding the meal, the captain proposed a toast to Billy and Simeon. It would have been easy to consume too much alcohol but the Captain adhered to the protocol regarding drink on board.

At the conclusion of the meal the Captain announced, 'We will be charting a course through the Red Sea into the Suez Canal. Once in the Mediterranean we'll sail to Limassol in Cyprus. From there you'll be bused to RAF Akrotiri to be flown to RAF Brize Norton. Our journey to Cyprus will take five days, giving you an opportunity to relax.'

Billy replied, 'Many thanks to you all.'

That night Billy and Simeon slept soundly.

Chapter 41

Staring out of the window as the Airbus accelerated along the runway Billy and Simeon watched landmarks whizz by. Passing by in a flash, suddenly the worms eye view changed to a bird's eye one where everything was beneath them. Britain was just over four hours away. Some of the Yemeni children were awe struck being on a plane for the first time creating an almost reverential fear in them. Many looked petrified at the experience of flying at 35,000 feet and travelling at over 500 MPH. Some were possibly thinking they were on their way to meet the Almighty.

A few started to chat incessantly, while those with fear etched on their faces sat in stony silence. Billy and Simeon deep in thought, contemplated the events of a week ago. Now safe and on their way home seemed a surreal experience, both men having to pinch themselves at what they'd achieved. In just over four hours they would be at Brize Norton. Unfortunately, Simeon's mind was in turmoil having not been totally frank with Antoinette about what they were doing in Yemen. His lack of honesty disconcerted him. How would Antoinette react? Would she ever trust him again? Annoyed by his dishonesty would she divorce him? All these thoughts went through Simeon's mind. Although filled with trepidation he couldn't wait to see Antoinette.

As the plane drew ever closer to home, his anxiety levels rose. Billy ruminated about his eventful life. Feted by many as a hero for what he'd achieved, this homeward journey gave him time to think about his own mortality. Yes, he had achieved well but he would have been another homeless person if it hadn't been for Simeon and Antoinette. Without them interceding to Pastor Robbins he would surely have been dead by now.

Rescuing him in this way provided Billy with the opportunity to fulfil his ability to help marginalised people. Being given this chance diverted his mind away from the trauma inflicted upon him by the Falklands War. Was he really such a hero? In the past he tried to commit suicide, lost his wife and broken up a family? Billy concluded he was no different from any other human being, having both strengths and glaring weaknesses. Thankfully, fate played a part in giving him the opportunity to use the assets he was born with to benefit others.

Billy concluded he had so much to be thankful for. Dwelling on the past would not change anything. Mind you rescuing these ten children more than compensated for the difficulties he'd encountered earlier in his life.

This period of deep thought was brought to an abrupt end by a steward who asked what they would like to eat and drink.

Speaking politely to Billy and Simeon he said, 'Gentlemen, I can recommend the curry and rice; we also have some excellent Kenyan coffee.'

'That'll be great for me,' said Simeon.

Billy lacked Simeon's classy demeanour and on occasions could unwittingly be rather rough and ready.

Crudely he said, 'Simeon, I'm so hungry I could eat a scabby dog.'

Here was another Billyism, the sort of statement capable of bringing a smile to people's faces.

Simeon commented tongue in cheek, 'I don't know whether a dog lover would be too pleased with what you just said, Billy.'

'You know I don't mean it, Simeon, that's what we used to say after a night out in Llanen when I was young.'

'We'll forgive you on this occasion. Do you think the children would like chicken, chips and lemonade?' the steward said sardonically.

'I'm sure they'd love that,' said Billy.

Billy and Simeon were famished, enthusiastically tucking into their curry. Billy commented, 'This is better than the Curry in the Star of India in Llanen.'

Politely the steward remarked, 'We'd like to think some of the best Indian chefs in the business prepare these.'

Attacking their meals with gusto the Yemeni children's first chip experience was an absolute winner, prompting them all to want second helpings. Obliging their every request the steward ensured the children's needs were met.

Impatiently looking out of the window Billy and Simeon were anticipating seeing the English Channel. As it came into view it was easy to distinguish the French and English coasts. Appreciating the plane was starting to descend, Simeon was again afflicted with pangs of guilt. Nervousness created butterflies in his stomach at the thought of meeting Antoinette who could well be spitting feathers. His decision to be economical with the truth might just be the last straw for her. He passionately hoped not.

Ecstasy at going home was tempered by the thought he'd mislead Antoinette causing Simeon to wear his unease like a veil. Billy on the other hand didn't need to worry about a partner being annoyed with him. Nevertheless, any agitation he felt was caused by anxiety about the reception they might get at the terminal. Touchdown was smooth. Braking hard the plane slowed ready to taxi towards the terminal. Silence pervaded the cabin until the plane ground to a halt. Billy and Simeon could hear the noise of the steps being wheeled alongside the door of the aircraft.

Using the plane's intercom, the pilot announced, 'Billy and Simeon to be off first, then the children.'

'I hope there are no customs issues, Billy,' exclaimed Simeon.

Billy laughed, jokingly saying, 'What are you on about, Simeon. I've smuggled 20,000 fags to sell in Tooting.'

Embarrassingly covering his face with his hands Simeon realised he'd made a really daft statement. Standing behind the steward Billy and Simeon were stunned by what they saw in front of them. Stepping into the sunlight, cameras began flashing. The story had really caught the British public's imagination. Obviously, there had been no media release until the children were safely aboard HMS Vanguard. Every national newspaper was represented at Brize Norton reminding Billy of film he'd seen as a child of the Beatles returning from their American tours.

Overwhelmed by the sight in front of them, both men were flabbergasted at the attention they were being given. For a week they realised they'd been in a bubble, isolated from what was going on in the world. The British public love a story with a feel-good factor. Newspaper photographers fought for the best position they could for a photo that would sell papers the following morning. Appreciating they would be headline news instilled both men with pride. Simeon still couldn't get out of his mind how annoyed Antoinette might be. He was desperate to see her. Nevertheless, apprehension about her reaction to what had happened was unsettling him. Would things be the same as they were last week?

Simeon remarked, 'Cor Billy, this is like when the Olympic Team returned from the Rio Games.'

'I think there's more press here, Simeon.'

Intoxicated by this moment Billy was swept along on a euphoric wave.

'Look Simeon there's a red carpet.'

As Billy finished commenting an RAF band played 'Congratulations.'

'Simeon, that's the Prime Minister Jonny Free Spirit by the terminal building.'

'Look at all the people, Billy. There are Government Ministers and look that's the Foreign Secretary.'

The moment Simeon had been dreading arrived. He caught sight of Antoinette dementedly waving and blowing kisses. Hopefully, she was not as annoyed as he had thought. Reassessing his original thoughts Simeon mused, maybe Antoinette was proud of his achievement. Suddenly riven with guilt again he wondered if Antoinette was not waving but shaking her fists. Surely not he thought to himself.

Press photographers wanted the group to organise on the steps in ascending height order for a photo. As all kids do, the Yemeni youngsters were all jostling for the best position. By the morning they would be headline news. Concluding the photo shoot, they stepped onto the tarmac. Moving forward the Prime Minister came over to shake Billy and Simeon's hands.

'Gentlemen, you've done the country proud. Saving the children has been a totally selfless action. The Free World are indebted to you. Countless lives could have been lost if IS had succeeded in brainwashing these youngsters. It is now our duty to see these children are properly catered for. Be content in the knowledge that you've plucked these youngsters from a future filled with despair to one of hope.'

Simeon did not need to look for Antoinette. She found him. Any reticence or guilt were replaced by joy at being reunited with his wife. Throwing her arms around his neck with a beaming smile on her face Antoinette announced, 'Wait till I get you home.'

Finally relieved to see Antoinette he was more importantly still in her good books. Mischievously Simeon replied, 'I wonder what you mean.'

Security men ushered the group into a side room where news reporters from television channels across the world expectantly waited to have their questions answered. What a story! Billy, Simeon and the children were on live television. They would be starring on global news programmes throughout the coming days. Members of the public would be following the children's story with great interest.

Once the media work had concluded Antoinette said, 'It's time for you two to come home.'

Chapter 42

May 2030

Eight years had passed since Billy and Simeon rescued the Yemeni children. Such a high-profile rescue mission ensured nationwide applications from people willing to provide a home for the Yemeni youngsters. Priority had been given to Muslim families, giving the children the opportunity to practise their faith. In addition, psychological assistance was provided for the kids to cope with the atrocities committed against their parents. Gruesome behaviour by IS against the children's parents was certain to have a devastating impact on the youngsters' lives.

Successive governments took their rehabilitation seriously. Initiated by the Prime Minister at the time of their liberation the children's mental health was considered a priority. Thankfully, his successors adopted a similar commitment to the children's welfare with politicians keeping their eye on the ball. Foster parents provided loving homes affording the children opportunities needed to adjust to British life. Some of the older children had miraculously coped with the trauma of their early childhood and started university, while others were in the sixth form after making good progress at school. Although Billy and Simeon had risked their lives rescuing the children, the superb outcomes had been worth it.

Billy was 66 years of age and was now drawing his old age pension, but despite advancing years he was still remarkably fit. During the last eight years Billy spent his time working at Tooting Evangelical Church where there was always plenty to keep him busy.

He was well established as a national treasure for his devotion to social justice and in particular he received widespread adulation for his leadership during the rescue of the Yemeni children. Advancing years demanded Billy lead a more sedate life. He continued to live at Tooting Church ensuring this progressive place of worship continued to thrive. Billy's willingness to help others, particularly the less fortunate in society was an important factor in its continued success.

Antoinette and Simeon forged successful careers. Simeon's humanitarian work in different global crises were well documented. Yemen was just one country with an unstable government where famine blighted the population. Other third world countries were afflicted by war, requiring humanitarian intervention to save lives. Simeon was now working for UNICEF (United Nations International Children's Emergency Fund) where his brief included coordinating famine relief in conflict hotspots.

Amir who Antoinette and Simeon fostered excelled at Galaxy High School, achieving top grades in his A-Levels. Academic excellence opened the way for him to fulfil his ambition to be a doctor and his career in Medicine was progressing well. Simeon's was a high-profile post, leading to his time being divided between London and the United Nations building in New York.

Antoinette's work as a researcher for the Liberal Party leader further stimulated her interest in politics. Having fully embraced the aims of the party she was nominated as a candidate in the 2030 General Election. Politics in the United Kingdom had polarised public opinion, paving the way for the rejuvenation of liberalism. Brexit in 2016 had been the single most important factor in the revitalisation of humanistic centred politics.

At that time elements in the country had been steadfastly preoccupied with the European Union's immigration policy as a reason for voting to leave this fusion of nations. Although a majority of leavers were concerned about the easy access to Britain for migrants, there was also a more sinister movement at work in the country. Far right extremists preyed on a small minority of misguided individuals who were recruited into these organisations.

Britain in 2030 was reminiscent of the growth of the far right during the last century when Oswald Moseley had become the leader of the British Union of Fascists. Although a thoroughly disreputable organisation it was able to attract a 50,000 membership during the 1930s using Black Shirts to police itself. Tommy Gunn a 21st century version of his predecessor exploited the fears of deluded individuals recruiting them to do his dirty work as Billy had found out to his cost when he was attacked. The organisation would ruthlessly try to impose its evil doctrine on people.

Viewing the Liberal Party as a force for good in British politics Antoinette was excited by the prospect of standing at the General Election, hoping that she would be the beneficiary of this division in British society. Individuals were attracted to Liberalism through the commitment of the party to an inclusive Britain, where all are valued. Thrilled that his two protégés were doing well in their professional lives, Billy was ecstatic they'd retained the caring side of their nature. Pleasingly people would tell Billy that although his friends held prominent positions in society, they still retained the common touch.

Unfortunately, there was a marked contrast with right-wing organisations who were agitated by Billy's efforts to integrate immigrants into British society. Organisations such as these were populated by narcissistic, macho men, taking or injecting testosterone in an effort to bloat muscles, seemingly giving these nationalists false confidence. Worst of all they completely lacked any morality. Displaying Union Jack tattoos in an effort to express patriotism they were the antithesis of what Britain represents as an inclusive country.

Historically the United Kingdom had welcomed suffering people from different parts of the world. However lacking any sensitivity some far right extremists had the digits 1 and 8 tattooed on themselves as a means of expressing devotion to the work of Adolf Hitler. Aiming to exclusively identify with white British people, marginalising all other ethnic groups was their primary purpose. Such extreme organisations gaining traction in modern day Britain proved a worrying development in a country priding itself on promoting freedom and equality for all.

Encouraging division, made these organisations exceptionally xenophobic. Additionally, integrated into their perverted thinking was homophobia and male chauvinism. Patriarchy was the far-right way, evident in all aspects of their work. Steadily influencing his followers Tommy Gunn's meetings involved indoctrinating his admirers with his philosophy.

Groups of men in Tooting with animosity toward different minorities found Tommy Gunn a persuasive character. Seeing Gunn as an engaging character, large numbers joined the British Loyalists far right group. Easily identifiable these neo-Nazis wore black jackets, baseball caps and dark glasses. Despite their frightening views they would brazenly carry the Union Jack with a skull in the centre as a symbol of their discrimination against minorities. Growing in both numbers and confidence they would openly flout the law, making Nazi salutes.

The British Loyalists were a paramilitary organisation, presenting their right-wing supporters at the upcoming General Election the opportunity to vote for their candidate in the Tooting constituency. Thinking she had her work cut out Antoinette hoped she had a few aces up her sleeve.

She went to speak with Billy asking, 'Will you help me with my campaign? With you and Simeon on my team it could give me a better chance of being elected.'

Having been a victim of this organisation Billy did not have to think hard. He proclaimed, 'There's no way I want to see the British Loyalists gain a Parliamentary seat.'

'Billy, your profile is so high you would be a real asset to my campaign.'

Although it was eight years since Billy rescued the Yemeni children, he retained his status as a high-profile figure. He was always modest, remembering how dire life had been as a homeless man.

'Antoinette, you might be surprised how many people will vote for you; this lot really are a nasty minority. They are chauvinistic and you might find their wives will probably vote for you. Remember it's a secret ballot and the British Loyalists' coercive behaviour will be obsolete once people get into the voting booth.'

'Billy, my vocation lies in improving people's lives. The opinion polls indicate a Liberal resurgence and I have great respect for Mary Broad, our leader.'

'You never know, Antoinette, you might be leader one day.'

'No Billy, I don't think so. I've not got the confidence.'

'Let's first get you into Parliament. Your confidence will grow as it has in the past. We need some of the British Loyalists wives to vote for you.'

'Do you think they will, Billy?'

'I do. They're so frightened of their husbands' violence towards them. This intimidation is so bad they won't divorce them. However, a General Election gives them the opportunity for some revenge.'

Antoinette was not convinced but she knew it would be foolish to dismiss Billy's counsel.

Hearing Billy Davies was part of Antoinette's campaign team enraged Tommy Gunn. His hatred of ethnic minorities meant he detested Billy's benevolence to these people. Treating migrants as fellow human beings who were born free and equal was repugnant for Tommy Gunn. It meant Billy was the inverse of what a true British citizen should be.

Tommy's nationalistic fervour ensured that he presented Billy as a hate figure. Desperately encouraging members to use intimidatory tactics Tommy Gunn would coerce people into voting for the British Loyalist candidate Richard L'Ucifer. Tactically this browbeating could easily backfire in the privacy of the voting cubbyhole. Followers were told to carry placards with 'Billy Davies is anti-British' and 'Billy Davies gives jobs to immigrants'.

Most disconcerting of all were placards stating, 'Liberalism belongs to the Past'. Such a drastic measure was an attempt to force the electorate into snubbing Antoinette. Fair-minded people saw this group as a worrying development in British politics which needed defeating.

Intimidatory tactics by the British Loyalists became the order of the day. At night thugs, their faces covered with Balaclavas threw stones through the windows of businesses owned by ethnic minorities. One far right criminal hurled a petrol bomb into The Himalayan, an Asian restaurant owned by the Patel family in Tooting High Street. Mr Patel had agreed to hang a Liberal Party poster promoting Antoinette in the window causing the British Loyalists to pay a hoodlum from outside London with similar political affiliations, to carry out the terrorist attack.

Using an outsider gave them the excuse to claim they had nothing to do with the attack. At 3:00 a.m., a stolen vehicle pulled up outside the restaurant and the perpetrator left the engine running and lit the rag stuffed into the neck of the bottle. He then callously lobbed it through the restaurant window. Having no regard for the outcome of his actions he coolly got back into the car and drove off.

Igniting instantaneously, it set the Patel's restaurant ablaze. Fortunately flames activated fire alarms alerting Mr Patel and his family who lived upstairs. Acting promptly, he hurried his wife and four children down the back stairs into the garden. Flames were visible to members of the public returning home late. One phoned the emergency services. At such a late hour a London street was relatively quiet, giving the fire tender an easy run to the property.

Spreading quickly flames engulfed the restaurant but fire doors prevented the inferno reaching the upper floor. Responding swiftly the emergency services prevented a complete catastrophe. Mr Patel, a Hindu, was an intelligent man with an outstanding knowledge of religious teaching. Pragmatically he quoted from the Jewish Talmud, 'It could always be worse.'

Of course, he was right but his young children quaking with fear did not quite see it that way. Crying uncontrollably their mum Lakshmi put her arms around them providing comfort.

Mr Patel declared to the police, 'Racism is an awful thing, but the rise of the far right is a growing problem in Tooting.'

Mr Patel's eldest daughter Anisha asked her dad, 'Why would people want to do this?'

'Anisha, ignorance leads to people behaving in this way. Many fascists blame ethnic minorities for taking their jobs. It's just an excuse. Many of these right-wing adherents believe it's their God given right to have work. Our family has worked hard to establish this business providing a good service to our clients. There's just no way they'll intimidate me.'

'Father, I feel the same way as you about this. Mum's named Lakshmi after the Hindu goddess of business and purity. Our family has always been hard working and honest. They will not drive me away either. It's my ambition to work in this business when I'm older.'

'Don't worry Anisha, the Lord Vishnu and his consort Lakshmi will protect and guide us. We will rebuild this business.'

Having driven from the crime scene, the arsonist made good his escape, dumped the stolen car, was picked up by his accomplice and disappeared. Absolute proof was needed if the police were to convict anyone, but their investigation came up against a wall of silence.

Nevertheless, Mr Patel received offers of help from local people. Antoinette and Billy visited the Patel family to lend support. Mr Patel's positivity and resilience delighted Billy following his own personal experience of the far right's attempt at intimidation.

Mr Patel's refusal to wither in the face of pressure elated Billy who demonstrated his admiration by saying, 'These people couldn't hold a candle to you, Mr Patel. Your determination epitomises all that is good in British people.'

Leaving the Patel's Antoinette was troubled and spoke to Billy, 'I asked Mr Patel to put a Liberal Party poster in his window, so I feel I'm the one to blame for the destruction of his business and home.'

Billy responded quickly alleviating any reservations Antoinette might have that she was responsible, 'Democracy is about people having a say in who should run the country. Persecution like this has no part in a free society. As far as the Patel's are concerned this is a terrible tragedy but they are insured and Mr Patel is determined to rebuild his business. It is important that this type of fascist poison is prevented from infiltrating society. Bowing to far-right coercion means they win. That cannot be allowed to happen.'

'But Billy, I think people will be frightened by their intimidation and won't vote for one of the main parties. Fear will drive them to the far right.'

'Antoinette, I honestly believe this menacing behaviour will be counterproductive for the British Loyalists. Even people holding prejudiced views will be shocked by what has happened to the Patel home.'

'I hope you're right, Billy.'

'Mark my words, Antoinette, you'll see.'

'You're right about letting this behaviour affect me. An aspiring politician has to defend our democracy against this menace and I will. However, I am worried they will target you.'

'Don't worry I've had to look after myself before.'

'You were younger then and I don't know what I would do if they killed you.'

'It takes more than a bunch of right-wing thugs to kill an 'old trooper' like Billy Davies.'

Unfortunately, Antoinette was not convinced by Billy's 'laissez faire' attitude to British Loyalist violence. One of the British Loyalists' most violent characters was nicknamed the Major who after buying into Tommy Gunn's philosophy was prepared to maim or kill to promote a school of thought that had no place in a civilised society. Linda, his wife was a pleasant lady who had a dog's life at the hands of her husband. He intimidated her so badly she had come to the end of her tether.

Unfortunately, she was the epitome of a battered wife, whose confidence had been eroded by constant browbeating at the hands of her husband's oppressive behaviour. Having watched a feature on television about domineering men terrorising their partners, Linda decided to speak out. Summoning up courage she visited Antoinette's campaign office. Entering the building she asked one of the campaign volunteers if the prospective MP was available to speak to a voter. Fully understanding the importance of every vote, the volunteer phoned Antoinette, informing her that a member of the Tooting electorate would like to speak with her. Antoinette left her office to meet Linda and both women shook hands.

Following the introduction Antoinette said, 'How can I help you, Linda?'

'I am pleased you've been able to talk with me, Antoinette. My husband is a leading member of the British Loyalists.'

'Not a nice organisation at all, Linda. Unfortunately, a throwback to a bygone era, making it really worrying that people like these hold such right-wing views.'

'It's almost certain the British Loyalists destroyed the Patel home and restaurant. We wives are not privy to information about the organisation's actions. Regarded as classified it's only available to a few people. As wives and partners, we have to do as we are told. Failure to follow our coercive husbands' instructions leads to us being physically hurt.'

'This is terrible, Linda; how can you possibly stay with a man who treats you like that?'

Linda began to cry, leading to her stuttering, 'I'm like many other women whose husbands belong to an organisation populated by macho men, who think nothing of using domestic violence to retain control. Many of us are at our wits end. We are all frightened to death at the consequences of not towing the line.'

'Linda, you should not have to suffer this type of behaviour in silence. If I win the election, I will use the law to rid this constituency of such a vile organisation. Voting for me would be a step in the right direction and if you have any influence over other women who've been abused you must tell them not to tolerate this behaviour any longer. Together we can work to change things for women.'

Encouraged by Antoinette's words Linda exclaimed, 'You will have my vote because it's desperate living in an environment where violence is the norm. If I didn't do as I'm told I would be living an intolerable existence. He will tell me to vote for the British Loyalists but the ballot box is confidential, giving me the freedom to vote as I want.'

'You must go to the police, Linda.'

'If you lived with one of them, you'd understand their mentality and what I'm up against. I will definitely have my own back on polling day. Count on me to persuade other women who have been terrorised to vote for you. Many are desperate for help.'

'I promise if I become MP for Tooting, Linda I'll do my best to help you.'

'Thank you, Antoinette, for listening to me. Good luck.'

Chapter 43

Campaigning tirelessly for Antoinette, Billy hoped his high profile in society would dent the aspirations of the British Loyalists. Constantly promoting his friend during the election campaign, Billy pinned his hopes on undermining the despicable efforts of this 21st century fascist organisation. Although there were considerable numbers of agitators in Tooting, the vast majority of people understood right wing organisations destabilised society. The aims of this divisive association were the polar opposite of Billy's objective where he wanted to create harmony in the community. Such a gratuitous attack on the Patel's restaurant induced a climate of fear in Tooting.

Billy wasn't fazed and his steely determination rubbed off on others. Tommy Gunn and his followers might have started as a threat to the established political parties, but extremist views and actions were making the electorate think twice about where they would put their vote in the upcoming General Election. It dawned on people that electing somebody like Richard L'Ucifer would be a retrograde step, introducing extremists with bigoted, disreputable, ethnocentric views into Parliament.

Thursday 9 May 2030 was Polling Day and Tooting's voting stations opened at 7:00 a.m. From early people were eager to cast their vote. British Loyalist members' black uniforms were in evidence on the streets but any intimidatory conduct was out of the question. Large numbers of police officers were watching for any menacing behaviour.

Six candidates were contesting Tooting. In addition to the Liberals and British Loyalists, Labour, Conservative and the Official Monster Raving Looney Party were competing for the electorate's votes. Lord Sutch had founded the Looney Party during the 1980s satirising British politics, bringing a touch of humour to a serious occasion with its memorable slogan, 'Vote insanity you know it makes sense.'

Judging by the constant flow of people into polling stations, Tooting's turn out would be the best ever. Antoinette's tendency to act as a glass half empty would have to change if she were elected to Parliament. Obsessive thought processes, where most people succumbing to distasteful covert tactics would vote for the British Loyalists, were at the forefront of her mind.

Contrast this with Billy's glass half full policy where he would say, 'Antoinette, I know they're voting for you.'

She would retort, 'I'm not convinced, Billy.'

'You wait and see.'

People were still voting at 9:55 p.m. but on the stroke of 10:00 p.m. the doors closed and polling in the 2030 General Election was over. The rush was on to open ballot boxes for votes to be counted. In a few hours, the result would be announced giving Tooting an MP. In what seemed an age waiting for the result to be announced, candidates assembled with their supporters. Ballot boxes arrived from polling stations throughout the constituency ready for counting.

Richard L'Ucifer with a smirk on his face gazed out at his arrogant intellectually devoid supporters. Although Richard L'Ucifer was academically gifted having studied at Oxford he unfortunately possessed a perverted worldview, making him a dangerous individual. Time dragged ensuring Antoinette's stomach turned somersaults. At 2:00 a.m. candidates and supporters eagerly anticipated the outcome. Displaying no emotion, the Returning Officer proceeded to announce the result.

Antoinette's supporters anxiously looked on; her face contorted at the thought of a British Loyalist victory. Swiftly delivering the result, deliriously joyful screams greeted the proclamation that the Liberal candidate had gained the most votes. Antoinette had realised her ambition to enter Parliament and Liberal supporters ecstatically hugged one another. Joyful scenes were swiftly followed by Antoinette's name being chanted in raucous football crowd fashion.

Glancing into the crowd Antoinette spotted Linda standing between Tommy Gunn and her husband, the violent Major. A cynical smile rolled across her face, carefully hiding her true feelings from the two glowering fascists either side of her. Linda's revenge was sweet. Ballot box secrecy had given her and other women who were victims of controlling behaviour, the opportunity to exact revenge. Symbolically pushing a knife between the shoulder blades of the British Loyalist organisation, Linda gloated at the thought she'd undermined this far right group.

Antoinette knew she would have to help Linda and many women like her by introducing the issue of domestic violence in Parliament. Richard L'Ucifer, puppet candidate of Tommy Gunn and his cronies was reduced to fourth place behind the three main parties. Still the emergence of this worrying trend in British politics produced enough votes to disconcert the authorities and the British Loyalists easily retained their deposit. Antoinette thought Carpe diem. Savour this moment. These problems can wait until tomorrow.

Going straight to Simeon and Billy, Antoinette said, 'I can't thank you enough for your undying love Simeon and Billy for your support which has been truly invaluable. You were right about the British Loyalists, Billy; winning tonight was really important for people like Mr Patel and Linda.'

Smiling from ear-to-ear Billy said, 'Well done Antoinette but a man of my age needs to sleep. Goodnight, all.'

Chapter 44

Partying until dawn with her supporters Antoinette and Simeon returned home where they listened to the last few parliamentary seats being declared. No party had an overall majority but the Labour Party had the greatest number of MPs. Inevitably a deal would have to be struck securing the majority needed to form a government. From Antoinette's point of view there had been a resurgence of support for the Liberal Party. Excitedly she said,

'Simeon, I think there could be a Lib Lab pact to form a government.'

'That's the most likely outcome. There's no way Labour would enter a coalition with the Tories. Their philosophies are poles apart but Labour and Liberals could be an effective force in government.'

'We'll have to wait and see, Simeon.'

Being a fledgling MP Antoinette was not privy to the wheeling and dealing taking place behind closed doors between negotiating teams from the two parties. David Graft the Labour leader walked out of 10 Downing Street to the lectern set up to face the British and world press.

He announced, 'I have agreed with Mary Broad leader of the Liberal Party, about forming a coalition to lead the country. This alliance would give the coalition an eighty-seat working majority.'

Antoinette was thrilled at the prospect of making her maiden speech in Parliament as a member of the Government and could not wait. Pondering her first appearance in the Palace of Westminster, Antoinette's phone rang. The screen indicated it was Billy.

She answered and Billy spoke excitedly, 'Great news Antoinette, you'll be part of the new Government. What an achievement!'

'I couldn't have done it without help. Your status has helped people realise right wing extremism is a divisive force in this country.'

'You're tailor made for this work, Antoinette.'

'It's not just your work throughout the campaign, Billy but your encouragement throughout the years.'

'I'm sorry for not staying to party. At my age I need my beauty sleep. I was there in spirit.'

'I hope you're free to attend Parliament for my maiden speech.'

'I wouldn't miss it for the world, Antoinette.'

'I'll make sure you get an official invitation.'

'I bet your phone hasn't stopped ringing, Antoinette.'

'Too true, Billy.'

'Listen, you've got a lot of people to talk to, so I won't keep you. We'll have a chat when things calm down.'

David Graft followed post-election protocol by travelling to Buckingham Palace to inform the King he was able to form a government. Everything was now set for the meeting of the new Parliament. Following the General Election, the House of Commons sat for a few days before the State Opening of Parliament giving Antoinette an opportunity to get a feel for her new job.

Parliament having re-selected the speaker of the house, Antoinette had to take the Oath of Allegiance. Brimming with pride, having achieved her lifelong ambition she was determined to serve the Tooting electorate as effectively as she could.

Antoinette repeated the following words as she took the Oath of Allegiance, 'I swear by Almighty God that I will be faithful and bear true allegiance to His Majesty, his heirs and successors according to the law.'

Sticking with tradition in recognition of her Christian faith Antoinette repeated the oath. Not having a religious faith other MPs affirmed their loyalty to the Crown. At the conclusion of these promises the State Opening of Parliament could now take place. Although Antoinette had seen this on television there was no substitute for the experience of being present. Filled with pomp and ceremony such an historic occasion would be a milestone in her life, one to treasure. She could not wait for the day to arrive so she could participate in this ancient tradition.

16 May 2030 was a momentous day for Antoinette. Following tradition, she assembled with the other MPs in the House of Commons waiting for the King to arrive. Arriving in the state coach the King presented a majestic figure in his ceremonial robes, promptly making his way to the House of Lords. Joining the peers in the Upper Chamber, the Monarch took his place. Easily distinguished

from the myriad of other important dignitaries, he wore the Imperial State Crown. Being such an elaborate occasion showcasing British history, culture and contemporary politics, it was an eye catching, amazing spectacle. Joining the Monarch and peers were the judiciary.

Antoinette waited with other MPs in the Commons ready to be led in by the speaker of the House. In anticipation she waited for Blackrod to approach the closed Commons door. Blackrod striking the door was an important aspect of the occasion, symbolising the rights of Parliament and its independence from the Monarchy. Hitting the door three times Blackrod announced the Monarch's summons, leaving Antoinette in awe of this ancient tradition. Such a prestigious ceremony left Antoinette thinking she might have to pinch herself to believe she was participating in it.

She cast her mind back to the sixth former who despite her privileged education totally lacked confidence. She owed her new-found conviction to a former homeless man who had helped build her self-belief. Fate had brought Billy Davies into her life, an encounter that altered her destiny. Her new status was something she would treasure and respect for the rest of her life. Humility and justice would be at the forefront of her actions, helping justify her elevation to such a lofty position.

Wonder struck by the pomp and ceremony of the occasion it was important Antoinette controlled any agitation she felt at being part of this prestigious occasion. If she began to fret now, how would she be when it was her turn to make a maiden speech.

Antoinette could hear Billy's voice, 'Keep calm Antoinette. You're as good as anyone. What's more you've only got to watch today. You're not actually participating.'

Controlling her emotions Antoinette decided to move from a terrified state of mind to one of reverential respect for the protocols of Government. Starting to perspire at the thought of addressing Parliament it stopped when she adopted a more measured approach to the occasion. Looking around at the other first time MPs she could see all the 'new kids on the block' were agitated. David Graft followed the Speaker into the House of Lords alongside the Leader of the Opposition. Behind him was Mary Broad Liberal leader, the new Deputy Prime Minister. Following on were 647 other MPs filing in behind the leading group.

Antoinette decided to walk in with a few other first time MPs. Picking out the experienced Members of Parliament was easy. To these this might not be old hat, but they'd done it numerous times, ensuring they were totally relaxed about the whole affair. Although near the back Antoinette was lucky to have a good view of His Majesty reading the pre-prepared Government speech, outlining governmental work for the year.

Antoinette thought to herself, 'We're going to be busy.'

Nevertheless, Antoinette calmed herself, enjoying the occasion realising an MP needs to be controlled at all times. Her next port of call would be the House of Commons chamber for the maiden speech. Quite a challenge!

Antoinette wrote her maiden speech, ripped it up, rewrote it again and again, logging it down numerous times. Frustrated she would bang the table, bringing a smile to Simeon's face, occasionally shouting, 'I hate you.'

Antoinette was referring to the paper but Simeon never once risked showing his amusement for fear of incurring Antoinette's wrath.

Finally completing the draft much to Simeon's delight, he playfully chided Antoinette saying, 'How many pens did you go through? What about the number of trees!'

Knowing Antoinette would be in a different frame of mind once she'd finished, Simeon was on solid ground with his comments.

Antoinette replied, 'Well, I had to get it right, didn't I?

'I realise how important it is, Antoinette. I'm really glad you've finished it.'

'All I've got to do now is deliver it effectively.'

'You worry, Antoinette, but you always come up trumps. Try to forget it, switch off and watch some telly.'

'That's a good idea, Simeon. I need to focus on something else. I'm going to try to enjoy the rest of the weekend.'

On Sunday evening Antoinette spoke to Billy having been scheduled to give her address in the morning. Speaking to her friend would give her the opportunity to release some of the stress she was feeling and Billy would always give plenty of encouragement. His calming effect enabled Antoinette to drop off into a deep sleep. Tomorrow would be a momentous day in her life. MPs regarded it as a rite of passage so Antoinette's discourse would be scrutinised by all members of the house.

Antoinette woke early filled with a cocktail of excitement and apprehension. She took a shower, dressed and went down for breakfast.

Simeon was already downstairs and asked, 'How are you feeling, love?'

'I don't really feel like eating anything, Simeon, but I'll have a black coffee.'

'It might be a good thing to eat and it'll help to settle your stomach.'

'I'm really sorry, Simeon, my stomach's in knots.'

'Feeling agitated can be a good thing, Antoinette and will almost certainly disappear when you start to speak.'

'I hope you're right, Simeon. I've spent hours preparing for this.'

'Let me tell you, Antoinette, if you're overly confident it wouldn't be a good thing. All football players feel anxiety about playing. As soon as the game begins, they're fine. Nerves are a good thing and natural.'

'You're right, Simeon. I'll try to eat a bacon sandwich.'

'Well done, Antoinette. You'll be fine.'

Finishing breakfast Antoinette left the house to catch the tube.

Simeon kissed her, wished her luck and said, 'I'll meet Billy and see you after the Parliamentary session is over.'

An hour later Simeon left home to travel to Parliament, calling at Tooting Evangelical Church for Billy who was looking a real toff dressed in his best suit. Beaming from ear to ear, Billy was pleased as punch. Antoinette had given him one of the two complimentary tickets for the Public Gallery. Together Billy and Simeon walked to Tooting tube station catching the Northern Line train to the Embankment. Walking the last half, a mile by the Thames the two men chatted excitedly. Both were experiencing pangs of anxiety at such an important occasion for Antoinette.

Simeon said, 'Oh, I hope she does well.'

'Don't worry about Antoinette, Simeon. Once she begins, she'll be fine.'

'Just what I told her last night.'

'Great minds think alike. Here's the entrance.'

Billy and Simeon entered Parliament through the Cromwell Green Entrance, passing through security and making their way to the Public Gallery. This was situated one floor above the chamber where Antoinette would deliver her maiden address to Parliament. Sitting alongside each other they looked down at the floor of the house. For both men this was a first visit and what an eye opener! From their vantage point they had a fantastic view of proceedings. Both were well aware that the seats in the House of Commons were green as opposed to those in the Lords which were red.

Billy asked Simeon, 'Do you know why the seats are green, Simeon?'

'I haven't got a clue, Billy. Is this a test?'

'Of course not, but I'm going to tell you. Green traditionally represented the bounty of nature and fertility. Then during the Middle Ages archers wore green. It was the colour of pasture and indicated how important the village green was to every community. Religious paintings used green in the background representing the virtues of faith hope and charity.'

'Billy, did you know that before today?'

'Of course, I didn't. I googled it out of interest before I came.'

'For a moment I thought you were a real clever clogs, Billy.'

Anxiously maintaining Parliamentary protocol Billy and Simeon whispered as they followed proceedings. Any excessive chatter would be unseemly as MPs indulged in the business of governing the country. David Graft the Prime Minister sat directly opposite the Conservative Leader with only the despatch boxes between them. Extensive political experience enabled these two adversaries to effectively joust with each other, expounding their political differences.

Simeon asked, 'Billy, do you think Antoinette will ever be Prime Minister?'

'Well, she's definitely honest and diligent enough. However, a lot depends on whether the Liberal Party can build on their considerable success at this election.'

'Antoinette thinks very highly of Mary Broad the Liberal leader who sees her as a politician with outstanding potential.'

'She will be a breath of fresh air. Her honesty will count for a lot. Nevertheless, she will need some luck as well to get to the top. There's so much uncertainty in the political world.'

Agitation began to affect Billy and Simeon as the time approached for Antoinette to speak. Billy, without thinking came out with one of his classics.

'Some of these speaking here are enough to put a glass eye to sleep.'

Simeon looked in amazement at him. He then broke into a smile and said, 'Billy only you could come out with something like that.'

Rising to her feet for the most important speech of her life Antoinette for all her self-doubt had real presence. As a symbol of good luck, Simeon's superstitious nature caused him to cross his fingers. She began by saying that she would serve her constituents to the best of her ability putting their welfare at the forefront of her thoughts. Her opening address left the House in no doubt about her level of commitment to British society.

Magnanimously, Antoinette praised her Conservative predecessor for his work in Tooting. Special mention was reserved for Billy Davies and his part in her rise to prominence in public life. Everyone in the house was well acquainted with Billy's humanitarian work, particularly his bravery rescuing the Yemeni children. Such a high-profile rescue was the single most important factor in propelling him into the public eye.

Consistently modest Billy had become one of the most acclaimed figures in Britain and a groundswell of public opinion thought he deserved greater public recognition for his work. Many thought his former lowly status as a homeless man was the reason for him being bypassed for awards. Cynics thought somebody from a privileged background who had achieved like Billy would definitely have received national recognition for it. His generous spirit created an impression with people even more than the considerable courage he'd shown.

Antoinette couldn't let the opportunity pass to express her disquiet at the rise of the far right in her own constituency and the country generally. Next Antoinette turned her thoughts to Linda, wife of the Major in the British Loyalists and other women who are the victims of domestic violence at the hands of their testosterone filled husbands. Such men were responsible for instilling fear into their wives, making Antoinette vow to eradicate the philosophy perpetuating this evil in society.

News programmes carried Antoinette's speech as their lead item because of her willingness to rock the boat rather than stick with convention where nothing controversial is said. One newspaper carried the headline, 'Parliament Welcomes the Boat Rocker.'

Filled with pride Billy and Simeon listened to Antoinette speaking so eloquently. Such an emotional occasion had a profound effect on Billy, causing tears to well up in his eyes when she mentioned his influence on her life. This was a particularly poignant moment for Billy, making him appreciate how much he had contributed to Antoinette's rise to prominence. After all they were sat in the British Parliament the place where one of the world's leading democracies makes its decisions.

Tears were not normally the Billy way, but he had reacted emotionally sitting on the capstan in Aden after rescuing the Yemeni children. Sitting in the Public Gallery he cast his mind back to the first meeting with Simeon and Antoinette, making him realise how closely his destiny was entwined with this couple. He never once took their friendship for granted; such was their influence on his life.

Chapter 45

Incandescent with rage Tommy Gunn bristled with indignation at failing to get Richard L'Ucifer elected to Parliament. He had intimidated British Loyalists' wives, business owners and other people in the community in an effort to force his views onto people. Fortunately, this tactic failed as voters found sanctuary in the polling booths, where they could vote secretly for their chosen candidate. Doing this they avoided detection.

Antoinette had been the beneficiary of the secret ballot when British Loyalists wives fed up with being subdued by their controlling husbands acted covertly when voting. In Tommy Gunn's world, immigrants and gay people had no place in modern day Britain. The beast now began plotting his next move. In Tommy's mind his failure to see women as equal with men meant females being reduced to the level of an inferior species. Female subservience was a pre-requisite of a British Loyalist's wife and it was their job to wait on men's every need.

In Tommy Gunn's opinion propagating the human race was their primary role. Women having a say in governing society did not fit with the right-wing British Loyalist agenda. Perceiving ethnic minorities as totally inferior human beings who should have no part in British society, the British Loyalist ideal for society was a country populated by a superior white master race. Tommy Gunn's thinking was straight from 1930s Nazi Germany and Hitler's autobiographical manifesto *Mein Kampf*, where he outlined his support for anti-Semitism. His face portrayed a man lacking compassion for any individual. Eyes as cold as steel made it easy for any fair minded individual to see he was totally evil, only respecting individuals who imposed their will on others through violence.

Stripped to the waist Tommy Gunn strutted across to the full-length mirror in his bedroom examining his drug-engineered torso. Constant steroid use pumped his physique giving him a false sense of security. Combined with the cosmetic effect on his body, the chemicals in these substances were playing havoc with his brain, making an already aggressive man even worse. Vulnerability had led to steroid abuse, highlighting Tommy's inadequacies. Chemical abuse compensated for this self-doubt. Like minded accomplices also participated in taking these muscle mass increasing substances. Short tempered, illogical thinking and a willingness to scapegoat immigrants for Britain's problems were the by-products of this misuse.

Hanging from the door in Tommy Gunn's spare room was a dart board with a photo of Billy Davies pinned to the bullseye. Readily picking up three darts, then hurling them at Billy's image was a way of alleviating the hatred he felt towards him. His photo was being treated as a Haitian voodoo doll with more puncture holes than a colander.

Dementedly, Tommy Gunn imagined inflicting physical injury on Billy such was his frustration at being outmanoeuvred by this former homeless man. All Billy did was help immigrants from different ethnic backgrounds adjust to British life, a philosophy contrasting with Tommy Gunn's parochial view. Right wing efforts in the past to maim or kill Billy had failed but now he possessed a high profile, attempting to harm him had become increasingly more difficult.

Intimidating the public during the General Election campaign had failed. Such was Tommy Gunn's hatred of minority groups he was determined not to give up. Right wing worldwide nationalistic groups used the dark web to infiltrate discontented young men's minds purveying hate messages to those who are easily led. Throughout the world people from all ethnic backgrounds protested against institutional racism. As hard as they tried to make their point, right wing elements in society attempted to impose their will.

Tommy Gunn, a high-profile figure among these fascist groups managed to operate on the cusp of the law, just avoiding police arrest. Despite this he was totally committed to the removal of those in Britain who failed to fit the right-wing template.

For days Tommy had been troubled by back pain. Intermittent, excruciating pain debilitated him. In his mind seeking medical help was a sign of weakness. Never giving a thought to his mortality Tommy was conceited and egotistical. His daily preening finished; Tommy picked up his mobile to speak to the Major.

Retribution was at the forefront of his mind and as the Major answered he said, 'I can't believe we lost that election so badly. With Richard L'Ucifer standing I thought, he was a shoo in.'

'Unbelievable Tommy, but I wonder if people have stabbed us in the back.'

'What do you mean, Major?'

'Well, I'm not certain about the bitch I'm married to. She'll say one thing but do another behind my back.'

'Listen now Major, if you're certain she's done something to harm us then give her a good hiding.'

'I'd break her legs if I knew for certain. The trouble is the ballot box is private and we've got no way of finding out.'

'See Major, too many of the whites in Tooting have been attending that church where Billy Davies lives. They're constantly filling their heads with shit like 'all men are equal' and 'all men are created in the image of God'.'

'Are they, Tommy? That's a joke. Our hero Adolf had the right answer to the immigration problem.'

'Major, it's time to get this immigration and gay problem sorted once and for all.'

'There's a few things we need to consider, Tommy. Propaganda needs to be an important tool.'

'We need to play on people's fears, convincing them that immigrants are taking their jobs.'

'Tommy, we need to sow seeds of doubt about gays in people's minds by telling them they're perverts who abuse children.'

'Great idea Major, we'll put those scum in their place. Britain should be like Germany was in the 1930s with an Aryan master race and minorities as our servants.'

'Turning the tables on the likes of Billy Davies is important. People need to know his thinking has created a huge problem for 'em.'

'Don't forget that immigrant loving bitch our new MP, Antoinette and her husband Simeon. They've made a lot of trouble for us, denting our ambitions.'

Tommy's blood pressure rose at the thought of individuals standing up to right wing intimidation. In the face of hostility brave people displayed courage alien to these fascists whose only means of coping was ingesting and injecting chemicals. Billy, Antoinette and Simeon might not be physically aggressive, but they possessed a steely determination, giving them the courage of their convictions. More importantly they would stick to their principles at all costs. Constant steroid use was having an adverse effect on Tommy's health, being egomaniacal he never considered it a problem. His only concern was to look the part. Possessing big biceps, triceps and pecs was all that mattered to Tommy.

He said, 'We need to get leaflets and British Loyalists posters done, Major.'

'Aye Tommy, we also need to use social media to rally our support. They've had their day. It's our turn now.'

'Bastard' shouted Tommy.

'What's wrong, mate?' Have I said something to upset you?'

'No Major, I've had this bad pain in my back coming on every now and again. I can't understand how someone in such good shape is having a problem.'

'You haven't been eating shit have you, Tom? It could be giving you wind.'

'It'll go. Now what were you saying, Major?'

'We were talking about propaganda, Tommy.'

'I know what I was going to say. We need to use every social media platform we can. It's important to sow seeds of doubt in people's minds.'

'Mind you Tom, we need to be subtle about the material we use.'

'That's important mate, I'm gonna get Richard L'Ucifer our intellectual right-winger to sort the propaganda out. It definitely helps to have someone who went to Oxford on our side. That right brainy sod will do it.'

'Aye Tommy, that brain box will keep us on the right side of the law.'

'That Oxford education of his is a big advantage for us. I'll speak to him.'

'Next thing Tommy, we need a big demonstration.'

'Yes Major, we need to show these people in Tooting that immigrants are taking over. You just need to look at the number of shops and restaurants they run.'

'Can't find a roast beef and Yorkshire pudding on a menu for love nor money.'

'Oh, flipping heck, Major. There's that pain again.'

'You've got to stop eating all those baked beans. You're full of gas.'

'Right Major, we need to get in touch with our branches around the country to get as many of our members as we can down here for the demo.'

'Good idea, Tommy. It'll look more convincing with a big demonstration.'

'Make sure our travelling supporters don't travel in their black uniforms. If they do people will realise, they're flying demonstrators.'

'Spot on Tommy, they need to change when they get to Tooting.'

'It'll make the silly buggers who support that immigrant loving tramp and that whore Antoinette and her husband who shouldn't be here, think twice about what they're doing to this country.'

'There's a lot to do, Tommy.'

'One of the most important things, mate, there must be no banners. I know we hate these immigrants being in our country but we can't break the law. Our uniforms will be enough for true patriotic British people to get the message.'

'Well done, Tommy, you think of everything.'

'Oh, bollocks that pain in my back.'

'It's lunchtime Tom, no beans!'

Chapter 46

1 June 2031

This was a worrying time for the police because in a fortnight they'd be facing a demonstration in Tooting. What they didn't know was nationwide British Loyalist supporters would be assembling in this part of London. Acting deviously the British Loyalists informed the police of their intention to demonstrate with Richard L'Ucifer using his considerable intellect to keep the organisation within the statutory requirements of the law. Totally unprincipled, he was able to tread a fine line between legality and prohibitive behaviour.

Such a degenerate individual took the unusual step of pre-empting any violence by informing the police that if any nastiness occurred on the day it would not be the British Loyalists but bystanders who caused it. Deliberately selective with information he conveniently forgot to tell the authorities that the supporters of this far right organisation would present themselves in intimidatory black paramilitary uniforms. Having scant regard for legality, he thought by informing the police of the demonstration it would mislead the authorities, throwing them off the scent.

Billy Davies experience of this degenerate organisation meant he was not fooled by their underhand behaviour leading to him calling a meeting of the London Council of Unity at Tooting Evangelical Church.

Addressing the group Billy declared, 'Freedom to demonstrate is enshrined in British law. This is being recognised by the police authorising this far right populist organisation to demonstrate. There's no doubt British Loyalists will be trying to incite trouble. Their passionate hatred of immigrants and other minorities is well known and has led to this paramilitary gathering.'

The Roman Catholic Bishop quickly supported Billy. He was equally concerned with the growth of right-wing extremism and responded by saying, 'There has been a racist undercurrent in Tooting for years slowly coming to a head. I totally agree with Billy we must have an appropriate response.'

Elaborating further he said, 'We must counter the motives of this far-right organisation and our response has to be peaceful in line with our religious beliefs.'

Billy pointed out, 'Richard L'Ucifer who stood as a candidate for Tooting in the General Election is reputed to be speaking for the British Loyalists.'

The Bishop continued, 'He definitely has the potential to ignite passion in the demonstrators which is why we must not respond to their goading. It's imperative we're on our guard. Our supporters must uphold peaceful principles demanded by our Christian religion. We must not get dragged into any sort of conflict.'

Billy was thrilled there was a consensus in the meeting for maintaining a pacifist standpoint and exclaimed, 'He's a slimy character, operating right on the edge of legitimacy, whereas many of the British Loyalist supporters are men who've been groomed and manipulated through their weak personalities. Many lack the intellect of Richard L'Ucifer who is a slippery individual. Rest assured he is bright with an evil side to his nature. It's a shame someone who studied at Oxford has such racist, warped ideas. He's dangerous and capable of influencing Loyalist followers with his vile rhetoric.'

Maintaining unity, the Anglican Archbishop spoke, 'This is going to be a difficult situation with the potential for emotions to spill over into violence.'

Billy had spent time thinking about this problem and outlined his plan for a counter protest. He said, 'We can mobilise large numbers of people to line the streets. It's essential every church leader encourages their congregation to join us. Contacting our brothers and sisters of other faiths is a priority. It's important to show we will not be intimidated by such a venomous organisation. Strength in numbers and unity will portray our determination to succeed. Lining Tooting's streets in an act of solidarity will show that we will not be oppressed by these extremists.'

'Do you think it might be appropriate to chant quotes from scripture or carry banners with biblical quotes on,' asked the Presbyterian leader.'

Billy had spent hours thinking about how to respond.

He put his plan forward to the meeting by saying, 'We should stand in total silence. If we encourage thousands of people to line the streets, this complete silence will be deafening. We need to turn their intimidatory tactics on them through a muted response. They might wear paramilitary uniforms but by linking arms with people from different faiths and ethnicities we'll show these fascists that we can't be beaten. When Richard L'Ucifer speaks we will sing verses from the song of the United States Civil Rights Movement 'We shall Overcome.' Our unity will flabbergast them, hopefully lighting a fuse to finish this discrimination once and for all. Our Liberal MP Antoinette will be with us.'

The Catholic Bishop was delighted with this non-violent direct action and said, 'Well done, Billy. I'm certain mass silence will reduce this bigoted group to a bunch of losers. We must prepare our congregations spreading the word amongst all fair-minded people in Tooting and those further afield.'

'It's time for a cuppa,' remarked Billy.

Chapter 47

14 June 2031

Tommy Gunn's day arrived when neo-Nazis from different parts of the United Kingdom began assembling in Tooting, swelling the numbers of far-right activists in this area of London. A menacing demonstration followed by Richard L'Ucifer's hate speech were designed to incite racial loathing. Tooting was always busy. However, on this day, there were unusually large numbers of cars arriving filled with distasteful looking characters sporting skinhead haircuts and covered in patriotic tattoos. These characters changed into black clothes as a mark of their allegiance to a contemptuous organisation, responsible for sowing seeds of hate between different groups of people.

Although some men had a cockney accent, there were a wide variety of dialects in evidence, a sure giveaway that numbers had been swelled by flying agitators. Just like Tommy Gunn, many of these men were grotesquely big through steroid abuse. Yesterday evening, Tommy injected steroids as he had every Friday for the last 10 years. Although he did some weight training, his sole purpose was to appear big to unnerve people.

Looking in the mirror Tommy's muscles might be bulging but, on this day, he was pallid. Both sides of his back were killing him causing him to take the painkiller co-codamol. He had not eaten anything responsible for causing this pain. Nevertheless, he was debilitated by it. Just like many young men Tommy failed to count the physical cost of his abuse. Pulling on a black jacket he knew he had to be fit to lead the march. Having arranged to meet at Garrett Lane, this show of right-wing fervour would march towards Tooting Bec then progress to Tooting Common where Richard L'Ucifer would address an expectant mob.

Thugs possessing distorted thought processes with violent, anarchist tendencies ingrained in them assembled at Coopers Lane. Such a formidable gathering presented a frightening sight for local people as they awaited the arrival of their mastermind Tommy Gunn. At 11:00 a.m. the two Tooting thugs arrived on cue; Tommy accompanied by his chief henchman the Major. They both stood at the front with countless other extremists lined up in a regimentally orderly manner standing behind them. Assembled under the pretence that it was a march about jobs, their mass gathering was a cover for a racist rally. Their behaviour was reminiscent of the white supremacist movements in other countries.

Turning into Tooting Bec the march resembled a lengthy, venomous, black snake displaying fangs like hypodermic needles, ready to propel venom at minority groups. The people being discriminated against were a greater asset to British society than this unpalatable mob. Slithering its way along the road, the serpent like gathering was confronted by a street lined with people from all ethnic groups and religions, linking arms as a sign of solidarity.

Having set out to intimidate people this venomous creature was squared up to by an anti-venom of people determined to stamp out discrimination, putting the boot firmly on the other foot. Such eerie quiet produced a stunning tranquillity, mesmerising this slithering black mass. The insipid, pastel coloured Tommy Gunn looked visibly stunned by this silent crowd glaring at the creeping monstrosity.

Police in riot gear waited for a disturbance to kick off but were not needed. When Billy gave the signal, the crowd began a rendition of 'We shall Overcome.' Acting as an anti-venom nullifying the poisonous effect, this black creature began to squirm. Unity and determination produced the desired result. Failure to cower to these bully boys halted the demonstration in its tracks.

Suddenly the head of the serpent Tommy Gunn, began to sway. Placing his hands on his back gripping hard in his kidney region he was obviously in discomfort. Finally, he collapsed in a heap, rendering any venomous threat useless. Steroid abuse caused this once intimidatory figure to crumble and pass out. Seeing Tommy Gunn sprawled on the road would remind some of the religious people in the crowd of the biblical quote from the *book of Samuel* following King Saul's death at the hands of the Philistines on Mount Gilboa. *'How the mighty have fallen'*.

Tommy Gunn's followers might have thought he was invincible. Here was a reminder to the neo-Nazis that all are vulnerable in this world. Steroid abuse had caught up with Tommy and his next port of call would be hospital. Seeing their leader in a heap on the floor and the overwhelming number of people lining the streets, making the point that far-right extremism had no place in British society caused these racist zealots to disperse. Well and truly humiliated, they scuttled to their cars, then disappeared with their tails between their legs to the motorway. Years of racial tension incited by a minority had been ended by the power of the people.

People just gazed at Tommy Gunn lying prone on the road with a mixture of disbelief and amazement that someone who'd brought misery to many, lay in a crumpled heap on the floor. Feared by many, admired by his supporters, his demise led to all abandoning him. Police on standby to quell any potential disturbance were delighted they hadn't been called upon to deal with a riot. A policeman summoned an ambulance for this prostrate villain who had fallen in the face of opposition from overwhelming numbers of tolerant people.

Many bystanders were committed churchgoers, but loathing for Tommy Gunn's contemptible behaviour had attracted support for Billy's counter peaceful protest from countless good citizens who'd never entered a church. Initial reaction from onlookers was someone as obnoxious as Tommy Gunn in their opinion didn't deserve to walk the face of the earth. His demise was warranted. Many were churchgoers adhering to fundamental Christian belief who literally interpreted scripture, 'An eye for an eye' believing Tommy Gunn had received his just desserts. Standing nearby a woman quoted from the epistle to the Romans, 'Revenge is mine; I will repay says the Lord.'

Billy could see the collapse of this hard-line racist prevented the British Loyalists from promoting their evil ideology, however he still saw Tommy Gunn as a human being worthy of help. First impressions were that Tommy Gunn was dead. Suddenly he began groaning in agony. He was alive but in need of immediate medical attention if he were to survive. Some churchgoers standing by realised that any initial feelings of revenge although innately human were inappropriate for people of faith. Rethinking their initial thirst for retribution, these people offered prayers for his survival, appreciating that justice and forgiveness were central pillars of Jesus's teaching. An ambulance arrived leading to Tommy Gunn being put on a stretcher and taken to hospital for assessment. Billy wondered if he would survive.

Chapter 48

Medical people at Saint George's Hospital were well aware of Tommy Gunn's notoriety creating a crisis of conscience for them. Irrespective of his despicable actions any personal feelings had to be side-lined guaranteeing Tommy Gunn being treated by medical staff. Specialists examined him concluding his demise resulted from a kidney problem. Although extremely weak he was able to inform doctors the pain had been in his back. Further investigation confirmed chronic kidney failure through perpetually ingesting and injecting steroids. Tommy's pasty colour bore testimony to the internal damage caused by his abuse. Ironically in view of his discriminatory behaviour an Asian Accident and Emergency consultant came to give him the news.

'Mr Gunn, you've chronic kidney failure.'

'What does that mean?'

'Unless we get you on to dialysis very quickly, you'll die.'

Previously conceited, egotistical behaviour had been replaced by a frightened, timid human being. Aggression was replaced by fear.

'I can't understand how this has happened.'

'Most steroid abusers fail to count the cost of their drug abuse. The desire to look good is the primary objective of their habit. Abusers forget about the significant side effects.'

'When will I go on to dialysis?'

'It will have to be straight away and then we'll do a further assessment. Oh, by the way a kidney transplant is the only long-term solution.'

'Will I be able to get one?'

'That's going to be difficult, Mr Gunn. You belong to the rarest blood group. People with blood groups AB are few and far between.'

Tommy's fear manifested itself through his silence. Inwardly he was scared to death. As he was examined, he blurted out, 'Doc, don't let me die.'

Failing to respond indicated the specialist thought Tommy's survival chances were slim.

Billy was pleased with himself for not wanting revenge. Although Tommy Gunn's behaviour was reprehensible, he could never wish another human being dead. However, Billy did wonder if Tommy Gunn would learn anything following his brush with death. Would it change the way he behaved making him rethink his philosophy on life?

Tommy Gunn's infamy warranted his demise making front page news. It would have been easy for Billy to deride Tommy. Instead, his innate goodness prevented him from giving a statement to the press or speaking to television reporters. Most people were quick to utter disparaging comments about this right-wing fascist. Many failed to understand why doctors bothered to save him.

Billy took the stance that Tommy Gunn's downfall countered his personal belief about his indestructibility. He no longer presented a threat to anyone. Never one to put the boot in when a man was down, Billy was adamant Tommy needed to survive so he could face justice for his crimes. Mr Patel's business had been destroyed by a British Loyalist petrol bomb. Although Tommy hadn't actually thrown it, he was the one who ordered it. Then there was the attempt on Billy's life where Tommy almost certainly had a role to play. By covering his tracks, he avoided being convicted for it.

News reports from the hospital updated the public about Tommy's deteriorating condition. Initially dialysis saved Tommy's life. However, after a fortnight his condition began deteriorating. Low blood pressure was a serious enough side effect, however life-threatening sepsis followed. Bacteria entering his blood stream caused toxicity leading to a renowned nephrologist coming to see him. He gave Tommy the news he was dreading, 'Without a kidney transplant you will not survive.'

Squirming with fear Tommy asked, 'How easy is it to get one, doc?'

This question was asked by a once brash, narcissistic, violent individual whose self-confidence had diminished to the point where Tommy Gunn was a quivering wreck.

Looking Tommy Gunn straight into lifeless eyes the nephrologist said, 'It's always exceedingly difficult, however in your case nigh on impossible.'

'Why is that?'

'Well, the best match for a kidney transplant is someone from your own blood group but yours is the rarest group. It's always difficult to find a donor in the AB group.'

Tommy Gunn's eyes filled with tears. Here was an intolerant, vindictive man who'd never shown any compassion towards anyone reduced to a quivering wreck.

'I don't want to die.'

The nephrologist replied, 'We'll do all we can to make you comfortable.'

A press release informed the public that this infamous right-wing extremist had contracted sepsis which in all probability would kill him. Some newspapers took the opportunity to express the sentiments of a large percentage of the population with headlines such as 'Good riddance to a Fascist.' Producing articles like these brought no credit to the press, with more discerning people referring to these articles as tabloid sensationalism.

At the end of the day Tommy Gunn was a human being. Information released stated that without a kidney transplant his death was inevitable. Many people bought into the opinions expounded by the worst elements of the British press, commenting online to editors where they expressed the sentiment Britain was better off without Tommy Gunn who should just be allowed to die.

One comment carried the heading, 'One less piece of pond life for society to deal with.'

Billy was watching television in the church when a reporter gave the news about Tommy's desperate condition. The correspondent commenting to viewers that his life could only be saved by a donor from the AB blood group. Tommy Gunn's plight really struck a chord with Billy causing him to think about his good fortune in life. His introduction to the church led to a Pastor taking a punt on Billy, giving him a home and a fresh start in life. If it had not been for Pastor Robbin's benevolence, he would have died a long time ago. Billy decided to phone Antoinette and Simeon. As usual they answered quickly. Their high-profile jobs resulted in incessant calls. Billy thought they must sit on that phone; they're so quick answering it.

Simeon answered before the first ring had finished saying, 'How's things, Billy?'

'How did you know it's me?'

'Well, I've told you before, it comes up on the screen.'

Billy was getting older making him a bit of a technophobe. His idea of a phone was an old pay as you go, something only Alexander Grahame Bell would recognise.

'Oh, I'm OK but I wonder if you would pop over for an hour. I've got something to tell you.'

'Yes, let's finish our tea and we'll pop straight over.'

'See you later.'

Antoinette and Simeon finished their tea then made their way to the church. If Billy wanted to see them quickly it must be important. Billy was not in the habit of disturbing their evening over a trivial matter. Walking through the church hall they could see Billy in the doorway.

'I hope you're both well," he said.

'We're fine, thanks.'

'I'll make us a cuppa.'

Taking their tea to the table the three friends sat down.

Billy asked, 'Did you watch the news and the announcement about Tommy Gunn?'

'Yes, he needs a kidney to survive. It's almost impossible because he belongs to the rarest blood group,' Antoinette commented.

Simeon added, 'Yes he's AB.'

Billy declared to his friends, 'I've decided to donate. I'm in the AB blood group.'

Exasperatedly Simeon pronounced, 'What do you mean? You have to be joking, after all he's done to harm you. What about the way he's intimidated other people?'

Billy was momentarily stunned by Simeon's response. After all he'd been brought up in the church where forgiveness was central to Christian teaching.

He exclaimed, 'Surely both of you don't think I'm making a bad choice.'

Antoinette added, 'Billy, we love you to bits, but you must be mad. There's no way he's deserving of such a precious gift.'

Antoinette's response showed her Christian values had also been temporarily side-lined, being replaced by a thirst for retribution.

'Everyone deserves to be given a second chance. Even someone like Tommy Gunn whose vile behaviour has affected the lives of so many people.'

'Not at the expense of you harming your body,' said Simeon.

Billy was anxious not to berate his friends. They were concerned about his welfare but nevertheless he thought they were missing a point.

'You've both been Christians a long time and central to the faith is Jesus died for human sin. Now I am not into organised religious services. However, my interpretation of Jesus's actions is that he died for everyone, good and bad people. Jesus did not distinguish between who he died to save. Rather he gave a chance to all people. I'm 67 years of age and determined to give Tommy Gunn a chance. You never know he might rise to a new life.'

Stunned silence, then followed a realisation, that their failure to attach any value to Tommy Gunn's life compromised their religious belief. Antoinette and Simeon appreciated they were wrong. Having been taught that no one is beyond God's love and redemption, they suddenly felt ashamed of their poor judgement in this matter.

Having thought about her misunderstanding of this issue Antoinette declared, 'Billy, you're quite right. Maybe we think we're better than we are. I'm really disappointed with myself.'

Billy smiled delighted by Antoinette's change of heart. He said, 'I'll go to the hospital tomorrow to see what I need to do.'

'Billy, you're a truly remarkable man,' declared Antoinette.

Chapter 49

Next morning Billy travelled to Saint George's hospital to make enquiries about donating a kidney. Having taken his details the receptionist told him, 'I'll see if someone's available from the transplant team. Just take a seat.'

Disappearing into a side room for a few minutes the receptionist returned to announce, 'Please go through. Mr Francis, the nephrologist will see you.'

Pushing open the double doors Billy went into the consultation area to find the specialist sitting at a desk. Peering over his glasses Mr Francis announced, 'I know you. You're Billy Davies. You've been acclaimed for your humanitarian work.'

'Well, I've just tried to do my best, Mr Francis.'

'Your achievements have been outstanding; it would have been appropriate for the authorities to recognise what you've done a long time ago.'

'Well, I never set out to get an award, just help people who need it.'

'I must say what you achieved in Yemen was absolutely remarkable. Rescuing the children in that way was immensely brave. No doubt the children have gone on to achieve well thanks to your courage. Going into a country torn apart by civil war was an audacious action. Thankfully, ten young lives were saved. Your profile in the United Kingdom is high, but despite that your modesty shines through all your achievements.'

'What can I do to help you?'

'I want to make a live kidney donation.'

'That's a really magnanimous gesture. Hopefully, you've thought about the implications of making such a gift. Can I just point out that long term complications are rare? Some donors have reported nerve damage and intestinal obstruction. Nevertheless, these are unusual and generally there are minimal long-term risks with kidney donation. It's a priceless gift for the recipient, giving the person an opportunity to lead a normal life.'

'I've thought everything through and I definitely want to proceed.'

'Have you anyone in mind. A live donation has a greater chance of succeeding.'

'Yes, I want to donate to Tommy Gunn.'

Initially Mr Francis the nephrologist was taken aback.

'Well, I find it difficult to believe what you've just said. I don't mean to be impertinent, but he's caused so much trouble with his Fascist views, I'm flabbergasted anyone would want to donate to him.'

'It might seem a strange request, however I believe everyone should have the opportunity to turn their life around. I'm in the same rare blood group as Tommy Gunn, meaning a greater chance of compatibility. Hopefully, it'll lead to a successful procedure.'

'In the light of the grief he's caused you, I find this an amazingly chivalrous gesture.'

Billy understood how people initially found it difficult to understand why he was giving such a gift. However, he'd been given a chance years ago by Pastor Robbins, transforming his life.

'You never know he might see the error of his ways, helping him appreciate we are all interdependent on one another. Hopefully, he'll realise we all belong to one human race.'

'This transplant will have to happen quickly, Billy. He's desperately ill. Without a kidney he's limited time left.'

'I'm ready whenever the team's ready.'

'We'll put the team on standby and inform Tommy Gunn of what's happening. There are important tests you'll have to undertake. I am sure everything can be set up in a few days.'

Billy left Mr Francis contented with the difficult decision he'd made. His action would give Tommy the chance to live but it might also encourage him to alter the course of his life. Mr Francis went to see Tommy Gunn in intensive care where machines and intensive nursing were keeping him alive. Tubes attached to many parts of his body were connected to monitors, alerting staff of any deterioration in his condition. So many machines made Tommy look like he was involved in some bizarre experiment.

'I've good news for you, Tommy,' declared Mr Francis.

'Look at the state of me. There can't be any good news.'

'A donor's come forward and he's a perfect match.'

Tommy was bemused knowing none of the thugs he'd associated with would give the gift of a kidney. For one of them to come forward a gun would have to be put to their head. Inwardly he knew none of them possessed either the physical courage or the spirit of generosity to make such an offering.

'Who is it?'

'Billy Davies has offered to donate a kidney. He's the same blood group as you.'

Ghastly white with red eyes looking like burning coals, Tommy Gunn sounded astounded, 'Why is he doing that?'

'Fortunately for you, he's not a man in a million but one in 100 million who thinks everyone deserves a chance.'

Stuttering Tommy Gunn found it difficult to get his words out.

'But I've.'

Mr Francis interjected, 'Yes, just be grateful and hopefully we'll do it in a few days.'

Mr Francis left Tommy Gunn in a quandary. Billy was a man he'd treated with disdain. Yet this special human being was prepared to give him a priceless gift. Even someone as hard hearted as Tommy Gunn began to think he'd misjudged people. Closing his eyes, a tear emerged from one, trickling down his face, reminiscent of a teardrop tattoo: an ironic moment as this single droplet both symbolised and acknowledged the abhorrent life Tommy had led. Such a lifestyle would lead to a prison sentence as recompense for his crimes once the operation had been completed.

Trickling down his face a water trail remained on his cheek, the diminishing tear drop eventually disappearing. Without Billy's gift Tommy's life would come to an end just as the tear had slowly ebbed away. Exhaustion caused Tommy to fall asleep.

Chapter 50

Four days later Billy arrived at the hospital in the knowledge he faced an operation to donate a kidney. Living with one kidney would present no long-term health problem. A few days in hospital to recuperate followed by a six-week convalescence should allow Billy to recover fully. Living in the church at Tooting, there would be a constant stream of people to care for Billy following his surgery. Worshippers were constantly reminded by the pastor that Billy Davies was a special individual who'd helped illuminate their lives.

As he entered the hospital Billy was presented with the consent form for the procedure to take place. Signing without making a comment Billy undressed, then put on the surgical gown he was given. As yet Billy had not seen Tommy Gunn but knew he must be in an adjoining room. Preoperative tests carried out confirmed Billy was physically fit enough to withstand the surgery.

When asked if he was anxious about the procedure Billy replied, 'No problem, I'm tough as old boots.'

'You're not worried about the surgery then Mr Davies,' exclaimed the nurse.

'Not at all. It's nothing compared to some of the things I've had to put up with.'

'Quite soon the anaesthetist will be in to see you.'

'Oh, I'm glad they are going to put me to sleep,' quipped Billy.

The anaesthetist, a distinguished, professional looking man came to the room. Although dressed in operating scrubs he gave the impression his patients were in good hands.

He addressed Billy, 'My name is Doctor Foster. It's my job to put you to sleep but there's really nothing to worry about. When you're under, I'll inject an anti-sickness drug, so you feel OK when you wake up. Are there any questions?'

'Just one. How long am I likely to be asleep?'

'If everything goes well it should be about three hours. If there are any issues it could take up to five.'

'Thanks very much.'

'Can I just say, Billy, it's a wonderful thing you're doing.

A few minutes later a theatre sister came to fetch Billy and he was able to walk to the operating theatre. As he walked along the corridor a bed with a sick looking man was wheeled in the same direction. Tommy Gunn who'd been sedated to relieve his pain was totally unaware of Billy's presence. Looking at Tommy it was easy to see a transplant operation was urgently needed, or he'd die.

Both men were taken to a side room to be anaesthetised. After looking for and finding a vein, a cannula was inserted into Billy's arm. Surgical lights emitted a bright white glare designed to help the medical people but temporarily dazzling Billy. Once the cannula was in Billy's arm the anaesthetist attached the line to administer the anaesthetic. Mr Foster the anaesthetist asked Billy to count to 10 but he managed to get to three before the lights went out.

'Billy, Billy wake up it's all over,' pronounced the nurse.

Billy was in the recovery room and as he came around, he thought to himself, 'I could have been out for two minutes, two hours or two weeks.'

A few metres away was Tommy Gunn. Billy still had the cannula in his arm when a nurse came in with a syringe and a phial of liquid. 'Mr Davies, I'm going to put this into your arm.'

'What's that nurse?'

'It's morphine to take the pain away but don't worry I'll put it into the cannula.'

Billy still groggy let out a grunt acknowledging he'd heard what the nurse had said. He presented his arm to receive the painkiller. Seriously weakened Tommy Gunn turned his head slowly to look at Billy.

He made a sound which Billy just about heard. 'Thank you,' uttered Tommy.

Billy befuddled and disorientated following surgery was ecstatic to hear Tommy's words of thanks. Drifting in and out of sleep the analgesic was now controlling Billy's pain. After two hours Billy was taken to his room by a porter.

Entering the lift, the porter exclaimed, 'Billy, there's not a person who doesn't admire what you've done but many find it difficult to understand why you've donated a kidney to such a distasteful character.'

'Throughout our lives we are making sacrifices to help people, whether it is a parent, teacher, doctor or porter. They're all giving a part of themselves hoping to change people's lives. Giving a kidney is just another example of a sacrifice hopefully transforming a man's life in more than one way.'

'I get what you're saying but I hope you're right, Billy and not going to regret what you've done.'

Wheeling Billy into his room a nurse came in to take his blood pressure, then made him comfortable. Finally, she checked the drain examining the fluid produced by the trauma of the operation.

'Everything's OK. Now you need to rest' she announced.

'Thanks very much, nurse.'

Billy was woken early next morning by the duty nurse who proceeded to check his observations. All were normal enabling Billy to have a light breakfast. Later that morning Mr Francis consultant nephrologist arrived to check on Billy.

'Everything went well Billy; I've just been in to see Tommy Gunn who is very anxious to see you. If you agree, I'll make arrangements to have you taken to his room.'

Billy was moved to a wheelchair, then wheeled 30 yards down the corridor to where Tommy was resting. Opening the door, the porter pushed Billy in, where he came face to face with Tommy Gunn who was propped up in bed. Once drawn and lacking vigour Tommy had been revitalised by Billy's gift. His complexion was no longer ghost like but now had a healthy glow. His physical transformation was indeed staggering. There was only one thing on Billy's mind. Would Tommy's worldview be reshaped to correspond with his physical change?

Tommy looked straight at Billy through bleary eyes. Emotionally charged Tommy uttered, 'I am so sorry. No amount of thanks can express my gratitude at what you have done. Without you, I'd have been a goner.'

'You're looking well.'

'I'm feeling better than I have felt for a long time. I realise that taking steroids to make myself look good was a big mistake.'

In an effort to lighten the mood with a corny one liner Billy said, 'I must say you looked offal before the operation.'

Tommy laughed as he said, 'I know.'

'Tommy don't worry, we all make mistakes. It's part of being human. Don't think everything in my life has been easy. When I was younger, I tried to commit suicide.'

'During the last few days, I've had time to think about my life and I now realise my behaviour has been criminal. Yet a man I hated saved my life. I now need to change.'

'That's just what I wanted to hear, Tommy.'

'I've had time to reassess my life, Billy. Although I was brought up in a violent home, I don't intend using it as an excuse for my hatred. People like me who experience violence, develop aggressive behaviour, seeing this as a way to control people and situations. Blaming minority groups, using them as a scapegoat for my own problems, was just a covering for my own deficiencies.'

Billy was overjoyed to hear Tommy had seen the error of his ways.

'Tommy, you've been very honest about your feelings.'

'It can't stop here, Billy. I've committed crimes and need to be punished to reconcile me with society. I am terribly sorry. I've seen the light. It was me who gave the instruction for you to be attacked and for the Patel's restaurant to be burnt down.'

'The change in you is astounding Tommy, making what I've done worthwhile.'

'I'm turning myself in to the police to take the rap for my crimes. A long prison sentence is a certainty before I can make a fresh start in life.'

Tommy overcome with emotion sobbed uncontrollably. Criminal behaviour where he had no concern for any other human being had been replaced by a man ready to confess and atone for his crimes. What happened to Tommy was a 'Road to Damascus' conversion, transforming his psychologically damaged persona. Billy returned to his room, his action totally vindicated by Tommy's reneging his criminal activity.

Chapter 51

Antoinette settled into her job as MP for Tooting. Following her maiden speech, she'd made a good start to her parliamentary career creating a favourable impression with MPs from different political persuasions. Expressing her distaste for the far right and the increase in domestic violence had certainly 'hit the spot' with her peers.

An unfortunate incident led to Antoinette profiting from a misdemeanour by the Minister for Women's Issues who was caught speeding by a fixed camera. Already having points on her licence, she claimed someone else had driven the car. Overwhelming photographic evidence proved the minister tried to hide the truth from the police leaving her position as a cabinet minister untenable.

Left with little choice her resignation was inevitable. As a public servant she failed in her duty to uphold high standards by attempting to deceive the authorities. As an up-and-coming politician Antoinette had the good fortune to be promoted to this Cabinet post. She was no longer on the bottom rung of the political ladder. Antoinette was embarking on a role in which she was qualified to excel.

At the same time soundings emerged from Norway that the International Court of Justice at The Hague had nominated Billy Davies for the Nobel Peace Prize. A humanitarian award was long overdue considering the work Billy had done. Although the Nobel Peace Prize is awarded for altruistic work during the preceding year, Billy qualified through his efforts in quelling racial problems in Tooting. His gift of a kidney to a far-right extremist who renounced his previous life also struck a chord with the committee. Eleven years previously Billy rescued the Yemeni children and this act of bravery had been bypassed at the time.

They were aware of his courageous action and Billy's subsequent work gave the committee an opportunity to retrospectively rectify this oversight. Following the completion of numerous reports by advisors scrutinising Billy's work they decided to nominate him for the Nobel Peace Prize. Conferred on him through Tooting being a hot bed of racist activity, such an award would be testimony to Billy's commitment in bringing harmony to the community.

Antoinette left Parliament to visit Billy in Tooting. Always thrilled to see Antoinette, he spotted her. Desperate to tell Billy the good news she found it difficult to contain her excitement.

'How's things going, Antoinette?'

'Well, I've got some good news for you, Billy.'

Tongue in cheek he exclaimed, 'You're not going to tell me there's a problem in Yemen, are you Antoinette?'

'No nothing like that, Billy. This is pleasing long overdue news. It's just been announced you've been nominated for the Nobel Peace Prize. What's more you're favourite to win it.'

'Good Lord, I don't believe that, Antoinette.'

'Your work hasn't gone unnoticed even though you are really modest about what you've done. I don't think you realise how impressed people are with your work and generosity.'

'If I win, will I have to go to Norway?'

'Yes, you have to go to Oslo.'

'I've never ever given the Nobel Prize a second thought. Will I have a certificate?'

'Yes Billy, you will have a diploma which is a unique work of art, a Nobel medal and cash prize of £800,000.'

'That's an amazing amount of money, Antoinette.'

'It is and it's up to you how you use it. You could keep it for yourself or give it to charity.'

'Because I don't have many savings, I'll keep a small amount for myself and the rest I'll use to fund projects for the homeless.'

'There are some really distinguished people who've been awarded this prize, Billy.'

'It's something I don't know much about. Who else has won the prize?'

'Desmond Tutu and the Dalai Lama are both Nobel Laureates.'

'They are both amazing humanitarians, Antoinette.'

'So are you, Billy. Not many people have rescued children from Yemen, quelled extremist action and donated their kidney to a right-wing extremist. Don't worry Billy, most people would think you are a more than worthy winner.'

'To be honest, I did these things because they seemed the right thing to do.'

'You might know this, Billy but there's been a number of controversies about past winners. Some members think the award has become politicised. If you win it Billy, no one can ever level that against the committee.'

'Which politicians have made the award controversial, Antoinette?'

'Well Billy, Mikhail Gorbachev and Jimmy Carter were two of the winners criticised for their political affiliations.'

'Well, I can understand why those awards caused dissent.'

'Unfortunately Billy, there's been some notable omissions. The most prominent person not to win the Nobel Peace Prize was Mahatma Gandhi.'

'That is unbelievable, Antoinette. His non-violent resistance stance made him an amazing example of a pacifist who worked for the good of others.'

'It's difficult to comprehend Mahatma Gandhi not being a Nobel Peace Prize winner. He's one of the most famous pacifist figures in history. How can you have the title 'Great Soul' and fail to win the Nobel Peace Prize. It beggars belief.

'How long will I have to wait to find out if I've won Antoinette?'

'Not long, the award is made on December 10th.'

'There are so many credible nominees that I'd be lucky to win.'

'As I said Billy, you're the bookies favourite. They don't often get it wrong!'

'Well in my opinion I'm just an ordinary Joe, Antoinette.'

'Coming from your background you're just what the award needs. There would be no controversy if you win it, Billy. It would mean the Nobel Committee's reputation would be upheld.'

At the beginning of November, the British Prime Minister David Graft was informed that former homeless man Billy Davies had been awarded the Nobel Peace Prize. What a coup for the British Government! Antoinette was given the responsibility of informing Billy of his award. Overwhelmed with excitement she set off for the church in Tooting. She couldn't wait to tell Billy, the bookies had it right. He was in the kitchen making a cuppa and although he had his back to her, he heard footsteps.

Turning around he welcomed Antoinette, 'Great to see you, Antoinette.'

'Unbelievable news, Billy. You've won the Nobel Peace Prize.'

Billy was astounded to hear this news.

'The bookies have probably lost a lot of money. I never thought for a minute I'd win. Billy Davies Nobel Peace Prize winner, yet Gandhi did not win one. It just doesn't make sense.'

'Yes, it does Billy, you've achieved amazing things. There's no doubt the great Mahatma will be looking down today applauding a first-class decision.'

'Antoinette, I looked up why the award is made on 10 December. It was the day Alfred Nobel died in 1896.'

'You'll be going with the Prime Minister; he has also asked Simeon and myself to come along.'

'Oh, Antoinette, I'll need a suit.'

'You're not buying one from a charity shop Billy.'

'Why not, I've seen some great ones in the charity shops on the High Street.'

'Forget that Billy, I'll help you choose one this time and it won't come from a charity shop.'

'I was only winding you up, Antoinette.'

'You're such a scoundrel, Billy.'

Laughing uncontrollably both hugged each other with Billy declaring, 'Come on gal, this deserves a special celebration. I'll boil the kettle. It's got to be Earl Grey.'

Chapter 52

Following his part in rescuing 10 Yemeni children in 2020 Antonio the United Nations Secretary General recruited Simeon to work for UNICEF, the Children's Emergency Fund. He and Antoinette had busy professional lives, involving spending long periods of time apart. Simeon regularly travelled to the United Nations building in New York, making time spent in London with Antoinette special.

Simeon had a two-week holiday coinciding with Billy's Peace Prize award in Oslo, allowing him to travel for the ceremony. Simeon and Antoinette met Billy at the church in Tooting on Tuesday 9 December for a taxi to transport them to Heathrow. A special reception had been organised by the Prime Minister's team. David Graft, the Labour Prime Minister was already in the reception area with his bodyguards, preventing any intruder getting near him. David Graft turned around and saw Antoinette.

He greeted her, 'Hi, Antoinette.'

Antoinette acknowledged him, 'I'd like to introduce Billy and my husband Simeon.'

The Prime Minister was eager to meet both men. Their humanitarian work had brought great credit on them.

'It's really lovely to meet you both. Billy, I've heard all about your remarkable life. Your achievements in Yemen were extraordinary and people still talk about it even though it was more than ten years ago.'

Simeon replied, 'Nothing would have been achieved without, Billy. He was the brains of the outfit.'

'I'm absolutely certain Billy would be quick to acknowledge the important part you played in the rescue.'

Billy was always quick to promote Simeon's part in the rescue.

'Yes Sir, I couldn't have done it alone. Simeon's role was vital.'

'Antoinette speaks highly of you, Billy. I realise you're a man of great integrity and society owes you a considerable debt. Your gift of a kidney to Tommy Gunn who caused you so much personal grief is astounding.'

'To be honest Prime Minister it has changed his life. Although he's in prison, Tommy accepts the sentence is justice for his crimes. On his release, he's determined to make a new start in life.'

'What a remarkable man you are! We need to open a bottle of champagne to celebrate your award. Billy you're the first British winner since John Hume and David Trimble from Northern Ireland for their part in the Good Friday Peace Agreement.'

'Thank you so much for your kind words, Prime Minister.'

Billy could not remember the last time he drank champagne. Feeling like crystalline pearls on his tongue the bubbles luxuriously tickled his taste buds, encouraging him to drink a second glass. Finishing his drink, a government official appeared to make an announcement.

'Prime Minister, the plane is ready for the flight to Oslo.'

Bodyguards walked in front of and behind the Prime Minister providing maximum protection for the British Premier. Antoinette, Simeon and Billy accompanied the party to the airbridge leading to a private jet. Entering the cabin, the Captain, First Officer and Cabin Crew greeted them.

Pampering was the order of the day on this two-hour flight where shortly after take-off drinks and canapes were served. Billy could never remember a time when he was treated in this way. He was being made to feel like royalty. It crossed his mind that it would be easy to get used to this type of treatment. A relatively short flight meant the plane soon touched down at Oslo airport. The party swiftly disembarked, to be greeted by the British Ambassador.

'Greetings Prime Minister, I'm delighted to have you all as guests for the evening. The cars are ready. They're over there to take you to the embassy. If the Prime Minister could go in the first car with the two bodyguards, Antoinette, Simeon and Billy in the second vehicle. At the embassy I have organised a special dinner in Billy's honour.'

Billy looked sheepishly embarrassed to be the centre of attention.

'You needn't have gone to all this trouble, Ambassador.'

'It's the least we could do for someone who's done so much humanitarian work.'

'It's a great honour for Britain to have a Nobel Peace Prize winner,' proclaimed the Prime Minister.

Dinner that evening was an opulent affair including rack of Welsh lamb and copious quantities of wine served in Billy's honour. All this luxury brought a smile to his face.

Antoinette whispered to Billy, 'This must all seem like a fairy story to you.'

'Too true. Sitting on the pavement in Clapham with a begging bowl in front of me, I would have been odds on to be dead by now.'

'If anyone needed help it was you, Billy. What you've given society is immeasurable.'

'Meeting you and Simeon was a turning point. Until you rescued me, life had been a real struggle for survival. Homelessness helped me empathise with countless millions of people in the world who need aid.'

Antoinette lightened the mood.

'If you were a Catholic, Billy, they would be canonising you.'

As quick as a flash Billy quipped, 'That's the last thing I would want to happen. I saw enough cannons in the Falklands.'

Both began giggling. Embassy officials wondered what had instigated the hilarity. Any mirth was brought to an abrupt end when the Ambassador made a speech, praising Billy's achievements. Self-effacement was one of Billy's characteristics making it difficult for him to recognise these traits in his own personality. Understandably, on occasions Billy would focus on the negative aspects of his life rather than the good he'd done. Virtuous accomplishments he'd achieved far outweighed the gloomy aspects of his life.

Simeon whispered to Billy, 'Praise that's well deserved.'

Concluding his speech, the Ambassador called Billy forward for the presentation to be made by David Graft the Prime Minister. Sheepishly leaving his seat Billy shook the Prime Minister's hand, taking a bronze plaque with beautiful impressions on it. Closely examining the images Billy became emotional realising what had been included on the panel. He could see his face engraved on it. Encircling it was the name of his birthplace Llanen, a small map of the Falkland Islands, his regimental badge and a logo for the London Council of Unity.

On closer examination Billy could see some special symbols. Swallowing hard to fight back tears, he identified a peacock which had been engraved into the plaque representing the Yazidi people. To the Yazidi's the peacock symbolises immortality, believing the flesh of this elegant looking bird doesn't decay. Yazidi culture adorns shrines, graves and places of worship with these graceful creatures. Another engraving showed a map of Yemen where Billy and Simeon had gone to rescue the children. A final symbol showed hands releasing a dove with an olive branch in its mouth in recognition of Billy's success in resolving Tooting's racial problems. Billy responded to the kind words spoken about him.

'I can't thank you enough for this amazing award. You've given me a gift encompassing the whole of my life. It will have pride of place in my room.'

Officials and dignitaries audibly muttered, 'Amazing achievement.'

Others exclaimed, 'Well done, well deserved.'

As the evening concluded Billy picked up the gift ready to go to bed. Placing the plaque on his bedside table he climbed into bed. No, he thought, it's not staying there. Getting out of bed he retrieved the plaque, climbed back into bed, grasping the plaque tightly to his chest. Billy contentedly drifted off to sleep.

Chapter 53

Billy woke bright and early, still gripping the bronze plaque tightly to his chest. Having clamped it to his chest all night had left indentations in his skin with the inscriptions branded into him. Quickly shaving, showering and dressing Billy went downstairs for breakfast. In no way was Billy possessive about things he owned but he was not going to leave such a valuable item in his bedroom. The award went with him.

Approaching an official at the desk he asked, 'Could you please put this plaque in the safe until I return from the ceremony?'

An adamant reply followed from the embassy official, 'Very wise because that's a lovely award.'

'Thanks a million. I'll pick it up later.'

Billy walked into the breakfast room to be greeted by Simeon and Antoinette who were already tucking into their meal. Simultaneously both said, 'Good morning, Billy.'

'Good morning both. Is the Prime Minister joining us?'

'No, Billy,' said Simeon.

Antoinette added, 'He'll be dealing with any urgent business; his job is 24/7.'

The waiter came over to Billy saying, 'What would you like for breakfast?'

'Have you any kippers?'

'Yes sir, they are a Norwegian speciality.'

'Oh good, would it be possible to have two?'

'A really wise choice, sir. They're the best in the world.'

Billy smiled and replied, 'I don't know whether a Scot would agree with you. I'm Welsh so I'll take your word for it. Oh, could I have some cereal and toast to go with the kippers.'

'You certainly can, sir.'

The cereal arrived immediately, followed by the kippers 15 minutes later. Salty, lightly smoked, delicately flavoured fish caused Billy to salivate. Mm he thought I might have to agree with the waiter. The kippers possibly are the best in the world. I would have to be careful how I'd play that card if I was ever in Scotland. Tucking in Billy wolfed them down, leaving two backbones on the plate with hardly a morsel of fish left. It was obvious to the waiter Billy had enjoyed his breakfast.

'Well, what did you think of those then?'

Ever the diplomat Billy said, 'Oh, I think you're right. They're better than Loch Fyne kippers. Mind you, I don't know whether I'd say that if I was in Aberdeen.'

Sniggering the waiter said, 'I told you they were good.'

Finishing his toast and coffee Billy said to Antoinette and Simeon, 'I'm just going to put my suit on, so I'll meet you in the foyer.'

Antoinette reminded Billy, 'We need to be in the foyer at 10:00 a.m. ready for the Prime Minister's car to pick us up.'

Billy returned to his room, put on his suit, then came downstairs at 9:45 a.m. There was no way he wanted to be late on parade, making him first in the foyer. Antoinette and Simeon arrived at 9:50 a.m. At one minute to ten the Prime Minister turned up flanked by bodyguards. As the clock struck 10:00 a.m., the official car arrived at the front of the embassy.

Observing protocol, the chauffeur opened the door for the three friends. Meanwhile the Prime Minister and his security guards climbed into the second car. Oslo City Hall was the destination for the ceremony. There are five Nobel awards, but the Peace Prize is the only one awarded in Oslo. Stockholm is the venue for the other four.

Arriving at the City Hall in the city centre it was easy to see this was a municipal building. Built of red bricks with two 60-metre-high towers this was the location for Billy's big day. He was receiving the prize on 10 December, the date Alfred Nobel died. Billy was Nobel Peace Prize recipient for 2031 and one of the conditions for the winner of the medal and diploma is to give a lecture.

Entering the building Antoinette proclaimed, 'I find it really unusual that the inventor of dynamite donates a Peace Prize when his invention has been used to maim and kill in war.'

Billy had researched Alfred Nobel's life.

'Nobel had invented an explosive more powerful than anything produced before. During the 20th century weapons of war became more destructive and modern conflict resulted in a great loss of life. To atone for this potentially ruinous accomplishment Nobel initiated the Peace Prize helping ease his conscience. He was a prolific inventor who held 355 different patents, but we also need to remember the positive aspects of dynamite used not only in war but for building projects. Becoming incredibly wealthy when he signed his last will in Paris in 1895, he set aside the bulk of his estate for the Nobel prizes to be awarded annually. I cannot believe I am the beneficiary of such a prestigious award and about to join a unique group of remarkable people.'

Antoinette adamantly replied, 'Billy, your achievements merit you belonging to a special group of people who've received this award.'

Taking his seat on the podium in the City Hall it was difficult for this man from such humble beginnings not to be overawed by the occasion. Reassuringly Antoinette gave Billy a squeeze, causing him to smile nervously. Hopefully, this would help settle his nerves as he waited to deliver a lecture to such an esteemed audience.

She encouraged him by saying, 'Billy, you're the one being given the award for your amazing achievements. Just tell them about your life and the struggle to get justice for people.'

'Once I get going, I'll be OK, Antoinette.'

Once again Billy began to suffer self-doubt.

'Oh, but what happens if I get tongue tied, Antoinette, the Norwegian Royal family are here.'

'Billy, I've never known you tongue tied. It's just like any other occasion where you've had to speak.'

First to speak was the chairman of the Norwegian Nobel Committee who told the audience why Billy had been chosen for the award. Calling Billy forward he was presented with the Nobel Diploma and Award. Moving to the lectern Billy began to deliver his lecture.

He opened with, 'Your Royal Highness, distinguished members of the Nobel Committee, British Prime Minister, citizens of the world, ladies and gentlemen, I am honoured to be here with you. I'm deeply grateful to the Norwegian Nobel Committee for recognising my contribution to the peaceful resolution of racial disputes in Tooting. I accept this award on behalf of all the victims of racism throughout the world whose lives have been affected by right-wing organisations.

Fate has brought me here as I was a PTSD victim of the 1982 Falklands War. Illness forced me into homelessness. I made my way from Llanen in Wales and following the breakup of my marriage ended upon the streets in London. Luckily, I met the two people who are here with me today and my life changed when their church took me in. Determined to pay back the generosity of this place of worship I have tirelessly worked for peace both in my own community and the wider world.

Racism demeans both victim and perpetrator. Being victims of oppression sufferers fail to reach their full capability. Those who see themselves as superior, always wanting to hold the whip hand don't recognise there's equality in creation. Victims of maltreatment are people who could if given the opportunity make a vital contribution to humanity. Fortunately, the leader of the neo-Nazi group in Tooting saw the error of his ways after experiencing an act of kindness. Subsequently he admitted his crimes to the police and is now serving a prison sentence.

On his release, he has vowed to make a fresh start. Tooting has become a much calmer place, where all ethnic groups are living in harmony. Individuals realise working together is the best way for people to enhance their life prospects, transforming society. I was delighted to be able to play a part in this reordering and I will treasure the Nobel Award for the rest of my days.'

A prolonged standing ovation followed Billy's address and he raised his hand to acknowledge the crowd.

Returning to his seat, Billy looked at the medal he had just been awarded. Alfred Nobel's head was on it, with a Latin inscription reading Pro Pace et Fraternitate Gentium [For peace and Brotherhood of Man]. On the reverse side he saw a group of three men forming a fraternal bond. Antoinette asked if she could see it. Billy willingly handed it to her. Once the presentation ceremony was over his stomach butterflies settled. Even someone like Billy who was a self-effacing man felt great pride at what he'd achieved. All that remained now was the banquet hosted by the Nobel Committee.

Billy thought to himself, 'I can manage that.'

In recent days, he'd developed a taste for champagne!

Chapter 54

Antoinette's dedication to her work gave rise to her becoming a highly respected cabinet member, endlessly striving to improve conditions for women. She was instrumental in guaranteeing women were given opportunities to reach the top in all walks of life. Antoinette's determination to further close the gender pay gap in the British workplace sealed her popularity among female voters. Another important aspect of her role was to end forced marriage and the despicable practice of female genital mutilation, which although illegal in Britain, could be a problem.

Simeon's work with UNICEF meant that he'd dealt with the issues of forced marriage and FGM (Female Genital Mutilation) on many occasions. His work gave Antoinette an insight into the pressures young girls were put under to conform to these practices. Antoinette was appalled that girls faced physical, emotional and psychological pressure to marry older men in some Third World countries. Young girls were often made to feel they were bringing shame on their families if they refused to follow their parents' instructions. Such customs had no place in a contemporary civilised society and needed to be curtailed from gaining a foothold in British society.

Forced marriage became illegal in 2014 and Antoinette was eager to stamp out the practice of taking a young girl abroad to marry or to be cut. Working wholeheartedly Antoinette brought these problems to the attention of the British public, enlightening people about the difference between arranged and forced marriage. Arranged marriage in Britain is legal, being prominent among people from South Asian cultures. Often a matchmaker is used but, in this tradition, the wishes of the son or daughter are respected making it an acceptable practice.

Antoinette's role as Minister for Women's Issues brought her into contact with a horrific form of child abuse mostly practised by people of African, Asian or Middle Eastern descent. The practice known as female genital mutilation or female circumcision occurs when the female genitals are cut without any medical reason. FGM Is usually carried out on girls between infancy and 15 years of age. Blood loss or infection can occur causing young girls to lose their lives. There are no medical reasons for carrying out this procedure and it is usually carried out by a person with no medical training. Using a razor or piece of glass, the girl's genitals are cut to control female sexuality.

Antoinette faced a difficult task outlawing this barbaric practice as there was great secrecy surrounding the custom, making families reticent about speaking out. Such cloak and dagger behaviour made it a difficult issue to stamp out. Antoinette appreciated this was an immoral tradition needing to be wiped out. People participating in this abuse had to be made to realise they were violating a girl's human rights. Education was a central pillar in Antoinette's strategy and she was acclaimed for her work, particularly speaking in schools regarding girls' basic rights.

The issue of forced marriage and FGM came to a head following a talk Antoinette gave at Simeon's former school. Being a multicultural educational community there were a diverse range of pupils attending this establishment. Many parents had come to Britain from African and Asian countries, retaining family ties in their homeland. Children from these countries faced the greatest threat from practices alien to British people.

Antoinette spoke in assembly to Years 9 and 10 girls about the issues of forced marriage and FGM and the illegality of these practices in Britain. An attentive young audience gave a polite round of applause at the end of the talk. Sitting listening was a young girl from Somalia named Astur who came to Britain from the capital Mogadishu. She was sitting by her best friend Belle whose parents had come to Britain from Jamaica. Both girls were in Year 10. Following the talk Astur confided to Belle that her parents were planning to take her to relatives in Mogadishu during the Summer holidays where she was to be cut.

Although her parents had told her this procedure was simple and would do her no harm, the talk by Antoinette had frightened her. During the talk Antoinette stressed that any instruments used were rarely ever sterilised and a lack of antiseptics often resulted in infection. Hearing that some girls bled uncontrollably had really startled Astur leaving her petrified at this prospect. Her parents had been economical with the truth withholding any of this information from her.

Astur confided in Belle, 'Belle, what am I to do?'

'We need to see Antoinette. I've heard that MPs hold surgeries at the weekend for people to discuss their problems. You need to go before it's too late.'

'If my parents find out they will say I've dishonoured the family and I'd be worried they might kill me.'

'Don't worry Astur, you can come to live with me. Think of all the fun we could have.'

'But Belle, it gets worse. After GCSE my parents have promised me to a man whose wife died.'

'What do you mean Astur, by promised? What's that?'

'It means I'm going to have to marry him.'

'That's against the law.'

'I know but it's in Somalia, so no one will ever know.'

'Well, do you like the man?'

'No, I've never seen him. All I know is he's 50 years old and his third wife has just died.'

'That's terrible, Astur. We've got to stop it.'

'I'm really scared because he killed his wife for not looking after him well enough. Women have no rights in Somalia. I'll become his property and he can do what he likes with me.'

'Look Astur, we'll make an appointment to see Antoinette. People say she's lovely and takes a real interest in them. We'll get the appointment for Saturday.'

Saturday couldn't come fast enough for Astur and Belle but there would be one problem. Astur's father was very controlling, wanting to know where she was going. On this occasion she told him that Belle was giving her a hand with homework. Astur's father had been so domineering that he didn't question her excuse, convinced that she would never disobey him.

Terrified at the thought of being cut, then owned by a much older man gave Astur the determination needed to defy her father. Antoinette's surgery was at Tooting library and the two girls had an appointment to meet her at 10 o'clock. Belle met Astur outside at 9:50 a.m. who was absolutely thrilled to have her best friend with her. It gave her the courage needed to speak out. As they sat outside Antoinette's office, both girls stared into space, scared at the prospect of meeting their MP. Belle knew she would want to listen to Astur's story.

At exactly 10:00 a.m. Antoinette came out of the office and introduced herself, 'I'm Antoinette Williams and your names?'

Astur was overawed at being in the presence of such an important person but Belle summoned up courage. 'I'm Belle and this is Astur.'

'Ah I remember the two of you. You were in the talk I gave the other day.'

Belle said, 'Yes, Mrs Williams.'

'Listen girls it's polite of you to call me Mrs Williams but there's no need. Everyone calls me Antoinette.'

This was just what the girls needed because Antoinette's relaxed manner put them at ease. Antoinette asked, 'What can I do for you?'

Astur burst into tears. Belle comforted Astur by putting an arm around her. Antoinette kindly took a tissue from a box and handed it to Astur.

'What can I do for you, Astur?'

'I listened to your talk about FGM and forced marriage realising how serious these issues are. My father is taking me to Mogadishu this summer to be cut. When you said how dangerous it is, I spoke to Belle who suggested we came to see you.'

Antoinette was shocked by Astur's frankness.

'Usually when a girl is cut, it is a precursor to marriage. Are you being forced to marry?'

'After my GCSEs I'll be taken to Mogadishu to marry a much older man who I've never seen. I'm really scared and I wondered if you could help me.'

'Too true, I intend helping. I wouldn't be doing my job if I let this go.'

'But I'm really worried, my family will kill me. They'll claim I've brought great shame on it which could well lead to an honour killing.'

Belle interjected, 'I know my mum wouldn't mind Astur coming to live with me.'

Antoinette was impressed with Belle's care and concern for her best friend.

'That's really kind of you, Belle. It might well be a short-term solution. In the meantime, we need to inform the police who I'm certain will pick up your father. As yet he hasn't committed a crime and it could be time to get him the help he needs. Although he's a British citizen he's still thinking as if he was living in Somalia. That's what we need to change. Your dad has to realise that a girl or woman is not a man's property and we'll get people to work with him to change his thinking. Please don't worry Astur, this will all be handed sensitively. Your dad will be given every chance to alter his mindset.'

'But what happens if this doesn't work, Antoinette?'

'Astur, I've introduced stringent FGM Protection Orders, preventing parents taking girls out of Britain to have this practice inflicted upon them and as for forced marriage it's been illegal for over twenty years. You don't need to worry. I'll be taking a personal interest in your case.'

Antoinette finished telling the girls what she intended to do. Immediately she called Tooting Police Station informing them that Astur's dad needed to be picked up for urgent questioning. She then phoned Belle's mum and asked her if Astur could stay with them for a short while.

Looking at the girls she said, 'Belle, what a good friend you are. Astur, you're so brave to speak out about an appalling practice which has no place in British culture. I will be taking a personal interest in both of you. I'm impressed and it won't be the last time we speak. A good friend of mine once told me that helping people is like digging in life's gold mine. With your help I think I've dug out a sizeable nugget today. Good luck, girls.'

The numbers of girls being forced into marriage and taken abroad for FGM reduced as a result of Antoinette's work reinforcing her status as a dedicated, committed politician. Astur's dad and mum received the support and counselling needed to adjust to British standards of life. After a period of time being looked after by Belle's mother, Astur was able to go home to her parents, to continue with her schooling, hopefully fulfilling her ambition to go to university. Antoinette's star continued to rise.

A cabinet reshuffle in 2034 installed Antoinette in the high-profile post of Home Secretary. David Graft Labour Prime Minister had been impressed with Antoinette's diligence in improving conditions for women and young girls. Mary Broad the Liberal leader endorsed Antoinette's promotion to one of the most prominent, high-profile cabinet positions.

The Lib Lab pact was working well and at the 2035 General Election Antoinette was re-elected in Tooting. Throughout Britain more seats were gained by the Liberal Party. Nevertheless, Labour still held the majority maintaining the status quo in Parliament. David Graft retained the Premiership, Mary Broad stayed as Deputy Prime Minister and Antoinette kept her position as Home Secretary.

As cabinet posts go Home Secretary is the poisoned chalice. There was always the potential for a metaphorical grenade to go off. One such explosion had occurred 17 years previously when the Windrush Scandal forced the incumbent Home Secretary to resign. Tackling immigration, cutting crime and keeping a grip on terrorism were all minefields with the potential to abruptly curtail an ambitious politician's career. Antoinette was honoured to do the job but it was not a role for the faint hearted. Fortunately, the once timid teenager had developed into a hard-nosed politician with an ingrained sense of justice. Always on the ball, Antoinette constantly monitored the work of civil servants, knowing one mistake could jeopardise any politician's career.

Fortunately during Antoinette's tenure, the Home Office ran like a well-oiled machine leading to crime figures dropping, making the United Kingdom the envy of Western Europe. Significant improvements were accredited to Antoinette's leadership. This ensured she was held in high regard. She attributed her good fortune to her friendship with Billy Davies. Even though Billy was 71 years old she regularly made time to seek his counsel.

Billy would say to her, 'You'll soon be in the top job.'

'It would be nice, Billy, but it's easy for things to go wrong in this job.'

'Antoinette, you turn everything to gold. Just keep believing and digging.'

'Even though you're retired, Billy, it's always nice to talk to you and I'll never forget how much I owe you. It was your counsel which gave me the confidence to apply to university.'

As Billy and Antoinette were speaking a bulletin came over the radio. The newsreader reporting some distressing news.

'It's just been announced that ill health has forced the Liberal leader Mary Broad to resign.'

Antoinette was taken aback by the announcement.

'I knew Mary wasn't well but I didn't realise she was that ill.'

Many ambitious politicians' first thoughts would have been it was their chance to step into Mary Broad's shoes. However, Antoinette's compassion meant she wasn't thinking about her next career move. Her first thought was for Mary Broad's welfare.

Antoinette said, 'I hope Mary's OK because we've got on really well. She's always supported me.'

'It's a real shame, Antoinette.'

'Sorry Billy, I'll have to contact my office. We'll speak later.'

Mary Broad was facing cancer treatment concluding that it was important for her to concentrate on the impending therapy. Fighting the illness would conflict with her role as Party Leader and Deputy Prime Minister. A new leader would have to be appointed using the alternative vote system favoured by the Liberals.

This voting structure involved all nominees being included on the ballot paper. Voters were then given the opportunity to rank order their choices. Any candidate with more than half the votes based on first choices would make that person the winner. Failing to achieve this, the candidate with the lowest number of votes is eliminated and concludes when one person has more than half the votes.

Later that evening Billy spoke on the phone to Antoinette.

'Antoinette, you must apply for the leadership.'

'Billy, I don't know whether I've the confidence and drive to do the job where the buck would definitely stop with me.'

'What does Simeon say?'

'He thinks I should apply.'

'There you are, Antoinette. Just remember a lack of confidence is a trait from the past, not something I associate with you now.'

'My knees knock at the thought of standing at the despatch box knowing I have responsibility for the party's policies and the answers I give will lead to my every word being scrutinised.'

'Antoinette, you've stood there before.'

'Yes, but not as leader. It's a great responsibility.'

'As Minister for Women's Issues you did a fantastic job.'

'Yes, I really thrived in that role. I was interested in it and thoroughly enjoyed the work.'

'You then took on the most difficult cabinet post making a 'really good fist' of being Home Secretary where the calculated risks you took paid off.'

'I suppose you're right, Billy.'

'I know I'm right, Antoinette. What's more you're favourite for the job.'

'Billy, you're making it sound like I've already got the job.'

'I walked past the bookmakers earlier on and the odds they were giving make you favourite; they rarely get it wrong. Never undersell yourself. You're a woman with an excellent intellect, an amazing work ethic and more importantly compassion for people.'

'You're always kind, Billy and after talking to you my confidence soars.'

'You'll be digging for gold for the British people if you get the job. I must say I think you're destined to be Prime Minister. Liberalism has come into vogue and you'll be the beneficiary.'

Antoinette made up her mind that Billy was right.

Chapter 55

In 2035 United Nations delegates acclaimed Simeon's outstanding work for UNICEF the International Children's Emergency Fund. These accolades presented Simeon with a dilemma because of his devotion to protecting the welfare and rights of children worldwide. From its inception in 1946, when UNICEF provided aid to refugee children in post war Europe, the organisation had been proactive during any global crisis.

Simeon had bought into the ideals of this organisation, tirelessly advocating children's rights. The provision of basic necessities had been at the forefront of Simeon's agenda. Growing opportunities for youngsters allowed Third-World children to fulfil their potential. United Nations delegates recognised Simeon as a devoted, indefatigable member with compassion and the ability to understand how young people suffered. Having initiated mass vaccination programmes in third world countries, he gave millions of children the opportunity to survive diseases which had the potential to kill any who were unprotected.

Another of Simeon's passions involved fulfilling one of the articles of the United Nations Declaration of Human Rights stating, 'All children have a right to an education.' He worked tirelessly aspiring to accomplish this principle. Investing in children's education presented a country with the opportunity to thrive. Simeon appreciated that basic survival for third-world peoples was top priority. After achieving that, looking after a child's long-term prospects meant providing education. This was an important factor in helping a poor country develop economic opportunities. Having this empathy led to Simeon being admired by fellow delegates.

Some Third-World countries attach little value to a girl's education but Simeon won international acclaim for his work in this field. His mantra 'Investing in Girls' Education Changes Countries,' impressed ambassadors from many regions of the world. The key pillar of his work involved raising awareness that educating girls strengthens economies, reducing inequality between first and third-world countries.

Many third-world societies stress the importance of girls working in the home. However, Simeon saw this as limiting and insisted educated girls contribute positively to the fields of science, medicine, music, literature and business. Simeon adhered to his philosophy, winning plaudits for his willingness to give all children the best chance in life.

His dilemma began when a vacant position became available on the United Nations Human Rights Council. Having promoted children's human rights, he was anxious to apply for this role. Simeon's courageous action participating in a mission to free ten children held captive by ISIS in 2020, guaranteed him being held in high esteem by the General Assembly. Election to the Human Rights Council involved internal wrangling between members but Simeon thought his experience would make him a real asset to this body.

He phoned Billy, 'Hi Billy, it's been a while since we spoke.'

'It's good to speak to you, Simeon, and it's excellent news that Antoinette is applying for the post as Liberal leader. One never knows, you could be married to a future Prime Minister.'

'Neither of us ever thought that would happen. Fortunately, Antoinette has taken to politics as to the manor born. Hopefully, she'll fulfil her ambition to be Prime Minister and I'm hoping to get a new job.'

'What is it, Simeon?'

'I'd like to get elected to the United Nations Human Rights Council.'

'That would be right up your street, Simeon. Surely the Council only needs to look at the work you've done.'

'Trouble is Billy, there's a lot of internal politics during the selection process.'

'Listen Simeon, there's no one better qualified than you. What you did in Yemen and your other efforts raising standards for children in poor countries should hold you in good stead.'

'The children were freed because you were there Billy.'

'Make no mistake Simeon, your part in our mission was equally important.'

'If I were to get the job, I'll be based in Geneva which means being closer to Antoinette.'

'That would be fantastic, Simeon. How do you get elected?'

'Well Billy, there are 47 members elected for a three-year term on a regional group basis.'

'You'll have to explain that process to me, Simeon.'

'It works like this, Billy. Africa has 13 members, Asia and the Pacific 13 members, Eastern Europe 6, Latin America and the Caribbean 8 and Western Europe 7.'

'So, you'll be elected for three years and what work will you do?'

'I'll be investigating human rights abuses by member countries.'

'What a really worthwhile job, that's right up your street.'

'Yes, the General Assembly began the Human Rights Council in 2006 as a response to a United Nations member country being accused of human rights abuses.'

'Don't let the opportunity pass you by, Simeon.'

'Thanks Billy, I'm definitely applying.'

Chapter 56

Tommy Gunn's kidney transplant was a resounding success. More importantly having shown genuine remorse for an incongruous lifestyle; Billy and others were pleased with the contrition he'd shown. Willingly cooperating with the police Tommy was tried at the Old Bailey. During his summary, the judge complimented Tommy for his sincerity and honesty but a custodial sentence for his crimes was inevitable. Justice had to be seen to be done.

Referring in his summation to Billy Davies as a unique individual, the judge heaped praise on this former homeless man for his compassion and forgiveness. Making a statement, Tommy Gunn pointed out that he was genuinely sorry for his appalling crimes and was ready to accept a prison sentence as just punishment. He was determined to use his incarceration profitably as preparation to serve society on his release. Sentencing Tommy to eight years in Wormwood Scrubs, the judge took the unusual step of wishing him well for the future.

Tommy's conversion from a life of crime led to him studying for an Open University degree while he was in prison. Studying would provide the foundation for a career as a social worker on his release. Tommy took advice from the prison education officer electing to study for a degree in psychology that could be completed in three years. An eight-year prison tariff would be reduced to four years with time off for good behaviour.

Tommy proved a model prisoner achieving a first-class honours degree after three years. Prisoners had plenty of time on their hands but Tommy didn't want to waste a year following the completion of his degree, so he wrote a book about the reasons why people enter a life of crime. These efforts showed him to be an academically gifted person who left prison in July 2035, a reformed human being. Demand for the services of this rehabilitated convict was high.

His book became a best seller, prompting local authorities to use Tommy to counsel youngsters who were in danger of 'going off the rails'. In addition, organisations paid him a hefty fee as an after-dinner speaker. Tommy's transformation changed a greedy self-obsessed man to a benevolent human being willing to donate large sums of money to various charities.

Admitting his criminal activity had been erroneous rejuvenated Tommy, making him more content than he had been at any time in his life. Tommy was a remodelled human being. The final piece of the jigsaw fell into place when he arrived at Tooting Evangelical Church, taking his place in the congregation.

At first worshippers were wary of this former right-wing extremist. It was glaringly obvious a remarkable transformation had taken place. People were astounded to see this former criminal who'd generated so much racial, homophobic and sexist hatred walk into the baptismal waters, emerging as a man ready to devote his life to God. Any who thought there was no place for someone like Tommy were reminded by Billy that forgiveness is a central tenet of the Christian faith.

Billy remarked, 'Remember the Gospel states, we are all sinners needing God's grace.'

Emphasising his point Billy used Jesus's words.

'Whoever is without sin let him cast the first stone.'

All nodded in approval at the reconciliation of a criminal finding the straight path in life.

Chapter 57

Four MPs were nominated for Liberal Party leader to replace Mary Broad. Among those included on the ballot paper was Antoinette who needed at least 200 party members spread across 20 different local parties to vote for her. Easily exceeding these figures, Antoinette was installed as favourite for the leadership. Party members now had to vote for their preferred MP. Media speculation was rife about who would be nominated as leader. Using his influence Billy encouraged Liberal members in Tooting to vote for 'their girl'.

As he walked around the constituency he would shout across to people, 'Make sure you take your vote.'

With a wink he would say, 'Don't forget, vote for Antoinette. She'll make a fantastic leader.'

Billy's commitment to Antoinette's cause brought a smile to people's faces. As an acknowledgement people would offer a quick salute in the hope of reducing his 'full on' enthusiasm. Billy would respond with a raised fist salute. Hustings were organised by the Liberal Party presenting candidates with the opportunity to promote their ideas. Although Antoinette was installed as favourite, Billy took nothing for granted.

He continued to forcefully encourage people to take no chances and vote. Just as the bookies expected, on Thursday 5 July 2036 Antoinette was appointed leader of the Liberal Party. She was 42 years of age having finally achieved her longstanding ambition. Liberalism had regenerated during the previous 15 years, raising the possibility that Antoinette might yet be Prime Minister at the 2040 General Election.

Simeon succeeded in his attempt to serve on the United Nations Human Rights Committee receiving a myriad of votes. Members viewed him as totally committed, giving people worldwide the opportunity to be treated with the dignity they deserve. Third world countries voted in large numbers for Simeon to serve on the committee, recognising his accomplishments in helping children from poorer regions of the world to improve their quality of life.

Although 16 years had elapsed since the Yemeni children were rescued, this remarkable incident was written into the United Nations annals. Modest at all times Simeon never took anything for granted but really his election was a dead cert. Hearing the news he had been elected, Billy phoned Simeon.

'How are you doing? I bet you're thrilled to bits with the new role. Well done, Simeon!'

'Thanks, Billy. I wasn't sure they'd elect me.'

'Well Simeon, you were an extra special candidate. If you hadn't got the job, there must have been somebody extraordinary standing against you.'

'The problem is I try not to take anything for granted.'

'You're quite right to think like that. Modesty has always been one of your great strengths.'

'Thanks, Billy. You've always been an inspiration and support to me.'

'Hey, you never know Simeon, you might be Secretary General next.'

'Unfortunately, that's not possible, Billy.'

'Well, I think you'd be great in the top job.'

'There's a problem, Billy.'

'What's that?'

'Nobody can be Secretary General if the country they represent has a member on the Security Council and Britain is a permanent member, so that rules me out.'

'I didn't know that, Simeon.'

'Not many people would realise it, Billy.'

'Well, well you learn something every day, even at my age.'

'I'm looking forward to being based in Geneva. It'll bring me closer to Antoinette so we can spend more time together.'

'That'll be fantastic, Simeon. How's things been going for Amir?'

Amir was the Yazidi boy who had been adopted by Simeon and Antoinette. Having been rescued, Amir had come to Britain where he'd attended Galaxy High School. Once Amir had settled, he excelled in his exams. Finishing school, he went on to study medicine at university.

'Amir's just been appointed as a paediatric consultant at Guys Hospital and he's doing really well, Billy.'

'That's the hat trick then.'

'Billy, it's been great to talk to you and when I come home, I'll be in touch.'

'All the best, Simeon.'

Billy put the phone down thinking to himself, 'What a lovely family! It's great to see them being so successful.'

Chapter 58

The Lib Lab pact governed the United Kingdom for five years. Following the dissolution of Parliament on Thursday 2 April, David Graft called an election for 10 May 2040. This coalition government had been successful in improving public services and the old two-party system had been replaced by a three-way fight for power. Even the bookies had difficulty predicting a winner. It was a distinct possibility the country could have its first Liberal Prime Minister since David Lloyd George in 1922.

Campaigning began in earnest confirming this period would be the busiest five weeks of Antoinette's life. Embarking on this important chapter of her time in politics, Antoinette would travel the length and breadth of the United Kingdom, canvassing support. Central to her campaigning would be her commitment to excellent public services.

In addition, Antoinette was anxious to promote the Liberal Party as progressives, advocating the civil and human rights of all individuals. Her first Cabinet role in charge of Women's Issues was certain to garner her a good proportion of the female vote, having addressed issues such as domestic violence, equal pay for women, FGM and forced marriage. Contentious issues as these were sure-fire winners in the eyes of anyone concerned with justice for all.

One cloud on the horizon was Billy's diminishing health. He was now 76 years of age. Unfortunately, he contracted a horrific chest infection. Failing to respond to antibiotics, Billy was admitted to hospital. Antoinette phoned Simeon to let him know Billy had been hospitalised.

'Hi, Simeon, I've some bad news. Billy's just been admitted to hospital.'

'What's the problem, Antoinette?'

'It started as a chest infection and giving Billy antibiotics hasn't improved it.'

'One of the problems, Antoinette, is that no one knows how much damage Billy suffered when he was living on the streets.'

'Yes, he was outside in appalling conditions. It was bound to affect his health.'

'I know you're busy with the election campaign, Antoinette but can you let me know as soon as possible if there's any news about Billy.'

'Although I'm concentrating on the election I'll be keeping in touch with the hospital about Billy's health.'

'Do me a favour Antoinette, just ring if there's any news about him'

'I'll definitely ring if I hear anything. Love you.'

'Love you too.'

'Speak to you soon, Simeon.'

Finishing the call Antoinette and Simeon were both anxious that their good friend was ill. They were certain Billy's philosophy would be to show concern, but life must go on. Simeon had to devote himself to improving human rights throughout the world, consoled by the thought that Billy would be a committed advocate of his work.

Billy would also insist Antoinette concentrated on winning the election as her brand of politics offered great hope to the country. She adhered to the principle that the gap between rich and poor in Britain needed to shrink, producing a more equitable society. Billy reassured himself that this approach would produce a more harmonious society and his rallying call would be 'forget me, get on with it'. This was difficult for Antoinette who owed Billy so much. It dawned on her that winning the election was a way of paying him back for the encouragement she'd received.

Using the Liberal campaign bus Antoinette travelled the length and breadth of the country meeting thousands of people. She shook so many hands by the end of the day the shaking caused her arm to ache. She would tell her aides much more of it would give her repetitive strain injury. However, Antoinette realised this was a necessary public relations act if people were to buy into her political philosophy. Maintaining a smile at all times she remarked her arm had been pulled more times than a Las Vegas one armed bandit.

Regularly throughout the campaign Antoinette returned to London, giving her the opportunity to visit Billy in hospital. Doctors and nurses were enthusiastic about conversing with her, readily volunteering opinions about improving the health service. Always making a mental note of these suggestions Antoinette listened attentively in the knowledge that any slip up could cost the Liberal Party votes. Hospital professionals were on the frontline of the health service, so animatedly engaging with medical staff gave Antoinette an insight into what was needed to provide a world class facility. It was on these visits to Billy she contended with a clash of interests. It was important to discuss these matters but she also wanted to spend quality time with Billy. Adroitly handling this situation politely, she knew Billy would want her to gain a comprehensive insight into providing the best healthcare possible for people.

On one occasion when she visited Billy's ward, he looked forlorn. Antoinette walked to the bed planting a kiss on his forehead. Billy wasn't his usual ebullient self and Antoinette had concern in her voice.

'Billy, you look a bit down in the mouth.'

'The specialist has been to see me and told me I've got exudative pleural effusion.'

'You'll have to explain that, Billy.'

'It means the pleura in my lungs have been damaged.'

'Did the consultant say what caused it?'

'Yes, I've had a series of infections causing me to produce too much pleural fluid.'

'What does that do, Billy?'

'All this fluid impairs my breathing, stopping my lungs expanding, making me short of breath.'

'Can it be treated, Billy?'

'There are various treatments, but it'll affect my organs, particularly my heart and kidneys.'

Anxious to lift Billy's spirit to instil some confidence in him. Antoinette remarked, 'I'm sure you'll be OK with treatment.'

'Antoinette, I'm not getting any younger so forget about me. More importantly, how's the campaign going?'

This was typical of Billy wanting to divert attention away from himself. Antoinette grew uneasy with his strategy, but she didn't want to upset him.

'It's been a positive campaign. I think a lot of women will vote Liberal.'

'I'm really not surprised with all the work you've done to improve women's conditions.'

'The opinion polls are showing the election result will be close between the three main parties.'

'Let's hope the Liberals have the greatest number of seats. Then it'll be down to you to strike a deal with one of the other parties.'

'If that were to happen Billy, I would like a coalition with the Labour Party. It'll give us an opportunity to continue the work done by the previous coalition. David Graft really respected my political beliefs and I will reciprocate these sentiments.'

'You get back to the crusade, Antoinette because I'm determined to be out of here for polling day.'

Putting her hand on Billy's shoulder Antoinette affectionately said, 'Billy, do as you're told.'

Billy gave Antoinette a wry smile, the sort that she'd come to love. She really knew Billy would do his own thing. Being desperately concerned about Billy's deteriorating health she left the hospital.

Chapter 59

On Friday 4 May Billy left hospital in time for Election Day. Tooting Evangelical Church was packed to the rafters on Sunday, the 6th. There was a significant buzz in the congregation knowing one of their own could potentially be Prime Minister by the end of the week. Voting with one's conscience was the theme of the sermon, but the Pastor gave a conspiratorial wink, wink, (straight out of the Billy handbook) indicating where he thought their vote should go. There was absolutely no need for the Pastor to worry, this was a captive audience.

Following the partisan sermon, prayers were offered for Billy, following his release from hospital. Members of the congregation were well aware that this illness had aged him and his chest was rattling. Church members quickly pointed out Billy was lacking his usual vigour; he was terribly short of breath. Being such a popular figure through his dedication to humanitarian work ensured he was never short of people to look after him. He'd given so much to society, people willingly gave their time to care for him.

Following his release from prison and transformation into a morally good human being, Tommy Gunn would regularly go into the church, cooking meals for Billy. Tommy's criminal days were behind him but he refused to forget the trepidation his behaviour caused the Tooting public. Realising he could not turn the clock back and never fully atone for his crimes, he did the next best thing by willingly dedicating himself to the church. Philanthropy was used as a way of easing his conscience, helping make amends for past misdemeanours. Tommy was a great example of a person renouncing their criminal past for a Christian way of life. People who'd once been circumspect about Tommy now trusted him implicitly.

Thursday 10 May arrived. This was the day many people in Tooting were waiting for. Polling stations opened at 7:00 a.m. and one of the first to arrive at the local school was Billy who went with Antoinette and Simeon to cast their vote. Picking up their voting papers in front of Antoinette were Astur and Belle. They were in the youngest group of voters and were full of enthusiasm.

Excitedly the girls shouted, 'Go, go Antoinette. You'll be Prime Minister. We're voting for you.'

Antoinette found it difficult to join in the premature celebrations, but she politely said, 'Thanks girls. You never know.'

An anxious wait followed to see if Antoinette's hectic campaign schedule had convinced enough voters to propel her to the foremost public office in the United Kingdom. Bookies rarely get things wrong, but a desperately close result was anticipated. Every vote would count if Antoinette were to be Prime Minister. A determined electorate kept Tooting's polling stations bustling with voters guaranteeing a record turnout for the election. Television channels indicated that these elevated figures were reflected right across the country.

Any voter malaise at past elections was replaced by a high level of public interest. Always the optimist Billy was confident Antoinette would achieve her ambition. His confidence contrasted with Antoinette's characteristic reticence about her chances. Leaving the polling station, the three friends went back to Simeon and Antoinette's place for coffee.

Simeon sipped his drink proclaiming, 'Antoinette, you've done all you can. It's now in the hands of the electorate.'

'Foregone conclusion,' said Billy.

Lightening the mood Antoinette pronounced, 'It's not over until Antoinette sings.'

Billy immediately jumped on the reference to singing.

'It'll be hymns and arias in the morning, Antoinette.'

Simeon added, 'You never know Billy, your next cuppa with Antoinette could be in 10 Downing Street.'

The three friends burst into a fit of the giggles knowing that Simeon's prophetic words could well happen.

Polling stations were busy throughout the day, leading to commentators predicting a record turnout for an election. People had taken a great interest in the election primarily because the Lib Lab coalition government made significant improvements to public services. Antoinette's concern for people's welfare had been a driving force in the advances made by the alliance government and people wanted more of the same.

Although people had probably made up their mind about their voting intentions Billy continued to remind people who they should vote for. Being such a prominent figure who'd achieved so much for society, his continual badgering was accepted with humour. Antoinette had overwhelming support in the Tooting area so her re-election as an MP was never in doubt.

Just after midnight the Tooting result was announced by the Returning Officer and Antoinette's re-election was greeted with unbridled joy by her supporters. Having secured an overwhelming victory Antoinette's concern switched to the other 649 seats in the country. The exit poll predicted seats would be evenly split between three parties. Would the Liberal Party have made up enough ground since the last election to hold the greatest number of seats? If this happened Antoinette would be in pole position to be Prime Minister.

By 6 o'clock in the morning Antoinette's zealous campaigning had borne fruit and the Liberal Democrats had the largest number of seats. A deal was now needed to form a government with a working majority. Political shenanigans were about to begin where promises would have to be made guaranteeing a working Parliamentary majority. Having the greatest number of seats, it was appropriate that Antoinette should be Prime Minister. The previous Lib Lab pact produced favourable results, so it was fitting that this coalition continued. This time Antoinette would lead the government.

People in Tooting were overjoyed at this news and worshippers at the Evangelical Church joyfully offered prayers for Antoinette's Government to be successful. Billy's thoughts turned to that cuppa in 10 Downing Street but his chest problems were worsening. Nevertheless, he revelled in the knowledge that a boy from Llanen had played a part in Antoinette's accession to Premiership.

Chapter 60

Billy's chest condition proved debilitating, consequently reducing his energy. This intuitive, astute human being, once filled with vigour was now a shadow of his former self, contenting himself with whiling away time reflecting on a previous full life. Much of his time had been devoted to helping others. His two close friends had reached the pinnacle of their respective careers and although Billy would downplay his part in their success, Simeon and Antoinette would not agree. Both attributed their separate triumphs to the help and encouragement Billy had given.

Although well looked after in the church Billy was beginning to find everyday tasks more difficult. Members realised how arduous Billy was finding looking after himself. In the true spirit of Christian love, people gave their time helping him cope with his deteriorating health. Having nearly reached 76 years of age Billy had had three spells in hospital during the last two months, when his lungs had filled with fluid. However, he made it plain and clear that hospital was not the place he wanted to be.

Billy was adamant he was not going to end his days in any infirmary, despite people telling him consistently that hospital was the best place for him. Billy would cantankerously say, 'Look, I know I'm on borrowed time but there's only one place it's all going to end. That's in the church so don't anyone send me to hospital.'

There was no point having an altercation with Billy. He was as determined as ever that hospital was not for him.

Antoinette was very aware that Billy would appreciate and relish the opportunity to go to Downing Street for a cuppa. It hurt Antoinette if she dwelled on the fact that Billy's life was drawing to a close. She fully appreciated the importance of getting this visit done. Having instilled her with confidence, the very least Billy deserved for the support, advice and encouragement he had given was for her to arrange a visit.

Antoinette spoke to Simeon, 'When you get back from Geneva, we'll bring Billy over to Downing Street for tea. Even though he's been there once before I know it's important for him to see me in my place of work.'

'Well, I'm on holiday from work in June, a week before Billy's 76th birthday.'

'Right Simeon, we'll set a date for Saturday 11 June. We will stay in London that weekend instead of going to Chequers Court. It will really give Billy something to look forward to.'

'I'll go to Tooting to get him ready. If you could send a car at 3:00 p.m., we'll get him to Downing Street.'

'It'll be lovely to have Billy here. We'll make it a really nice occasion for him.'

'He'll be so excited, Antoinette. Hopefully, there'll be an added bonus because it'll possibly perk him up.'

11 June arrived; Billy could not contain his excitement. Arriving in Tooting at 2:00 p.m. Simeon found Billy ready in his best suit, sporting a huge grin from ear to ear. Throughout his time in Tooting Billy had always been really happy but the last few years had been pain filled on occasions causing irritability.

People understood the distress his lung condition was causing him. All were filled with sympathy but Billy hated any fuss. He was exhilarated at the thought of the official car turning up for him. In true governmental fashion his transport arrived at exactly 3:00 p.m. Billy refused a wheelchair, determined to struggle with crutches.

Perseverance was one of Billy's fortes, prompting him on this occasion to say, 'I'm no quitter and there's no way I'm going in a chair. If it takes me an hour to walk 10 yards, I'll do it'

A government official held the door open for Billy, politely greeting him.

'Good afternoon, Mr Davies.'

Feeling chipper and in typical Billy fashion. He replied, 'Forget the Mr Davies just call me Billy, everyone else does.'

'Come on Billy, let me help you in.'

'Cheers.'

There was real animation in his voice for the first time in ages.

Feeling a million dollars Billy was thrilled as the car whisked him through London's streets to the gates of Downing Street. Immediately recognising the car, the police waved it through to a parking spot outside Number 10. Billy's spark temporarily returned but he'd have to be careful as over eagerness could so easily result in a fall.

Having watched the scene many times on television, Billy was now playing the starring role as it would be him going through the famous black door. Antoinette was waiting just inside the door. Billy moved painstakingly slowly towards her using his crutches. At this low point in his life, it was difficult to envisage a man who had been filled with abundant vim and dynamism. Antoinette stepped forward to meet Billy and the friends warmly embraced.

Grateful for the invitation Billy spoke, 'Thanks very much for inviting me over. It's not every day I'm invited out for tea, let alone an invitation to 10 Downing Street.'

'Billy, you've always wanted to come to tea here. There was no way I was going to let this opportunity pass.'

'You've got a country to run, Antoinette. You shouldn't be spending your time thinking about an old codger like me.'

Gently scolding him Antoinette playfully said, 'There's no way you should be calling yourself an old codger. You're still the same Billy to me.'

As Antoinette finished, Amir the Yazidi boy who had been adopted by Antoinette and Simeon stepped out of the shadows.

'Hi Billy, it's been a long time since we've met up. I've been really busy with my medical work.'

'Yes, I've heard how successful you've been, Amir. It's nice you're now a consultant paediatrician at Guys hospital.'

Warmly hugging Amir Billy regarded this as a magical moment. What could be better as Billy was shown to the Pillard Room where he met some civil servants, before going through to the dining room. Here he enjoyed a glass of champagne, then tucked into sandwiches and cakes. Antoinette knew Billy was desperate to see the staircase where black and white photos of Prime Ministers were mounted on the wall. She escorted him there.

Awestruck, moving his eyes between the different portraits, he fixed his eyes on the photo of Winston Churchill, noticing that he was the only Prime Minister with two photos. Quickly thinking, Billy assumed there were two photos because he was regarded as the greatest of Prime Ministers. Taking an extended look at these two portraits Billy thought it better to keep his counsel regarding the ill feeling towards Churchill in the old mining communities of the Welsh Valleys. People there had long memories. When he was Home Secretary Churchill sent the army in to support the police who were failing to control miners taking strike action over low pay. This incident resulted in Churchill not getting the acclaim in Wales he enjoyed in other regions of the British Isles. Nevertheless, Billy thought it better to keep his mouth shut.

Averting his gaze from Churchill, Margaret Thatcher came into Billy's eyeline. Highly regarded by many people for Billy she was a real Marmite character. Seeing her photo his mind was transported back to the Falklands War which had left an indelible mark on his life. Billy's mind focused on the bombing of the Sir Galahad and the carnage of Sapper Hill. Then there was the 1984 Miner's dispute when colliers went on strike for a year in an effort to prevent pit closures.

Welsh Valley communities including his beloved Llanen were decimated as a result of an industry being hastily terminated. Mines had sustained valleys villages for many years. Images of hungry, desperate children with buckets knocking doors begging for food came into Billy's mind. As he stared at the photo his thoughts went into overdrive, momentarily seeing kind teachers and kitchen staff who went into schools at the weekend to provide meals for famished children. Resonating in his thoughts were the words of an Oscar winning MP who castigated Thatcher in Parliament after her death for insensitivity to the mining communities.

Margaret Thatcher's single-minded determination to draw a line under this industry left a bad taste in the mouths of the inhabitants of these communities. Just like Winston Churchill there'd be no warm welcome in the hillsides for this giant of British politics. It made Billy realise politics was a business where difficult decisions had to be made; sometimes they could be unpopular with elements of the electorate.

He knew Antoinette had a steely attitude, but she was extremely sensitive to the needs of others. Billy was convinced she could cope with the constant demands of the job. There was no doubt her moral compass would guide any decision making. This new incumbent was certainly no Thatcher. There was no way she could ever put political ambition before the financial security of village communities. Antoinette would fight tooth and nail improving conditions for people particularly those in poverty.

Billy gazed intently at these photographs but was brought back to reality by Antoinette announcing, 'There's my photo, Billy. What do you think?'

'You look superb Antoinette, really dignified.'

Time flew by; all too soon the visit was over. Billy was driven back to Tooting with the memory that this had been a lovely occasion, a real honour to visit such a prestigious venue again. Contentedly Billy went to bed that evening. Unfortunately, he woke in the night, struggling to breathe. In the morning one of the church members who looked after Billy could see he was distressed. Billy's ailing health caused him to bark an instruction.

'There's to be no ambulance. I'm not going to any hospital.'

The church member announced, 'Well, let me get the doctor. We need to have you examined.'

'If you say so but there's to be no hospital.'

Arriving swiftly the doctor examined Billy and exclaimed, 'We need oxygen to help Billy breathe. His lungs are full of fluid.'

At that moment, the Pastor came into the room to speak with the doctor. The Pastor wanted to respect Billy's wishes and pointed this out to the doctor.

'Billy said he won't go into hospital. We've enough church members who hold him in such high esteem, they'll organise a rota to look after him.'

'Pastor, I don't think he's got long left.'

'We are praying he lasts the week because he'll be 76. It was my predecessor Pastor Robbins who gave Billy a home here in 2012. He was homeless and nobody ever thought he would live this long. Billy is a remarkable man, a real gift to people. We will nurse him.'

'Ring the surgery if you need anything. We'll give you all the help we can.'

Billy's birthday arrived and he was struggling to breathe. Simeon and Antoinette had been contacted with the news that his death was imminent.

Chapter 61

Church members waited anxiously for Simeon and Antoinette to arrive. People were attending to Billy, making him as comfortable as possible. Attendees became disconcerted as Billy's breathing grew more laboured and intermittent. Nevertheless, despite the air of inevitability there was also expectation that Billy's two friends would arrive in time. People said little, constantly looking at their watches. Simeon and Antoinette had still not turned up.

Enormous strain radiated from the faces of those present, knowing Billy's death was imminent. The thought that Antoinette and Simeon might miss the passing of their great friend, created unimaginable tension in the room. The strain was tangible, anticipation hanging heavily in the air as the situation grew increasingly more stressful. Church members exuded a nervous agitation created by a situation becoming increasingly tense.

Suddenly a dishevelled figure opened the door. It was Simeon and one could feel the release of strain from the people attending to Billy, now Simeon had arrived. His normally immaculately coiffured hair was unusually frizzy, resembling someone having a bad hair day. Simeon's shirt was out at the back, his tie strung over his left shoulder. Normally fastidious about having a straight tie Simeon rushed to Billy's bedside. On meeting, there was a warm embrace between the two friends but Simeon avoided squeezing too hard because Billy was weak.

Billy opened his eyes and although barely audible he said, 'You've done really well Simeon. Not bad for a boy from a block of council flats in Tooting. Cor I'm really proud of you.'

Tears welled up in Simeon's eyes knowing that Billy's time on earth was nearly up. Despite being elderly Billy's passing would be harrowing for Simeon knowing he'd been the biggest single influence in his life. Billy wouldn't accept it, but Simeon knew the rescue of the Yemeni children in 2022 was the most important factor in him achieving the status he enjoyed today. That rescue could not have succeeded without Billy's ability to weigh up a situation and act accordingly. It seemed to Simeon anything Billy undertook appeared to alleviate the difficulty of the situation. For some reason, a difficult and potentially life-threatening situation ended positively just because Billy was there. On more than one occasion Simeon would say Billy led a charmed life.

A few minutes later a government car drew up outside the church. Antoinette stepped out, flanked by her security people. Immaculately dressed, carrying herself with real poise, this was Antoinette's most important assignment of the day. Whereas Simeon rushed into the building, Antoinette's role as Prime Minister ensured she was conditioned to avoid panic. This trait was infused into her persona. No doubt the image she portrayed was not the full picture because of her affection for Billy.

She walked into the church, down the stairs, opened the door and approached Billy's bed. Ever alert security men stood behind her, armed to the teeth, reflecting how vital it was to protect such an important political figure. Antoinette owed Billy so much that any protocol was discarded. One could see her hard, outer exterior begin to melt, as a tear appeared in the corner of her eye, eventually trickling down her cheek. Any amount of training for presenting a British stiff upper lip could not prepare Antoinette for the emotion of this moment. Billy struggled to get his words out.

'That's my girl, you're a real star.'

'You're the real star. If I had not met you, I'd have achieved nothing. You're perfect, Billy.'

Continuing to struggle Billy wanted to put his life in perspective.

'I'm not perfect, Antoinette. Nobody's perfect. I regret having been involved in the Falklands War, killing the ISIS guard when we rescued the Yemeni children and the breakup of my marriage.'

'Billy, you had no choice, you joined the Army and had to fight, then when you went to Yemen, children were saved because you killed one monster and as for your marriage you were really ill at the time and had no medical support to counter the problems. No human being could have withstood the pressure you were under, so there's no need to reproach yourself.'

Struggling to speak Billy just managed to get his words out, 'That means I'm just like everyone else suffering through Original Sin.'

Billy's breathing grew shallow, his impending death was a moment of great sadness for all at Tooting Evangelical Church. The remnants of his diminishing physical strength finally faded and Billy took his last gasp, ending an exceptional life. Antoinette manically grabbed Simeon's hand. At this moment, a resolute, determined woman was momentarily overcome by insecurity. Even though Simeon and Antoinette had high flying careers they passionately loved each other but at this moment they were overwhelmed by a realisation that their achievements were down to Billy entering their life, instilling confidence in them when they were young.

Through bleary, teary eyes Antoinette proclaimed, 'I still say Billy was perfect. He helped so many people and if he wasn't flawless then he was unquestionably the quintessential gold digger.'